Dear Reader,

Scarlet is now two months old and I was delighted by your response to last month's launch. From your reaction, it seems that *Scarlet* is just what you've been waiting for, so I hope that you'll enjoy the four books I've chosen specially for you this month.

There's a questionnaire at the back of this book and, if you didn't complete and return one last month, I'd be delighted if you'd do so as soon as possible. When we receive your completed questionnaire, we'll be happy to send you a surprise free gift.

This month, *Scarlet* is offering you a book set deep in the heart of Texas, another which takes place in Canada and two with English backgrounds. Do you like this mixture of locations? What's *your* favourite setting? And how do you like our covers?

Because we want you to remain a *Scarlet* woman, we'd like your views on what you like best about our new list, so do drop me a line.

Till next month,
Best wishes,

Sally Cooper

SALLY COOPER,
Editor-in-Chief – *Sca*

A Question of Trust

MARGARET CALLAGHAN

A QUESTION OF TRUST

Enquiries to:
Robinson Publishing Ltd
7 Kensington Church Court
London W8 4SP

First published in the UK by Scarlet, 1996

A copy of the British Library Cataloguing in
Publication data is available from the British Library

ISBN 1–85487–473–X

Printed and bound in the EC

10 9 8 7 6 5 4 3 2 1

Part One

CHAPTER 1

'Okay, lady. What are you doing?'

The voice came out of nowhere and Billie jumped, losing her grip, the panic surging as she began to slither downwards. She didn't like heights at the best of times and, as wild fingers scrabbled for a hold, the realization dawned. She was going to fall. The flimsy boughs couldn't possibly take her weight. She closed her eyes, shutting out the world and the garden below that swayed so alarmingly. Then it hit her. She was still, she was safe, but a good twelve feet from the ground – she was well and truly caught.

'I said, what the hell do you think you're doing?'

Flying kites, she almost retorted, the sarcasm honed by nerves, only she didn't. Something in the voice, deep, male and angry, hinted at a warning, the sort of warning even Billie couldn't miss.

'Well? I'm waiting. And believe me, lady, I'm rapidly growing bored.'

Impatient. Yes, definitely impatient, Billie

3

decided. And in the absence of anything better to say, opted for the truth. 'I didn't think anyone was home,' she explained, peering dizzily through the foliage.

Cold black eyes stared back at her. 'You don't say,' he drawled, not a hint of a thaw on the handsome face.

'The cat – '

'Ah, yes, the wretch that's ruining my flower beds,' he growled. 'Along with his anti-social owner. Nice of you to drop in.'

'I'll make good any damage,' she snapped, his mocking tone goading.

'Too right you will. Every bulb, every seedling, each and every shrub will have to be paid for – by you.'

'If Smudge is to blame, I'll happily pay,' Billie conceded coolly. 'Just send round the bill. I live next door.'

'At raggle-taggle cottage?' he sneered. 'I'd never have guessed.'

Billie flushed. He was right, the cottage *was* a mess, and so was the garden. She hadn't the time – or the money – to do much about it, not with the nursing home fees eating into her savings. But that didn't give him the right to judge and find her wanting. 'You're welcome to call,' she heard herself inviting. 'The cottage may be shabby, but it is clean, neat and tidy and more than fit for visitors.'

And it's mine, she added silently. Buckingham Palace it would never be, but it was home and she was happy there, and no one, least of all this disconcerting stranger with his mocking eyes and mocking words, could ever take it away from her.

'Thank you, but no. I don't think so.'

Surprise, surprise, she silently jeered, her gaze slipping past his tall, powerful form and focusing instead on the house beyond. Gone were the ruins she'd explored as a child, and in their place a fairy tale come true. Oh yes, in three short months he'd turned it around, three months and a small fortune, Billie acknowledged, lips tightening in unconscious disapproval. He had the lot, she bitterly observed, dark, brooding looks and a fortune to match. And yet, why fall into his trap? Why judge him and find him wanting? Underneath that cool exterior could beat a heart of gold. Unlikely – but possible, she allowed, half smiling at the thought.

'I'm glad you find it amusing,' he ground out. 'Since it is my garden you're managing to spoil, you will understand if I don't see the funny side?'

Billie stiffened. 'I don't think – '

'No,' he interrupted. 'You don't think. Hence the mess you're in now. Supposing I call the police, prosecute for trespass?'

'I've offered to pay for the damage,' she reminded.

'Correction. You will pay. For every blade of

5

grass. And then you and your menagerie will hopefully leave me in peace. Well?'

'Well, what?' Billie stalled.

'Aren't you going to rescue the little wretch? That is what you're doing perched in my tree?'

His garden, his flower bed, his tree. 'Possessive, aren't you?' she heard herself sneer. 'I wonder why?' And his lane, too, she remembered, the moment the comment was out. It was his lane she'd been trundling up and down for the past four years, his *private* lane, the newly painted sign clearly underlined.

Fool, fool, fool, Billie berated herself as she realized what she'd done. He was angry enough in the first place without sassy remarks from her. So, bang went that favour she'd needed to ask. Her own fault really. She should have called round at the start of the week when she'd noticed that someone, this exasperating man presumably, had moved in. But it was too late now. She'd blown it. Give him the satisfaction of turning her down? Oh, no. She'd go the long way round in future, set out for work fifteen minutes early.

'You know,' he murmured confidentially, folding his arms and smiling grimly, 'I've half a mind to remove that ladder – *my* ladder,' he emphasized coldly, 'and leave you to stew. Two or three hours perched like a parrot should be enough to teach you some manners.'

'Like, "Please, sir, can I have my cat back"?' she said scornfully.

'Ah, yes,' he agreed. 'I do believe you're learning. The lines are word perfect, in fact, but there's a certain something missing from the tone: humility, submission, the unmistakable ring of sincerity. Still – ' He broke off, shrugging eloquently. 'If madam wants to call my bluff . . .' And he shrugged again, reaching for the ladder and placing it flat on the ground before sauntering back across the lawn, whistling annoyingly, uncaringly, into the air.

Billie stifled the panic. He wouldn't leave her stranded, she consoled herself, gauging the distance to the ground and going dizzy at the thought. He wouldn't. Oh yes, he would, she realized, as he reached the edge of the terrace. And once he disappeared into the house . . .

She took a deep breath. 'Wait! Please!' she called out with what she hoped was casual unconcern. Too casual, she discovered, as she lost her grip, slipped and had to make a grab for the final layer of branches. Regaining her hold, Billie clung on, like a limpet on a rock, closing her eyes as she choked back the nausea. Time passed. Nothing. Not a sound, not a movement. Nothing.

Frightened by the silence, Billie opened her eyes. He'd reached the house, had propped himself against the wall and was watching her, his expression cruelly unrelenting. But he was there, she acknowledged as the relief poured over her. He hadn't abandoned her yet. And all Billy had to do now was swallow her pride and ask. Leastways, that's what she was hoping.

'Please,' she murmured weakly, and still he didn't react, didn't blink, simply stood silent and unbending. Your move, his body language stated eloquently. Apologize? Billie bristled. She'd done nothing wrong, for heaven's sake, but nine feet from the ground was hardly the place to argue the point. 'I'm sorry,' she conceded, the words almost choking her.

The man half smiled. 'Strange,' he called out provokingly. 'I'm sure I heard a little bird begging for mercy. But there again . . .' He angled his head, an elaborate pretence of listening, and then he shrugged. 'I must have been mistaken.' And he moved off again as Billie's surge of anger finally broke through.

'You can't!' she shrieked, blocking out the fact that she was inches away from danger. 'Are you listening, damn you? You can't!'

He halted, spun round, raised a single enquiring eyebrow. 'Can't I?' he queried, oh so softly. 'Lady, just you watch me.'

'No!' Billie screamed. And again in her mind, no! no! no! But at least the note of hysteria had managed to touch a chord.

He moved back into view. 'You called?' he murmured drily, sharp eyes logging the panic, her cheeks devoid of colour. 'There's something you wanted to say, something along the lines of: please, sir, I'm sorry, sir, it will never happen again? Or is this a ploy to keep me talking, wear me down, appeal to the better side of my nature?'

If you have one, she derided, but she was pushing her luck just by having the thought. Annoy the man again and he'd simply disappear into the house, leaving her to stew. And once he returned, *if* he returned . . .

'Look, I'm sorry,' she began as reasonably as possible. 'I know I shouldn't be here but Smudge disappeared and then I heard his cries. He was terrified – ' Just like me, she could have pointed out, but didn't. 'And since no one was home – '

'You trampled the flower beds, hijacked my equipment and made yourself at home in my tree? How perfectly ill-mannered,' he drawled. 'But thank heavens for small mercies. Faced with an empty house, you could have taken it into your head to throw a party for half the village.'

Billie ignored the barb. 'Are you going to replace that ladder?' she demanded with asperity.

'Tut, tut. Are you going to replace that ladder, *please*?' he chided, but the hard edge had left his tone and Billie sensed that the danger had passed. Like a cat with a mouse, he was toying with words,

9

and when the game grew tiresome, he'd relent.

And then he surprised her, propping the ladder back against the trunk without waiting for Billie to grovel.

Sending up a silent payer of thanks, Billie began edging towards it.

'Haven't you forgotten something?'

She paused, nonplussed, her eyes searching his in silent enquiry.

'The cat,' he reminded. 'The reason you're here.'

'Oh!' She glanced up, spotting the frightened animal several feet above her. She licked her dry lips. 'I don't think I . . . Oh hell, couldn't you?' she asked with rare humility.

'No,' he retorted coolly, folding his arms. 'Your cat, your problem.'

Bilie's heart sank. He meant it, too. And yet Smudge had barely moved from the spot she'd been inching towards before the interruption. She'd have managed it then, but now –

'I'll break my neck,' she warned. 'And then you'll be sorry.

'I'll wring your pretty neck,' he vowed, 'if you don't get a move on. I'll count to ten and then I'm going, taking the ladder with me. And since I'm driving down to London it could be a long, lonely weekend. Chilly too, according to the forecast. Shall I go on?'

'Don't bother. I think I get the message,' she

conceded huffily and, bracing herself for the worst, began the slow climb back to the cat. Steeling herself not to look down in case the dizziness swamped her, she reached out at the exact moment Smudge backed away, discovered his own line of escape and, in three graceful leaps, reached the ground before skittering across to the hedge.

He laughed. In other circumstances Billie would have joined him. But not today. Wretched animal. Wretched, wretched man! But if the cat was safe, she wasn't, and she was forced to swallow yet another sharp retort as she crawled her way back to top of the ladder. 'I can manage, thank you,' she bit as he stepped forward to help.

'Suit yourself,' he allowed pleasantly.

So far, so good, Billie realized when the top rung took her weight, and the relief poured over her. And then the ladder lurched, pitching her sideways, and Billie screamed as outstretched arms and a powerful body helped to break her fall.

'Like I said, nice of you to drop in,' he murmured drily, recovering first.

Billie didn't move. She couldn't. And she didn't want to. Strong arms had closed round her and she was shockingly aware of the man cradling her in his lap. And she was drowning, drowning in a pair of laughing black eyes, such wonderful eyes tinged with flecks of gold and fringed by lashes a girl would happily die for.

11

'Next time, lady, do us both a favour. Send for the fire brigade, hey?' he chided, and Billie flushed, the velvet timbre of his voice creating strange sensations in the pit of her stomach.

'I – '

'Didn't stop to think,' he reminded her tersely. 'Are you always so pigheaded?'

'Pigheaded? Me?' Billie spluttered. 'If you hadn't come marching across in the first place,' she reminded huffily, 'I'd be safe and sound at home by now.'

'If you hadn't been climbing trees, other people's trees,' he needled, 'you wouldn't be sprawled like a hoyden in the grass. You little fool, you could have been killed.'

'I was perfectly safe till you arrived,' she pointed out coolly.

'In *my* garden.'

'Ah, yes.' Billie smiled grimly. 'Your garden, your tree, your ladder. My apologies, sir, how could I have forgotten?'

'Knowing you – ' He paused, shrugged, spread his hands. 'It's probably second nature.'

'But don't forget,' she retorted. 'You don't know me at all.'

'No.' He dropped his gaze, a slow, heated glance that reached out to touch her, quickening the pulse at the base of her throat as his sultry eyes moved lower, lingering for a heart-stopping moment on the

12

rapid rise and fall of Billie's breasts against the cotton fabric; down, then up, triggering fresh waves of panic deep inside her. 'No,' he said again softly, just the hint of a smile at the corners of his mouth. 'But believe me, lady, I'm learning fast.'

Billie bristled. She pushed herself free, scrambling to her feet.

The man followed, an unhurried return to the realms of normality, and then she had to crane her neck to meet his gaze, that mocking gaze that seemed to reach to the centre of her soul. Five feet nine herself and long used to towering above the males of her acquaintance, Billie's fluster doubled.

Time to leave, she decided grimly. Only how? Take the short cut and crawl through the hedge like a hoyden – hoyden! she berated herself, painfully aware of the sight she must present in the lived-in jeans and crumpled cotton T-shirt. Or walk the length of the garden, skirt the house and be escorted to the gate by *him*? Suppressing the urge to follow the cat and bolt across the lawn, Billie turned to face him.

'I – guess I'd better go,' she murmured awkwardly.

He seemed to read her mind, black eyes slipping past to scan the hedge behind, but he didn't speak, fell into step as Billie began to stroll towards the terrace.

'I think I can find my own way out,' she murmured coolly, careful to leave space – a lot of space – between them.

'I don't doubt it,' he acknowledged drily. 'Since you found your way in easily enough.'

'Don't worry, it won't happen again,' she retorted, risking a glance at the arrogant profile.

'Tell that one to the cat,' he replied with the merest hint of steel.

Billie increased her speed, striding ahead, aware of his eyes burning holes in her back yet unable to relax and feign the sort of unconcern she normally donned when feeling threatened. It was – disconcerting, this churning response to a man she barely knew. A tall, dark and handsome man, she silently mocked herself, while at the same time remembering the comforting touch of his arms about her shoulders, the heat, the glance, the ripples of excitement.

She quickened her pace, was conscious of nothing but the man who matched her step for step without seeming to hurry. He clearly couldn't wait to see the back of her and, as far as Billie was concerned, the feeling was mutual. As she stepped onto the terrace she gave another spurt, but the soles of her shoes were wet from the grass and she slipped, lost her balance and would have gone sprawling but for his arms, those disconcerting arms closing round her again.

14

'Hey, slow down,' he murmured, amusement threading the velvet. And he took her weight, pulling her against him, the powerful lines of his body moulding naturally to hers.

Billie gasped, attempted – gently – to wriggle free, not wanting to squirm and appear nervous, yet the grip simply tightened, increasing the panic as warm lips brushed against her ear.

'Manners, my lady,' he growled. 'Don't forget the magic words.'

Magic words? What on earth – ? And then the penny dropped. Billie stiffened. 'Thank you,' she ground out huffily, yet still he didn't release her. The nearness, the maleness, the unique body smell honed her sense of danger. Then another sound broke the silence, the tap, tap, tap of stiletto heels on concrete.

'What is it, Travis?' a husky voice enquired as tiny hairs on the back of Billie's neck rose like the hackles of a cat.

A woman rounded the corner of the house, the exquisitely made-up face registering surprise: surprise, curiosity and, last of all, contempt shadowing her features. 'Oh, I see!' Green eyes flashed their derision, missing not a thing, Billie was sure: her hot and guilty face, the torn and grass-stained jeans, the man's arm about her waist. 'A village urchin,' she scorned. 'How tiresome. Travis, darling, I do hope you've sent for the police.'

'No.' Firm male lips twitched again and Billie twisted free, her cheeks burning. 'Not yet,' he added provokingly, a wealth of knowledge in the laughing black eyes.

Alert green eyes narrowed at once and the woman's face hardened. 'In that case, Travis, we're wasting time. I'll do it now.'

'Easy, Cleo,' he soothed. 'The girl's done no harm.'

'Not this time, maybe,' she grudgingly allowed. 'But you know these village kids. Give them an inch and they'll take a mile, not to mention the apples that are missing from the trees.'

Apples? At this stage in the season? Billie smothered her derision. 'Not guilty, I'm afraid,' she said instead. Village kid? The nerve of the woman. Okay, so Billie didn't look her age at the best of times, but she was sharply aware that it was more than that. It was the contrast, chalk and cheese; smart town-mouse upstaging country cousin; the chic designer clothes that had clearly cost a fortune, not to mention the petite, china-doll figure that made Billie feel clumsy.

She folded her arms, nursing the tattered shreds of her dignity as the woman swept past in a cloud of perfume, her expression fleetingly ugly as she moved to claim her prize. Arms linked possessively through his, she gazed coyly up at him before turning the heady smile of triumph over to Billie.

16

The light in Billie's mind died. 'Can I go now?' she demanded curtly, switching her gaze.

'Be my guest,' he invited. 'Turn left at the gates, follow the road for a hundred yards or so and you can't miss it. The cottage with the cats,' he tagged on provokingly. 'When they choose to stay at home.'

'Only one,' she tossed out huffily. 'And he will.'

'For your sake, lady,' he all but growled, 'he'd better. Next time I won't be so understanding.'

Billie flushed but didn't reply. He was right, she supposed. She was in the wrong and since cats will be cats, the damage to the flower beds could be down to Smudge. More expense, she realized, her heart sinking. But she'd pay for every scrap of damage if it broke her.

It was the longest journey of her life, crossing the terrace, conscious of their eyes burning holes in her back, the arrogant stranger – neighbour, she supposed, half smiling at the image of cosy chats over coffee in her clean but shabby kitchen, and his equally arrogant girl-friend. Unless, of course, Billie mused, testing the idea and not liking it at all, unless she was his wife.

As she reached the corner of the house the woman's angry voice drifted across. 'You're a fool, Travis Kent, letting her get away scot-free. Before you know it, every Tom, Dick and Harry in the village will be running amok in your gardens.

17

When we're married – ' But the threat was lost, muffled by the sound of careless laughter, and Billie paused, hating herself for the weakness, but forcing herself to turn and watch, to witness the kiss, the casual embrace that drove the breath from her body for a reason she didn't want to analyse.

And then he raised his head, his gaze locking with Billie's.

'Don't worry,' he reassured as Billie looked on in silent misery. 'There won't be a next time. I'll have the holes in the fence put right while we're in London, and as for the girl – ' He paused, deliberately, provokingly, the challenge clear, in those mocking black eyes. 'Believe me, sweetheart, she won't be back. She might be a kid, but she got the message. No one, but no one, crosses Travis Kent.'

CHAPTER 2

'Kid! Can you imagine it. Twenty-two years old and he thinks I'm a kid.'

Anna smothered a smile, grey eyes crinkling at the corners. 'Look on the bright side,' she pointed out wryly. 'When you get to my age, Billie, you'll take it as a compliment.'

'*If* I get to your age,' Billie murmured, sipping her coffee. 'Unlike Smudge, I'm blessed with only one life and that could be in danger if the arrogant Travis Kent catches me again.'

'Well, he's certainly made an impression and, where you're concerned, that takes some doing. I can't wait for the next instalment,' Anna tagged on provokingly, walking her fingers across the table to the plateful of biscuits Billie had just put down.

'There won't be a next time,' Billie insisted. 'You must have noticed? His precious garden's safe inside a solid six-foot wall.'

'Good.' Anna licked her fingers clean of chocolate. 'You won't mind four abandoned kittens then. Just for a week or so,' she coaxed with a smile.

'Orphans?' Billie queried, not needing an answer. 'What happened this time?'

'Half-drowned, poor little souls. They were dumped in the canal, but a couple out walking heard their cries and managed to fish them out. Come and take a look. They're in the back of the car.'

'And here's me thinking this was a social call,' Billie sighed.

'And so it is. Me, and four homeless mites,' Anna agreed, taking the dig in good part. 'I'd keep them myself, but with two dogs, five cats and half a dozen kittens waiting for homes, I'm a bit short of room. What I need is a place in the country. Something like this,' she explained, waving a hand, 'for when I retire. If you ever thinking of selling, Billie, give me first refusal, won't you?'

'You're on. The thought of an animal sanctuary, right under the nose of a certain insufferable man, is almost irresistible. And talking of irresistible, how could anyone be so cruel? Oh, Anna, they're delightful.'

Anna had lifted the lid and four startled kittens stared up at them, tawny eyes wide with fear. They cowered in the corner of the box as Billie reached down, picking out the smallest, cradling it securely against her chest, her soothing words taking effect as the kitten nuzzled into the fluffy fabric of her jumper.

'Five weeks? Six?' she asked, gauging their ages.

'They're lapping milk so they're probably weaned. I'll advertise for homes,' Anna explained as Billie placed the kitten back in its nest and carefully lowered the lid. 'But in the meanwhile, if you could keep them here, you'd be doing me a favour.'

Billie smiled. It wasn't the first time and it wouldn't be the last. Rarely a month went by in the spring and summer without one of Anna's calls for help; at least these little mites were almost independent. Three- or four-hourly feeds with a mouth syringe took some doing, especially when working but, as Anna had explained, these were quite advanced. How Smudge would take to the new arrivals, though, was anybody's guess. And thinking of Smudge, Billie felt a twinge of unease. It must be an hour since she'd seen him last. Not that she was particularly worried. Travis Kent's fortress was impregnable.

Or rather, that's what Billie was hoping as she watched her godmother's car trundle down the driveway. Reaching the road, Anna turned left, avoiding Mr Kent's precious private lane, and Billie raised her arm in cheerful acknowledgement.

She went inside, checking the kittens were safe and sound in the spare bedroom – more a junk room, really, since Mum had moved out – and she was humming to herself as she rooted round for dishes and raided the cupboard for kitten food and milk. She was just snipping open the carton when an unexpected rap on the front door made her jump and she knocked the carton flying.

'Hell!' Smothering her annoyance, Billie grabbed a cloth and mopped frantically at the ocean of milk, before hurrying out to the hall. To her surprise, there was no blurred human figure framing the frosted glass. She halted, nonplussed, and was about to go back into the kitchen when an eerie sound made her blood run cold. Then she realized.

'*Smudge!*' She darted forwards, flinging open the door, almost tripping over the box at the top of the steps. The cat was howling pitifully, frantically clawing at the cardboard in an effort to break free. Sensing the animal's panic, Billie took the box inside before raising the lid. Smudge bolted upstairs, leaving a bemused Billie kneeling in the hall, her relief giving way to anger as realization dawned. Someone – that insufferable man next door, who else? – had deliberately trapped her precious Smudge. And then she saw the note, the bold scrawl almost leaping off the page.

'Returned, one hellcat – like its owner, out of control. Perhaps the enclosed will prove that I mean business, and that Travis Kent always keeps his word.'

'The enclosed' was a bill for damage, long, detailed – and to Billie's mind, unbelievable.

She saw red. 'Right, Mr Kent. If it's a fight you're wanting, it's a fight you'll get.' And she marched stiff-necked out of the house, down the straggly path, a hundred yards up the lane, pausing merely to draw breath as she reached the impeccable driveway. The wrought-iron gates stood open, a clear invitation to enter, Billy decided. So she did. Climbing the steps, she rang the bell and hammered away on the heavy oak door, the sound echoing in her mind, goading, taunting, until what was left of her patience snapped. Throwing back her shoulders, she headed round the side, coming up sharp as a set of iron fingers grasped her wrist.

'You again!'

'Don't sound so surprised,' she reproved, twisting free and standing her ground, although her insides were churning. 'After this morning's charming note, you must have been expecting me.'

'It did cross my mind. And sooner rather than later,' he drawled.

'Well?'

'Very well, thank you,' he stalled.

'Don't play games, Mr Kent. You know perfectly well why I'm here.'

'Ah yes. The little matter of damage to my garden.'

'Little? With a bill as long as my arm? Smudge is

23

a cat, not a herd of rhinos. And if the damage was so slight,' Billie challenged sweetly, 'why the hefty sum?'

'You've had the invoice; why not judge for yourself?'

'I intend to. In person. Every bulb, every plant, every seedling, each and every shrub.'

He smiled coldly. 'Be my guest,' he invited, waving an airy hand. 'In fact, don't stand on ceremony, make yourself at home. You've managed it before often enough.'

'Twice,' Billie bit back. 'And with never a blade of grass disturbed, I can assure you.'

'But let *me* assure *you*, the damage has been done.'

Impasse. Two sets of eyes, one cold as ice, the other hard as tempered steel. Billie held her ground, determined not to blink, to show any sign of weakness. It was hard; a vague unease was eating away at her. It wasn't the man, more the aura of power he seemed to exude. He was on home ground so the advantage was his; yet still she didn't waver, didn't move, hardly drew breath. Then he smiled, a cold, mocking twist of much too generous lips.

'I'm a busy man, Miss . . .?'

'Taylor. Billie Taylor,' she supplied coolly. 'And heaven forbid that I should keep you. Believe it or not, my time's valuable too.'

'Good. Let's keep it brief. A cheque to cover the

damage and we're quits. You *did* bring your cheque book?' he queried coldly.

'No, Mr Kent. I didn't see the need. I'm not paying. Not now, not tomorrow, not next week, not ever. Understand?'

'No, Miss Taylor, as a matter of fact I don't. Perhaps you'd better spell it out for me.'

'I just did. Here's your bill and here's what you can do with it.' She produced the sheet of paper and folded it in half and then in half again before ripping it into smaller and smaller pieces, her satisfaction growing with each and every tear. Blue eyes oozing defiance, she opened her palm, allowing the scraps to flutter through her fingers and scatter like confetti at his feet.

Your move, she challenged silently.

Black eyes hardened at once and Billie felt a *frisson* of unease. Neighbour or not, he was a perfect stranger, and the house and cottage were the only ones for miles. She sensed danger, the hairs on the back of her neck prickling out a warning, the fight-flight surge of adrenalin pumping through her veins.

'You know,' he murmured confidentially, folding his arms and watching her from under heavy brows. 'You could be sorry you did that. You could be sorry for a lot of things, but most of all,' he silkily informed her, 'you could rue the day you chose to cross Travis Kent.'

'You don't say,' Billie drawled provokingly, aware that she was playing with fire, that she was all alone with a man she barely knew and, if the worst came to the worst, she could scream herself hoarse and there'd be nobody to hear. She licked her dry lips as darting eyes gauged the distance to the terrace. Recognizing sickly that his long, lean legs would be sure to outstrip hers, Billie made a decision. After all, what had she to lose? And she sprang away, but the gesture was futile since, quick as a flash, he snared her again. Only this time the iron grip bit, held and refused to allow her to wriggle free.

'Not so fast,' he murmured, tugging once, twice, three times, each nonchalant jerk pulling her nearer and nearer to that scornful face, those frigid eyes, the grim line of his mouth. 'Like it or not, you and I have some unfinished business to discuss.'

'You can talk till you're blue in the face,' Billie informed him huffily. 'I'm not obliged to listen,'

'Wrong!' he contradicted coolly. 'You'll listen, you'll understand, and you'll never darken my door again. Leastways,' he added carelessly, 'not if you've any sense.'

'Are you threatening me?'

'Not threatening, merely stating facts.'

'Ah, yes, but whose version?' Billie enquired saccharine-sweetly. 'The truth according to the mighty Travis Kent or the truth, the whole truth and nothing but the truth? Why not admit that you're bluffing? Smudge breached your highly expensive security system and you're peeved. Damage? He's a six-month-old cat, for heaven's sake. He wouldn't hurt a fly.'

'Wouldn't he? In that case, lady, explain this.'

He turned, pulling Billie with him, and she had to run to match the pace that he set, dragged like a rag doll the length of the house and into the garden.

'You're hurting me,' she protested hotly.

'Good!' came the grim reply and the steel band tightened, bruising her skin, as Billie's vague unease gave way to alarm.

'Well?' he demanded, pausing at a rose bed, voice dripping poison.

'I – oh, no!' Billie's heart sank. Rose bed it may have been once, but she hadn't the words to describe the carnage. Not a single shrub was intact, with petals scattered to the winds like the torn scraps of paper she'd so recently flung in his face, yet he didn't give her time to think, setting off again at the same punishing pace.

'If it's the truth you want,' he informed her frigidly, 'it's the truth you'll have. Take a good look, my dear, and tell me what you see. Well?'

Billie shrugged. 'It's a mess,' she admitted stonily, absent-mindedly rubbing at her wrist, too shocked to notice that he'd released her.

'My, my, progress indeed. The lady sees things

27

my way.' And he smiled again, another cold, sneering curl of the lips.

Billie flushed. 'Wrong, Mr Kent. I was simply being honest. It's a mess all right, but it's nothing to do with me – or my cat.'

'No?'

'No!'

Another charged pause, black eyes locked with hers, smouldering with rage. He was angry, but he was wrong, although Billie could see why, could understand his need to blame, to hit out at someone for a mindless act of spite. And it had to be spite, she acknowledged sickly. Village kids perhaps, annoyed that the orchard of trees they'd traditionally poached was suddenly out of bounds. But he was wrong. He was blaming Billie and he was wrong. But how to make him believe it?

'Look – ' she began, as reasonably as possible.

'I did,' he reminded her. 'It was difficult to miss. One newly planted garden – ruined. I was less than an hour,' he almost spat, 'and you didn't waste a moment.'

'You can't seriously believe that I'm responsible?' Billie challenged, eyes widening at the thought.

'Why not? You're just next door, the only house for miles, in fact. Who better to know when there's no one home? You had the time, you had the motive.'

'Motive?' Billie gasped, stunned. 'What motive?'

28

'Isn't it obvious? You're peeved. Raggle-taggle cottage acquires a new neighbour and your pert little nose has been pushed out of joint. A touch of the green-eyed monsters, perhaps.'

'Jealous? Of you?' Billie laughed. 'Come off it, Mr Kent. You'll have to do better than that.'

'Wrong again. The logic can't be faulted. Tell me, how long has it been since anyone lived so close? One year? Ten? Twenty? Ah, yes, I thought so,' he added provokingly as Billie started, coloured and realized where the softly spoken words were leading. 'You're used to isolation, having things your own way, and you can't accept the thought of someone next door – in a brand-new house with brand-new gardens. Shall I go on?'

'Oh, I think you've covered all the angles,' Billie conceded coolly, folding her arms in turn and regarding him through a veil of lashes. 'You're quite a man, aren't you?' she sneered. 'Arrogant, rich – and smugly convinced that you have all the answers.'

'If you say so,' he acknowledged with another mocking smile.

'I do!' she snapped, aware that he was goading, that by rising to the taunts she was provoking the scorn, and she hardened her face, clamping her lips together in an effort not to rise.

Surprisingly, he smiled, a ghost of a smile that caused strange stirrings deep inside her body.

Confused by the signals, Billie turned away, her eyes scanning the garden, from the trampled beds of plants and the manicured lawns, to the damaged shrubs that led down to the orchard, which was a tangle of bushes and trees. Though the ground had been tidied, the trees had been left intact – such a contrast to the rest of the garden that Billie vaguely wondered why, the idea of the arrogant Travis Kent running out of money so absurd she was forced to smother a smile.

Sensing her amusement, he followed the line of her gaze, his anger and hostility for the moment set aside.

'It's quite something,' he explained on a lighter note, crossing to stand beside her, and Billie glanced up, the sudden nearness unnerving. 'I'd have bought the land for the orchard alone.'

'You mean, you're going to keep it?' she queried absurdly.

'Of course. Don't sound so surprised. Even the arrogant Travis Kent knows when to bow to nature.'

'I'm glad,' she approved, ignoring the barb in the self-mocking words. 'About the orchard, I mean. We had the run of the place as kids – and we did no damage,' she added defiantly.

'Your brothers and sisters?' he probed, refusing the bait in Billie's heated words.

'No.' Billie half smiled. She'd been an only child

of doting parents – a lonely child in many ways, but there'd been too many compensations to waste time on self-pity. 'Just me – and the other village urchins,' she explained with another show of defiance.

'You were lucky, then. I was brought up in a busy town and I never had the chance to roam free and arrive home grubby but happy.'

Poor little rich boy, Billie jeered, and yet her heart went out to the lonely child the simple words had conjured. Because she didn't know this man at all, she realized she could be wrong, and miles out in her assessment. For all she knew, Travis Kent could be a self-made man, hard-working, clawing his way up to the top by sheer determination. She found herself wondering just what he did for a living. Nothing mundane, judging from the house. The land alone must have cost a fortune, and as for the building . . . Billie shrugged. It was as plain as the nose on her face that no expense had been spared; she wouldn't mind betting Travis Kent had never known the taste of poverty. Everything about him screamed money: from the crown of that handsome, well-groomed head to the tip of his toes, neatly encased in the hand-made Italian shoes. He was a wealthy man – and it showed. And money, she was all too aware, went hand in hand with power – the power to destroy.

The memories flooded back: her father's struggle to hang on to the business he'd spent a lifetime building, her mother's pain when her world fell apart. And Billie hadn't known. Just sixteen and in the middle of her exams, she'd been blissfully unaware that anything was wrong because her parents had been brave, too brave, concealing their worries so Billie wouldn't suffer. She was their little girl and must never know how close they'd come to ruin. Until it was too late, much, much too late.

Billie felt the sob rise, the unexpected trickle of tears that she dashed away with the back of her hand as she struggled for control, hugging her arms to her body. She was vaguely aware that Travis Kent had moved closer, the handsome face no longer mocking but shadowed with concern.

'Billie?' he murmured softly. The familiar sound of her name on a stranger's lips sent currents of heat swirling through her veins. And again, equally softly, 'What is it, Billie? Tell me what's wrong.'

'Why?' she demanded, turning to face him, the surge of anger catching her off guard. 'Why should I? Why should you even care?' she all but spat, nostrils flaring white. 'You don't know me and that's the way I'd like to keep it.'

'Fine,' he conceded coolly, spreading his hands, the shutters coming down over strangely probing eyes. 'If that's the way you want to play it – '

'It is!' Billie hissed, wanting to hurt, needing to pierce that grave composure, to hit back at someone – anyone – for her father's death, her mother's illness. 'We inhabit different worlds, Mr Kent,' she heard herself condemning – unfair of her, she knew – yet she was powerless to stem the vicious flow of words. 'How could you possibly understand how normal people live, how they struggle to cope with the hand that fate has dealt them? Does this matter?' she railed, an outstretched arm sweeping the garden, furiously dismissive. 'Does it? Does it really? Twenty pounds, fifty, a hundred. You could replace it all tomorrow and never blink at the cost. But that's what matters to you, isn't it?' she rasped, eyes pools of contempt. 'Not people, other people's lives, their worries and their ups and downs. No,' she reinforced bitterly, 'as long as your precious world is safe, nothing else matters.'

'So – it was you?' he growled, snatching at her arms, fingers digging deep as he swung her back to face him. 'And I was right about the motive. Jealousy. Spite. Sheer resentment of someone else's success.'

'Wrong, Mr Kent,' Billie spat. 'Wrong! Wrong! Wrong! On every count.'

'Am I?' He shook his head, his black eyes holding hers, oozing condemnation and Billie squirmed. The heat from his strong fingers scalded her sensitive skin, spreading out, creating wider and wider ripples of heat that soothed and stirred, shocked and thrilled. Billie was confused, her reeling mind unable to cope with the conflict of signals. She felt the urge to bolt, to put distance between them, a lot of distance, but it was completely outweighed by the weakness in her knees as strange longings flooded through her. He shook her none too gently. 'Am I?' he repeated, his voice devoid of emotion.

'Oh, yes,' she rasped, beginning to struggle, needing to break free of his restraining fingers, yet the more she fought, the deeper the fingers bit.

'You're lying!' He dipped his head, condemning eyes much too close for comfort. 'You're lying to me and worse than that, you're lying to yourself. Who else had the time, the perfect opportunity? The postman? The milkman? Uncle Tom Cobbley and all? Don't be so naive,' he sneered. 'We're miles from the village, you little fool. It had to be you.'

Billie smiled grimly. 'Really?' And resisting the urge to laugh in his face, she shook herself free, rubbing at the skin where his iron fingers had left an impression. She was a mass of raw emotion: resentment, anger, incredulity, battling against newer, stranger, more fragile sensations. How dare he? How dare he condemn her out of hand? The whole idea was ridiculous, laughable almost and yet, judging from those frigid black eyes, he really did believe it.

'Oh, yes, really,' he repeated.

Billie raised her chin. 'Well, on that point,

Mr Kent, we'll have to agree to differ. I know the truth and without an ounce of proof, you'll just have to take my word – won't you?'

She didn't wait for a reply, simply swung away, heading for the gate, aware of his eyes boring holes in her back.

'I can wait,' he tossed out mildly, the calm assurance goading, and Billie spun round, raising her chin in defiance as Travis Kent smiled his now-familiar smile. 'Walk away by all means,' he invited with a sneer. 'But you'll be back; we both know you'll be back. You're a bitter woman and it shows. But next time I'll be waiting, and next time, Billie Taylor, I'll make you pay for every scrap of damage.'

'And what if you're wrong?' Billie demanded stonily.

'About you? My dear,' he informed her with another taunting smile, 'you really must learn that when it comes to women, Travis Kent is never wrong.'

CHAPTER 3

'Sounds like you had fun.'

'Fun? *Fun*?' Billie repeated, almost choking on her coffee. 'That's the last thing I've had. Ten days of peace ruined, all because that man doesn't like cats. I've never been so glad to get back to work in all my life.'

'You might change your mind when you hear the latest news.'

'Oh?' Billie queried, apprehension prickling.

Anna's face was sober. 'Rumour has it the company's in trouble and one of the big firms is showing an interest.'

Billie's heart sank. Not again – not another small family business swallowed up by some soulless, faceless company. Yet, if she was honest, it wasn't a surprise. The order books were anything but full and hadn't been for months.

'So, when shall we know?' she asked, pushing her cup away, the sour taste at the back of her throat nothing to do with the coffee.

36

'Straight after lunch. The Boss has called a special meeting. My job's bound to go, along with the other part-timers, but the full-time staff should be safe, subject to interview.'

'Oh, Anna. What can I say?'

The older woman gave a shrug of resignation. 'I'll manage. I was retiring soon in any case so, in a way, I'm glad they've forced my hand. I can do what *I* want to do, spend time with my animals.' And she shook her head, soft grey eyes full of compassion. 'No. That's not worrying me.'

'Oh?' Billie said again, alarm bells ringing. 'What is it? There's something else, something I'm not going to like?' And she racked her brains for the sort of news that could make Anna look so grave.

Anna nodded, leaning forwards, her eyes never leaving Billie's face. 'You're bound to hear sooner or later, so I'd rather it came from me. The offer's come from Giddings.'

'*Giddings*? Are you sure?'

'I'm sure.'

Billie went cold. She didn't believe it. A takeover bid was bad enough, but this was history repeating itself – literally. 'Right!' she muttered grimly. 'That settles it.'

'Oh, Billie, Billie, don't take it to heart. Please, don't do anything foolish.'

'Like resign before they sack me?' she asked bitterly. 'Oh, Anna, I can't work for Giddings.

37

Work for the firm that destroyed everything good in my life? Surely you understand?'

'Of course I do. It turned my life upside down as well, remember?'

'Ruined it, more like,' Billie reminded, her voice oozing scorn.

'No.' Anna shook her head. 'I was lucky. I found another job and I've had six happy years here.'

'And for what?' Billie railed with an angry toss of the head. 'To be pushed around, discarded, dumped on the scrap heap?'

'I'm not in my dotage yet, miss,' Annabel chaffed.

'No,' Billie hissed. 'But Mummy is, thanks to *them*.'

She couldn't believe it. Giddings of all people. The very name was enough to haunt her. Oh yes, she remembered it well. Giddings, bully-boy tactics, and dozens of lives thrown into turmoil – again. So what if jobs were safe, some of them, at least? Big deal, she scoffed. It didn't change a thing. They'd have her resignation by the end of the afternoon.

'And what good will that do?' Annabel chided when Billie voiced the bitter thought. 'Think, Billie, think. You need the job, need the money – '

'Not *their* money,' she hissed. 'Blood money. I'd rather starve.'

'And break your mother's heart? Oh, Billie, you couldn't.'

'I'll find another job,' she pointed out stiffly.

'Here? Designing? Doing what you're good at? Have some sense. You'd have to move away and you'd be leaving behind everything you loved – '

'Giddings destroyed everything I loved six years ago.'

'Not quite,' Anna reminded gently.

Billie swallowed hard. 'No,' she admitted with a catch in her voice. But her mother had never recovered from the shock of her father's death. She'd gone to pieces, lived in a twilight world of her own, Billie's visits a heart-breaking waste of time. Most days Marianne Taylor barely recognized her daughter, or the life-long friend whose worried gaze now rested on Billie's heated face.

'You couldn't leave, Billie,' Anna reminded softly. 'Marianne needs you. You're all that she's got left now.'

Although it wasn't strictly true, Billie could have argued, but didn't. The memories of her aunt were somewhat hazy. Hardly surprising, since Janey had settled in the States with barely a thought for the sister left behind. A birthday card, a Christmas card, but precious little else had winged its way across the Atlantic in the past eighteen years. And yet, had she cared to take an interest, Janey Housman-Steele had the means to make Marianne's life so much easier.

'Please, Billie,' Anna repeated softly. 'Don't turn

your back on Felbrough. Marianne's settled but she needs to know you're close.'

'York, Leeds, London – or Timbuktu itself,' Billie retorted harshly. 'She's my mother. She'll cope.'

'She's my friend,' Anna reminded. 'And you know full well she wouldn't understand.'

'She doesn't understand now, remember?' Billie flared. 'She's only half-alive – thanks to Giddings.'

'But, thanks to you, she's never lost the will to live.'

Maybe, Billie acknowledged with another stab of pain.

She turned to work, hiding the bitter thoughts behind a calm exterior. It was pure routine, attaching swatches of fabric to the sketches she'd been working on before her short break. Ten days. How much can happen in just a few short days. When she'd last opened her sketch block, Billie had been doing a job that she loved and thought was safe. And now? She sighed, pushing the nagging fears to the back of her mind as she flicked through the sample books, a ridge of concentration furrowing her brow.

It was a modest house with little scope for design, so Billie had kept things simple, with plain pastel walls and tiny print fabrics to help create an illusion of space. Everyday work – bread and butter work, her father had called it. Thinking of her father, Billie felt the tears well up. He'd had plans, such grand plans to expand the business: hotels, stately homes, 'Buckingham Palace itself, if the Queen will let me,' he'd boasted often enough.

But the hotels had been few and far between and the stately homes even more elusive. Yet he'd been happy, happy enough to wait for Billie to finish her education and then join him in the business, a business that didn't exist any more – thanks to Giddings. And now, incredibly, the company responsible for his death was about to ruin Billie's life all over again.

'So you see,' Peter Grace explained apologetically to the staff assembled in the cutting room, 'we didn't have much choice. Accept the offer or go bankrupt. Thirty jobs lost or a rescue package with half of them saved, more if we're lucky. The interviews start tomorrow morning, when the new man arrives; in the meanwhile, if there's anything you need to discuss, I'll be here for the rest of the day.'

Just a few short hours, Billie realized, and her carefully constructed world would never be the same again.

She turned away as the buzz of noise began, voices strangely subdued and heavy.

'Billie?'

She flushed, aware of the compassion in the older woman's eyes. 'Anna?' she stalled, equally aware of the concern behind the unspoken question. Billie

41

needed time, and yet time was the one thing Giddings wouldn't give. It wasn't even up to her, she realized. If she swallowed that pride and asked to stay, the final decision was out of her hands. By nine-thirty tomorrow morning Billie Taylor could be surplus to requirements. It all hinged on the interview. 'It's all right, Anna,' she found herself relenting. 'I'll give it some thought. I won't do anything foolish, I promise.'

Anna's grave expression lightened. It almost made up for the pain of having to swallow that pride.

Billie turned over, reaching for the clock, jerking wide awake in an instant. Oh, no! Of all the days to oversleep. Her lips twisted. Ironic, really. She'd spent half the night arguing it out in her mind and now fate intervened and made the decision for her. At least, that's the way it was looking. But since she *had* promised Anna . . . She pushed back the duvet, heading for the bathroom.

She'd had it all planned, her one decent suit hanging ready on the wardrobe door, the rarely needed make-up bag open on the bathroom shelf. She rifled the contents in a vain search for a lipstick. Ah well, they'd just have to take her as they found her, wouldn't they? Fresh-faced and eager. Eager? Her lips twisted again. Hardly. She was wasting her time, she convinced herself, dragging a comb through her hair and darting a critical glance in the mirror. But win or lose, Billie Taylor was going down fighting.

Five minutes later, the car wouldn't start, another five wasted while she coaxed the engine into life. The car shuddered up the drive, Billie over-revving as she paused at the top in an effort to stop the engine cutting out again. It was overdue a service, another expense she could well do without, she acknowledged wryly. She glanced at her watch. Eight twenty-five. She could be a devil and nip down the lane and be there by quarter to. Or take the road and risk being horribly late.

'Sorry, Mr Kent,' she murmured, swinging the wheel round to the right and setting off without a second thought, 'but my need's greater than yours.' Besides, at this time of day the lane would be empty.

Only it wasn't. She should have known. It wasn't her day, she decided as, taking the final bend just a shade too fast, she was forced to brake when she spotted the car ahead. Bracing herself for the worst, Billie clung grimly onto the steering wheel, sending up a silent prayer of thanks as the Escort slowed, juddered across the loose chippings – and then slithered into the back of the gleaming white Mercedes.

There was an awful clunk of metal on metal, the melodic cascade of shattering glass, and Billie closed her eyes, not daring to look, half-afraid she'd have shunted the white car out into the middle of the dual carriageway, creating carnage, but no, the Mercedes had moved forward all right, but she was lucky. The grass verge had absorbed much of the impact. Lucky! Billie took one look at Travis Kent's thunderous face as he swung himself out from behind the wheel and prayed for the road to open up and swallow her.

'Would sorry help?' she murmured, winding down the window and wincing at the fury in his eyes.

'No, madam. Sorry wouldn't help. What the *hell* do you think you're playing at? First your dratted animals, and now you creating chaos. My car could have been a write-off and all because you haven't the least regard for other people or their property. And in case you hadn't noticed,' he pointed out tersely, 'this is a private lane, *my* lane.'

Billie saw red. She was late. She faced an interview with a man she didn't know for a job she wasn't sure she wanted, and she was shaken, far more shaken than she had thought. And Travis Kent was worried about a few scratches and a couple of smashed tail lights on a car he could probably afford a dozen times over and never even blink at the cost! As for the Escort . . . she'd be lucky if it started, let alone limped into town for more repairs she could ill afford.

'You're right, of course,' she acknowledged heat-

edly. 'It's an organized campaign. My cat's deliberately ruined your garden and I'm hellbent on
destroying everything else. Well, I'm sorry,' she
spat, choking back the tears, damned if she'd cry in
front of this dreadful man, who could have been
killed, she realized with mounting hysteria. 'Yes, I
was driving too fast but I was late. And thanks to
you, now I'm even later – so late I'm probably out of
a job,' she railed. 'So if your precious car's acquired
a few dents, you will understand if I don't cry
bucketfuls. It could have been worse and the car
will mend. And *don't*,' she hissed, as he attempted
to speak, 'don't say a word. Along with the damage
to the garden, Mr Kent, just send me the bill.'

She'd put the car into gear as she was speaking;
now she turned the ignition, praying for a miracle
and getting one for once, and drove off, leaving him
standing, a stunned expression on his face. But he
was safe, she told herself as she slowed the car in an
effort to calm her frazzled nerves. She'd damaged
his car and dented his pride, but Travis Kent was
safe. So all she had to worry about now was the cost
of the repairs weighed against the loss of her no-
claims bonus. Oh, yes, and the little matter of her
job.

The buzzer rang, short, sharp and impatient. Peter
Grace's secretary smiled apologetically. 'Sorry to
keep you. We're running a bit late. I'm afraid. But if

you'd like to go though, it sounds like he's ready.'

Good of him to spare the time, Billie thought scornfully. Although she'd been glad of the delay. She had used the time to pull herself together, to put the morning's disaster to the back of her mind. And though she couldn't wipe the incident clean, she'd face Travis Kent, and his horrendous bill for damage, when they arrived.

So she paused outside the office – Giddings' office now, she supposed. For two pins she'd turn around and walk away without so much as a backward glance, only she couldn't. She'd promised Anna and, in a strange sort of way, she'd promised her mother. Straightening her back and lifting her chin, Billie knocked quietly on the solid oak door.

'Come in.' A strong voice, strong, vibrant and just vaguely familiar.

He was sitting behind the desk, head bent, engrossed in some writing, and didn't look up as Billie crossed the floor. She came to a halt, unsure of what to do, staring at the crown of a clearly arrogant head. Had it been Peter Grace, she'd have known to take the chair, but this man, this stranger . . . He glanced up.

'You!' Billie almost staggered backwards.

'The very same,' he acknowledged: for a moment, a fleeting imaginary moment, he was as startled as she. Only Travis Kent recovered fast. 'Won't you sit down, Miss Taylor?'

'Where's the point?' she challenged bitterly. 'I'm the last person Travis Kent wants or needs.'

'Your opinion – or mine?' he queried politely.

'Take your pick,' she invited frigidly.

'In that case, Miss Taylor, for the next five minutes at least, I'll keep an open mind.'

And then I'm out on my ear, she realized starkly, only her pride, that insufferable pride, stopping her from walking out there and then. Let him see that she was bothered? Oh, no! Billie was made of sterner stuff than that.

She took the chair, sitting rigidly upright, legs crossed primly at the ankle. Despite the rush, she'd tried to dress with care in her burgundy linen suit that echoed the darker glints in her honey-brown hair, the short jacket and knee-length skirt hugging the contours of her body. At eight o'clock this morning, she'd felt smart, sophisticated almost, but now she felt gauche, like an anxious teenager out on her first date. Though she tried to appeared as relaxed and unconcerned as he, her nervous tongue moistened dry lips, a gesture surely not missed by those sharp black eyes. Billie flushed, attempting not to squirm, returning the gaze with her own unblinking regard.

'So . . .' Travis Kent took up his pen. 'You're the girl wonder.'

'The girl *what*?' Billie almost choked.

'Come now,' the dry voice chided. 'Don't be modest. You must be aware of your worth.'

47

'I work hard, if that's what you mean,' Billie retorted tartly.

'A virtuous habit, indeed,' he agreed. 'But hard work alone doesn't guarantee success. At Giddings, we demand a lot of our staff: efficiency, reliability, the ability to cope under pressure and, in the case of our designers, lashings of talent and flair, the sort of flair that comes highly recommended. In short, Miss Taylor, you.'

'Are you making fun of me?' she demanded coldly.

'And what makes you think that?' he asked, folding his arms and regarding her from under drawn brows.

'Oh, just an impression, a vague idea.'

'Woman's intuition, in fact.'

'If you like,' she acknowledged grimly, her chin snapping up in defiance. 'But feel free to belittle that as well.'

'And incur the wrath of a very plucky lady? How could I dare?'

'Knowing you?' Billie shrugged. 'Without a qualm.'

'Ah yes, but don't forget,' he reminded coolly, 'you don't know me at all.'

Billie flushed. He was paying her back for an earlier gibe, and he was right. She didn't know him, didn't want to know him. Young, good-looking, rich, not to mention the lashings of arrogance, he

48

could vanish from her life tomorrow and she'd never grant him a second thought. Or that's what she told herself, blue eyes oozing defiance as she locked her gaze with his. She stopped short of the sort of candid, assessing glance he'd given her at their very first meeting. Common sense, she wondered idly, or cowardice?

Appearing to read her mind, Travis Kent smiled. 'So, Miss Wilma Jane Taylor, we both know where we stand.'

'On opposite sides of the fence,' she flashed. 'Remember?'

'For the moment,' he agreed pleasantly. 'But enough of the small talk, let's get back to business.'

Small talk? Ha! Talk about bowling a girl over. But he was right. They were wasting time, and time meant money.

'So – ' taking up his pen, he pinned her with his steely gaze ' – you know the score. Thirty people, twenty jobs. Why should you be one of the lucky ones?'

'Something to do with my lashings of flair?' she enquired with heavy sarcasm.

'Well met,' he acknowledged drily. 'But if you really want this job, Miss Taylor, you'll have to do better than that. You'll have to sell yourself – to me.'

'But if you want the best, shouldn't you do the bidding, or risk losing out to one of your rivals?' Billie reminded sweetly.

'What happened to the modest, unassuming Miss Taylor who knocked timidly on my door ten minutes ago?'

'She doesn't exist, as I'm sure you know.'

'Ah, yes. Quite an act. But not what I was expecting from Peter Grace's notes. "Hard working, conscientious, the best young designer I've known in a lifetime spent in the trade,"' he quoted lightly. 'An infant prodigy, no less.'

'It runs in the family,' Billie snapped. 'Though your precious company didn't seem to care six years ago.'

'I beg your pardon?'

'It doesn't matter.'

'So why the barbed comments, the face like sour milk? Though on second thoughts,' he added tartly, 'sour grapes is nearer the mark.'

'Meaning?'

An eloquent shrug of powerful shoulders. 'The green-eyed monster,' he silkily reminded. 'I'm this side of the fence, and you're that.'

'And that's the way you'd like to keep it, hey, Mr Kent?' Billie challenged.

'Strangely enough, no. But I don't expect you to believe me. So . . .' He turned back to the resumé, glancing down the page, giving Billie time to study him for a change. He was formally dressed, of course, the lightweight, steel grey suit, expensively cut yet worn with ease. He simply oozed money in that quiet, understated way that only a strong personality could carry. Look at the man, not the fine garments, Travis Kent was saying. And why not? The attractions were obvious and only a fool would try to deny them. Tall, slim yet powerfully built, he'd be used to women falling at his feet in droves. And yet, Billie remembered with a strange stab of pain, Travis Kent was spoken for, was engaged to be married to just the sort of woman Billie would have expected, someone in his own league, young, beautiful – and rich. Her lips tightened.

'If you've quite finished . . .'

She gave a nervous jump, realized she'd been staring, rudely, realized too that he'd been aware of the scrutiny and was vaguely amused as if reading her mind again. Billie flushed, discovering it was her turn as those cool, assessing eyes travelled the length of her, down, then up, missing not a single detail: the hostile face devoid of make-up, the generous curve of breast beneath the fitted jacket, her long, slender legs sheathed in black.

Resisting the urge to wriggle like a worm under a microscope, she held her breath as Travis Kent finished his inspection. With a nod of satisfaction, he raised his arms to the nape of his neck and leaned back in the chair, perfectly relaxed, perfectly at home.

'Welcome to Giddings, Miss Taylor.'

51

'Isn't it polite to offer the job first?'

'I just did. Don't tell me – you're about to turn it down.'

'As a matter of fact,' she informed him coolly, 'that's exactly what I'm doing.'

'You can't.'

'Can't I?' She smiled and, reaching for her handbag, rose leisurely to her feet. 'Just you watch me.'

'Is that wise?' he enquired softly. 'Think, Miss Taylor, think very carefully. Walk out on me, and you're finished in the trade.'

'Oh, I think I'll find another job easily enough,' she countered coolly, already turning away.

'And I think not,' came the equally cool reply. 'I'll make sure of it.'

Billie spun round. 'You're threatening me?'

'Not threatening. Just spelling out the facts. This company needs talent, your sort of talent. And if you think for one moment I'll allow that talent to escape to one of our rivals, then you're a bigger fool than I took you for.'

'And how do you propose to stop me?' she sneered. 'Handcuff me to the work bench?'

'Nothing so crude, I assure you,' he drawled. 'The answer's simple. No references.'

'I don't *need* references.'

'Everyone needs references these days,' he stated as a matter of factly.

'Then I'll see Peter Grace.'

'Don't waste your time,' he scorned. 'Peter will toe the company line – a neat guarantee that the sale goes through. In accepting the role of consultant, Peter's aware that his job, plus another twenty, depend on his co-operation.'

'In other words, blackmail.'

'No, my dear, just sound business practice.'

'Business practice? Oh, no. You're bullying me, probably bullied Peter. But Billie Taylor won't be pushed around. I'll go it alone and I'll survive.'

'As an ex-employee of Giddings? An ex-employee with no references?' he emphasized softly. 'Have some sense. There's not a company in the world will touch you.'

'But that's where you're wrong,' she pointed out sweetly. 'I don't work for Giddings, never have, never will.'

'Correction, Miss Taylor. You've been working for Giddings since nine o'clock yesterday morning.'

'You're lying!' she spat, sickly aware that she was clutching at straws. Travis Kent had nothing to gain from misleading her. 'You're lying!'

'Am I?'

There was a loaded pause, two people, two minds, two rigid iron wills. Billie glared back at the man behind the desk, anger and fear gripping her because she was afraid. Oh, not for herself – despite the veiled threats, Billie would survive, was one of life's fighters – but if she really did have to leave, find work in another town, how would she explain it to her mother?

'So – ' Travis Kent broke the stalemate ' – what's it to be? Common sense – or professional suicide?'

She supposed later that the unfortunate choice of words, following on from the morning's disasters, had been the final straw. She didn't think, didn't give herself time to think, her reactions pure reflex as she moved to the desk, eyes shooting daggers, nostrils flaring white.

'That's right,' she castigated coldly, the advantage hers as she towered above him. 'I might have known you'd find it amusing. Laugh, sneer, treat life as a joke. But whose life is it you're calmly rearranging? Mine! *My* life, *my* hopes, *my* future – if I have one,' she tossed out bitterly. 'But why should you care? With Giddings behind you, your cosy little world's all safe and sound. Isn't it? Isn't it?' she repeated, her balled fist hammering the desk as the anger spilled over, needing an outlet, itching to wipe the knowing expression from a much-too-handsome face. 'But that doesn't give you or anyone else the right to push me around. I'm flesh and blood, Mr Kent, not just a number on a payroll. I live, breathe, hurt and cry, like all the others whose lives are ruined by people like you. Only not this time. Believe me, this time it's not going to happen.'

'Have you quite finished?' he interrupted icily as Billie paused for breath.

'Finished? Finished?' she repeated frigidly. 'I haven't even started.'

'Then why not sit down, make yourself at home? It could be a long and bitter battle, my dear. Because when you've had your say, it's my turn. Only fair, don't you think?' he queried mildly. 'An eye for an eye, a tooth for a tooth – and an insult for an insult. And believe me, Miss Taylor, by the time I've finished with you, you'll wish you'd never been born.'

He smiled, a chilling snarl of the lips that made her blood run cold.

But it was suddenly all too much for Billie. The interview, the accident, the knowledge she could have caused carnage out on the road. Delayed reaction maybe, but the tears welled up, her control snapping as the anger waned. Fool, she sniffed, swinging away and heading blindly for the door.

Only the man out-thought her, outpaced her. 'Whoa there, lady, I can't let you leave like this,' he growled as Billie careered full pelt into him.

'Let go of me!' she spat, struggling to be free of iron fingers, fingers that sent currents of heat swirling though her.

'All in good time,' he murmured, and though he did relax the hold, he refused to allow her to pull away.

Billie shivered, aware of the man, his maleness, the tang of expensive aftershave. The touch was firm yet strangely tender. Despite the turmoil, it crossed her mind that had it been anyone else, she'd have welcomed the contact, would have allowed her body to melt against his, would have raised her face in expectation of a kiss. But Travis Kent stood for Giddings, everything bad in her eyes, and she scolded herself for giving it a moment's thought. Fool, fool, fool, had she no sense, allowing her guard to drop and handing him the chance to despise her? Travis Kent was spoken for, wouldn't dream of wasting time on some insignificant *hoyden* like Billie.

She sniffed and, in the midst of her misery, he relented, smiled, then dipped his head. Billie's heart turned over as she mis-read the signal.

'Here, take this. Your need's greater than mine,' he murmured, pulling a crisp, white square of linen out of a pocket and pressing it into her hand.

He turned away, giving Billie time to pull herself together, and she was extremely aware of every movement, every rustle of silk. He moved to the window, pushing aside the blind. Though Billie kept her back turned, in her mind's eye she could see the man framed against the light, the outline of a powerful body, the angle of his head. The knowledge that he had the power to turn her blood to water was unnerving and exciting.

'Better now?'

The sympathetic tone was almost more than she could take. Blinking back the tears, she crumpled the handkerchief into a ball and then spun round, blue eyes swimming with derision. He probably had her down as another hysterical female who'd reached the wrong time of the month. 'Yes. Thank you,' she murmured. 'And you needn't worry, I shan't embarrass you again.'

Expressive eyebrows rose but he didn't reply, simply waved a hand to the easy chairs grouped around the coffee table. Billie moved automatically, legs like jelly, her nervousness increasing as he took the seat beside her and pulled it in close.

'I make a good listener,' he surprised her by saying, 'if you'd like to talk.'

'And waste even more of your valuable time?' Billie shook her head.

'If you're going to work for me, you'll have to learn to trust me,' he chided.

'Work for Giddings, you mean? I'd rather rot in hell.'

'You might have to. It's a cold, harsh world out there and you can't afford the luxury of turning me down.'

'And how would you know?' Billie flashed, too raw to hide the pain. 'Or care?'

'I care. You might not believe it, but I care about people.'

57

'Working for Giddings? Come off it, Mr Kent, all they care about is the end-of-year balance sheet.'

'Maybe so,' he agreed tightly. 'But that doesn't rob me of feelings. I'm human, too.'

'If you say so,' she bit out.

'I do! Hell, woman!' he railed with unexpected vehemence. 'I'm a man, not the devil incarnate. Walk out of here by all means, Billie, if that's what you've decided, but don't make me your scapegoat.'

Billie flushed, a twinge of conscience pricking as her gaze collided with dark, glowering pools. No wonder he was angry. She'd caused a scene, embarrassed them both, and though he could have taken the easy way out and simply let her go, he'd been concerned enough to calm her down, repeat the offer of a job. And he was right. She didn't have a choice. Without a job, and a well-paid one at that, Billie could never afford the nursing home fees, could well end up on the breadline. And as for her mother . . . Billie swallowed hard.

'So – it's settled then. We have ourselves a deal?'

Billie glanced up. He'd been watching the shadows chase across her face and now he'd reached his own conclusions.

'You're so sure, aren't you?' she scoffed. 'You've been certain all along.'

'About you?' A ghost of a smile crossed his features. 'Strangely enough, Miss Wilma Jane Taylor, no.

'Well, you should be. Because if the offer's still there, the answer's yes. Satisfied now?'

'Not entirely. But I've sense enough to know to quit when I'm ahead. Tell me, though,' he entreated lightly. 'What exactly have you got against Giddings?'

Her face closed up at once, lips clamping together, and catching her reaction, Travis spread his hands.

'Okay,' he soothed. 'You're right, it's none of my business. But if you change your mind, I'd be interested to know. In the meantime, we'll forget it and I'll order some coffee.'

'Why?' Billie asked, instantly wary. 'I thought we'd finished.'

'Finished?' He shook his head, and watching him, slivers of fear snaked into Billie's mind. 'Oh, no. This is just the beginning. You and I, Miss Wilma Jane Taylor,' he reminded solemnly, 'have the slight matter of the damage to my garden, the damage to my car and the slightly more serious matter of business to discuss.'

CHAPTER 4

'Travis Kent's assistant? But you're a designer, not a secretary.' Tony Massie raised a puzzled eyebrow.

Billie smiled: 'Exactly. A good designer, one of the best. As Travis Kent's right hand, I must be – mustn't I?' she queried softly, hardly daring to believe it. And twenty-four hours on, she was still half convinced she'd dreamed the whole episode.

She'd left the office in a daze, her thoughts in a whirl, Travis Kent's words echoing in her mind. 'I'm a designer, too,' he'd reminded her. 'But I'm a man. I see things from the male perspective. And two heads are better than one. If a job's to be done well, I need someone I can trust to give an honest opinion, an honest *informed* opinion.'

'From the kid who supposedly ruined your garden?' she'd jeered. 'And who nearly killed us both in this morning's little shunt, how far do you think you could trust me?'

60

'In a professional capacity? Peter Grace's word is good enough for me.'

Of course, she'd acknowledged bitterly. In a professional capacity she had no choice. Throw a spanner in the works and she'd out on her ear faster than she could breathe.

She could hardly breathe now, she realized, smiling happily across at Tony's rugged face. She'd taken the job, she'd been promoted and, last but not least, she'd been given a hefty pay rise.

'And not before time,' Tony declared. 'But I wouldn't mind betting you're still worth double. You're wasted in Felbrough. Why not take a chance, move to London? You'd be making a fortune and be close to me. Yes, why not?' he urged, leaning forwards, clear blue eyes fastened on hers. 'There's plenty of room in the flat, Billie, and face it, we're good for each other. We could make it work, you know we could.'

'Maybe.' Billie smiled again, but sadly. She shook her head. 'It's a nice idea, but I couldn't leave Mum. She wouldn't understand.'

'She doesn't understand now,' he reminded her. 'Admit it, Billie, Marianne's ill and she won't be getting better.'

'But we don't know that for sure,' she chided softly. 'No one does. And you know what the doctors have said. A week, a month, a lifetime maybe, but there *is* still a chance that Mummy will improve.' And though she logged the doubt in Tony's eyes, Billie closed her mind, refusing to believe that Tony was right; warm-hearted, generous Tony who'd never let her down.

They'd grown up together. When other friends had moved away and left their roots behind, Billie and Tony had drifted together, not so much in courtship as a comfortable brother/sister pairing which had managed to survive Tony's move to London. There was the odd twinge of conscience when she suspected Tony's view of things was different to hers but, for the most part, Billie was content. She had one of those twinges now; the hint he'd dropped had been unmistakable.

'Stay for supper,' she urged, hoping to divert him. 'It's only quiche and salad, but there's a bottle of wine in the fridge that I've kept for a special occasion. And this *is* an occasion,' she pointed out brightly.

Tony checked his watch. 'Sorry, Billie. I'm meeting a client at eight. But that's not a problem. Why not come along?'

'And be in everyone's way?' Billie shook her head. 'I don't know a thing about hospital supplies.'

'Tomorrow then, before I head north? I'm due in Glasgow first thing Friday morning, and if I swing this deal,' he confided with a fierce touch of pride, '*I'm* in line for promotion too.'

Billie smiled delightedly. 'It couldn't have happened to a nicer guy,' she pronounced, hugging him and leading the way down the narrow hallway.

'It hasn't happened yet,' he reminded, and he paused on the doorstep, his expression serious. 'But when it does, Billie,' he told her solemnly. 'I'll be back, and you know what I'll be hoping.'

Billie nodded. *Could* she change her mind, she wondered, closing the door and leaning against it? Leave the village she'd grown up in, not to mention her mother and her job and the dynamic Mr Kent? *He* wouldn't take no for an answer, she knew instinctively. Or wait around for a girl to change her mind. He'd walk in and take control, would insist, cajole, charm his way through the problems. And he'd get what he wanted by fair means or foul. Oh yes, she acknowledged with a twist to her lips, the Travis Kents of this world always got what they wanted.

And working side by side with a man like Travis wasn't going to be easy. Which led her to the next disconcerting thought. Smudge, she realized with a jolt of alarm, hadn't been in for his tea . . .

'Cats will be cats,' Anna reminded her. 'And you might as well get used to it. He'll turn up when he's hungry.'

'But supposing he's hurt, lost, stuck up a tree, locked in a shed? Anything could have happened. And supposing *that man*'s hurt him?' she hissed in an undertone.'

63

'That man, as you insist on calling him, is our boss, and since he's just walked in, why not put your mind at rest and ask him?' Anna responded calmly.

'And warn him that Smudge is on the loose for the fourth time in a month?' Billie scowled. 'No thanks, Anna, I'd rather go to hell.'

'I wouldn't bother. It looks to me like someone's already been there.'

Billie glanced across. Anna was right. Travis did look out of sorts; furthermore, he was heading straight for their corner. Billie's heart sank. Who'd upset him this time?

'Good morning, Travis. And how's the garden?' she enquired brightly.

'Cat-proof,' he retorted crisply. 'I hope.'

'Good. Let's hope it stays that way.'

'It will,' he informed her curtly. He switched his gaze to Anna. 'If you'll excuse us,' he murmured, flashing her the sort of smile that made Billie go weak at the knees. 'I need to talk to Billie.'

'Of course,' Anna demurred as Billie's hackles rose.

'I haven't finished my coffee,' she pointed out coolly.

'I'll order some fresh. My office. Go ahead, I'll be with you in a moment.'

Yes, sir, no, sir, three bags full, sir, Billie silently sneered as she made her way down the newly carpeted corridor.

The office had changed, too, in the month that Travis had been there, Peter Grace's heavy oak furniture giving way to matt black, smoked glass and tubular steel. The easy chairs were low and matching leather and Billie paused, unsure of which to choose – the desk chairs or the easy chairs. Then she shrugged. It *was* her coffee break, after all. And she sank down onto the luxurious grey leather sofa, resisting the urge to snap bolt upright when the door swung open and a tight-lipped Travis reappeared.

He glanced across and then moved to the desk, pulling out a second chair before taking his own.

The gesture was unmistakable. Move, and move now, the body language stated baldly, and Billie felt a twinge of unease. She had the sneaking suspicion that, if Travis was annoyed, it had to be down to her. But conscience clear for once, she'd be damned if she'd worry – or jump to attention like a child. She glared across, returning his gaze with her own steady regard before rising leisurely to her feet and joining Travis at the desk.

There was another strained pause and then the coffee arrived.

'I take mine black,' he informed her, clearly expecting Billie to pour.

She bit back the comment that sprang to her lips, depressing the plunger and pouring the drink in silence. 'Sugar?' she enquired silkily. 'Or are you sweet enough?'

He darted her another cold look. 'Two, please,' he conceded and then, barely giving Billie time to fill her cup, 'You do know why you're here?'

'Haven't a clue,' she admitted. 'But it must be important since you've dragged me away from my well-earned break.'

'Ah, yes, but is it, though?' he challenged coolly.

'Is it what?' Billie snapped.

'Well-earned. Or is this the start of some sly campaign, the warning shot across the bows perhaps?'

'Meaning?'

'Come now, Miss Taylor. You're playing games. You know full well what I'm driving at.'

'As a matter of fact, I don't,' she informed him, subconsciously noting the use of her surname. 'Where work is concerned I never play games.'

'Pellaton Hall,' he prompted softly. 'We've lost the contract.'

'We didn't have a contract,' Billie reminded him. 'Just an initial consultation.'

'Which we've lost – thanks to you.'

'And how do you make that out?'

'Lady Catherine is a friend of mine. I couldn't believe it when she phoned. Naturally, I've tried to talk her round.'

Oh naturally, Billie mimicked silently as Travis paused, his face tight-lipped and grim, and watching him, Billie went cold. He really was annoyed –

understandable, she supposed. Rumour had it the hall was a designer's dream, completely unspoiled by progress, the original rugs and hangings the perfect template for the modern replacements. It was a once-in-a-lifetime chance to preserve the air of a fine old building and, since research could be cut to a minimum and tassels and trimmings ordered at once, the house could be transformed in a fraction of the time normally required. Only now – thanks to Billie – Giddings would never have the chance. Only that wasn't fair, she silently railed. But how to convince Travis? And then she stiffened. Why the hell should she? Either he trusted Billie to make decisions or he didn't. And since he clearly didn't . . .

'So – ' his tone was arctic ' – hadn't you better explain?'

'I *could*,' Billie conceded coolly, 'but I'm not sure that I want to.'

'You mean, you can't?'

'I mean exactly what I say.'

Another screaming silence, with Billie white-faced and tense on the edge of her chair, and Travis cold and controlled in his vantage position at the head of the desk.

This was it, she realized starkly, knuckles clenched tight in her lap. Unless she came up with a plausible explanation, she'd be out on her ear – jobless and unemployable. And yet she loved the job, had always loved the thrill of transforming even a modest shell of a house into a home to be proud of.

She'd enjoyed working with Travis, too, despite the strain of coping with his forceful personality. He was a true professional, hard working, tireless – ruthless, she wouldn't mind betting, though until now he'd kept that facet under wraps. But, best of all, their ideas had coincided. She and Travis had formed a team that other firms would find difficult to match. And maybe, just maybe, she'd allowed herself to hope, her future was secure. Once she proved herself in Travis's eyes, she could ask for that reference and escape from the company she'd spent six long years hating.

'Well?'

'Well, what?' Billie countered, resisting the urge to lick her dry lips.

'I'm waiting, Billie, and I'm running out of patience – fast.'

But of course, the arrogant Mr Kent snaps his fingers and the whole world jumps to attention. The whole world apart from Billie. She sat tight.

Travis smiled grimly. 'Nothing to say? Nothing to add? Come now, Billie, this just isn't you,' he berated. 'Spitting fire, yes – rightly or wrongly you've always held your own, but sulky defiance?' And he shook his head, waiting, still waiting, as Billie returned his gaze with her own unblinking stare. She was hurting inside, but she'd be damned if she'd let it show, damned if she'd explain either. She wasn't a child, for heaven's sake, They'd had a problem and she'd dealt with that problem and if Travis didn't like it, then tough. He'd just have to sack her. And yet . . . that was the last thing she wanted. Pride, Billie, pride, she chivvied herself, and she took a deep breath as Travis beat her to it.

'Hell, woman. Have you nothing to say? Don't tell me I've got to – '

'Fire me? Is that what you want?' she interrupted shrilly, her head snapping up in alarm. 'Well, go ahead. Don't let me stop you.'

'I was going to say, drag the story out of you,' he countered mildly. 'But I'm wasting my time, aren't I, you fool? You're digging in your heels and sealing your fate with your silence.'

'Wrong, Travis. *You*'re sealing my fate. You and your Giddings' ideals.'

'Why blame Giddings for your own shortcomings?'

'I *did* nothing wrong.'

'Then why can't you explain?' he riposted.

'Would you?' she demanded, politely, in the circumstances. 'Would you account for each and every move you make in my absence?'

'That isn't the same and well you know it. I'm the – '

'Boss?' she supplied with an angry toss of the head.

'The one who carries the can when something goes wrong. Damn it, Billie, you're not being fair.'

'Why? Because I refuse to be bullied? Because I believe in trust? Remember trust, Travis? Team work, trust, and a dozen empty words that aren't worth the paper they're written on.'

'Maybe you're right,' he conceded calmly. 'But how can I judge when you won't give me the facts.'

'Lady Catherine gave you the facts,' she reminded bitterly.

'Kate gave me her view. What I'd like now is yours.'

There was a long, loaded pause, Travis's black eyes fastened on hers, Billie's gaze equally unwavering. Stalemate.

Until Billie sighed. Why not? Why not get it over and done with? She tilted her chin in a gesture of defiance. 'Fine. Lady Catherine phoned. She was booked in for Friday and wanted to change it, wanted fitting in at once, in fact. No real problem except you were away and I was involved in the Dawson plans. When I offered to send one of the juniors, her ladyship pulled out.' Though not before she'd bruised Billie's ears with a string of pithy comments, Billie recalled, her face burning at the memory. And just to make sure she'd hammered the point, Lady Catherine had slammed the phone down.

'And is that it?'

'Isn't it enough?' Billie countered evenly.

'Kate said you were rude.'

'Lady Catherine was rude. Believe it or not, I was the soul of discretion.'

'But we've still lost the contract.'

'We didn't *have* a contract,' Billie needled. 'Just an initial consultation.'

'Which we've lost, thanks to you.'

Billie saw red. 'I might have known you'd see it her way. Walk all over the menials, why don't you?'

'And what's that supposed to mean?' he demanded.

Billie spread her hands. 'Peter Grace, Giddings, the whole shabby set-up. Not to mention Anna this morning.'

'Anna? Now what are you driving at?' he murmured incredulously.

'You were rude,' Billie accused. 'She might be working her notice but that doesn't mean you can trample all over her.'

'I was curt maybe. But never rude, I assure you.'

'And I assure you, that's how it seemed. You barely gave her the time of day. And why should you? She's just a number on the payroll and in a few short weeks she'll be living on the breadline.'

'Aren't you forgetting your facts?' he enquired mildly. 'The twenty-first century is just around the corner. Redundancy, retirement, the welfare state.

71

If Anna ends up on the breadline, it won't be down to Giddings.'

'No, of course not,' Billy scorned. 'The pay-off's more than generous, I'm sure.'

'Believe it or not, yes.'

'Oh, yes?' Billie niggled. 'Just like the last time.'

'Last time?' Travis queried, puzzled.

'Giddings. The big bad wolf of the trade. Gobbling up the smaller opposition.'

'And Anna lost her job, is that what you're implying?'

'Among others, yes.'

Travis shrugged. 'If Giddings was involved, Anna wouldn't have suffered. The company's generous to a fault in a merger.'

'I might have known you'd defend them. After all, they pay you to manage, and pay you well at that.'

'And is that a problem?' he enquired deceptively mildly. 'Or another case of the green-eyed monster raising its ugly head?'

'No, Mr Kent. No! No! No!'

'But from where I'm sitting, Billie, it's yes, yes, yes. I don't believe you.'

'Believe what you like,' she invited coldly, glaring back, matching glance for stony glance.

The atmosphere thickened. Billie didn't blink, didn't breathe, the room no longer in focus. Just the man, the much-too-handsome face with its sneering conviction that he knew best. And why not? Clearly a force to be reckoned with, in and out of the office, an aura of power oozed from the pores of his skin – power and control. Success was written into every arrogant line, the heady scent of power more than matched by the stunning looks and the undeniable appeal of a long, lean body. Not that Billie would admit to having noticed. Tight-lipped, back ramrod straight, she swiftly applied the brakes to that direction her mind was taking.

The phone rang, slicing through the tension.

'Yes?' Travis barked, and then his expression changed. 'Cleo, darling! What a surprise. Busy?' His dismissive gaze flicked aross the desk to Billie. 'For you, honey, I'm never too busy.'

Billie reached for her bag.

'I haven't finished with you yet,' Travis murmured, covering the mouthpiece as Billie headed for the door.

'Fine. But I need to powder my nose and then I'll order fresh coffee – if sir doesn't mind?'

He nodded and then swivelled the chair round, Billie instantly forgotten.

Having escaped, she took her time. She'd missed out on her coffee break and the cup on Travis's desk had lain untouched, forming a thick, unappealing skin as it cooled. Besides, she'd no intentions of playing gooseberry, third party to a love scene, and she lingered in the Ladies', glaring at her reflection in the mirror. Cleo, darling, she found herself deriding as she dragged a comb though her long, straight hair, didn't know the half of it. The man was impossible. Self-centred, arrogant, completely impossible, there weren't enough words to describe him. The lovely Cleo was welcome to him. And then something struck her, snaking in from out of nowhere. Jealous? Of Cleo? Billie felt her cheeks burn. Oh, no! The idea was ludicrous. Travis Kent was everything she hated in a man, *and* he stood for Giddings. As far as Billie was concerned, he and Cleo were made for one another

She forced a brittle smile as Travis's vibrant voice responded to her rap upon his door.

'Ah, Billie. Where were we?' he enquired pleasantly, the loving interlude clearly a mellowing influence.

Billie felt her hackles rise. 'Niggling about Giddings, as I'm sure you know.'

'The hand that feeds you,' he chided, jumping up and leading her away from the desk and formality. A tray of piping hot coffee graced the low table and Travis waited patiently for Billie to take her place on the low-slung sofa before slipping in beside her, unnerving her with his nearness. 'Never heard of loyalty?' he pointed out mildly. 'If you're so anti-Giddings, why stay?'

'References,' she reminded. 'You threatened me.'

'Threatened, Billie? Surely not.' There was the sudden flash of gleaming white teeth. 'Call it a timely reminder of the cold, harsh world outside.'

'Call it what you like, I recognize the truth when I hear it. You threatened me, refused to allow my talent and flair to go to another company. If I don't work for Giddings, I'm out on my ear.'

His mouth tightened. 'What is it with you? Do you have to be so negative? It's a good firm, Billie, one of the best.'

'That's right, defend them. You'll be telling me next to buy company shares.'

'Why not? With a personal stake in the group, you might even suffer a change of mind.'

'And be seen to condone their bully-boy tactics? Thanks, but no thanks,' she derided.

'Bully-boy *what*?' Travis spluttered. 'Now you're being ridiculous.'

'Am I? You don't deny it, I see.'

'Deny what? That Giddings succeeds where others fail? This is business, for heaven's sake. I work hard, everyone here works hard. That's the idea. Why should I feel guilty when someone less efficient folds?'

'So that's why you've dragged me back, to lecture me on the finer points of business management?' Billie needled, reaching murky waters and refusing to be drawn.

Surprisingly Travis smiled, one of those broad, disarming smiles that Billie was just being to place for what it was – a signal for danger. 'As a matter of fact, Billie,' he almost purred, 'no.' And then he paused, poured the coffee, slid a cup across to Billie, sugared his own and stirred the granules with slow deliberation as he drew out the moment. Watching him, Billie felt a prickle of alarm.

And then he explained.

'You are joking?' she enquired politely.

'Where business is concerned, I never jest.'

'But – ' Billie was flustered. 'I'm busy. I've work to do here, a dozen and one things demanding my attention.'

'Correction. We've got work to do at Pellaton. And believe me, Billie, if it takes till midnight, we'll smooth things over with Kate. This contract's important.'

'But – ' Billie felt the panic grow. Travis couldn't know it, but it was the one evening in the week when her mother could be sure that Billie would visit. She'd go straight from work, stay for supper, sit in the gardens if the weather was fine, read, knit or watch TV – the ordinary, everyday things that a mother and daughter would do at home. And though Marianne seemed not to notice that Billie was there, the doctors were convinced that the routine helped.

She jumped up, crossing to the window, needing

time to think, folding her arms and hugging her body, suddenly chilled, though the office was warm. 'I can't work over,' she said without turning. 'Not today. I have – responsibilities,' she explained coolly.

'Ah yes, the flashy BMW. Quite a responsibility.'

Tony's new car, Billie acknowledged, startled. His consolation prize for missing out on that promotion. 'You don't miss much, do you?' she sneered, angling her head, her expression arctic.

'When it affects me, or the company,' Travis agreed pleasantly, 'no.'

'This has nothing to do with you – or the company,' she reminded icily.

'Wrong, Billie. The first rule of business, the customer's always right. And Kate's expecting us, expecting us both. And if I can talk her round, you'll stay and do the work.' No fine words, no persuasion, just a thinly veiled threat. Billie would stay. Or else.

'Fine.' She smothered the spurt of anger. Why make another scene, give Travis the satisfaction of goading her again? 'But I need to make a phone call.'

'No problem. Help yourself.' He nodded at the desk.

Billie flushed. Discuss her private affairs here, with Travis soaking up every word? 'Thank you. But that won't be necessary. I've a perfectly good phone of my own. If you've quite finished?' she added politely.

'Oh, quite,' he agreed, but tawny lights danced in laughing black eyes and Billie flushed, aware that he'd seen through her. 'In fact,' he added easily, unravelling long, lean legs and rising casually to his feet, 'since the day's planned, the sooner we leave the better. If we need to talk, we can talk in the car. We'll go in mine.'

Naturally, Billie mimicked. Expect the arrogant Travis Kent to make do with her old banger? And as for her driving skills . . . Billie's annoyance vanished. There had been no real damage to either car, she'd been relieved to discover, so when the bill arrived, she'd barely been out of pocket.

He walked her across to the door and she was very aware of Travis beside her, ever the gentleman as long, tapering fingers reached out for the handle.

She halted. 'Is this likely to happen often?' she asked, forcing herself to meet his gaze, that mocking gaze that seemed to see to the very centre of her soul.

'It's possible,' he agreed as Billie's sinking spirits settled somewhere near the floor. 'Is that a problem?'

She shrugged. 'It could be,' she admitted frankly, and the vague unease turned to alarm as Travis smiled, another mocking, taunting, goading smile that turned her blood to water.

'In that case, Billie,' he pointed out slyly, folding his arms and leaning back against the wall, 'it looks like you've a problem. What's it to be?' he invited calmly. 'The job – or your social life?'

CHAPTER 5

'Now what are you doing?' she demanded as the powerful car pulled off the road and into the pub car park.

Travis grinned, teeth flashing white in the August sunshine. 'Relax, Billie,' he entreated. 'It's a beautiful day, the sun is shining, the birds are singing and you and I deserve to be spoiled. Homemade steak and onion pie,' he informed her. The best in all Yorkshire. You'll love it.'

'I normally skip lunch,' she explained, the thought of sharing a meal – any meal – with Travis filling her with panic.

Travis groaned. 'Not another foolish female starving herself in the name of fashion, surely?' he derided, his contemptuous gaze flicking over Billie as he killed the engine. 'You're all skin and bone, child,' he pronounced carelessly. 'The slightest puff of wind and you'd blow away.'

Child? Billie bristled. Did he have to be so – so –

so impossibly condescending? she asked herself, biting back an angry retort.

Travis held the door, helped Billie from the car, the hand at her elbow sending currents of heat pulsing through her veins, and though Billie had the urge to shake herself free, she let the touch remain, the need to appear cool, calm and collected – and anything but a child – overriding the nerves.

Passing from the glare of the sun into the grey stone building, Billie paused on the threshold, her eyes adjusting to the gloom.

An impatient Travis tugged her inside. 'Mrs Bridges,' he requested as they reached the bar, 'a glass and a half of your finest beer for two parched and weary travellers, if you please.'

'Travis!' The plump, rosy face beamed her approval. 'My dear, it's been a long time.'

'Too long,' he agreed ruefully. 'But now that I'm back, wild horses wouldn't keep me away.' He introduced Billie. 'She needs fattening up,' he explained in an audible whisper as Billie stood and fumed. 'What would you recommend?'

The landlady nodded. 'Just leave it to me,' she insisted in a broad Yorkshire burr.

'Your local?' Billie enquired with heavy sarcasm as Travis picked up the glasses.

'Hardly,' he murmured, weaving his way through the lunchtime crowd, nodding at one or two friendly faces as they passed. 'But I like to call in, when I'm in the area.'

He led the way into a small, secluded garden, the borders a riot of colour, and Billie joined him at one of the rustic wooden tables, thankful they weren't alone. Her relief lasted a whole thirty seconds, the time it took for the young, besotted couple to leave hand in hand.

'So – ' she licked her dry lips ' – what are we doing here?'

'I've told you. It's lunchtime and I, for one, am starving.'

'And I need fattening up?'

'It wouldn't do you any harm,' he admitted, his heated glance candidly assessing Billie's slender form.

She felt the colour creep into her cheeks. Just like a child, she found herself deriding, aware that the more she tried to shake the annoying habit of blushing, the deeper the colour ran. 'And what about work?' she demanded, taking a welcome sip of beer and glaring at Travis across the rim.

'Work can wait. This is important.'

'Work *is* important,' she needled. 'Pellaton Hall, remember, and the lovely Lady Catherine?'

Travis spread his hands. 'Half an hour. You wouldn't begrudge me that now, surely?'

Billie would, but as the steaming platefuls of food arrived on cue, she held her tongue. She was hungry, she discovered, and Travis was right: the pie was delicious. Served with fresh local vegetables and an excellent gravy, there was little room for the cheese and apples that followed. Travis, she noted with interest, consumed the lot. Skin and bone he'd never be, but she was all too aware there was little spare flesh on his long, lean form.

'So why the faddy diet?' he demanded once the plates had been cleared.

'Who mentioned diets?' Billie stalled, checking her watch and hoping he'd take the hint.

Travis shrugged. 'You did. If a woman doesn't eat in the middle of the day, there has to be a reason.'

Time, Billie could have explained, but didn't. Most days she'd too much to do to stop and eat, but Travis didn't need to know. He was her employer, not her keeper; as long as she was back at her desk on the stroke of one, Travis had no room for complaint. Besides, if she was engrossed in her designs, she preferred to work through or catch up on some research in the library. Giddings, like Grace and Son before it, did well out of Billie. And as for the spot of freelance . . . Billie shrugged. Even by the widest stretch of the imagination, designing clothes was hardly the same.

'Another drink?' Travis enquired when Billie drained her glass.

'No. Thank you.' And when Travis made no

move to finish his own, 'Shouldn't we be going?'

'In a hurry, Billie?' he queried, clearly amused. 'Now why, I wonder.'

'You know perfectly well why,' she admonished.

'Ah yes, the lovely Lady Catherine. Don't worry, her bark's worse than her bite.'

'It had better be. A second blast from that sharp tongue would try the patience of a saint.'

'And that's something you'll never be, hey, Billie?'

Billie flushed. Travis was teasing. In another man she'd suspect that he was flirting, but with the glamorous Cleo hanging on his every word, Travis had no excuse for playing games, not those sorts of games, at least.

The garden filled with a group of students dressed for walking and harassed parents with their brood of small children, and still Travis sat on, an impatient Billie curbing her annoyance, allowing the drone of the bees and the warm August sun to soothe her. Ten minutes, twenty, half an hour, it hardly mattered now. To anyone watching, they were just another couple enjoying the hot summer spell. And since Travis was surprisingly easy to talk to away from the strains of the office, it was nothing like the ordeal Billie had been expecting.

He was relaxed for a start, the morning's anger forgotten, jacket carelessly slung on the back of a chair, shirt sleeves pushed to the elbows exposing the lightly tanned flesh beneath a mass of dark hair, a casual effect that Billie found disturbing. So he was her boss, the new broom still to be tested – her wariness was natural, surely? And yet it was more than that, Billie acknowledged. She tried to pretend that she'd have felt the same had he been fifty, fat and bald but she was painfully aware that she'd be lying.

'So, Miss Wilma Jane Taylor. Now that you've had time to get used to the idea, how do you like working for Giddings?'

'Giddings – or you?' she stalled, biting back the comment on the tip of her tongue. Miles from Felbrough and alone with Travis, she wasn't about to provoke another niggle. There'd be no more niggles, she'd finally decided. She needed to escape, and once Travis had settled in and Billie had proved her worth, she was determined to ask for that reference. She'd pick something up in York, she'd been thinking, and she'd soon get used to commuting. It was hardly a desk job in the first place, given the time spent visiting clients, so as long as Billie had a base, she'd get by. Giddings paid the bills for now, but Billie couldn't come to terms with her conscience. By working for the firm that had caused her father's death, she'd set the value on his life at thirty pieces of silver.

'Both, I suppose,' Travis conceded. 'At the end of the day, isn't it the same?'

Billie shrugged. 'Not exactly. I can put a face to your name,' she explained, mindful of the need to keep that fragile peace. 'But mention Giddings and there's something missing.' The personal touch, she could have told him, but didn't.

'So working for Grace and Son was different? I don't see how,' he challenged when Billie nodded. 'It can't have changed much in the space of a month.'

'No-o,' she allowed. But there were plans, ideas that took her breath away. Wallpaper, paints, fabrics, the intricate trimmings that added just the right touch, to name but a few. One way or another, Travis seemed determined to make his mark on the Giddings organisation.

'Why dilute the profits?' he'd explained before the ink had dried on Billie's new contract. 'We broaden our base, cut out the middle man and we produce the goods. Small factory units with nothing mass produced, just individuality, Giddings individuality – at a price. And Giddings will have arrived, will be *the* name in interior design.'

And Billie had been stunned, the vision poles apart from anything her father could have imagined.

Travis would do it, too, she'd conceded bitterly. And all the fine words in the world wouldn't change the way she felt. Cut out the middle men and trample the opposition – bully-boy tactics, the same bully-boy tactics that had cost Billie her father.

'Something tells me Miss Wilma Jane Taylor doesn't approve. Of me, I wonder, or the company?'

Billie glanced across, flushing under Travis's knowing stare. 'My name's Billie, for heaven's sake. Do you have to keep trotting out that ridiculous list?' she demanded irritably.

'I happen to think it has a ring to it. Billie makes you sound like a tomboy.'

'Well, maybe I am. I've climbed enough trees in my time,' she reminded him.

'Past tense, Billie? Or present?' he enquired slyly, and Billie's stain of colour spread.

'Ah. So you'd noticed. And I thought I'd been discreet.'

'You were. Why else would I turn a blind eye?'

Why else indeed? she asked herself, relieved to know the cat had caused no damage.

'He never had,' Travis confessed when Billie put the thought into words.

'You mean – you've known all along and let Smudge take the blame?'

'Hardly a crime,' he pointed out lightly. 'And if you hadn't blown your top, gone up like Vesuvius, you'd have worked it out for yourself. After all, you were the one who gave me the hint.'

'I did?' Billie queried.

'Village kids,' he explained. 'They've had the run of the copse for years. And as long as they stick to the far end of the garden, I'm happy to turn another blind eye. I don't need the fruit and they're doing no harm.'

'Isn't it time we were going?' she demanded tartly, the glimpse of the man beneath the steel suddenly disconcerting. 'After all, the sooner we get there, the sooner we'll get away.'

Expressive eyebrows rose. 'You *are* in a hurry,' he accused.

'No, Travis. *You* are. To salvage this contract. And since the afternoon's half gone and we haven't even arrived, I dread to think what time we'll make it back to Felborough – '

'Oh, so *that*'s what's eating you,' he acknowledged mockingly. 'The need to get home. Now why, I wonder? Got a date, Billie?' he enquired slyly. 'Someone special? Anyone I know?' And he leaned back in his chair, hands linked at the back of his neck, black eyes far too knowing. 'The rugged Viking perhaps, sweeping you off your feet in the flashy BMW?'

'Mind your own business,' she retorted, amazed that he'd noticed not just the car but had seen enough of Tony to give a fair description.

'But it is my business. Since I'm paying for your time, the least I expect is one hundred per cent attention.'

'Which you've got,' she acknowledged. 'If it takes till midnight, remember? But at this rate,' she hissed, blue eyes shooting flames, 'it will be midnight tomorrow.'

'Suits me,' he drawled provocatively, ignoring Billie's scowl.

Billie felt her cheeks flame. Impossible man, she silently proclaimed, snatching up her handbag and flouncing to the Ladies'. This time she didn't dawdle. Give Travis the chance to accuse *her* of wasting time? Oh, no! And she dragged a comb through her hair and added a light coat of lipstick before striding back outside.

Travis was waiting, propping up the wall, and as Billie reappeared, he pointedly checked his watch. Billie ignored him, swinging away and heading for the car park. She reached the doorway, the sudden glare of the sun blinding and she pulled up short, giving Travis time to come up behind.

'This way, my lady,' he murmured, taking her hand and tugging her forwards.

'I'm not a child,' she protested, shaking herself free,

'No?' Travis halted at the car, the only car left, she noticed, the thought vaguely alarming. He shook his head. 'Child? No, Billie. I never for a moment took you for that,' he murmured huskily and he reached out, fingers closing round her shoulders as Billie went rigid, the heat spreading out at once, tiny currents that pulsed from every point of contact. Billie had to fight the urge to pull away, to bolt, to put distance between them, a waste of time in any case since Travis held her, the hands but a gentle restraint as the black eyes pinned her. 'Oh, Billie,' he murmured softly and he dipped his head, his mouth brushing hers, a fleeting touch but enough to send the heat flooding through her veins.

Billie went weak. She swayed against him, felt his arms close round her, heard Travis murmur something low and urgent and she parted her lips, an eloquent invitation that Travis couldn't resist. Then his mouth was moving against hers, lips now gentle, now persuading, now hungry and demanding, his tongue sweeping though into the warm, moist depths of her mouth, swirling across the soft, sensitive inner flesh of Billie's lips, and she moaned aloud as Travis growled, as the tip of his tongue explored the tip of hers, danced with hers, fresh darts of pleasure filling her with heat.

And while mouth explored mouth, his hands moved down the lines of her body, following the curves, into her waist and over the swell of her buttocks, tugging her even closer, and Billie gasped at the contact, felt the hardness against her groin, felt the thrill run through her. She wanted him. Impossible, she knew, but oh, how she wanted him, and her mind soared skywards as she realized Travis wanted her every bit as badly.

And the kiss went on, his lips nibbling, teeth biting, her own response pure instinct as she raised her arms to the back of his neck, allowing her breasts to lift, to brush against his chest, her nipples hardening at the contact, Travis growling at the contact as he tugged her even closer.

'Billie, oh, Billie,' he murmured, and his hands were kneading and caressing, urging her into the hard lines of his body, and Billie moved her hips against him, fuelling the need, stoking the flames, and as Travis groaned aloud Billie gave a throaty chuckle of delight.

'Easy, sweetheart,' he entreated thickly, and Billie smiled inside, relaxed the pressure of her hips, her fingers kneading the skin at the nape of his neck, reaching upwards to rake through the thick mass of his hair. And as her hands reached upwards so did his, gliding into the curve of her waist, and higher still until his thumbs were stroking the soft underswell of Billie's breasts, breasts screaming out to be touched, nipples rigid and tingling as Travis denied her, stroking, caressing, filling her with heat yet denying her the contact that she craved.

A lifetime passed and then he gentled his lips, calmed the frenzy, and Billie smothered the disappointment as his arms closed round, holding, enfolding, and they stood together, heart to heart, cheek to cheek until the day came back into focus.

Billie glanced up, all of a sudden very, very shy.

'Not so skinny after all,' Travis murmured, and he smiled down into her face, Billie's heart turning over as their glances locked. 'And definitely not a

91

child. Oh, Billie, Billie,' he crooned. 'I've wanted to do that for weeks, ever since you first dropped in on me, in fact. But it was definitely worth the wait, my little tigress. Oh, yes,' he reinforced smokily, 'the waiting was part of the fun.'

Fun? Billie stiffened. Was that all? Was that how he viewed it – just a kiss, a casual embrace, an idle moment of pleasure?

The surge of anger drowned the disappointment. 'You shouldn't have done that,' she flashed, pushing herself free, and though tears scalded the backs of her eyes, Billie blinked them away. 'You had no right.'

'Right?' Expressive eyebrows rose. 'Don't be so ridiculous,' he scorned. 'What rights are involved in a man kissing a pretty woman, a woman who didn't seem to be raising any objections?'

Pretty? Oh yes, Billie railed as the pain scythed through. Put her side by side with the elegant Cleo and guess who'd pale into insignificance? And thinking of Cleo . . . 'You *are* engaged,' she hissed, 'in case you'd forgotten. And I – '

'Have the rugged Viking to think about? But he wouldn't begrudge me a kiss, surely, Billie? And what the eye doesn't see, the heart can't grieve for.'

'The Travis Kent philosophy of life,' she sneered.

'Not at all. But these things happen, Billie. So if you feel the need to run and tell, salve your guilty conscience, don't let me stop you.'

'I've done nothing to be ashamed of.'

'No? Well, that makes two of us. But at least I'm not afraid to admit that I enjoyed it, each and every moment in fact – just like you.'

'And what if I did?' she allowed, his easy words goading. 'I'd have to be made of stone not to respond to someone as skilled as you. Had a lot of practice, Travis?'

'No more than any other normal, healthy male,' he growled. 'And you're a normal, healthy woman judging from your reactions. All woman, in fact.'

'But not your woman,' she reminded.

'No.' Generous lips twitched and Billie flushed. 'Wishful thinking, Billie?' he slipped out slyly. 'Doesn't the rugged Viking come up to scratch?'

'Leave it, Travis,' Billie snapped.

'Only asking,' he conceded coolly and then he shrugged, slipped a hand and into a pocket and fished out his keys. 'We're late,' he reminded as the strident central locking tone declared the incident over. 'Get in.'

Billie winced at the curt, derisive note and the tears welled up again, hovering on her lashes. As the car swam out of focus, she swung away, a hand on her arm bringing her up short. She glanced down, then up, frigid blue eyes glistening with contempt.

'Don't overreact,' he entreated, the easy words pouring salt on an open wound. 'It was – just a kiss.'

Just a kiss? A moment of magic to Billie but just a kiss to a man of the world like Travis.

She angled her head. 'Fine. You keep your distance, I'll keep my cool.'

'And miss out on the fun, Billie?'

'Fun? Yes, I might have known you'd see it that way. The prerogative of the ruling class,' she sneered.

'Meaning?'

'Meaning precisely that. You're the boss, I'm a mere employee. You pay the piper, you call the tune.'

'And Billie Taylor doesn't like being told what to do, is that it?'

'Doesn't like being pushed around, by you – or that unscrupulous firm I have the misfortune to work for.'

The moment the words were out, Billie realized she'd gone too far. His face changed, anger replacing the sneer.

'What is with you?' he demanded, snatching at her arms and tugging her close. 'You never miss a chance do you, Billie? Carping, sneering, sly insinuations about Giddings. Why, Billie, why such a warped view?'

'You wouldn't understand,' she insisted, struggling to be free but locked in grip of tempered steel.

'I might, if you gave me some facts. But you can't, can you?' he demanded. 'The big bad wolf doesn't exist – except in your mind.' He shook her roughly, black eyes raining scorn. 'Admit it, Billie, you've nothing to go on but rumour.'

'Let go of me,' she spat, logging his anger, the flared nostrils, the contempt raining down from frigid black eyes.

'When I'm good and ready,' he rasped. 'And not before. Face it, Billie, you're living in a dream world.'

Dream world? Ha! A nightmare, more like, a nightmare created by Giddings. Her mind slipped back, remembering the day they'd told her, the day her safe little world had come crashing to an end.

She'd been at school, in the middle of an exam, and the police had arrived. Just two of them, a man and woman. Strange, really, that Billie should have raised her head just as the car had pulled onto the drive. She'd vaguely wondered why and then she'd glanced at the clock, had decided time was running out, completely unaware that that's how it had been for her father. While Billie's mind had been grappling with the events of the Industrial Revolution, her father's will to live had already died. Thanks to Giddings.

'Well?' The single word held a wealth of menace and despite the heat, Billy shivered. 'Are you going to behave like an adult or do I have to talk some sense into you?'

'That's right,' Billie goaded, her chin shooting

up. 'Threaten, bully. Just like Giddings, if you can't buy what you want, take it by force.'

'And what's that supposed to mean?'

'House of Marianne,' she spat. 'Six years ago.'

'House of – ? Oh, yes.' Generous lips curved in derision. 'A tuppeny-ha'penny firm,' he pronounced scathingly. 'I remember it well. And Giddings bought them out. All above board and legal,' he emphasized grimly. 'Believe me, I know.'

'But I know different,' she hissed. 'And Anna – '

'Lost her job? Survived? Now works for Giddings?' he supplied with a lightning flash of logic. 'But since Anna doesn't object, why should you?' There was a pause, black eyes oozing scorn and oh, so confident. 'Well, Billie?' he prompted softly. 'Answer me that – if you can.'

And if she did, Billie allowed as the anger turned to pain, what difference would it make? At the end of day, it was much, much too late.

She shook herself free. 'We're late,' she reminded in a voice devoid of emotion. 'We'd better go.'

'Oh, no!' His mouth was grim and Billie stumbled backwards as Travis closed in again, pinning her against the car. 'I've had enough,' he rasped. 'You've spent weeks and weeks sniping at Giddings but this is the end of the line. So – decision time, Billie. Bury your resentment and work for me – or go. Giddings or the scrap heap,' he reinforced softly. 'And I want to know now.'

CHAPTER 6

It wasn't the easiest three weeks she'd ever endured, but Billie made the best of it, the outward calm hiding a wealth of emotion as she buried herself in work and fooled the world that she was happy. Only Anna, caring, wise Anna wasn't deceived.

'What is it?' she asked. 'Something's bothering you. It can't be problems here or half the staff would be aware of them, so it has to be something else. Your mother?' she probed. 'The nursing-home fees? I know it can't be easy, Billie, but if you're finding it a struggle, I'd be more than happy to help, you know I would.'

Oh, Anna! Billie was choked. As if Anna didn't have worries enough of her own. And what could she say that would make any sense? Tell her – tell her what, for heaven's sake? That Travis had kissed her. That she'd responded, overreacted like a school girl? Just a kiss. An insignificant kiss between a man and a woman. But it had turned Billie's world upside down. She brought her gaze back to Anna. 'It isn't Mum. It's nothing really,' she insisted, forcing a smile. Aware of the shadows in Anna's grey eyes, she added lightly, 'It's probably my hormones. I'll be fine in a day or so, you'll see.'

'Hmm. Well, if you say so,' she allowed and leaned across to squeeze Billie's hand. 'Always remember, Billie, I'm here if you need me. Marianne – work – whatever's on your mind, I'm more than happy to listen.'

Billie felt the sudden sting of tears. 'I know,' she acknowledged with a catch in her voice. 'And thank you. You've no idea how much that helps.'

It did, too. Simply knowing Anna was there was enough to keep her sane. And though the nursing-home fees were an ever growing problem, as long as Billie kept her head – and her job – she'd get by.

Her job. Bury the resentment or go, Travis had insisted. The devil or the deep blue sea. A rock or a hard place. And since she hadn't any choice, she'd choked back the tears and swallowed her pride. But it was never going to be easy. Not working so closely with Travis.

Travis. Face it, Billie, she urged, the sketches on the block little more than a blur. Travis is the problem, not Giddings. The arrogant Travis Kent with his laughing black eyes and his easy smile.

'It was – just a kiss,' he'd carelessly conceded. Nothing more, nothing less.

To him, maybe, Billie had allowed, the knife blade twisting. But he'd awakened needs that she'd never suspected. She wanted him, wanted the touch of his arms around her, the magic of his lips exploring hers, and strange longings stirred in the secret, sensitive parts of her body. It was madness. He didn't want Billie. The Travis Kents of this world didn't waste a thought on women like Billie. They used them, took the goods on offer, gave nothing in return. Except a moment's pleasure. Such exquisite pleasure, she had to admit. Yet with Cleo in his life, that's all it would ever be. And though she'd gained his respect, it was something much more basic that Billie craved.

'You're quite a woman,' he'd surprised her by admitting on their drive back from Pellaton. 'No tears, no sulks, no touching pleas for mercy. Just a curt assurance that the job wouldn't suffer, and several hours spent proving it. Very impressive.'

And Billie had flushed, turning her head, allowing her eyes to lock with his. She didn't bother explaining she'd had plenty of practice, that she'd lived with pain so long that burying hurt was almost second nature. He didn't need to know, and he wouldn't understand. As Travis had tacitly acknowledged, as long the job was done well, nothing else mattered.

'It wasn't done for you,' she'd reminded coolly. 'It was done for the good of the firm.'

'That's my girl,' he'd laughingly replied, taking the dig in good part, and Billie had bristled. Travis Kent's girl? Some chance, she'd derided.

He was quite a man himself, she could have riposted. From the moment they arrived at the Hall, Travis turned on the charm. The lunch, the kiss, the angry words might never have taken place as the true professional swung into gear, his easy words more than a match for the thorny Lady Catherine.

'Kate, my love, you haven't changed one bit,' he'd declared warmly, and the woman's stony face had softened.

'Fiddlesticks!' she'd retorted tartly, but beneath the gruff tone she was visibly pleased. The sharp grey eyes had darted to Billie.

'My assistant, Billie Taylor,' Travis had supplied speedily.

'Ah, yes. The young woman I spoke to on the phone. Rude, I seem to remember.'

'As it happens,' Billie had demurred, risking a sideways glance at Travis, 'I wasn't. But if that's how it seemed, allow me to apologize.'

There'd been a pause, a tense, electric moment when Billie was sure that this time she'd blown it. Bye-bye job, she'd convinced herself, praying for the ground to open up and swallow her. And then amazingly, unbelievably, Lady Catherine had nodded, linking her arm with Travis and leading the way up the steps and into the house.

'She'll do,' she'd pronounced as Billie fell into step behind. 'I can't abide mealy-mouthed misses who wouldn't say boo to a goose.' And she'd poked him playfully in the ribs. 'Keeps you in your place, I hope?'

'Billie has her moments,' he'd admitted drily, and he'd turned his head, black eyes locking with Billie's. You promised, they'd reproved silently, but Travis needn't have worried. For the rest of the day at least, Billie had played safe. Not to mention busy as room after room had been photographed, discussed, dissected, Billie's sure fingers rapidly sketching the intricate details of plasterwork and fittings. And all the time she'd been keenly aware of Travis at her elbow, keeping overwrought nerves taut as bowstrings.

And then the journey home, equally tense, Travis strangely silent. Just the parting comment, his grudging admiration . . .

Billie banished the cobwebs. This won't do, she silently admonished as the phone rang.

It was Travis, his velvet tone music to her ears. 'Billie? I've hit a snag. I'm stuck in York for the rest of the day but I've an afternoon appointment. The Old Brewery at Allerton. The fitters have nearly finished but there's a last-minute hitch. Be an angel and pop across and sort it.'

An angel? Billie swallowed a smile. Not so long

since he'd declared she'd never be saint but it was a welcome diversion, an excuse to leave the office – and thoughts of Travis behind. And yet, as she collected the heavy file from Travis's tidy desk, she was horribly afraid that was something she could never do.

'What the *hell* do you think you were playing at? The place was almost finished, Billie. It was perfect, damn you, and now – ' His face darkened and Billie flinched, shrinking into the fabric of her chair as Travis tossed a heavy file onto the desk in front of her.

Allerton Old Brewery. Billie's heart sank. She might have known. The moment peace was declared, World War Three would inevitably break out. Would they never settle to trusting one another? And that's all it came down to, Billie decided. Trust. Or in Travis's case, lack of it. Despite the promotion, the pay rise, all the fine words about Billie's skill as a designer, Travis simply didn't trust her to make the right decisions.

She licked her lips, eyes darting from Travis's stormy face to the box file and back again. 'Is there a problem?' she asked absurdly, hooking a stray lock of hair behind an ear and tugging at an earring in a giveaway gesture.

'Too right there is,' he all but snarled, black eyes pinning her. 'You!'

'And what have I done this time?' she stalled,

flinching as he leaned across the desk, the granite features much too close for comfort.

'You know! Don't play the snow-white innocent. You know exactly what you've done, don't you, Billie?'

'To the Old Brewery plans? I made a few changes, if that's what you mean,' she admitted.

'Minor changes? A light bulb or two? The odd window catch? Or something really trivial like a whole new interior?' His voice was heavy with sarcasm.

'I just did as I was asked, ironed out the problems. And the client seemed pleased.'

'No doubt.' Generous lips curled in derision. 'The client doesn't foot the bill – we do.'

'What bill?' she asked as alarm bells sounded.

'The penalty clause. The twenty per cent reduction if we're late completing. And we will be late, won't we, Billie? Thanks to you and your grand ideas.'

Billie bit her lip. Better late than never, she countered silently, wondering what Travis would have said if she'd lost them the rest of the contract, a string of conversions that stretched the length of the country. And though the threat had been veiled, it had been there. Besides, if the client made the request, the time clause wouldn't apply. That is, Billie didn't know for sure, simply crossed her fingers and hoped.

'I thought – '

'Wrong, Billie,' Travis contradicted. 'You didn't think. Hence the mess we're in now.'

'A couple of hundred pounds – '

'Thousands, more like. Not to mention the cost of the fabric. Have you lost all sense?' he asked incredulously. 'You know Giddings' policy; if we can't make it ourselves, we use our own suppliers.'

'If we can,' she stated reasonably, logging the racing pulse at the base of his throat, the dark hint of stubble on the strong, angular jawline. 'This time we couldn't.'

'No? Well, there's a surprise,' he scoffed. 'Giddings couldn't supply because someone – *you* – had to opt for something outlandish. What are you trying to do,' he asked in a voice of tempered steel. 'Put us out of business?'

Billie's chin snapped up. He couldn't be serious. Angry, yes. Annoyed, yes. But to think that Billie would stoop so low . . . 'I don't believe you said that,' she stated quietly.

'No? Well, more fool you. Because the more I think about it, the more sense it makes.'

'Sense? For whom? The idea's ludicrous. If Giddings folds, I go too, remember.'

'Ah yes, but you're a rebel with a cause, Billie. A six-year crusade for House Of Marianne. And when fanaticism flies in, out goes logic.'

'Along with my conscience? Don't be absurd. If I was stupid enough to risk my own job, Travis, I'm hardly likely to risk everyone else's.'

'Unless the end justifies the means.'

'Meaning?'

'Like I said, it's been a long crusade but if you really are hellbent on revenge . . .'

'I'd be cutting off my nose to spite my face. The idea's laughable.'

'But not impossible. And you're not exactly falling over backwards to deny it, I see.'

'Well, if that's all that's bothering you, let me put your mind at rest. No, Travis,' she reassured coldly, sitting back and folding her arms, 'this isn't a one-woman plot to put Giddings out of business. Happy now?'

'Hardly. But in the absence of proof, I guess I'll have to take your word.'

'Big of you,' she needled.

'Not at all. I deal in facts. And you do have this irrational response where Giddings is concerned. Let's just say that when things go glaringly wrong, everyone comes under suspicion.'

'Ah yes, but with Billie Taylor's name at the top of the list?'

'Not necessarily.'

'Don't lie, Travis. You've insulted me enough as it is. But at the end of the day it all comes down to trust – or in your case, lack of it. Given your very high opinion, I'm surprised you allow me to rustle up the biscuits for the mid-morning coffee break. This isn't going to work, is it?' she asked bitterly. 'And I guess we've both known it all along.'

'What are you saying?'

'You know what I'm saying. You've got this enormous doubt at the back of your mind. So, innocent or guilty, sooner or later, I'll be forced to go. But maybe that's what you've been angling for – thorny Billie Taylor out of your hair once and for all?'

'Don't be ridiculous. I wanted you to stay, remember?'

'Did you? Did you really?' she challenged. 'True, you didn't *have* to keep me on, but you could hardly sack Grace and Son's best young designer out of hand. This way I quit, and clever Travis Kent is in the clear.'

'Now you're being paranoid – '

'*I'm* paranoid? That's rich, coming from you,' she sneered.

'And what's that supposed to mean?'

'A certain subtle ploy to put Giddings out of business,' she reminded him, her voice dripping sarcasm. 'Not to mention Pellaton Hall three weeks ago.'

'Maybe,' he acknowledged coolly. 'And maybe not. But with the best will in the world, Billie, you *have* cost us money. The penalty clause for a start.'

He was right, she admitted, as the anger gave way to weary resignation. She hadn't known about the clause and she should have done. 'I'm sorry,' she murmured softly, slumping down into her chair.

'Sorry? It's a bit too late for that. You're my right hand, Billie. You know the way we work. And as for leather!' The sneer was back in his tone. 'The idea's insane.'

Billie stiffened. 'I don't agree. The client wasn't happy with tiles. He wanted something warm.'

'Have you never heard of cork?'

'Too soft,' she parried, regretting the impulse to sit while Travis towered above her. Travis Kent. Mr Perfection. Tall, good looking, dressed like a million dollars in the hand-made, Savile Row suit, and overendowed with charm – if and when he chose to use it. And never wrong. Just like now. Billie's lips twisted.

'Lino?' he queried politely.

'Too common – the customer's words, not mine,' she tagged on defiantly.

'Carpet, then?'

'Unimaginative.'

'Pine?'

'Out of character.'

The battle went on, Travis's clipped suggestions, Billie's cool replies. And, despite the cost, Billie was glad she'd thought of leather.

The building was superb, a converted brewery

with a sitting-room running from end to end. And with the top floor removed to create acres of space and a bank of double-decker windows, Billie had known at once that quarry tiles would be arctic, that cork just wouldn't wear. It had to be leather. Immensely practical and tough as old boots, there simply wasn't another material to touch it.

'You have an answer for everything, don't you, Billie?' Travis sniped when the sparring ran out of steam.

'When I know I'm in the right? Too true I do,' she conceded coolly. 'And I guess that's the real problem, isn't it, Travis? That's what's really eating you. Not the money or the delay, just the simple fact that my ideas were more acceptable.'

His face darkened. He moved, looming over the desk again, taking his weight on his hands, and Billie's mind flashed back, remembering the day a particularly nasty teacher blasted a child who could not read. The girl had crumbled beneath the tirade, her sobs echoing round the room. The rest of the class, Billie included, had hardly dared to breathe, had kept their eyes firmly fixed on the desk in front, each one afraid that if she caught the master's eye, she'd be next. And Billie, twelve years on, banished the scent of panic with a massive surge of anger. Sit here and allow Travis to reduce her to shreds with his softly spoken words and thinly veiled threats? Oh, no! She jumped up, snatching up her briefcase and heading for the door.

'Running away, Billie?' the low voice goaded. 'Leaving? Quitting? Surely not?' he sneered. 'Don't forget,' he reminded slyly, 'there's such a thing as working out your notice.'

She spun round, an icy finger touching her heart. 'Are you sacking me?' she asked as the colour left her cheeks.

'Should I need to?' he replied, his arrogant features impassive.

'You're the boss,' she reminded curtly. 'You tell me.'

Travis shook his head. 'Oh, no. You're not wriggling out of this one so easily. *You* tell me,' he invited softly, spreading his hands. 'And give me one good reason why I shouldn't.'

There was a loaded pause, Billie's mind in chaos, the atmosphere so thick she could have cut it with a knife. He couldn't be serious. The penalty clause, yes, he probably had a point. But the accusation, the thinly veiled threat to sack her . . .

Travis smiled, another cold and evil twist of his lips.

'Go to hell,' Billie snapped, throwing caution to the winds. 'You're impossible. And I'm late for my appointment. And time,' she reminded with a defiant tilt to her head, 'costs money. Giddings' money.'

'The same Giddings' money that keeps you in a

job,' Travis needled. 'Always assuming you have one.'

She didn't reply, simply turned on her heels and left, the sound of mocking laughter following her down the stairs and echoing horribly inside her head.

She was crying inside but Billie didn't slow the punishing pace, reaching fresh air, heading for the car purely by instinct. She climbed behind the wheel, the windscreen a blur, and dashed the tears away with an impatient sweep of hand. Starting the engine, she eased the car onto the road before the first sob escaped her.

She stifled it. She had her pride. Allow Travis Kent to upset her? No chance. He might never know but Billie would. For two pins she'd quit here and now. Go home. Leave her client high and dry. Let Travis salvage the contract. She'd had enough. She couldn't do right for doing wrong and she'd had enough. She couldn't take the strain of working with Travis. He never gave her a moment's peace and, despite the resolution, the hot trickle of moisture on her cheeks gathered pace.

Steering blind, she pulled in to the side of the road and, uncaring of the traffic speeding past, lay her head upon the dashboard and cried as if she'd never, ever stop.

'Billie?'

She glanced up, going hot then cold, the colour

draining from her cheeks as she logged the grim expression. This was it, then. The moment she'd spent the afternoon dreading. Quit? Who was she kidding? Telling Travis to go to hell was a luxury she couldn't afford. She needed the job and now she'd blown it.

'I –'

'It's gone six,' he interrupted. 'If you're not rushing off somewhere, let me buy you a drink.'

'Why? So you can carry on where you left off this afternoon – insulting me?' she queried brusquely, not about to go without a fight. 'Thanks, but no thanks.'

'I'd like to explain.'

'Apologize, you mean?' she couldn't help but needle.

'If you like,' he conceded, velvet eyes bottomless pools. And when Billie didn't move, didn't blink, but continued to glare back defiantly, he added, 'Come on, Billie, we can't talk here.'

He turned, not waiting for a reply, clearly expecting Billie to follow. Only she didn't. Travis could wait, and she took her time as shaking fingers shuffled the papers she'd been working on into a neat pile. Locking the files away, she glanced around, impressing on her mind all the things she daily took for granted: the pale cream walls, the warm oatmeal carpet, the assortment of pot plants framed by the window. A huge part of life was in this room and

Billie was painfully aware of what the next few minutes could bring. One word from Travis and her life at Giddings would be over. Travis. She braced herself. Ah, well. Might as well quit stalling.

He was waiting at the car and for once the impatient air was missing. 'We'll go in mine,' he explained as Billie approached with leaden footsteps. 'The Dog and Gun. It's not far. Don't worry, yours will be perfectly safe here.'

Billie bristled. He was doing it again, issuing orders, expecting the world to jump to Travis Kent's tune, but she smothered the comment that sprang to her lips, allowing Travis his way.

Five long, silent minutes passed before the car pulled off the road and then he led her inside, not touching, simply walking beside her, Billie's instincts screamingly aware of the nearness.

'So – ' he murmured politely, having bought the drinks and settled down beside her. 'How did Harden House go?'

'You've been checking up on me!' she challenged flatly.

'Just taking an interest,' he countered. 'When you said you were running late, I checked your diary and phoned to explain that you'd been delayed.'

'Big of you,' she needled, irrationally annoyed at his common-sense approach.

'Hardly. More a guilty conscience, Billie. If it hadn't been for me, you'd have made it on time.'

Guilty conscience – or sound business sense, Billie mocked, but silently, vaguely aware that Travis had called a truce. And she'd been thinking. She'd spent the afternoon thinking, dissecting, analysing. And maybe, she'd probed, she wanted Travis to sack her. Subconsciously, of course. Because she was torn. She needed the job, yet hated working for Giddings, being part of the firm that had ripped her family apart. And maybe, just maybe, niggling at Travis was Billie's way out. By forcing him to sack her, she acknowledged frankly, Giddings could be blamed for yet another ruined life.

She glanced up. He was watching her carefully, and Billie flushed, half afraid the thoughts were written across her face.

'Another drink?' he asked, and Billie checked her glass, amazed to find that the double gin and tonic had somehow disappeared.

She nodded, opting for orange juice and the need to keep her wits. If stone-cold sober she could talk herself out of a job, heaven only knows how she'd behave once the barriers came down.

He was less than a minute and this time, to Billie's consternation, he took the chair opposite, leaning forwards and capturing Billie's hands.

'I'd like to apologize,' he murmured, intense black eyes locking with hers, refusing to allow her look away.

'For what?' Billie stalled, aware of the touch of skin on skin and the strange expression in his eyes, eyes she could happily drown in. She tried to pull away, but his sensitive fingers held her fast, his velvet gaze pinned her and Billie was shockingly afraid he was reading her mind, seeing to the centre of her soul.

'For today,' he said simply. 'You were right. I trusted you with the job and I shouldn't have blown up when you did what you're paid to do and used your initiative.' He shrugged. 'We've lost two big contracts in the past few days because of problems with suppliers; when the Brewery invoice landed on my desk, I guess it caught me on the raw.'

'The kick-the-cat syndrome,' Billie acknowledged, dropping her gaze, homing in on Travis's tanned skin, the shadow of hair on the backs of his hands. He didn't wear a ring, she noticed. He was engaged, not married, but even so it came as a surprise that Cleo hadn't stamped her ownership with a signet ring at least, an eighteen-carat-gold Keep Off sign.

'And will you?' he asked on a lighter note.

'Will I what?' she enquired, risking an upward glance and finding that the corners of his mouth were smiling.

'Take it out on Smudge?'

'What do you think?' she challenged as the atmosphere eased.

'I don't think, I *know*. Anyone who daily risks their neck for such an ungrateful wretch couldn't hurt a fly.'

'Hardly daily,' Billie demurred, and as Travis reached for his glass, releasing one hand, she seized the chance to disengage the other.

'So – I am forgiven?'

'Are you asking, or telling?' she stalled, wondering vaguely if she was flirting.

'Just hoping,' he countered, velvet eyes full of dancing lights.

'Ah, yes, but do you deserve it?' she teased, and this time she didn't wonder, she knew. She *was* flirting. A dangerous occupation where Travis was concerned. After all, hadn't she'd seen him in action? He could charm the birds from the trees without so much as the crook of a little finger, and she felt the blush creep into her cheeks at the knowledge that he could stir her. And yet, why the surprise? His tall, slim, yet powerful form was more than matched by stunning good looks and Billie would need to be made of stone not to notice. Casually dressed or formal, Travis Kent was out of this world.

He pushed back the cuff of the elegant steel grey suit. 'Seven o'clock. Are you hungry?' he asked.

'Why?' she stalled, instantly wary.

'Because the night's still young and I haven't finished explaining. We could go back to my place, pick up some food on the way. There's an excellent Chinese in the village,' he pointed out.

Billie froze, the hairs on the back of her neck prickling out a warning. Supper with Travis? At his place? Alone? She licked her dry lips. She'd always wanted to see inside the house but . . .

'Or your place, if you'd rather,' he allowed, cutting through the tension. And then he smiled, the kind of smile that was meant to reassure but did nothing of the sort. 'Come on, Billie, loosen up a little – hey? Be a devil.'

It didn't take long, with the powerful Mercedes eating up the miles and a bottle of wine and food collected on the way. And Billie sat rigid beside him. Loosen up, Travis had urged. But it was easier said than done, and as they ground to a halt outside her front door, fresh waves of panic rose up to choke her. Was she mad? Allowing Travis into her home, into her life? And yet, she reproached herself with a flash of common sense, why the wild reaction? Such an innocent occasion, supper with the boss.

Grow up, Billie, she admonished, leading the way up the steps. But as Travis crossed the threshold, his massive presence filling the hallway, the panic came back with a vengeance. Irrational or not, Billie couldn't shake the notion that after tonight, life would never be quite the same again.

CHAPTER 7

'Raggle-taggle cottage,' Travis teased, glancing round the small, simply furnished sitting-room. 'I'm impressed.'

Billie flushed. 'After that wonderful house next door,' she reminded him, 'don't be ridiculous.'

Travis shrugged. 'Wonderful it may be, but it's an empty shell – a show house, if you like. This, Billie, feels like home.'

He made himself at home, too, insisting he could manage. Billie perched on the edge of her sofa, acutely aware of Travis moving about the kitchen, opening drawers, clattering plates – cosy, everyday sounds that Billie, living alone, had almost forgotten.

And once the debris had been cleared and the plates washed and put away, Travis faced her across the coffee table, long legs stretched comfortably beneath, glass of wine in hand and a warm smile mellowing his face.

He *was* at home, his expensive jacket discarded in

the hall, the open-necked shirt a casual touch that Billie found disturbing. And, since her gaze was drawn again and again to the dark shadow of hair at the base of his throat, and lower, her thoughts took on a mind of their own, passing through the fine lawn fabric stretched taut across his chest and imagining the body beneath. She imagined her hands caressing that body, keeping her nerves in a permanent state of frenzy.

Smudge appeared in the doorway, pulling up short at the sight of Travis comfortably ensconced in *his* favourite chair. With swift animal intuition he summed the stranger up, the lightly raised hackles flattened as the cat ran forwards into Billie's outstretched hand.

'Hello, boy,' she purred as he brushed against her legs. 'Hungry? Come on, then.'

She was less than a minute, so was surprised to find that Travis had moved to investigate the shelf in the corner. There was little of interest really, a couple of framed photographs, a glass paperweight, and a delicate Wedgwood vase that had been her mother's pride and joy.

Sensing Billie's return, he spun round. 'Your parents?' he queried, holding out the largest of the photographs, and Billie nodded, swallowing the lump in her throat.

'My father died,' she explained painfully. 'When I was at school. And Mother never got over the shock.'

'Pity. She was a beautiful woman. I can see where you had your looks from,' he added, as Billie registered the use of the past tense. He thought her mother had died as well, and she was on the point of explaining when she changed her mind. Was Travis so wrong? she wondered, bitterly. Her mother was alive, sure enough, but it was a strange, twilight existence.

Billie sat down, her pulse rate soaring alarmingly as Travis slipped down beside her. Side by side on her minuscule settee meant elbow room only. She had to fight the urge to jump up and take the chair opposite, aware that Travis dominated the room, would dominate the room whatever the seating arrangements, the way he was beginning to dominate her thoughts.

'So – ' she blurted out, smoothing out the creases in her skirt, which was new and shorter than she normally wore, part of a smart navy suit she'd been able to buy thanks to the generous increase in salary negotiated by Travis. And though she'd tried hard not to look the gift horse in the mouth, she had yet come to terms with the freedom the extra cash was giving her. 'What else did you want to say?'

Travis grinned broadly. 'That's right, Billie. Say it like it is. Don't bother hinting or probing or skirting round the subject. Why not get straight to the point?'

'That *is* why you're here,' she needled, cheeks

beginning to glow; blushing, with Travis around, was almost a permanent feature.

'Maybe,' he allowed. 'And maybe I simply felt the need to share a meal with a beautiful woman, a beautiful, fiery woman.'

'Who calls a spade a spade,' she reminded him, his easy words unnerving.

'She certainly does,' he acknowledged, 'as I've discovered to my cost. This afternoon's little niggle,' he obligingly explained. 'The Old Brewery. You were right, treated leather's perfect for the floors. Unusual maybe, but perfect. And something I'd never have thought of.'

'Oh!' The colour flared again. A compliment from Travis. Progress indeed. 'But the cost,' Billie needled him as the imp inside her surfaced, 'at least a thousand pounds.'

'Nearer three, according to the invoice, but that won't be a problem.'

'Oh?' she murmured, amazed to note that Travis had the grace to look ashamed.

'I've had the company lawyer check our position. According to the small print, the client is liable for the late completion. But . . .'

'But?'

He shrugged. 'We'll waive it. Arkwright's a pain in the neck. I've worked for him in London. It's worth a few thousands to keep him off my back. So . . .' He paused, amber lights dancing in liquid

120

black eyes. 'It would seem, Miss Wilma Jane Taylor, you're overdue an apology. Am I forgiven?'

'Until next time,' she murmured drily, warming at the words. 'And knowing you, Travis, there will be a next time.'

'Am I so impossible to work for?' he asked, with a lightning change of tone.

Billie was startled. How to answer *that* without creating waves on a newly calm sea? So she cradled her glass, swirling the pale yellow liquid round and round, searching for inspiration.

'No,' she said at length, strangely aware she was giving him the truth. Travis was – hard-working, demanding but scrupulously fair. He asked nothing of his staff that he wouldn't do himself, and tonight had proved he could own up to his mistakes. But on a personal level, she realized starkly, simply being with Travis was hell. 'No,' she said again, raising her head, her gaze unwavering though her insides were churning. And then she smiled. 'Not impossible – but definitely bordering on it!'

She escaped to the kitchen to rustle up some coffee, and was humming lightly under her breath as she carried in the tray. 'My, you're honoured,' she acknowledged, pausing in the doorway. Smudge had climbed onto his lap and was curled up in a ball.

'All part of my natural charm,' Travis admitted wryly. 'Cats – and their owners – just can't leave me

121

alone. You wouldn't believe the hours they spend exploring trees in my garden.'

It was Billie's turn to smile. 'Wouldn't I?' she murmured, aware of the colour stealing back into her cheeks. 'Well, if you say so.'

'Not that I mind,' Travis conceded. 'This little fellow's made himself at home. And as for you . . .' Black eyes were innocent pools, innocent pools with treacherous depths. 'Next time, why not ring the bell and invite yourself in for coffee?'

'An open invitation,' Billie stalled. 'You could be sorry.'

'I doubt it,' he countered, as Billie's glow deepened.

Smudge stirred, circled, settled down again and Billie absent-mindedly reached out to stroke him. The cat responded, and as he arched his neck to rub against her, he nudged her fingers down onto Travis's thigh. Like a scalded cat herself, Billie snatched her hand away.

'He's a lovely animal,' Travis acknowledged, seeming not to notice. 'Where did you find him?'

'Anna,' Billie explained, glad of the chance to change the subject. 'She has a passion for cats. And dogs. And most four-legged creatures, come to think of it. And every now and again she farms a batch of orphans out on me. So when she couldn't find a home for this little guy, guess whose arm she twisted?'

'Anna means a lot to you, doesn't she, Billie?' Travis mused.

'Hardly surprising since she's my godmother.'

'Ah! So that explains it. The resentment about Giddings and House Of Marianne. No wonder you took took it so hard when Anna lost her job. It makes sense now,' he half-stated, half-queried.

Billie shrugged, aware of the truth hanging heavily between them. She wanted to explain, but the pain had grown with the years, fuelling the resentment. Confide in Travis? Invite his pity. He might understand, but why on earth should he? Young, successful, rich – and clearly a rising star in the Giddings organization? Oh, he'd say the right words sure enough, but he'd never understand. No one could. Except Anna.

Smudge began to purr as Travis stroked the smooth fur, the sound filling the silence and giving Billie something to focus on.

'You've made a friend for life,' she observed, wondering how on earth she'd have survived such a tense evening with Travis without the comforting presence of the cat. 'He's very particular about his humans. Tony never gets a look-in.'

'Tony? The rugged Viking? The boyfriend, Billie?' Travis queried slyly.

'I – yes, I suppose so,' she admitted, aware of Tony's secret hopes, her own misgivings.

'You *suppose* so?' The tone was scornful. 'Good

heavens, child, don't you know? Talk about love's young dream. Is it passion running in his veins or lukewarm water?'

'None of your business,' she replied, refusing to be drawn. Travis could think what he liked. Her friendship with Tony suited Billie. It didn't suit Tony, she was beginning to think, but Travis didn't need to know that, and if it gave Travis the impression that she was spoken for, even better.

She collected the cups and saucers and stacked them on the tray before clambering to her feet, the need to get away making her clumsy. The tray tilted, the noise of sliding crockery frightening Smudge, who bolted, allowing Travis to shoot out a hand to steady her.

'I can manage, thank you,' she ground out, her eyes firmly anchored on the sugar bowl.

'No doubt,' he murmured drily, ignoring her protests as he took the tray from her. 'But you made the coffee; the least I can do is help clear away.'

Billie bit her lip as he walked off into the kitchen. Judging from the sound of running water, he was doing more than clear away, but she didn't move, simply stood and waited, counting the minutes till Travis reappeared.

'I'll be off, then,' he murmured, shrugging himself back into his jacket and allowing a subdued Billie to lead the way down the hall.

They paused at the front door, the moment suddenly awkward; Billie racked her brains for something to say, something trite and light to ease the gaffe of overreacting – the story of her life, she was beginning to think, where Travis was concerned. 'See you in the morning,' she said instead, hoping Travis would remember the promise of a lift to work.

'Eight o'clock sharp,' he agreed solemnly and Billie pushed past, reaching for the handle. She didn't make it. The brush of skin on skin sent currents of heat surging through her body, and she froze, aware of the sharp hiss of indrawn breath as Travis responded. Then she was in his arms, strong arms that closed round, not restraining, simply holding her as Travis dipped his head, his lips brushing lightly against her mouth. Billie's lips parted with the shock. It was an unconscious invitation for his tongue to slide in and there was an electrifying pause, a moment of sheer incredulity. Then Travis groaned, gathering her to him, the rasp of his stubble against her chin strangely erotic, his lips at first gentle and persuading, then hard and demanding as Billie moaned deep in her throat.

It was the most natural thing in the world. Billie didn't stop to think, didn't need to think as mouth moved against mouth, his tongue exploring, sweeping languidly arosss the sensitive underside of her lip and then on into turbulent depths where Billie's tongue entwined with his, each and every touch heightening the tension, stirring the blood in her veins.

She was in heaven, her mind soaring skywards as her body responded; driven by instinct, she was kissing, touching, tasting, her hands caressing as she raked the silk of his hair and, consumed by a need too wonderful to question, she pressed her body shamelessly against his. And he wanted her! Billie's heart was singing. He wanted her, needed her – all the proof she'd ever craved was here beneath her fingers. He wanted her. And prim and proper Billie Taylor, she acknowledged with wonder, wanted him.

'Billie! Oh, Billie!' he groaned and the heat of his breath fanned the flames as he nibbled the corners of her mouth, a delicate touch that sent delicious shivers dancing the length of her spine. As his lips caressed, so did his hands, sliding down to the curve of her waist and spanning it as he tugged her urgently closer. Billie gasped afresh at the contact. Hip against hip, the force of his arousal drove the breath from her body.

And still the kiss went on, the need spiralling out of control as his hands swept upwards, thumbs brushing the undercurve of Billie's straining breasts and she swayed back, wanting Travis to touch, needing Travis to touch, to trigger fresh waves of heat pulsing through her body. Only

Travis, tantalizing Travis, continued to deny her. As his mouth wreaked havoc, his hands created needs that Billie had never suspected, her nipples hardening, aching, straining for the touch that Travis *almost* allowed. Almost. So near, yet so far, the denial exquisite torment as Travis pulled away.

Her lids flew open, the bubble of happiness popping as mocking black eyes gazed back at her.

'Oh, Billie,' he chided, his heated glance sweeping the length of her, down, then up, and lingering for a heart-stopping moment on the nipples straining against the fabric of her blouse. 'Do yourself a favour. Find yourself a man, a real man. The lukewarm Viking hasn't the fire to hold you.'

'Hasn't he?' she snapped, sickly aware that Travis was right. Tony was a friend, a good friend, but if she'd had her doubts before, Travis had confirmed them once and for all. Not that she meant to admit it. Clinging to the threads of her dignity, she stepped back, angling her head, blue eyes cold as ice. 'Hasn't he?' she repeated, swallowing hard. 'Well, maybe that's for me to judge. But since Tony Massie's a gentleman, I'd hardly expect the cheating Travis Kent to understand. Cleo,' she reminded him pointedly. 'Heaven help her, she doesn't know the half of it.'

Travis ignored the barb. 'Oh I see, a *gentleman*,' he sneered, raising a mocking eyebrow. 'Fine manners, fancy words and – ' he snapped his fingers in a curt, derisive gesture ' – no fizz.' He moved as he spoke, backing her against the wall, the cursory brush to her lips enough to ignite her and Billie trembled under the blast of Travis's knowing gaze. 'Lie to *me* by all means, Billie,' he entreated frigidly, 'but when you're lying to yourself . . .' He shrugged, the scorn almost more than she could bear, then walked out the door and climbed into his car. As Travis drove away, she slumped against the door jamb, shame burning in her cheeks, shame – and another churning emotion Billie's mind instinctively shied away from.

'Come on, Billie. Let's go for a drink. I'm due back in London tomorrow and heaven only knows when I'll have the time to see you again.'

'Oh?' Billie looked up from the dress she'd been sketching, Tony's petulant tone an unwelcome interruption. 'Has something happened?' she enquired politely. 'Is it the job? I thought you were happy now that you've had the chance to settle in.'

'I was – am,' he corrected crossly. 'But everyone's under pressure. The market's not moving, Billie, and without the orders, no one's safe. And since I'm the new guy, I'm the one whose job's on the line.'

'I'm sorry, I didn't realize.' She gave a reassuring smile. 'Half an hour,' she entreated. 'It's Heather's show next month and I promised these designs by

128

the weekend. And since it's Thursday now . . .' She shrugged apologetically.

Tony's scowl deepened. 'And that's another thing. You shouldn't allow Heather to take advantage. You have enough to do, working full time for Giddings.'

'Maybe,' she agreed pleasantly. 'But dress design is a bit of light relief. And I benefit, too, don't forget.'

'Huh!' Tony's voice was scornful. 'Half a dozen outfits you could easily afford to buy if you earned a decent wage.'

'Not quite,' Billie corrected. 'But you know where the money goes and I don't begrudge a penny. Thanks to Heather, I can dress well *and* take care of Mummy.'

'But if Giddings paid what you were worth, you wouldn't need my sister's charity.'

'Not charity,' she explained patiently, not bothering to point out that she'd already had a more than generous pay rise. 'Just a favour repaying a favour.'

An ideal arrangement in fact, Billie acknowledged, remembering how it had started. As Tony's guest at a Christmas ball, she'd been horrified to learn that evening dress wasn't so much expected as a treasonable offence punishable by death for defaulters. And, since money was tight, Billie had made her own, an unusual design that caught Heather's eye. When Heather had made her proposal a few days later, Billie had jumped at the chance. As far as Billie was concerned, designing clothes was a bit of light relief that had benefited her as much as Heather. And, if the need wasn't quite so urgent now, thanks to Giddings, Billie wouldn't dream of letting Heather down.

Tony continued to glower and, watching him, Billie felt a spurt of irritation, a response she hastily smothered. She leaned across. 'You *are* out of sorts, aren't you?' she teased, trying to coax a smile. It didn't work and a ripple of unease ran through her. This wasn't like Tony at all. She pushed the pad away. 'Come on,' she chivvied. 'The designs can wait. Let's go for a drive.'

Not a good idea, she realized later. Tony's bad mood had deepened, making the drive into the countryside anything but peaceful. He'd hammered away at Billie's world. Giddings, her mother, the freelance for Heather – nothing seemed to please him. And as for getting married . . .

'Married?' Billie had been horrified.

'Don't sound so surprised,' he'd growled. 'You know I love you, Billie, so it's only a matter of time. You'll come round, you'll see.'

Only Billie hadn't, Tony's smug conviction was enough to try the patience of a saint. Hardly surprising, then, that they'd quarrelled, parting in stony silence, a concerned Billie wondering what Heather would make of her brother's state of mind.

'He'll come round,' she reassured her when Billie popped into the boutique with the designs. She ran a critical eye over Billie's sketches. 'The best yet,' she declared warmly. 'I'm beginning to think you're wasted at Giddings. If ever you need a new career, Billie, this one's ready made.'

Billie laughed. 'Thanks, Heather, but no thanks. Dress design is fun, but my heart isn't in it.'

A strange choice of words, really, because if Heather was serious, it *was* a way out. Escape from Giddings – and Travis. And in that case, Billie probed, why didn't she jump at the chance to do exactly that? And, though her mind skittered away from the answer, Billie was aware that, in hiding from the truth, she was embarking on a course for disaster.

Travis's phone rang. Billie paused on the threshold, half tempted to ignore it. She'd only popped in to pick up a file and, with Travis away for the day, Billie needed every minute to herself. Smothering her impatience, she crossed the floor and palmed the receiver. 'Yes?'

'Get me Travis,' the chilly voice demanded rudely, a chilly female voice that Billie recognized at once.

'I'm afraid Mr Kent isn't available,' Billie replied, the hairs on the back of her neck prickling out a warning.

131

'I think you'll find, Miss Super-Efficient Secretary, that for me Mr Kent is always available.'

Billie stiffened. Secretary? The cheek of the woman. And then she realized. The call had come through on Travis's private line. Cleo, she wouldn't mind betting, wasn't used to dealing with anyone but the great man himself.

'If you'd like to leave your name,' Billie murmured pleasantly, 'I'll have Mr Kent get back to you.'

'Didn't you hear?' the cold voice threatened. 'I said I wanted Travis and I want him now.'

'But I'm afraid you're out of luck,' Billie retorted coolly. 'Mr Kent won't be back till late this afternoon. If you'd like to leave a message – '

'As it happens, I don't, but since his mobile's not responding, I'm left with no choice. About the weekend,' she rasped, 'something's come up and I just can't make it. You *can* remember that?' she tagged on insultingly.

'Of course,' Billie retorted. 'Mr Kent will be told the moment he arrives, Miss – ?'

'Oh, he'll know who was calling, never you doubt,' came the acid reply and she rang off, leaving Billie holding the handset. She shrugged. The arrogant Cleo, she decided sourly, scribbling a note to Travis which she left in the middle of his desk where he couldn't possibly miss it, suited the arrogant Travis down to the ground.

It was a busy afternoon, with Billie ever conscious of the minutes flying by.

'You're the one with the flair,' Travis had reminded her, tossing a file onto her desk. 'See what you can do with this in a hurry.'

'This' turned out to be a hotel, one of an international chain in need of revamping, and, if the Giddings' bid was successful, quite a feather in their cap. Though Travis's ideas were good, he wasn't happy with the overall effect. There was something missing, he'd insisted. Something elusive that would set it apart, give instant recognition worldwide.

The door swung open. 'Any luck?' Travis asked, dropping his briefcase onto a chair and joining Billie on the floor.

She pushed a stray lock of hair out of her eyes, leaning back on her heels, the colour creeping into her cheeks as Travis scanned the scattered papers.

She nodded. 'It's a bit of a gamble but – ' She filled him in. 'It's the first impression that counts,' she emphasized. 'White marble floors, off-white leather sofas and velvet walls panelled with glass. No plants, no gimmicky fountains, just lots of space and cool, clean luxury. And, if the foyer makes an impact, everything else falls into place. Unless you think it's too cold?' she added doubtfully.

'Cold? Billie, it's perfect. I knew you could do it. You finish off here and I'll put GUS on standby for Monday.'

Billie smiled. GUS was Travis's new toy, state-of-the-art technology, a multi-media computer system with graphics so clear the effect was photographic; since it had been installed, half the workforce had been queueing up to use it. It was probably worth expanding, Billie had realized, wondering whether to mention it or leave Travis to work it out for himself.

He popped his head round the door. 'Come on, Billie. You can't improve on perfection. Pack away now and we'll check the plans on Monday.'

Billie gathered the papers. 'I still don't see what the rush was. The bid doesn't close till the end of next week.'

'Officially,' Travis conceded, taking the file and locking it away. 'But word on the grapevine says otherwise. And since it doesn't hurt to be the first as well as the best, the Giddings portfolio guarantees both. Leastways,' he added, hugging her briefly, 'it does now. And if it hadn't worked out,' he explained with a smile, 'I'd have waved goodbye to my weekend, not to mention another lucrative contract.'

'Oh?'

'A stately home. One of Lady Catherine's recommendations. I'm a house guest till Sunday – assuming Cleo ever arrives,' he added with an impatient glance at his watch.

Billie felt the colour drain from her cheeks. 'Oh hell,' she muttered weakly.

'Oh, hell, *what*?' Travis enquired, sharp eyes raking Billie's guilty face.

She swallowed the urge to lick her dry lips. 'Cleo rang. She can't make the weekend. I thought you knew,' she ended lamely.

Travis's face darkened. 'And how could I know, since you didn't bother telling me?' he rasped as the temperature dropped.

'But I did. I left a note on your desk,' Billie explained, damping down the panic. With the heat from Travis's casual hug still running through her veins, his lightning change of mood was causing chaos in her mind.

'I haven't been near my desk since I got back,' he pointed out tersely.

'But I wasn't to know that.'

'You should have phoned,' he insisted tightly, black eyes frigid. 'When Cleo rang. If I'd known earlier, I could have worked something out. But now – hell, Billie!' He checked the time again. 'I'm due at Fleet in less than ninety minutes.'

'You can still make it,' she pointed out calmly, a lot more calmly than she felt. She was sharply aware of his tight control, of the anger simmering just beneath the surface and, if she was honest, she was equally aware that she was in the wrong. She should have remembered to tell him the moment he arrived.

'Alone?' His voice oozed derision. 'Don't be ridiculous. The invitation states Travis Kent and guest, *female* guest. That's the protocol. And since I phoned to confirm this morning, pulling out now sends out all the wrong signals. Damn it, Billie,' he repeated. 'You knew where to reach me. Why didn't you call?'

Billie shrugged. 'It – didn't seem important. She didn't even leave a name,' she stalled. 'I just assumed it was Cleo,' she ended lamely.

'Who else could it have been but Cleo? What do you take me for – a playboy?'

Billie shrugged again. 'One girl, two, a dozen. Your private life's your own concern. And you can't be short of friends, female friends,' she slipped out slyly.

'No. But that's in London. This quaint corner of the world hasn't the same advantage. Unless . . . Ah, yes!' He smiled and, watching him, Billie felt a prickle of alarm. 'Why, thank you, Billie,' he almost purred. 'What an excellent idea. You can come along instead.'

'Me? You're mad! I've other things arranged.'

'Then cancel them.'

'No.' Billie's tone was mulish.

'Yes, Billie. You got me into this, the least you can do is help me out.'

'That's right, blame me,' she railed, feeling guilty enough as it was without Travis hammering home the point. 'But you'll have to think again. I'm not going. I've other things to consider.'

'Such as?'

'Smudge for a start.'

'Ask the lukewarm Viking to feed him.'

'Not possible. Tony isn't around this weekend.'

Travis nodded. 'Good. That way he can't object if I borrow his girlfriend.'

'No, but I can. I'm not going,' she repeated, folding her arms, blue eyes unblinking and defiant. 'End of discussion.'

'Agreed. We haven't time to stand and argue. You've no choice.' And he smiled again, oh so confident. 'I'll make it worth your while,' he offered matter-of-factly. 'What's the going rate for weekends – double time? Triple?'

'That won't be necessary,' Billie retorted coolly, her eyes firmly fixed on the knot of Travis's silk tie.

'Maybe not, but if you're working for me, you'll take the money on offer.'

'Wrong again, Travis. I work for you all right – Monday to Friday,' she reminded, and she raised her head, tilting her chin in defiance.

'With overtime, if and when required,' he underlined softly. 'And in case you don't believe me, it's there in the small print. So – ' Chill black eyes brimmed with assurance. 'I'll pick you up in forty-five minutes.'

'Just like that?'

'Just like that.'

Billie bristled. 'But – I can't go. I've nothing to wear for a start,' she added absurdly, clutching at straws.

'Typical female vanity,' he mocked. 'It's a house party, not the Lord Mayor's ball. Worry not, Billie, you won't need a crinoline.'

'I won't *need* anything. I'm not going.'

'Forty-five minutes,' he repeated coolly. 'If that's long enough?'

'You mean I have a choice?' she queried, and, since reasoning with Travis was a complete waste of time, Billie turned and flounced out.

She wouldn't go. Spend a weekend with Travis? He could go to hell as far as Billie was concerned. She seethed as she made her way along the maze of corridors, down the stairs and out to the car, glad to find that everyone else had gone. Heaven only knows how she'd have reacted to the usual cheery calls of 'Have a good weekend'.

Twenty minutes to reach the cottage allowed Billie's simmering temper to come to the boil. The cheek of the man. Drop everything and go. Just like that. Well, had she got news for Travis. He could call, he could spend the night camped on her doorstep, but Billie Taylor was staying put. Or rather, that's what she told herself, bracing herself for the worst.

Bang on time, the doorbell rang.

Billie ignored it, the sharp, shrill tone echoing

138

horribly inside her head. It came again, only this time Travis's patience snapped, his finger glued to the bell in a non-stop whine that quickly reduced Billie's fraught nerves to shreds.

In a whirl of fury she headed for the door, flinging it open and shrinking beneath the sudden blast of chill contempt. She flattened herself against the wall as Travis strode past.

'You haven't packed,' he stated frigidly, eyes darting round the tiny lounge.

'I don't need to pack,' she countered, nervous fingers plucking at a thread on her sleeve. 'I'm not going,'

'Wrong, Billie. You're coming with me if it takes all night to convince you,' he contradicted starkly.

And message delivered, he flung himself down on the sofa and reached for the evening paper. Five whole minutes passed before he glanced up.

'Shouldn't you be packing?' he enquired with galling confidence.

'Why? Why should I do anything for you?' she challenged, holding his gaze.

He'd changed, she noted inconsequentially, the formal office suit having given way to tailored trousers and an open-necked shirt with sleeves pushed up to the elbows. Casual. Too casual for Billie's wayward mind, which made the jump from work to pleasure to the implied intimacy of a weekend away with Travis.

'Why?' he queried lightly. He turned a page, folding the paper with smooth, easy movements that did little to soothe Billie's taut nerves.

How could he sit there and be so calm, so self-assured, so confident? she wondered, as an ice-cold glance flicked back to her face.

He raised a hand, fingers snapping into place. 'Because I've said so. Because Giddings pays your wages. Because you haven't any choice. Because I need you,' he stated coldly, adding curtly, 'Need I go on?'

'But if I agree – *if*,' she emphasized, as the knife blade twisted – need her? Oh yes, she thought. He needed her all right, just like any other Giddings' accessory – 'If I agree,' she pointed out sweetly, 'we'll be horribly late. Why not simply phone and explain you can't make it?'

'But I can. And I will. With you. Better late than never,' he reminded her. 'And the sooner you accept that, the sooner we can go. Besides – ' He paused, black eyes oozing scorn, and Billie felt a shiver of apprehension.

'Besides, what?' she prompted, and she held her breath as he glanced around the room, slowly, deliberately, logging the clean but shabby furniture, the threadbare carpet, the woodwork badly in need of a fresh coat of paint.

The wandering gaze came back to Billie and then he smiled, an ugly curl of the lips that froze the blood in her veins. 'Use your imagination,' he invited, spreading his hands.

'You're threatening me.'

'Not threatening. Reminding. I need you. You need me. Simple.' He smiled again and, glancing at the clock on the mantelpiece, he added softly, the poisoned words almost a caress, 'You've five minutes to make up your mind. Five minutes exactly. After that I leave, and you know what that means – don't you, Billie . . .?'

CHAPTER 8

'For someone with nothing to wear, you look out of this world,' he informed her solemnly, his heated glance travelling over Billie's slender form.

She flushed. The dress was classic, a sleeveless black sheath teamed with matching jacket, the clear cut lines hugging the contours of her body and, since the skirt was daringly straight and short, it showed Billie's long legs off to perfection. Five years old and dateless, it was the perfect choice for every occasion, though occasions like this, she silently acknowledged, were few and far between. Mentally thanking Heather for the gift of the design, she forced a smile.

'Thank you.'

He looked out of this world himself, she could have added but didn't, her tongue thick and dry as they made their way along the maze of corridors, heading for the sound of voices, the tinkle of laughter and crystal glass, the dozen sets of critical strangers' eyes that Billie had braced herself to meet. And yet with Travis at her side, she had nothing to be afraid of. It might be a sham, a weekend away with this tall, handsome man, but no one here could know that, would secretly despise her. And in that case, she told herself, willing the butterflies to calm, why not simply make the most of it?

Turning a corner, the noise level rose suddenly and, aware that they'd arrived, Billie risked a glance at Travis's aquiline profile. He caught the gesture, black eyes fleetingly mocking as their glances locked. Then he relented, the smile strangely tender as he bent his head to hers.

'Relax,' he whispered, his breath a warm flutter on her ear. 'Just be yourself. You'll knock them for six, you'll see.'

Unconvinced, Billie nodded, her head beginning to swim a little. They paused on the threshold, the noise and colour just a swirling, whirling mass to Billie, but an overwhelming urge to turn and run was more than matched by the weakness in her knees. And then Travis slipped a hand around hers, his long fingers unexpectedly reassuring, equally disturbing as the steady grip held, helped propel her forwards.

'Smile,' he commanded as a hush descended and someone – their hostess, Billie assumed – swept towards them, her smile so warm that even Billie's nerves began to calm.

'Travis, you're here at last – and since Kate's told me so much about you, I simply *must* call you Travis,' Lady Bea insisted, offering her cheek for the kiss which Travis obligingly gave.

He laughed. 'Knowing Kate, the words don't bear repeating, but – ' He shrugged, the rueful smile disarming. 'Now that I'm here, you'll be able to judge for yourself.' He introduced Billie.

'Billie! What a lovely name. So modern,' Lady Bea pronounced, her pert nose wrinkling as she leaned forwards, the confidential air strangely appealing. 'I'm stuck with Beatrice, you know. Quite Victorian.' And she linked a friendly arm through Billie's. 'Come along and I'll introduce you to everyone.'

It was a hectic few minutes, a blur of names and faces to Billie whose cheeks soon began to ache from the smiles, but the greetings were warm, the glances curious rather than critical. Once dinner was announced, she found herself seated, Travis beside her, glass of dry white wine at hand. Sipping the ice-cold liquid, the apprehensions eased. The worst wasn't over yet, but they were here and she'd survived the tense journey with Travis, a tense, informative journey as Travis had filled her in on the background.

They were guests, he'd stressed, so business wouldn't be mentioned but she did need to know the history of the house and family, would need to

mix, make conversation, be at ease. At ease! Billie
had choked at the thought and yet, with Travis to
support her, it shouldn't prove too difficult. Travis.
Ah, yes. Billie's lips twisted. The house, the high
society, the beautiful, rich, and undoubtedly pampered women with their equally suave companions
were sure to be a strain, but if she was being honest
it was Travis, handsome, powerful, arrogant Travis
who really unnerved her.

As the soup was being served, Billie allowed
herself to glance the length of the exquisitely set
table, the silverware and crystal catching the facets
of light thrown out by the magnificent chandeliers.

Everything had happened so fast that she was
finding it hard to believe that less than an hour ago
she'd been at home.

Five minutes Travis had allowed and five minutes he'd given, precious little time to contact Anna,
wonderful Anna who'd sensed the strain but hadn't
stopped to question. She'd simply listened, reassured, and calmly taken charge. She'd phone the
nursing home, she'd visit Marianne and she'd look
after Smudge. There had been nothing for Billie to
do but pack, her frugal wardrobe dictating the
choice of clothes so that, bang on time, she'd
reappeared in the lounge, defiance blasting out
from each and every pore. And Travis, exasperating Travis, had simply nodded.

'Good,' he'd murmured, taking Billie's case and

heading for the car. 'I didn't think you'd let me down.'

Billie hadn't replied. What could she say that wouldn't provoke a niggle? Things were fraught enough without another war of words. And Travis was wrong. He could go to hell for all she cared, but she'd be damned if she'd let herself down. It was work, pure and simple. Unconventional overtime maybe, but as Travis had reminded her, it was there in the small print. And, despite her qualms, the extra money would come in handy – oh, not for herself, she'd swiftly amended, almost choking at the thought. But it had given her an idea.

And so they'd arrived late, of course, but Travis had phoned ahead to offer their apologies. And though Billie's nerves were honed, there hadn't been time for the panic to strike.

That came later, after the exquisite meal, the coffee, the brandy and liqueurs. They'd walked together upstairs, heading for their rooms, their *bedrooms*, she realized as the implication hit her. He'd be just next door, a few feet away, just a few, tantalizing feet away from Billie.

She paused outside her door, the butterflies chasing round her stomach, strange longings filling her mind. She wanted Travis to kiss her. Didn't want Travis to kiss her. Didn't know which was worse, the need to feel his arms around her or the need to deny the Judas touch. He worked for Giddings, after all, and she meant nothing to Travis, nothing beyond his cold, professional, single-minded determination to promote the Giddings' image.

'So . . .' His eyes were deep, bottomless pools. 'I'll say goodnight, then.'

Billie nodded, her tongue sticking to the roof of her mouth, her eyes shying away from the knowledge that lurked in his. As she reached for the doorcatch, Travis put out a hand to stop her.

'Running away?' he challenged, and her head shot up in alarm. 'Tut, tut,' he teased as she tried to pull away. 'Haven't you forgotten something?'

'Forgotten – ? N-no, I don't think so,' she stammered, every instinct shockingly attuned to Travis; his eyes, his generous mouth, his powerful body, the evocative tang of aftershave.

He smiled, a lazy, heart-tugging smile that set the blood pounding in her ears. Billie stumbled backwards as the grip held and long fingers circled her wrist, tugging her forwards, closer and closer, resistance futile as the narrow gap between them disappeared.

'Oh, Billie,' he crooned, and he pulled her against him, his arms closing round to hold and enfold. 'I do believe you've forgotten how to say goodnight – the real way, my little tigress.' And he kissed her, briefly, fleetingly brief before raising his head, eyes locking with hers, smoky with promise, heavy with desire.

'No, Travis!' she cried, struggling to be free, yet another waste of time as Travis laughed, the sound music to her ears, the touch of mouth against mouth stifling the protest as his lips took possession, as the madness spread, the need to kiss and touch, kiss and be touched, filling her mind, her body, blocking out the reality.

She swayed against him, hips skimming hips, thighs matching thighs, his taut muscles rippling at the contact, her own thrill of satisfaction fanning the flames. She wanted him. Heaven help her, but she wanted his mouth exploring hers, his lips caressing, teeth nibbling. And though she craved his hands on her body, Travis denied her, simply held her close, so close she could feel the heat, the hardness, the need that Travis, tantalizing Travis, kept under taut control.

With a surge of frustration, Billie moved her hips, and Travis laughed, his mouth a warm growl against her ear, and yes, he moved his hands, simply skimming the swell of her buttocks and holding her fast against him, both giving and denying since she was powerless to move, was in heaven and hell together because the need was there, his need every bit as urgent as hers.

She heard a sound, a haunting, moaning, exquisite strain of music that came from somewhere deep within her. And as his tongue swept through into the secret, moist corners of her mouth, Billie trembled, eddies and whirlpools of delight rippling outwards and inwards, heightening the need, fuelling the need, the screaming, aching, frustrating need to make her body part of his.

And yet, it was madness. As long, sensitive fingers raised goosebumps on her skin, as exploring lips caressed, bruised, nibbled, the distant corners of her mind were clinging to the threads of sanity. He wanted her. Now. This moment. He wanted her. And just like the last time when he'd proved his point with brutal eloquence, Travis was playing games. He didn't love her, didn't need her, simply wanted her. Young, handsome, rich, he'd be used to taking what he wanted when he wanted, and then he'd move on. Oh, yes. He'd take what she was offering and he'd move on, with never a thought for the pain he'd caused, for Billie's bruised heart or the fragile blossom of emotion.

She pulled away, the force of pain and anger taking even Billie by surprise. 'Leave me alone,' she hissed, eyes locking with his and brimming with emotion. She stepped back, coming up short against the wall, eyes shooting flames, cheeks glowing like embers, her body shockingly aware of the man, the need, the longing. Smothering the longing, she raised her chin. 'Are you listening, Travis?' she entreated coldly. 'Leave me alone, stop playing games.'

'Who's playing?' he drawled lazily.

Her colour deepened. 'You are,' she replied with a calm she was far from feeling. 'But not with me. Understand, Travis? You're engaged to Cleo and I – '

'Have the lukewarm Viking to console you?' And he folded his arms, eyeing her with calculating scorn. 'Some consolation,' he jeered.

'And how would you know?' she challenged back, the words too near the truth for comfort.

He moved, a lightning reaction too quick to parry, and powerful hands gripped her shoulders as Travis kissed her, a sneering invasion of mouth and mind that was over before it began. Billie stumbled backwards, the sudden sting of tears shaming as black eyes rained scorn.

'You want me,' he stated flatly. 'I know it. You know it. And only a fool would choose to deny it.'

'You're wrong,' she contradicted, pride blurring the hurt, masking the reality. 'You're wrong.'

But Travis simply shrugged. As he turned away, Billie groped her way into her room, leaning back against the door, tears hovering on her lashes. She gulped, hate, anger, fear battling for position, the truth weighing heavy. The truth. Ah, yes. And even now she didn't want to believe it. She loved him. Fool, fool, fool. She loved him, had probably loved him all along.

The sob rose, choking her and, with a huge effort of will, Billie dashed the tears away, refusing to wallow in pity. Pity. Travis's pity. If she couldn't have his love, she had to be strong to keep pity at bay. Allow Travis to know? To pity and despise her? True, he'd logged her reactions, physical reactions to a physical man, but he must never, ever, know how deep her feelings ran. She swallowed the pain. She needed a drink. Glancing round, she spotted the drinks' tray, then spotted something else she hadn't had time to notice earlier. A door. A connecting door. Oh, hell! Travis was just next door and must have the key.

Without pausing to think, she marched across, flinging open the door in a blaze of indignation. Travis glanced up. He was sprawled fully dressed on the bed, glass of brandy beside him, note book at hand. Logging Billie's heated face, he raised a mocking eyebrow.

'Do come in,' he drawled and, swinging himself upright he patted the bed. 'Sit down, make yourself at home. Brandy?' he offered with perfect unconcern.

'I've come for the key,' she stated baldly, ignoring the invitation.

'Key?' he queried. 'What key?'

'That key,' she snarled, pointing to the door.

'Oh, *that* key,' he acknowledged, with maddening insouciance. 'Sorry, no can do.'

Billie went cold. 'What do you mean, no can do?'

'Exactly what I say. I don't have a key. Rooms

151

'like this don't, you know,' he confided solemnly. 'That's the whole idea.'

'What is?' Billie snapped, pushing a lock of hair out of her eyes and glaring across the space between them. 'Stop talking in riddles, Travis. What are you saying?' she demanded, her heart sinking. Less than six feet away from Travis, with an unlocked door the only barrier, she'd never be able to sleep. And she needed her sleep to keep her wits.

'Think, Billie, think,' he chided lightly. 'We're here as a couple. They couldn't put us in a double room – it's not the done thing in polite society. But in the fun-loving nineties . . .' He paused, shrugged, amusement playing about the corners of his mouth. 'Side by side, with a door that doesn't lock, what could be more natural?'

'But – you must know where the key is,' she insisted tightly, damping down the panic. 'You're hiding it somewhere.'

'And why on earth should I do that?' he asked incredulously.

'Oh – I don't know. Any one of a dozen reasons. To worry me,' she tossed out absurdly.

'Worried that I might creep in?' he challenged softly. 'Or worried that I won't?'

Billie gasped, turned crimson, saw the laughter brimming in his eyes and clamped her lips together in prim and proper disapproval, before flouncing out and slamming the door behind.

There was a heavy wooden chest beneath the window. Wincing at the noise, she dragged it across and pushed it against the door, breathing a huge sigh of relief that lasted all of twenty seconds, all the time it took for Travis to rap on the door, fling it open and stand framed in the jamb, his smile widening as he surveyed Billie's futile attempt to keep him out.

'Thought I'd better remind you,' he drawled, eyes bubbling with suppressed amusement. 'The door opens my way. But worry not, Billie,' he reassured tartly. 'I won't be stealing into your bed the moment you close your eyes. If and when I need a woman,' he explained cruelly, 'there's no shortage of offers.' He raised his glass. 'Goodnight, Billie,' he toasted drily. 'Sweet dreams.'

Despite tossing and turning, convinced she'd never sleep, Billie woke refreshed to a pot of freshly brewed tea and a maid drawing the sprigged muslin curtains.

'Good morning, ma'am. Breakfast in thirty minutes,' the young girl informed her pleasantly, her quick bob of a curtsy amazing Billie who was forced to stifle a giggle.

It set the tone for the day – sheer luxury, unashamed luxury, a world Billie had never suspected still existed, and wasn't sure she'd want to live in on a day-to-day basis. Yet despite the thorny presence of Travis, she enjoyed the experience of being pampered for once.

A ramble in the park was followed by lunch, the conversation turning to horses.

'Lady Bea keeps an excellent stable,' Travis had explained on their journey in. 'I don't suppose you ride, by any chance?'

'You don't suppose right,' she'd confirmed flippantly. On my sort of budget, horses and riding lessons don't get a look-in.

'Pity,' he'd acknowledged. 'An interest in horses might have helped swing the deal.'

'While Cleo, of course,' she'd challenged scathingly, 'rides to hounds and would have been there at the kill?'

Surprisingly Travis had laughed. 'As a matter of fact, no,' he'd admitted. 'Cleo's city-born and bred. She'd never take to life in the country.'

An interesting snippet for Billie to mull over. Felbrough was hardly the back of beyond, she would allow, but if Cleo *did* crave the bright lights, Felbrough, with or without Travis, didn't fit the bill.

While the others rode, Billy explored.

'Feel free to browse,' Lady Bea had insisted when Billie declined the offer of her company. Since Bea adored riding, Billie could hardly risk the wrath of Travis by keeping her away from it. And though she took her at her word, she was careful to keep to the public rooms.

It was amazing. No wonder Travis was determined to land the commission. The entrance hall alone was enough to take her breath away, with wonderful marble columns and acres of space. It had been built in 1780 and was less grandiose than Pellaton, more delicate, more elegant. And, though in need of decoration, the furnishings were superb – not to mention worth a king's ransom.

Billie was almost afraid to breathe lest she damage the patina of the beautifully preserved Chippendale and Louis XVI furniture. And yet this was a home, she acknowledged, not just a a miniature palace. Every sofa, every chair, each and every occasional table was clearly in use.

The research would have to be thorough, Billie realized, pausing in front of an exquisite Reni painting. But she was sure that Giddings could do it.

With ideas teeming in her head, she headed outside for a breath of fresh air. It was mild for late September, the autumn colours of the park reflected in the glassy calm of the lake. She was vaguely aware of the riders in the distance, the sound of laughter, cheery voices, the gallop of hooves. And Travis. Oh yes, never forget Travis. He filled her mind, dominated her thoughts, an ever-present torment. And though she wanted him, needed him, loved him, she was living a dream. Travis belonged to Cleo, and treated Billie as little more than a mild irritation, a thorn to be endured for the company's sake. She could walk out tomorrow and Travis would curse her – and then promptly forget her as he found himself another designer, she understood starkly.

Caught up in her thoughts, Billie didn't notice the sudden commotion, the raised voices, the thunder of hooves, the wild snort of a frightened pony. And then she smelt the danger.

Heart in mouth, she spun round. It was a child, Lady Bea's four-year-old daughter, and her pony had bolted, careering away from the others and heading straight for the lake – and Billie. A surge of panic caused Billie to freeze and she closed her eyes, incapable of moving as the animal bore down on her. There was a huge splash as the pony veered away and hurtled into the water, but Billie's relief was fleeting. The child screamed, panicked, floundered and, as the pony swam for the bank, she disappeared below the chill, grey surface.

Without stopping to think, Billie plunged in, the icy cold water paralysing her mind. She was a strong swimmer, but her quilted jacket slowed her down. It gave buoyancy, but filled with air, ballooning up and hampering her frantic arm strokes. And it was cold, mind-numbingly cold.

Reaching the spot where the girl had disappeared, she groped blindly beneath the surface, frantic hands connecting with something solid. Praying as she'd never prayed before, Billie heaved with all her might and the girl's head broke the surface. Billie didn't pause, but simply turned and struck out for the bank, towing the unconscious figure securely behind as reinforcements arrived at the water's edge.

The next half hour was a blur – Lady Bea's tearful thanks as the child spluttered, coughed and cleared her lungs of water, Travis's strong arms cocooning Billie, his jacket across her shoulders as he whisked her inside.

'You need a hot bath,' he insisted tersely, dragging her away from the tableau by the lake. 'Come on, you little fool, before you catch pneumonia. Don't worry about Daisy. She's fine. She'll be fine – thanks to you.'

'All thanks to you,' Lady Bea echoed later. It seemed to take a lifetime, but normality returned and dinner had gone ahead, the small child tucked safely up in bed, none the worse for her ducking and sleeping as soundly as an angel while the grown-ups downstairs relived the drama.

'She'd have drowned but for you,' Lady Bea insisted as they gathered for drinks in the library. 'We'd never have reached her in time, wouldn't have known where to look.' She swung round to Travis, placed an imploring hand on his arm. 'Your fiancée's worth her weight in gold, Travis. You will take care of her, won't you?'

Fiancée? Billie almost choked on her wine, the heat running through her like a brand, and she opened her mouth to speak as Travis's solemn gaze locked with hers.

'Don't worry,' he insisted softly, flashing a bright, reassuring smile at their hostess. 'I intend to.'

'Fiancée? Hah! You've got a nerve,' Billie hissed later, checking they couldn't be overheard.

Travis shrugged. 'So I didn't explain. Hardly the crime of the century. You're here, you're with me, and if people jump to the obvious conclusion, why worry? It's hurting no one and it's a natural mistake. And Bea's unbelievably grateful. We're bound to swing that contract now, Billie.'

'Is that all you're concerned about – the money?' she fumed.

Travis's mouth tightened. 'Don't knock it. Money opens lots of doors – and besides,' he added slyly, the atmosphere changing like the wind, 'I don't notice you turning up your nose at the benefits.'

'Meaning?'

'That dress. Last night's stunning little number. They cost money, Billie. Lots of money,' he emphasized softly. 'You didn't find those in Felbrough High Street.'

She had, as it happened, thanks to Heather. But she wasn't about to tell Travis that. 'It's none of your damn business,' she snapped.

158

'Correction. You work for Giddings – that makes you my business. And you've not averse to pocketing the extras, are you, Billie? This weekend's fee for a start.'

'I've told you, keep your money.'

'*Your* money now,' he reminded her. 'And quite a sum for a weekend's work. Tell me,' he entreated with a sneering curl of the lips, 'how will you spend it? On the raggle-taggle cottage, perhaps? Or yet another designer outfit to dazzle the lukewarm Viking?'

'Like I said, mind your own business,' she snarled, swinging away and losing herself in the crowd of chattering guests. The words had stung, but Billie was damned if she'd explain and she bottled the pain along with a mass of other emotions that were centred on Travis. Despite the sneering enquiry, he neither knew nor cared how Billie spent her money, but her conscience was clear. She didn't want the money, Giddings' money, but she'd take it, would use it to give her mother an overdue holiday. It was something Billie had never been able to afford, but now, thanks to Travis, Marianne could have a much-needed break.

It was midnight before they headed back upstairs, Billie lightheaded from the unaccustomed wine and the vintage champagne that had been opened in her honour.

'Quite the belle of the ball,' Travis teased, though

not unkindly, taking her hand and guiding her upstairs. Billie didn't bother trying to wriggle free. Experience told her that what Travis wanted, Travis took, yet she was achingly aware of the touch of skin on skin, of Travis's unique body scent, and fresh waves of longing swept over her.

They paused outside her room. 'A night-cap?' he suggested, producing a bottle of wine as if by magic.

'Where on earth – ?' she began and then broke off. Of course. No need to ask. The Travis Kent brand of charm had clearly worked on one of the maids.

'Your room – or mine?' he challenged, the message loud and clear in tawny-flecked eyes.

Lightheaded and reckless, Billie smiled. 'Mine, I think,' she decided, leading Travis inside. She was playing with fire, but his mocking tone was galling. And besides, she'd been thinking, it was high time she proved herself. Despite the inner turmoil, her mind was in control and one way or another she'd prove it. She willed herself to relax as Travis filled the glasses.

'Here's to Giddings,' he toasted solemnly, coming to sit on the bed beside her, creating fresh waves of panic, 'and to Wilma Jane Taylor who stunned us all with her heroics.'

'Don't!' Billie insisted. 'Don't mock.'

'Oh, I'm not mocking,' Travis explained, taking the glass from her trembling fingers and placing it carefully on the bedside table. He moved in close, so

160

close Billie was half afraid to breathe, his nearness unnerving. The urge to reach out and touch, kiss, offer her mouth to Travis was so acute that she dug her fingernails into the palms of her hands in an effort to stay in control. 'Believe me, Billie,' he insisted solemnly. 'I'm not mocking, simply stating – ' He broke off, leaned forwards, allowed his lips to brush hers, a wonderful taste of wine-flavoured lips. 'That you're a brave – ' Another kiss. 'Recklessly brave – ' Another pause, a lingering caress, a heart-stopping moment. 'Stubbornly brave – ' Mouth against mouth, lips hungrily devouring as Billie shivered with the heat of expectation. 'Extremely beautiful, extremely desirable young lady. And I want you,' he murmured huskily, raising his head, eyes locking with hers and gazing to centre of her soul. 'Understand, Billie? I want you. And I want you now . . .'

CHAPTER 9

Time slipped. Billie gasped, the heat from Travis's fingers scorching her skin as he urged her back against the covers, her frightened eyes fluttering open, searching for his, searching for love and reassurance, her heart turning a somersault at the intense, smouldering gaze that came back at her.

'I want you,' he said again, black eyes smoky with promise. Billie trembled as he stretched out beside her, burying his face in her hair, kissing her hair, kissing her neck, nibbling her earlobes, nibbling, sucking, biting.

'Billie, Billie, Billie!' he murmured and Billie writhed against him, aware of his hands, magic hands gliding over her curves and creating waves of pleasure, currents of heat surging through the flimsy fabric of her dress, every touch a brand, every touch exquisite, the need too real, too right to ignore, to suppress, to deny. Her mind was floating on a cloud of love. She loved him! She loved him, needed him, wanted him! And Travis, wonderful, wonderful Travis wanted her!

The kiss deepened, the pressure increasing, as Travis plundered her mouth, his lips hard, bruising, punishing, his teeth nibbling almost to the point of drawing blood. Billie mewed piteously as Travis eased the pressure, his lips now persuading, inciting, his tongue slipping through into highly charged depths, exploring, caressing, sweeping languidly across the soft inner flesh, and back again to tangle with her own.

Billie was in paradise, lived for the moment, revelled in the moment, and she gasped aloud as sensuous fingers caressed the tingling skin of her bare shoulders, the chiffon bodice but a feeble restraint as Travis gently tugged, freeing Billie's aching breasts. And it was Travis's turn to gasp, the sharp hiss of indrawn breath dissolving the final threads of doubt in Billie's mind.

'You're very beautiful,' he murmured thickly, pausing, raising his head, eyes fastened hungrily on Billie's glowing face, her diamond-bright eyes. He nodded solemnly. 'Oh yes, you've very beautiful.'

He dipped his head, tasted her mouth, briefly, too briefly, Billie's protest provoking a throaty laugh as his lips moved down, gliding across the heated stem of her neck. A pause, a breathtaking pause to nuzzle her throat before he moved on, downwards again, slowly, inevitably downwards, nearer and nearer, his mouth tantalizingly close, hands and fingers tantalizingly close, and closer still and closer. And yet still he denied her, circling the heated skin, tiny kisses that scorched and soothed, scorched and excited, his thumbs an erotic glide across the plains of her belly.

'Travis! Oh, Travis!' she cried, arching towards him and he laughed again, drawing back, the message in his eyes filling her with joy.

'Easy, sweetheart,' he murmured, shrugging off the dinner jacket, sure fingers snapping at the buttons of the white silk dress shirt.

Billie watched, smiled inside as with slow, deliberate movements Travis tugged the shirt from the waist band of his trousers, exposing the thick, dark mass of hair across a powerful chest, and all the time his smouldering eyes were fastened on hers, the need, the desire, the naked promise in their depths making Billie's blood boil. Travis wanted her. He wanted her!

A moment later he was beside her, half-naked, his lightly tanned flesh gleaming in the soft glow of the bedside lamp. And Billie reached out, hesitantly, her fingers raking through the mass of hair that covered his powerful chest and Travis laughed, caught at her hand, nuzzled the palm before raining tiny kisses the length of her arm, across her shoulders and down again, and as Billie arched towards him he dipped his head, fastening his mouth on the straining bud of her nipple. He nibbled, nuzzled, tongued and teased, circling each breast in turn, almost gliding from one peak to the other, merely pausing to nuzzle the valley between. And while his mouth created havoc, such wonderful havoc, his hands ranged her body, easing her skirt and tights and petticoat away, leaving Billie completely naked but for the tiniest wisp of lace at the junction of her legs.

Another pause, electricity crackling in the air as Travis pulled away, gazing down, drinking his fill. And then his eyes moved back to her face and Billie's heart flipped over as she read the message, misread the message, until Travis smiled, banishing the fear, creating urgent needs as he touched her again, skin against skin, long fingers caressing the smooth, white flesh of her inner thighs, filling her with heat, filling her with dread. Because she wanted him. She wanted his hands to explore her body, wanted this man's touch with a fever she couldn't control. Because it was right. It had to be right. It was too wonderful to be anything but right and Billy gasped aloud as Travis pulled her against him, the strength of his arousal sending shock waves pulsing through her body.

'Oh, Billie,' he murmured, his lips nibbling hungrily at the corner of her mouth. And she was exquisitely aware that his hands had moved on, had reached the line of her lacy black briefs.

165

There was a pause and her eyes flew open, irises dark with fear, fear and a raw need that was reflected in Travis's sultry gaze. As Billie smiled, Travis smiled and a single finger slid slowly beneath the hem of her panties.

'Oh, God!' she moaned as Travis probed, parted the curls, found her moist and hot. And she writhed as Travis urged her back onto the bed, the scrap of lace the final, irritating barrier because she wanted to be naked, shamelessly naked, needed Travis to see, to touch, to inflame, to make her come alive. She needed him.

And yet, common sense, unwanted and unbidden, snaked in to remind her that that was all it was – just a need. A physical need on his part, an aching, mind-blowing, soul-destroying need on hers. And she was cheapening herself, offering her body, denying the needs of her mind. The need was tainted. And the biggest shadow in Billie's mind was Cleo.

The battle continued to rage as Travis knelt beside her. Billie lay quite still, gazing up into his eyes, black eyes smoky with desire, the taint of desire that mirrored her own. And oh, how she wanted him. It was wonderful, too wonderful to be wrong, surely? she asked, willing herself to believe it. And she was alive, shockingly alive, her body dancing, pulsing, aching, responding. She wanted him, needed him, loved him and she moved her hips, arching against his hand, his probing fingers, the pain in the pit of her belly exquisite hell as Travis paused, smiled, then began to draw the panties over her hips. He dropped his gaze; as the eye contact severed, something vital in Billie's mind snapped.

'No, Travis, no!' she cried, twisting away, seeing the shock, the hurt in his eyes, and hating herself for allowing it to happen. She sat bolt upright, folding her arms protectively across her naked breasts, eyes full of silent pleas as she locked her gaze with his.

Simmering anger came back at her. 'You bitch.' He spat the words, quietly, viciously, and then he swore. Billie blanched, shrank away, the iron grip of his fingers pulling her up short. A lifetime passed before he spoke. 'Oh, Billie,' he castigated coldly and, as he spoke, he tugged her close, so close the heat of his breath was scorching her cheeks. Billie closed her eyes, shutting out the man but not the words, the softly spoken words of poison. 'You want me,' he stated coldly. 'You might not want to believe it, but your body doesn't lie, *this* doesn't lie.' And he snatched her to him, the touch of his lips a fleeting, bruising insult that sent waves of heat pulsing through her veins. 'Are you listening, damn you?' he berated, and he shook her roughly, his fingers biting deep. Billie's lids flew open in alarm. Catching the scent of panic, Travis smiled, a contemptuous snarl of lips before he pushed her away with a gesture of distaste.

She slumped on the bed, watching as Travis retrieved his shirt, slung it carelessly across his shoulder and then strolled across the room, slow, easy movements that seemed to take for ever.

He reached the door, the door that led from her room to his and the fact that he chose to use it underlined the contempt he didn't try to hide. She wanted him. She wanted him and she was just next door, and if he chose, he could take her . . . If . . . Billie closed her eyes as the softly spoken gibe screamed across the space between them.

'Who'd have believed it?' he sneered. 'Billie Taylor, the modern-day miss, turns out to be a prude.' And, as Billie squeezed back the tears, struggling to hang on to any shreds of self-control, he tagged on cruelly. 'And since a virtuous woman is priced above rubies, let's hope the lukewarm Viking appreciates such a gem.'

Luckily Sunday was busy, too busy to spend brooding as extra guests arrived for lunch and, with Daisy's escapade the main talking-point, Billie found herself the unwilling centre of attention. Only Travis, saturnine, knowing Travis kept his distance, a nervous Billie aware of his every move, every smile he chose to bestow on the stunning blonde who stuck like a limpet to his side. And

168

Billie was jealous. Jealous of Cleo, jealous of the girl. And knowing that Travis didn't care didn't help one bit. The girl was unimportant but the message was plain. If Travis chose to snap his fingers, he was demonstrating cruelly, the girl, like Billie, was his for the taking. Oh, yes, Billie acknowledged grimly, the man she loved could have his pick of women.

And then came the bombshell, the girl's careless query drifting down the table. 'Giddings? But I'm sure I've heard that name before. Yes, of course,' she trilled with another bright smile. 'Roma Giddings, the famous designer.'

'My mother,' Travis acknowledged as Billie went cold, faces around the table blurring as the anger surged. Working for Giddings was bad enough, a nameless, faceless company, but to work side by side with a Giddings, to take money from a Giddings, to love this man . . . Billie felt the nausea rise.

With a muttered excuse she scraped back her chair, the need to get away suddenly overpowering. Reaching the terrace, she leaned against the wall, taking huge gulps of clean, fresh air in an effort to stay in control. She wanted to escape but had nowhere to go, had the rest of the day to endure, hours and hours of making polite conversation with a houseful of people, and then the journey home, another nightmare ride with Travis. She felt the sob rise, dashed the tears away with an impatient brush of her hand and then froze as she sensed a movement beside her. She didn't need to turn her head to know that Travis was close, too close, and the knowledge that she loved him, hated him, loathed him, needed him filled her with shame.

'Billie?'

'Go back to your lunch, Travis,' she murmured flatly.

'Fine,' he agreed. 'As long as you come with me.'

'I- I'm not hungry,' she explained, the mere thought of food enough to make her stomach churn.

'Maybe not,' he agreed pleasantly. 'But the least you can do is sit and talk, join the conversation while you push the odd potato round your plate.'

Billie gulped. She took the hint. Do the job she was paid for, he meant. Sparkle, shine, socialize. Heaven forbid business should suffer. Business came first, always first, with a Giddings.

Like an obedient child she turned, felt the touch of skin on skin, Travis's light grip scalding her. She pulled up sharply, angled her head, eyes brimming with silent misery.

'What is it, Billie?' Travis asked, the soft words almost her undoing.

'Nothing,' she hissed, aware of self-control hanging by a thread. 'Nothing for you to worry about. Let's go in, Travis. You lunch will be getting cold – not to mention the slight matter of business.'

* * *

170

It was a tense, frigid journey back, Billie shrinking into the rich white upholstery, her mind churning. What a fool she'd been, allowing Travis close, and just how close she realized by replaying the scene on her bed that was etched deep in her mind. She'd almost given in, allowed Travis to make love to her – love, hah! What a mockery of love their coupling would have been. Sheer indulgence, physical indulgence, the need so raw that even now Billie had to fight the urge to reach out, touch, caress, invite Travis's heated gaze to travel her body. Had she no shame? she silently upbraided herself. Wanting a man, this man, this man who'd helped to destroy her family. And though she had had the sense to stop before things got out of hand, the need refused to go away. It would fill her mind in the daylight hours, tear her apart in the long, lonely midnight moments in her bed, because the need refused to go away. The raw, aching, shameful need she had of Travis.

Caught up in her misery, Billie failed to notice that Travis had slowed the car, brought it smoothly to a standstill, the sudden silence deafening. She glanced around, aware of nothing but darkness, not a light, not a sound, not another vehicle, and then the panic surged as Travis snapped off his seat belt and swung himself round to face her.

'Right – now talk.'

'What about? The weekend? Quite a success,

don't you think?' Billie trilled, her voice overloud in the silence.

'Quit the sarcasm, Billie. It doesn't become you. And yes, you're right, the weekend was a success – thanks to you.'

'All part of the job I'm paid for – and paid well, remember?' She couldn't help but goad him.

He smiled grimly. 'I'm sure you'll manage to spend it – somehow. On the house, maybe. Heaven knows, the raggle-taggle cottage deserves a new look. Except, of course, designer clothes and the lukewarm Viking have first claim.'

'Leave Tony out of this. In fact, leave Tony alone, full stop.'

'Why? What's so special about the boyfriend that the subject's taboo? He's human, isn't he? He lives, breathes, works for a living just like the rest of us. What's so special about a salesman, Billie?'

'You've been checking up on me!'

'Hardly. I've better things to do than pry into other people's lives.' Travis shrugged. 'But since he comes and goes, he must travel around. Unless, of course,' he hinted slyly, black eyes narrowing, 'unless there's a wife lurking in the background?'

'Now you're being ridiculous.'

'Am I? It was – just a thought. But if you know better . . .' He shrugged again. 'In that case, Billie, I was right in the first place. He's a rep, well paid and highly successful. Either that or he's found himself a gold mine.'

'Meaning?'

'Meaning you. You've a good job, your own home, no family commitments – and precious little to show for it. Apart from the boyfriend. The one with the flashy car,' he pointedly added as Billie gasped at the implication.

'I'm not listening to this,' she informed him stonily, staring rigidly ahead. 'I've had enough.'

'Good. That makes two of us. I've had enough. More than enough of your juvenile behaviour.'

'Juvenile? Ha! So these are the thanks I get for giving up my time – '

'My time, Billie, since I'm picking up the tab.'

'*My* time – paid or otherwise,' she contradicted.

'My time,' he reinforced firmly. 'I pay the piper, I call the tune. Which is why we're here now. I want to know what's wrong. You haven't said a word since we left the house.'

'Because I've nothing to say. We've nothing to say. Not to one another.'

'I don't agree. There's something on your mind, something I could help with if you'd let me. Why not spit it out, save me the trouble of dragging it from you?'

'Because there's nothing to tell.'

'You're lying.' The words were harsh but the tone was mild. He paused, spread his hands. 'The

173

scene at lunch, the journey home. There's something eating away at you. Come on, Billie, spit it out before it chokes you.'

Billie turned her head, looked at him then, allowed her eyes to rake his face, the familiar features that were etched into her mind. Why not? Why not get it over and done with? They were finished, finished before they'd started, and now the job would go, Billie would go, could never live with the shame of working for a Giddings, of working for Travis, loving Travis, hating Travis, knowing Travis belonged to someone else.

She took a deep breath. 'You lied,' she stated coldly, accusingly, her fingers rigidly clasped in her lap.

'About what?'

'Who you are, for a start. You're a Giddings.'

'And is that such a crime?' he asked as Billie's sensitive ear registered vague amusement.

She stiffened. 'Maybe. Maybe not,' she allowed. 'But the plain fact is, you lied. And how,' she berated him coldly,. 'you let me believe you were just another employee. You know full well I'd never have agreed to work for a Giddings.'

'But why, Billie, why?' he demanded incredulously. 'Not some imaginary slight paid to Anna, surely?'

'Hardly imaginary – '

'She survived, found another job – '

'And then lost it – thanks to Giddings.'

'She took early retirement. You said yourself she was loving it.'

'She hadn't much choice, had she, Travis? And you know Anna, always one to make the best of things. Faced with retirement or the sack – '

'She wouldn't have been sacked,' he explained with the patient tone of a parent addressing a difficult child.

'Like the last time, you mean?' Billie said scornfully.

Travis sighed. 'I'm wasting my time, aren't I, Billie? You've closed your mind, closed it years ago if the truth's known. You're just not prepared to listen.'

'To more lies?' Billie shook her head. 'No, Travis. Save your breath. I'm not listening. Not any more.'

'Not ever, you little fool. You're stuck in a time warp. Because life for Billie Taylor ended years ago.'

'Six years ago to be exact. When Giddings, *your* family, *your* business, ruined House of Marianne.'

'No, Billie. You're wrong. It wasn't like that.'

'No? Well, that's where *you*'re wrong. But Travis Kent won't admit it because, lo and behold, Travis Kent is a Giddings.' She looked at him then, eyes nuggets of hate, six long years of hate blasting out from rigid features. But no more. Because Billie Taylor had finally had enough. 'Goodbye, Travis,' she murmured coldly, releasing the catch of her seat belt and picking up her bag. 'It's been – quite an experience, but this is where it ends.'

'What are you doing? Are you mad? We're miles from the nearest town, Billie. Shut the door and show some sense.'

'I'd rather rot in hell,' she snarled. She climbed out, resisting the urge to slam the door, and without a backward glance, set off at a tearing pace in what she hoped was the right direction.

It was raining, she noticed belatedly, a soft soaking mist that found its way inside the neck of her jacket. Only showerproof to start with, it had already suffered a ducking in the lake and would need to be reproofed. Cold, wet, bitterly unhappy and with high-heeled shoes not meant for hiking, Billie's punishing pace soon faltered. And once she slowed, reality hit her. Thanks to her pride, she was stranded miles from heaven knew where; her misery increased with every passing moment. Tears welled, cascading unchecked down her cheeks. Why not? Why not cry, let the hate pour out? There was no one to see her. No one to care. Not Travis. Oh no, not Travis, safe and sound in his cosy little world. A sob escaped her, and then another. Then Billie was crying, really crying, as she stumbled blindly on, the noise in her head masking the sound of the engine as Travis pulled in beside her.

'Billie!'

'Leave me alone. Go away,' she muttered angrily, ignoring the open door.

'Get in, you little fool. You're soaked. You'll catch your death.'

'Fat lot you'll care.'

'Of course I care. Hell, woman!' He cut the engine, swung out, had crossed the road to block her path before Billie's numbed mind had time to react. She swerved to avoid him, not caring where she went, striking out blindly across the verge as Travis shot a hand out to halt her, the hands on her shoulders sending rivulets of heat surging through her. She was soaked and vividly aware of the sight she must present, hair plastered to her face and head, eyes red and swollen from the tears she'd shed, tears that continued to rack her. 'You little fool,' he said again. 'Of course I care.'

Billie sniffed loudly, miserably, and Travis swore lightly under his breath, hands slipping from her shoulders, cupping her face, cradling her face, the expression in his eyes unfathomable. Then she was in his arms, felt the heat of his mouth as his lips met hers, the warmth spreading outwards and inwards, a wonderful surge of emotion that Billie hadn't the strength – or the will – to fight.

Travis raised his head, hands holding, caressing, cradling. 'I care, Billie,' he repeated softly. 'But you must understand. I can't help who my family are – any more than you can.'

177

'You lied,' she said accusingly, but the anger had died and the ice around her heart had started to melt. He did care. She wanted to believe it. Because if Travis cared, nothing else in the whole wide world mattered.

'I didn't lie,' he insisted, black eyes softly pleading. And though his hair was plastered his head, the aura of power increased as Travis shrugged off the rain. 'I just didn't explain. How could I?' he asked. 'Since you'd made your feelings plain, you'd have walked out weeks ago if I'd told you. And I didn't want to lose you. I still don't want to lose you.'

He hugged her, briefly, reassuringly. Billie's heart soared again. He loved her! He was telling her that he loved her and her eyes shone with tears, tears of love, a love given and returned. 'I don't want to lose you,' he repeated softly, fingers linked with hers as he drew her back inside the car. 'You're the best designer I've got.' And he smiled. As something vital died in Billie's mind, Travis smiled. 'Surely you understand, Billie. I just can't afford to lose you.'

CHAPTER 10

Monday morning. Another Monday morning. Billie woke early. If the truth were known, she'd barely slept at all, was beginning to feel the strain of playing a part whilst working close to Travis. It was a sham, the air of calm she donned like a mask the moment she walked into the office. But it helped her face the day, face the man she loved. Love! What a fool she'd been, imagining Travis could love her. Travis Kent wouldn't know the meaning of the word. He was a Giddings; Giddings, she knew to her cost, had time for nothing but business and the end-of-year balance sheet.

The weekend at Fleet seemed an age away; though she'd wanted to resign, something held her back. Her mother, she supposed – her radiant smile, when Billie mentioned the holiday, all the thanks she'd needed for the hurt and the pain churned up by Travis's careless words. Walk out cold and it would be Marianne who'd suffer, not Billie.

She checked the clock. Seven-fifteen. She ought to make a move, face another day – and Travis. She smothered a sigh. And then the doorbell rang, shattering the silence. Who on earth – ? And then she remembered. Tony. He'd turned up on her doorstep the night before, and after an awkward start, they'd finally cleared the air. Tony, she was glad to find, would settle for being friends, the first friendly gesture Billie's when Tony's car refused to start. With garages in Felbrough few and far between, she'd offered him a bed on her sofa.

The bell went again, short, sharp and impatient. Tony's mechanic, she decided, pushing back the duvet and reaching for her robe. Though how Tony managed to sleep through such a commotion was anybody's guess.

She reached the top of the stairs as a dishevelled Tony appeared from the lounge. 'It's bound to be for you,' she said as Tony opened the door. Only she was wrong. It was Travis, a struggling Smudge in his arms.

Travis's gaze swept from Tony, fully dressed but clearly unshaven, to Billie frozen at the top of the stairs, and then back to Tony. He smiled. At least, his mouth did. The expression in his eyes was arctic. 'Yours, I believe,' he murmured tersely, not bothering to mask the contempt. And as Smudge scrambled free and darted up to Billie, he added, 'I can see now why you were too busy to notice that your cat spent the night howling in my garden.'

Work was hell. She didn't know which was worse, Travis's frigid silence or the clipped words that never moved beyond the the task in hand. They worked together yet alone, ideas politely put, just as politely turned aside or accepted.

It had puzzled her at first, such a fierce reaction. What right had Travis to judge and find her wanting, to condemn her out of hand? And then she'd realized. Pride. Travis didn't love Billie, but he'd have taken what he could and then tossed her aside with never a moment's thought. Only he hadn't. Because she'd rejected him. *She*'d rejected him. And the arrogant Travis Kent wasn't used to rejection.

Anna saw the shadows beneath her eyes. 'What is it?' she asked, a frown creasing her brow. 'Is working for Giddings getting you down? I know Travis wasn't completely honest about his background, but you're not still fretting about that, are you, Billie?'

Billie swallowed hard. 'Not really. It's – something and nothing,' she explained, forcing a smile and receiving a playful rap from Anna for being evasive.

But Anna, wise old Anna, knew better than to press her. Instead she changed the subject. 'I don't like to impose, but there's no one else I can trust. I need a surrogate mother.'

'Kittens!' Billie's eyes lit up.

'Just for the weekend,' Anna explained. 'It's a long-standing invitation that I can't wriggle out of. So, if you could help out . . .'

'Of course I can. I'll love it, you know I will.'

'You might have second thoughts when you have all the facts.'

'Oh?' Billie murmured warily.

It was Anna's turn to smile. 'They're just three weeks old. And you know that that means?'

Billie nodded. Three- or four-hourly feeds with a mouth syringe. Day and night. Not to mention the other intimate tasks normally done by the nursing queen for her kittens. 'It doesn't matter. I'll cope,' she insisted. And with luck, she decided, it would keep her mind off Travis.

It didn't. And, by the time Monday morning dawned, the lack of sleep was catching up with her. But at least, she consoled herself, orders were slack. She'd be able to take things easy for a change. Yet another misconception quickly nailed.

'We'll need to work late,' Travis informed her crisply. 'For the rest of the week, at least. I assume that won't be a problem?'

Billie nodded. With Tony away, Heather in London showing her autumn collection and her mother on holiday, there was only Anna likely to notice and she was wrapped up in her kittens.

By Friday lunchtime Billie was on her knees, a throbbing head adding to her misery. It was a relief when Travis announced he'd be out for the rest of the afternoon.

'I've an appointment in York. But I'll be back about six. We'll go over the Grey portfolio then.'

'Yes, sir,' Billie snapped, giving a smart salute to Travis's retreating form. Her heart sank. Bang went that three o'clock finish. She turned back to her sketch, the page blurring before her eyes. It was no good. She didn't feel well. She'd be better off at home in bed. Only Travis would be back and he'd expect to find her working.

She was, but the design he needed wasn't finished. His mouth tightened in eloquent disapproval.

'I'm sorry,' Billie murmured wearily. 'I had a busy weekend and I guess I haven't recovered yet. I was up half the night with – '

'If you were up half the night,' he interrupted tersely, 'I can probably guess why. But don't forget, you work for me, you're paid by me, and in future, Billie,' he cautioned her coldly, 'you put work before your love life.'

Or else. He hadn't said it, of course, but the threat was there.

The tears welled as Travis closed the door and Billie let them hover, the luxury of simply letting go, of laying her head in her arms and pouring out the misery, almost gaining the upper hand. Till pride came to the rescue. Damn Travis. Damn Giddings. She'd do the work if the effort nearly killed her.

She didn't notice the time, didn't hear the door or the footsteps muffled in the thick pile of carpet, looked up in surprise when she heard Travis's voice.

'Billie? What on earth are you doing? Don't you know it's late? You should have gone home hours ago.'

'I – didn't want to let you down,' she explained as something in his tone triggered the tears. Only this time Billie couldn't contain them and the floodgates opened.

Travis moved fast, cradling her in his arms, murmuring words, soothing words while Billie sobbed against his shoulder, the touch familiar, his unique body smell filling her nostrils, filling her mind, the ever-present need running through her like flame. Simply touching Travis, being close, being held, was enough to trigger the tides of her treacherous body. Only Travis was simply being kind, allowing the warm, human side to show through the man of steel.

He held her, consoled her, dipped his head to kiss away away the tears, each delicate touch creating fresh explosions, the sharp hiss of his indrawn breath sending signals of hope whirling through the misery.

There was a pause, a screaming, shrieking, bittersweet moment when Travis raised his head, allowed his eyes to lock with hers and the message was transmitted, received, acknowledged, returned, and then his mouth was tasting hers, the hunger spreading, outwards and inwards, the pressure bruising, lips bruising, Travis's need shocking as he crushed her against him, sending tongues of desire licking through her body.

Billie's mind smiled. She'd caught the heat, the hardness, and this time she was sure that he wanted her and the headache was forgotten as the knowledge filled her mind. Travis wanted her, needed her, loved her. The proof was here in the hands that stroked, the thumbs that teased as he brushed the swell of her straining breasts. Oh yes, he wanted her and, though the pressure of his lips eased as Travis calmed the frenzy, Billie was over the moon.

He raised his head, his smouldering gaze locking with hers and as he smiled, a tender tug of generous lips, Billie's heart flipped somersaults. 'Come on,' he murmured softly, pulling a crisp white handkerchief out of a pocket and patting dry the residue of tears. 'I'll run you home. You're in no fit state to drive. And next time, Billie,' he solemnly warned her, cupping her face in his hands and gazing down into her eyes, an open window to Billie's soul, 'next time, don't let me bully you. Bite back. You're more than capable of putting me in my place – aren't you, my love?'

My love. He'd called her his love! And yet, she acknowledged, swallowing hard, he was simply being kind. And the next time she weakened . . . Heaven knew, she'd come close to giving in at Fleet, to indulging the needs of her body, the yearnings of her mind. It was only a matter of time, she thought starkly. She wanted Travis. Travis wanted her. A need primeval and basic. Was it so wrong to yield to the temptation?

Yes! she insisted in stronger moments, Cleo's presence yet another cruel reminder that in wanting Travis, Billie was living a dream.

'I know you,' Cleo had hissed down the phone line, stunning Billie with the venom. She'd been working in Travis's office, had automatically reached for the handset, forgetting the chaos she'd caused the last time she'd taken a call on his private line. 'I knew I'd heard that voice before. You're the tomboy. The one with the cats.' The words had been relentless, Billie's ears reeling from the poison. She didn't know why but Cleo was jealous, jealous of her, was warning her to stay away from Travis! Billie had almost laughed. Travis's beautiful Cleo, jealous of her!

And, not content with the phone calls, Cleo had taken to dropping by, the fact that Travis was out and wouldn't be back for the rest of the day clearly unimportant. She'd make herself at home, order coffee as if she owned the place and then she'd slip away, but not before she'd made a point of reminding Billie that she loved Travis, that Travis belonged to her.

And so the hell went on, the hell of working with Travis, being with Travis, wanting Travis.

'You look dreadful,' Heather told her frankly when Billie called in with some designs. With the Felbrough Charity Fashion Show just a few weeks away, Billie had spent long hours at home sketching page after page of exquisite clothes, the need to fill the time and deaden her mind driving her to the point of exhaustion. 'I could have read this wrong,' her friend murmured softly. 'But this isn't down to Tony, surely? I know he's taken a job in Scotland, Billie, but I thought you'd parted friends.'

'We have. It's all right, Heather,' Billie reassured. 'It's not Tony.'

'I'm glad. But I wondered. You and he were close and since Tony had hopes – '

'Of us getting married?' Billie supplied. 'It wouldn't have worked. We were friends, never lovers, and it wouldn't have worked. Tony understood.'

'Hmmm.' Heather looked thoughtful. 'Well, something's eating away at you. Giddings?' she

187

queried shrewdly. 'The powerful Mr Kent?' She picked up Billie's sketch pad, sifting through the papers and then she glanced up, grey eyes narrowing. 'You know, Billie, these are first class. You're wasted at Giddings. I can't afford to pay what they do, but if the place is getting you down, why not come and work for me?'

Billie looked startled. Leave Giddings? Leave Travis? And yet, why not? She'd never escape the knowledge, but she could escape the daily torment of being with Travis, of living and breathing a Travis she could never hope to possess. She took a deep breath. 'If you're serious, Heather, then you're right. I need to get away. I'll hand in my notice first thing tomorrow.'

'You're *what*?'

Billie winced. She'd known it wouldn't be easy but Travis's shocked expression took the wind from her sails.

'I'm resigning,' she repeated, a nervous tongue moistening dry lips. 'I'm sorry, Travis, but I can't work for Giddings any longer.'

'But why?' he asked, swinging himself upright and moving round the desk, a towering six feet three inches of sheer incredulity.

Billie stumbled backwards, needing space, needing room to breathe, Travis's powerful body as always unnerving. Her darting eyes travelled the room, looking anywhere but at Travis – the geometric design on the carpet, the clean-cut steel and glass furniture, Travis's expensively shod feet placed squarely before her. How to explain? How to explain without giving him the truth?

'Is it the money? Aren't I paying you enough?' he demanded, running his hands through his hair in a strange, distracted gesture that caught at her heart strings. But he didn't wait for a reply, rushing on before Billie had time to reply. 'Hell, Billie, that's not a problem. You don't need to leave. We'll talk it through. *You* decide what you're worth.'

'It isn't the money,' she stalled, inwardly wincing. How mercenary he thought her! The assessment hurt, hurt more than she'd have believed.

'Then what? Giddings? Me? You're not still blaming me for what happened years ago, surely?' he demanded incredulously.

'Yes! No! You wouldn't understand,' she cried, twisting her hands together in an effort to stay in control.

'You've found another job, is that it?' he demanded. 'But whatever they're offering, Billie, Giddings can match it. You can't leave. I need you here.'

The knife blade twisted at Travis's choice of words. Trial by fire. But Billie was growing stronger and this time when she spoke, she was calm, icy calm. 'No, Travis. You don't need me. You've never needed me.'

189

'Wrong, Billie. You're one of the best – '

'And you can't afford to let me go to another company,' she said with quiet irony. 'It's all right, Travis,' she reassured him drily. 'I won't be setting up stall in Felbrough High Street. As you've told me more than once, when I leave Giddings, I'm finished in the trade.'

'But – it doesn't make sense. You've got to live, for heaven's sake. You can't exist on fresh air, unless – ' He broke off, black eyes narrowing in speculation. And then he whistled under his breath. 'Ah, yes! I get it,' he sneered. 'The luke-warm Viking's finally popped the question?'

'Tony?' Billie laughed. 'Oh, Travis. You're miles off target. Tony's the last man I'd want to marry.'

Travis's expressive eyebrows rose. Surprise, relief, delight flicked across his features – a fleeting, imaginary glimpse of Travis's soul that Billie swiftly denied. Because that's what she wanted to believe – that Travis cared about Billie the woman, not Billie the designer, but she was kidding herself.

He moved, his hands shooting out and catching at her shoulders and Billie's legs turned to water. How could one man cause such a fierce reaction? she wondered, fighting for control as the ripples of heat began, ever-increasing circles in the pit of her stomach that grew stronger and stronger till they promised to devour.

'Then what is it?' he demanded fiercely. 'How do

you plan to live? You're no fool. If it isn't Tony, you must have something lined up.' And he shook her roughly. 'Look at me, damn you, and tell me you haven't found another job.'

She swallowed, raised her head slowly, tracing the long, lean outline of Travis's powerful form, the expensive Italian suit, the white silk shirt with its carelessly knotted tie, lingering for a moment on the stubborn set of his jaw with its dark hint of stubble, before dragging cloudy eyes to his with an awkward show of defiance. She winced, the blast of knowledge on Travis's tight face tearing her apart.

'So – ' He released her, the gesture strangely weary. 'I was right in the first place. You're walking out on the job you love, and you're walking out on Giddings – because of me. Aren't you, Billie? You're blaming me for something I can't help?'

'No! You're wrong.' She darted forwards, willing him to believe, willing him to see the truth she could never put into words and yet afraid, so much afraid that she was damned if she told him the truth, damned if she didn't. But at the end of the day, she realized starkly, if she couldn't have his love, she didn't want to live with his pity. 'I'm sorry, Travis,' she murmured softly. 'I can't explain. But if it helps,' she added pleadingly, willing him to look at her, to understand, to allow her to leave without rancour, 'it has nothing to do with the fact that you're a Giddings.'

His cold glance bridged the chasm between them. 'You're lying,' he said without emotion. 'You're lying to me and you're lying to yourself.'

Billie shrugged. If that's what he chose to believe . . . Better that than the truth, she acknowledged silently.

It was a tense few days, with Travis's eyes silently accusing whenever Billie happened to glance across. And, she had to admit, his thoughtful gaze came her way unnervingly often. But she was busy, was able to escape, to spend long hours in her office on last-minute sketches for a very special project, a feather in Travis's cap, the biggest contract yet for Giddings.

Three o'clock. It was nowhere near home time but she'd done as much as she could without referring it back to Travis. Bracing herself for a tense half-hour, Billie picked up the file. Reaching his door and hearing his voice, Billie paused, rapping softly on the panel before popping her head round.

He was on the phone, his back to Billie, but sensing her presence he spun round, beckoned her forwards, the conversation clearly over as he replaced the handset, the angle of his head speaking volumes.

'What is it?' Billie asked, aware of the anger simmering in his eyes.

'The Haige Restaurant scheme. We've lost the contract. Heaven knows how,' he acknowledged, crumpling a fax sheet into a ball and letting it drop unheeded. 'But someone's undercut us – stolen our ideas and simply undercut us.'

'But how?' Billie asked, automatically taking a chair. 'We've kept it under wraps. Nothing's gone to the workroom yet and you haven't programmed GUS. It doesn't make sense.'

'That's what I keep telling myself,' Travis mused as long tapering fingers absentmindedly reached for a cut-glass paperweight.

He balanced it in his hand, as if mentally weighing the problem, and Billie sat quite still, hardly daring to breathe as she shared his disappointment. It wasn't his week: first her resignation, and now this. They'd worked on the designs together. Travis had been confident that Giddings would land the contract, a world-wide restaurant refurbishment that could take the company into another dimension. Only now, the contract, along with the planned expansion, was lost. And it didn't make sense.

'It doesn't make sense,' he said again, echoing her thoughts, 'No one knew the details, Billie. Just you – and me.'

'And since we've been so careful, locking everything away – ' She halted, her mind racing, an awful thought taking hold.

'Just you and me,' he repeated softly, his gaze focusing on the heavy piece of glass beneath his fingers.

The paperweight dropped as his glance whipped across, the sound shattering the silence. Billie jumped. Travis smiled, an awful parody of a smile that made her blood run cold.

'Oh, I get it. No wonder you resigned in such a hurry. You mistimed that, didn't you, Billie? A few more days and you'd have pulled it off. You'd have gone, leaving Giddings high and dry.' And he leaned forwards, pinning her with his gaze, that awful gaze with its chill blast of judgement. 'Tell me, my dear,' the soft voice invited. 'What did they offer? A job for life? A place on the board? Or something much more basic like cold, hard cash?'

'No! You're wrong!' She sprang up, facing Travis, the nausea in her throat almost causing her to swoon and she groped for the edge of the desk, leaning forwards, the moment of weakness taking her face closer to his, closer to that cold, accusing stare.

Travis shook his head. 'Not this time, Billie. It's the only explanation – the only logical explanation,' he chillingly underlined. 'Only two people had access to those plans, me – and you!'

'But – ' Billie was stunned, the fact that Travis could doubt her – worse, could actually believe she could do such a thing – leaving her numb. 'But – but what have I to gain?' she cried.

'In your twisted mind?' Travis laughed, a cold, empty sound that was to echo horribly inside her head for days. 'You don't need a reason, you've never needed a reason. You're hitting back at me – at Giddings. That's the only reason Billie Taylor ever needed and don't think I don't know it.'

He looked at her then, his face so full of hurt and disbelief that Billie wanted to reach out, touch him, tell him how wrong he was, tell him how much she loved him; yet the expression in his frigid black eyes condemned her. Something vital died. Travis believed it. It was enough. She was too proud to beg, too proud to protest.

'Get out of my sight,' he muttered wearily as she dropped her gaze, sealing her guilt with the silence. 'You're finished here. And you're finished in the trade – I'll make sure of it. Now go. Just go. Are you listening, Billie? Get out and stay out.'

Part Two

CHAPTER 11

The phone rang. He raised his head, wondering where the noise was coming from, the intrusive, imperative ringing tone. And then he realized. Shaking off the lethargy, he reached for the receiver.

'Mr Kent?'

'Yes, Donna. What is it?'

'Mr Arkwright of Allerton Old Brewery. Shall I put him through? He says it's urgent.'

'He would,' Travis murmured drily, running his fingers through his hair, unseeing eyes gazing across the wide expanse of desk with its overflowing in-tray and the crumpled fax that would damn Billie for ever in his eyes. He smothered a weary sigh. Why not? Might as well get it over and done with. One problem raised, one problem solved. At least this one should be solvable. 'Put him though, Donna,' he instructed with a marked lack of enthusiam. 'And then hold any further calls. If the Queen herself decides to phone with a commission for Windsor Castle, I'm out.' I'm just not here, he added silently.

And though he dealt with the hitch, managed to appease the troublesome Arkwright without too much difficulty, it was all in a dream, the automatic pilot swinging into force.

Get out of my sight.

The words echoed horribly inside his head. Had it really been as brutal as it sounded? he wondered grimly. And she'd gone. Not a word. Not a plea. Not a single excuse. She'd simply gone. But not before he'd seen the hurt, felt the pain. Because of what she'd done? he wondered fleetingly. Or because he'd found her out?

Oh, Billie! Billie! What have you done? And *why?* he asked himself incredulously. After all that we've been through, all that we've shared. Why? Why? Why?

He sprang up, wandering across to the window and pushing aside the blinds, gazing down with half-unseeing eyes. His office overlooked the car park and he found himself unconsciously scanning the neat ranks of cars, half hoping the familiar battered Escort would be parked in its usual spot beside the front steps. But no. It had been raining and the patch of dry tarmac where the car should have been was silent, mocking testimony. Billie had gone. She'd gone, and rightly or wrongly, she'd never be coming back.

And the knowledge hurt. It hurt like hell. Because he'd trusted her. Worked with her, fought with her, laughed with her, loved her almost, in that unfulfilled moment of magic at Fleet. But, most of all, he'd trusted her. But never again, he vowed. Once bitten, twice shy. And Travis Kent had had his fill. Trust. He dropped the blind, let it fall back into place, the pendulum swish-swish unnaturally harsh in the silence.

He checked his watch. Three-fifteen. He needed a drink. Three-fifteen in the afternoon and he needed that drink. Giving silent thanks for all-day opening, he strode purposefully through the workroom, nodding grimly at the one or two unsuspecting souls whose cheery greetings froze on their lips.

He reached the car as the mobile phone in his pocket began to trill.

'Travis, sweetheart – '

'Sorry, Cleo.' He cut her off abruptly. 'I haven't time now. I'll phone you.'

'But tonight – '

'Can't make it. Sorry, honey.' He cut the connection, disconnecting the phone at the same time.

It took the strident central-locking tone to bring him partly to his senses. When he said drink, he meant drink. And in that case he'd walk, call in at the nearest pub, the Dog And Gun, he recalled, the memory of the last time he'd been there scything painfully through his mind. He needed a drink. And he'd have that drink. And the next. And when he'd had enough, he'd take a cab home. Only, he could never have enough. Not enough to deaden the pain, the hurt, the screaming, aching, rawness of Billie's deception.

'Afternoon, sir.' Customers being few and far between, the publican's greeting was warm. He placed the glass he was polishing back amongst the stack and moved smartly down the bar to Travis. 'Lovely weather for ducks by the look of things.'

'Is it?' Travis's tone held no cosy invitation to chat. 'Brandy, please. No, on second thoughts, better make it a double.'

He carried it across to the corner, their corner, and since the pub was almost empty, Travis could sit and brood without fear of intrusion from curious eyes.

Billie. He couldn't escape. Despite the second, equally large brandy, he just couldn't escape. She'd seemed so pure, so true – prickly as a hedgehog where her pride was involved. But as honest as the day was long. Or so he kept telling himself. And he swirled the golden liquid round and round the balloon of the glass as the thoughts swirled round and round inside his head.

'Is this seat taken?'

Travis glanced up. He hadn't noticed the woman

approach, was surprised she would risk a pickup when the pub was so empty. She was young, quite well dressed for a hooker, long, bleached blonde hair, make-up just a shade too heavy, skirt just a shade too short, and a strange expression in her eyes – almost a plea, he decided absurdly, and for a moment, a fleeting, mad moment, he was sorely tempted to take whatever she was offering, half an hour's meaningless conversation over another drink, and a half-hour fumble in some anonymous motel room. And then the waves of loathing swept over him.

He shook his head and the hope in the girl's eyes died. 'It's – nothing personal,' he said, attempting to soften the blow. 'I'm – waiting for someone.'

And it was true. He was waiting for Billie. Would always be waiting for Billie. Why, why, why, Billie? And worse, why did it matter? He'd lost contracts before, more than he cared to remember, in fact. And yes, he'd been angry at the time. And then the realist would surface, the business man, the man of steel, and the disappointment would be swept away with the next batch of plans, plans that *would* be successful. Until now. So – better face it, old man. This time it's Billie who's stuck the knife in and turned the blade. So – why should Billie make such a difference?

He drained his glass. Four-thirty. Two double brandies in less than an hour had done nothing to deaden the pain, but had allowed the germ of an idea to escape from the dungeons of his heart. Billie. But, of course, fool, he cursed himself. He should have known, had probably known all along, but had buried the knowledge. Because all the signs had been there. Even that first afternoon in the garden all the signs had been there and he'd simply refused to face them. And yet, how ironic. How mockingly ironic. Travis Kent does the one thing he'd vowed he'd never, ever do.

He grimaced as he threaded his way between the tables and back to the liquid comfort of the optics. Oh, yes. He was a prize fool.

'What the hell do you think you're playing at, Travis? I had to lie, lie to the Finchley-Bakers. Probably the most influential family this side of London and I had to let them down. And all because you couldn't be bothered keeping our date.'

'I told you, Cleo. Something came up.'

'Oh yes? Something – or someone?' she asked with an unusual flash of perception.

Travis glanced up. Cleo was furious, green eyes spitting fire, twin spots of colour burning in her cheeks. She stood before him, hands on hips, every line of her petite, expensively clad form quivering with indignation.

And he was tired. Too tired to argue. Too tired to reason. 'Go home, Cleo,' he murmured wearily, picking up the discarded newspaper and folding it pointedly open at the business page. 'It's been a long day and I'm tired.'

'Oh, no!' She moved, darting forwards and snatching the paper from him and Travis felt a surge of annoyance. And yet, why take his anger out on Cleo? She'd done nothing wrong, had simply picked the wrong moment to hassle him. So he folded his arms and raised an enquiring eyebrow instead, the placid expression he carefully assumed a red rag to a raging bull.

'Well?' she hissed at him.

'Well, what?' he replied, aware of the dull thud at his temples, the remnants of the blinding headache that he'd woken to. Countless double brandies and the bottle of red wine he'd later downed at home had exacted their own painful revenge. But he'd slept. And for a time at least, he'd forgotten. And after an unrewarding day at work, the atmosphere grim in the wake of Billie's shock departure, the last thing he needed was Cleo in one of her rare but famous tempers.

'Well, what? *Well, what*?' Her voice rose, the high-pitched whine grating in his head. 'You stand me up, you're abominably rude when I phone, you disappear for half the night and can't be reached on the mobile. You force me to lie to some very dear friends and now you have the nerve to sit there and pretend you don't know what's wrong.'

'Look, sweetheart, I know you're disappointed – '

'Huh! Now there's an understatement. Disappointed, hurt, angry, confused. We're engaged, for heaven's sake. We're a couple. We're supposed to share things – '

'And we do – '

'So *why* can't you explain?'

'I just did. Something came up. Business.'

'Business – or Miss Snooty-Assistant Taylor?' Cleo queried, clearly not in the mood to be sidetracked.

'Ah!' Travis smiled despite himself. So that's what was eating her. Not the broken date, the cancelled meal with the Finchley-Bakers. Jealousy. Just a simple case of the green-eyed monsters. And yet, how ironic. How mockingly ironic, he acknowledged. Cleo was jealous of the one woman in the world who wouldn't be seen dead in his company. The woman who hated him enough to want to destroy not just him but everything he stood for.

Billie. It was there again, that knife blade twisting in his belly. He needed a drink. Despite the headache that was back with a vengeance, he needed a drink.

'Brandy?' he queried, crossing to the tray of bottles that graced one end of the long, modern sideboard, the seals on most unbroken.

Cleo glanced at her watch. 'At this time of day?

206

No, thank you,' she murmured primly, eyes cold, her mouth a thin and angry line.

Travis shrugged, pouring himself a generous slug and adding a perfunctory splash of soda. 'Coffee, then? Or a fruit juice if you'd rather?'

'I don't *want* a drink. I just want an answer.'

'Fine.' Travis took his time. He swirled the amber liquid round and round his glass at the same time regaining his place on the huge, richly upholstered sofa. 'Sit down, Cleo,' he told her pleasantly.

'I don't want – '

'Yes, you do. You said you wanted an answer. Remember?'

Impasse. Two sets of eyes, anger, indecision, the unaccustomed shadow of doubt in Cleo's, an unfathomable expression in his. And then he smiled, breaking the tension, waving Cleo to the easy chair opposite.

She flounced down, though not without a defiant toss of her head.

'So . . .' He paused, raised his glass and took a thoughtful sip, his eyes fastened on her face the whole time. 'What exactly do you want to know?'

'You make me sound like a nosy, suspicious bitch,' she stalled, having the grace to look ashamed.

'When we both know that you're none of those,' he observed mildly, too mildly, the veneer of sarcasm lost on Cleo.

'Well, no, but – '

'Ah, yes, but . . .' He smiled again, though the light didn't reach his eyes. 'Always the but,' he murmured half to himself. And then he drained his glass, held it up with a theatrical flourish for Cleo's inspection before putting it carefully down on the smoked glass coffee table between them. 'If you must know,' he conceded into the screaming silence, 'I was out getting drunk.'

'Alone?' she queried incredulously.

Not, *why*, he noted, though doubtless that would feature somewhere in the general inquisition.

'Of course, alone. What do you take me for? No gentleman worth his salt would drag another – man or woman – into the mire.' And he had reached rock bottom, he remembered clearly. Could do with another drink now, as a matter of fact. He half rose at the silent suggestion but – His lips tightened. Ever the gentleman. For the moment at least.

'But – ' Cleo frowned, leaning forwards, fingers nervously fiddling with the huge sapphire and diamond ring she wore on her left hand. 'I don't understand.'

'You and me both,' he stated drily.

Cleo's flash of anger returned. 'Will you please stop talking in riddles?' she snapped.

'Certainly. If you're sure that's what you want. I got drunk. There was a problem at work and for once I took the easy way out and drank myself into oblivion.'

'Work?'

'Yes. You know, my place of employment. The nine-till-five occupation that helps pay the bills.' Not to mention the sapphire and diamond engagement ring and the dozens of other expensive little trifles that had found their way into Cleo's jewellery collection.

'Thank you, Travis. Believe it or not, I do get the picture.'

I doubt it, he derided, but silently. 'So – ' He held her gaze. 'That's it. Simple.'

'That's it? End of explanation. Just like that?'

'Just like that,' he agreed offhandedly.

'You're lying!'

'My dear.' He looked her up and down with thinly veiled contempt. 'If you know me at all, Cleo, you'll know that I never lie.'

'But I don't, do I?' she hissed. 'Not in this mood, at least. And as for last night – '

'Yes, Cleo? About last night? Come along now, don't be coy. Spit it out, whatever it is that's choking you.' And he folded his arms, sank back into the cushions, raised that supercilious eyebrow again.

'Oh – you! You're impossible!' She flounced across the room in an angry swish of skirts, heading for the drinks' tray.

'Make mine a brandy,' Travis called out provokingly as she helped herself to a vodka and tonic. 'It doesn't do to drink alone. One glass leads to another and before you know it, bingo! It's the morning after the night before and an army of little men are hammering away inside your temples.'

'Good. It's no more than you deserve,' she informed him witheringly, placing the brandy before him and regaining her place on the edge of her seat. It was Cleo's turn to raise a glass. 'Cheers,' she murmured evilly, adding, only half under her breath, 'I hope it chokes you.'

'It won't.'

They lapsed into silence, Travis completely uncaring of her anger simmering just below the surface. Poor Cleo. Poor, spoilt Cleo who couldn't cope when the world suddenly stopped revolving around her. She had it all, if only she but knew it. The single, pampered child of wealthy parents, she'd probably never done a day's real work in her life. And yet, that was unfair, he realized at once. Cleo filled her time easily enough: shopping, visits to the hair salon, the beauty parlour; expensive luncheon parties with a long string of girl friends; night clubs, charity balls. She didn't need to work, had been brought up with the expectation of enjoying life and landing an equally rich and preferably titled husband. And she certainly knew how to live life to the full, her fun-loving ways and normally sunny nature ensuring a never-ending flow of invitations. And she *was* fun to be with, usually, a welcome splash of frivolity in Travis's ordered world. Only sometimes, just sometimes, he'd found himself searching for something more. Something – or someone? he asked himself, the sudden thought sobering.

He reached for his glass. More soda than brandy, he note, polishing it off with a grimace of distaste. Probably as well, really, but the night was still young and why not have another, and another, finish the bottle if that's what he wanted. After all, it was his life, his brandy, his problem. Billie. His problem. His. No, never his, he acknowledged bitterly. Never, ever his.

'How many of those have you had?' Cleo enquired disapprovingly, breaking into his dangerous thoughts.

'Not enough,' Travis quipped.

'I don't agree,' she contradicted primly. 'You're drunk.'

'No. Not yet. But I'm working on it.'

'Why, Travis, why?'

Ah yes. He'd wondered how long it would take for the sixty-four-thousand-dollar question to occur. 'Why?' He shrugged. 'Who knows? Believe me, Cleo, it doesn't make sense to me either.' He grinned. Leastways, his mouth did. The light didn't spread to his eyes.

'But you won't tell me what's wrong,' she murmured petulantly. 'How can I help if you won't explain?'

'But, my dear, you didn't ask, didn't want to know *why*,' he emphasized coldly. 'You simply assumed I was out on the town with someone else. You see, Cleo,' he explained enigmatically, 'it all comes down to trust. She didn't trust me. I didn't trust her. You don't trust either of us.'

'So – I was right,' she said tearfully. 'It was another woman – *that* woman. You rat!'

'If you say so,' he mocked, equally unmoved by the tears and yet another flash of temper. It helped getting drunk. It took the edge off the pain, took the sting out of the niggles. He grinned again. Perhaps he ought to try it more often. Reaching into a pocket, he drew out a clean, folded square of linen. 'Here. Use this,' he entreated, dropping it into her lap and rising leisurely to his feet. 'I'll make some coffee while you pull yourself together. And, Cleo,' he added softly, the warning veiled but the meaning crystal clear, 'you will pull yourself together.'

He took his time, half hoping she'd have taken the huff and gone but no, she hadn't moved from the armchair, her back ramrod straight as Travis recrossed the room, footsteps muffled in the deep pile of the carpet.

Sensing his approach, she raised her head, just the dark circles beneath her eyes betraying the earlier flood of tears. And she was beautiful. Despite the smudges of mascara, she was beautiful.

'That's my girl,' he approved, wincing at his unconscious choice of words.

'Am I, though?'

'Are you what?'

'Your girl. Or has the ever-efficient Miss Taylor managed to dig her claws in?'

'You're wrong, Cleo.'

'Am I? I doubt it. I saw the way she looked at you that afternoon in the garden, and as for work, in a few short months she's made herself indispensable. You've said it yourself often enough, so deny it if you dare,' she challenged him with an aggressive tilt of the chin.

'Wishful thinking, Cleo. You're wrong on every count. Billie's gone.'

'What do you mean, gone?'

'Gone. Left. Quit. No longer works for Giddings.'

'You mean you've sacked her?' Incredulity, delight, a gamut of emotions chased across the exquisite china-doll face.

'I mean she's gone, left the company and won't be coming back.'

'But I never – ' She broke off, flushing in confusion.

'Never *what*, Cleo?' Travis asked sharply.

She shrugged, reaching for the coffee, deliberately taking her time as she poured, added cream to her own, sugar to both before pushing a cup across to Travis. 'Well, well, well,' she murmured, raising her cup to her lips and sipping thoughtfully. 'Who'd have believed it?'

'You never what, Cleo?' Travis persisted, oh so softly, his black eyes pinning her, refusing to allow her to look away.

She smiled, a brittle smile that was never intended to reach her emerald eyes. 'Oh – you know. I just never expected it, I suppose,' she explained with ill-concealed glee. 'What did she do? Nothing trivial, I hope?'

'Bitchiness doesn't become you, Cleo.'

'No. But sometimes it's fun. Remember fun, Travis? We used to have fun,' she told him wistfully. 'When we lived in London and before you moved to this one-horse town. Fun! Fun! Fun!' she trilled, jumping up and sweeping round the room as if swaying in time to some hidden, haunting melody.

Travis watched her warily. There was something not quite right, some vague unease at the back of his mind. And yet, Cleo's surprise was genuine enough. And he raised his arms, linked his fingers behind his head, assessing her as a stranger would. Petite, perfectly proportioned with a peaches-and-cream complexion, she'd be an asset to any man. And he was sharply aware of how lucky he'd been. Given her parents' well-publicized aspirations, he'd done well securing their consent to the engagement. And being unashamedly ambitious, Travis had enjoyed showing Cleo off around the most influential dinner tables in the country. She could smile, sparkle, keep the conversation flowing with the right word at the just the right moment, and could charm the birds from the trees if she was in the mood. And she was beautiful . . . and spoilt . . . and petulant . . . and a tiger in bed.

Bed. His mind slipped, remembering the smoky expression in a pair of deep velvet eyes, the halo of honey-brown hair fanned out across the pillow. Billie was perfect and there'd been an aura of innocence that had stoked the fires of his desire. And he'd wanted her. Hell, how he'd ached for her. And yet he'd been afraid, almost afraid to reach out and touch in case the vision disappeared like a mirage in the desert. And she'd smiled, the shadows in her eyes mirroring the shadows in his. Because the want was there, the need, along with the fear of the unknown. Because for once, he really was afraid. Travis Kent, who'd bedded his first girl on his sixteenth birthday, had been afraid. Because he'd wanted Billie like a man in a desert craves water. Every touch, every taste, every kiss had been nectar. He'd wanted her and needed her, yet instinctively he'd known that to move too fast would be a mistake. He would frighten her. And it would break his heart to startle her.

It had taken every ounce of self-control but he'd reined himself in, the rigid control heightening the tension as he'd slowly undressed her, sliding the flimsy chiffon bodice across those creamy shoulders and down, allowing surprisingly full breasts to spill free. He'd wanted to bury his head in the valley between them but still he hadn't touched; simply looking was enough, a tantalizing feast. Skirt, petticoat, tights had been stripped away and then she'd been naked, just the lacy black briefs that concealed, yet revealed all, bestowing the dignity of modesty.

And then he'd touched her. Travis groaned as he remembered, every tiny detail etched in his mind: the room, the soft glow of lights, the bed, Billie. Wonderful, wonderful Billie who'd looked so young, so fresh, so pure. And he'd tasted the nectar of her mouth, had caressed every inch of her quivering, fragrant body. And then when he'd touched her mound, it had been heaven. Heaven and hell. To want her with an urgency he hadn't known existed, to suppress it, to deny it.

And then to touch, to finger the petals of that most exquisite bud, to tease the petals open –

'Travis? *Travis?*'

He shook his head, disappointment scything through him. Yet the image refused to disappear. Billie was there, inside his head. He could see her, touch her, smell her, and yet she didn't belong, she'd never belong.

'Travis!'

He ran his fingers through his hair, attempting to focus on the scowling woman who'd planted herself squarely before him, arms folded angrily across her pert little breasts. He gave a shaky laugh. 'Sorry, sweetheart. I guess I was miles away.'

'The far side of hell, judging from your face. Daydreaming, Travis? That's not like you.'

'No. Like I said, it's been a long day and I'm tired.'

'Too tired to take a girl out to dinner?' Cleo's scowl deepened and Travis smothered a weary sigh.

Not another niggle. He wasn't in the mood. If Cleo pushed her luck, his temper would explode and Heaven only knew what damage that would do.

And then, amazingly, the storm clouds vanished and Cleo smiled. 'I know,' she murmured, moving round and sidling behind. She leaned over the low back of the settee, bringing her head close in to Travis, her hands sliding over his shoulders and down to his chest, her thumbs idly brushing against his nipples.

Travis froze, the hairs on the back of his neck rising like the hackles of a cat.

'How about,' she murmured huskily, her breath a warm flutter on his ear, 'I pop down to the village for a take-away while you raid the fridge for a chilled bottle of wine? And when we've eaten, and just because you're tired, of course,' she sug-

217

gested playfully, her long, slender fingers skilfully kneading the contours of his chest and sliding between the buttons to scratch at the skin beneath the fine lawn fabric, 'how about we slip upstairs and climb into that enormous feather bed?' She kissed the corner of his mouth, the point of her tongue darting between his lips in moist and steamy invitation. 'Bed,' she repeated meaningfully. 'Just you and me, Travis. All night long.'

CHAPTER 12

Six o'clock. Time to go home. With Cleo arriving at seven, he was already cutting it fine. And still Travis sat on, the computer screen blurring before his eyes.

Hell, he was tired. Tired enough to sleep for a week. Only he wouldn't. Not unless he drank himself into oblivion and there'd been too many nights like that already. Long, lonely, empty nights.

But at least with Cleo away on holiday, he hadn't been forced to play a part. Only now she was back. Time to play the loving fiancé. Not to mention happy families.

'Dinner with Mummy and Daddy,' she'd announced brightly over the phone, catching him off guard. 'They're staying over with some friends for a day or two, so Daddy's booked a table at The Swift. Eight for eight-thirty.'

Travis grimaced. The Swift. York's showpiece five-star hotel. And then Cleo had sprung her own surprise.

'And, since it's Saturday tomorrow, I thought we'd stay on. At the hotel, I mean. Just the two of us. It will save the drive home and after all, darling, it's been weeks since we've been together.'

Five weeks. Five weeks since Billie had walked out. Five weeks since that most disastrous night when he'd been incapable of making love to Cleo and had come close to telling her the truth. He didn't love her. He probably never had in retrospect, but they'd been good for each other. Past tense, he amended sadly. He was living a lie and not sure he had the stomach to keep the pretence going. Not now. Not knowing the way he felt about Billie. So, sooner or later, he realized, yet shying away from the hurt it would cause, he would have to let Cleo down.

He cleared the screen, backing up the data and closing down the network. It had been one of Billie's ideas, expanding GUS into the workroom.

'The technology's there, why not take advantage?' she'd pointed out logically. 'It's a cutthroat world in business and Giddings can't afford to be left behind. Just a few thousand pounds, Travis, and Giddings stays ahead of the rest.'

And he'd had to admit it made sense. But, coming from the girl who'd openly resented the big bad wolves of the trade for gobbling up the smaller opposition, the idea had been tantamount to sacrilege.

Billie. He shook his head. Would he ever understand? he wondered, as he hurried through the deserted building, his footsteps echoing eerily in the silence.

Everyone else had long since gone, the Friday-afternoon practice of finishing at three one of the perks Travis had no intention of curtailing. The first rule of good management. Treat people well and they'd reciprocate. Treat them like dirt and they'd rebel. But, despite the theory, there'd been rumblings in the workroom for weeks now and Travis was convinced that someone with a grudge was deliberately stirring up trouble. It was something else that didn't make sense but, since one bad apple could taint a whole barrel, as soon as Travis could identify the culprit, he – or she – would be out on their ear.

A door slammed in the distance, and Travis halted, more surprised than worried. The cleaning staff running late? he mused, straining to hear. Or the security guard starting his rounds?

He checked the time again. No time to waste. Straight home, then. So why the detour, the main road that took him past Billie's gate? The cottage was in darkness, as it had been every night for the past five weeks. She'd gone. Heaven alone knew where, but there hadn't been sight or sound of anyone. No cars, no callers, no cat. Travis inwardly groaned. What he'd give to see that familiar black-

and-white face, with its smudge of a nose, peeking down from one of his trees.

But – no time to brood. Home. Shower. Dress. Brandy. Overnight bag. Pack. Bang on time, the doorbell chimed.

'Travis! Darling!'

She launched herself into his arms, the heady cloud of perfume unexpectedly cloying.

He returned the kiss, his arms folding round her automatically, feeling the warmth and softness of her body as she pressed herself against him, and inhaled the musky fragrance of her hair. Yes, he'd missed her. Like any established couple, they'd grown to know one another, the moods, the needs, the fears. The passion hadn't died, he frankly acknowledged, gazing down into Cleo's smiling face, aware of his manhood hardening. Just the love. So maybe, just maybe, he could pick up the pieces, push Billie to the back of his mind and start all over again with Cleo.

'How was Scotland?' he asked as he braked, swung Cleo's sleek Lotus Elise into the flood-lit car park and cut the engine. It was the first time in forty minutes he'd been able to get a word in sideways.

The uniformed attendant sprang forward and Travis relinquished the keys, held the passenger door open for Cleo and then led the way up the canopied steps to where the top-hatted doorman stood ready. With an obsequious nod of respect, he almost bowed them across the threshold and Travis winced. All part of the service, he knew, but for once he found the attention overpowering.

'Oh, you know.' Cleo gave a moue of resignation. 'Scotland was – wet, wild and windy. But Mummy loved every moment. She swanned around like the Queen at Balmoral and spent most of the journey down today nagging Daddy about buying their own little place north of the border. And for little,' she added tartly, 'substitute several thousand acres.'

Travis laughed. 'Scottish estates don't come cheap,' he pointed out, his hand on her elbow as he guided her through the opulent foyer and along to the cocktail lounge. 'Not these days.'

'Thank heavens,' Cleo responded with an impish grin. 'Honestly, Travis. Can you really see me settling down in the middle of nowhere?'

He didn't reply. According to Cleo, Felbrough was the back of beyond and, since he'd moved in, there'd been more niggles than he cared to remember. Cleo was a city girl, happy to spend her days shopping till she dropped in the exclusive stores of Mayfair, Kensington and Knightsbridge, not to mention the regular jaunts to the boulevards and piazzas of Paris, Milan and Rome. And, when the sun went down, there were restaurants and night-clubs, a never-ending stream of wild parties and Cleo's definite ideas on how to have fun.

Could Cleo settle in Felbrough? he wondered. Or would the bright lights of London constantly beckon? And yet, wouldn't that suit them both? Combine the best of both worlds and give plenty of space for each to go their own way?

'Cheer up,' Cleo murmured, mistaking his silence for sombre anticipation of the evening ahead. 'Mummy's in a super mood. Lord and Lady Snelling have invited them for Christmas and that lets you and me off the hook. We can do what we please, when we please, where we please. And, since you haven't had time for a holiday,' she reminded him pointedly, 'I thought we could go away. Somewhere hot and sunny and as far away from Scotland as I can make it. Still — ' she squeezed his hand conspiratorily, a gleam of speculation in her eyes ' — we'll talk later. And not a word to Mummy and Daddy.'

It was one of those meals that seemed to last for ever, with Cleo's mother, Suzanne Rossington, loving every moment. Queening it. Yes. Travis hid a smile. Cleo's earlier remark had hit the nail on the head. An older, more brittle, version of Cleo, there was none of Cleo's warmth or spontaneity. Suzanne Rossington was a social climber, a prize bitch, Travis wouldn't mind betting, seeing the heady glint of triumph in the older woman's eyes. And, having spent two weeks touring Scotland and another two as guests of one of the country's foremost families, she was like the cat that got the cream. Satisfied. Very self-satisfied. But there was no doubting her beauty, nor the stares of approval that had followed the two women across the crowded restaurant, the frank, assessing glances that hadn't been meant for Cleo alone. From a distance, Travis decided, they'd probably be taken for sisters.

Something struck him and Travis tensed, reducing the freshly baked roll between his fingers to a sorry heap of crumbs. Looking at Suzanne, he was seeing Cleo in twenty years' time. Hard and brittle. Because he'd have cheated her.

'Travis?'

He realized Suzanne had been speaking, that to all intents and purposes he'd been staring, and flashing her a rueful smile, made an effort to pull himself together. 'Sorry,' he murmured apologetically. 'I was miles away.'

'I'm surprised your ears aren't burning, all the wonderful things we've been saying about Giddings. Last month's magazine spread. *Homes and Gardens*,' she explained when Travis didn't respond. 'I showed the article to Lady Mary and she was most impressed. Quite a feather in Giddings' cap, the commission for Harden House.' And she leaned across, placed her hand on his arm, a surprisingly unattractive hand, he found himself thinking inconsequentially, the fingers short and

225

dumpy despite the lacquered nail extensions. An enormous cabouchon sapphire winked up at him. 'But not a single photograph of you,' she chided, patting him reprovingly. 'Such a disappointment. What on earth were you thinking of, allowing your assistant to take all the credit?'

'Just being fair,' he countered as the pain sliced through. 'Billie handled the refit. I could hardly step in and steal her thunder. Besides, she's prettier than me,' he added with a forced attempt at lightness that didn't quite come off. 'Much more photogenic.'

'Past tense, Travis,' Cleo pointed out coldly, 'since she no longer works for Giddings.'

'Present tense, Cleo,' he added equally coolly, switching his gaze from mother to daughter. 'A former employee she may be, but there's no denying Billie's attraction.'

'For some, perhaps. Personally, I always found her a plain sort of thing. Too tall for a start and quite the tomboy.'

'Oh?' He let his napkin fall to the side of his plate, sat back in his chair, folded his arms across his chest. 'I don't recall you meeting Billie often enough to form an opinion,' he half-mused, half-queried as the temperature dropped. He was niggling, he knew, and he was on dangerous ground, but Cleo's catty remarks had stung.

'Come now, Travis. The girl's half wild. The

little matter of climbing trees in other people's gardens. Your garden. I was there, remember?'

'Once,' he acknowledged. 'So on the strength of that, you're prepared to condemn Billie out of hand?'

'Why not? She hardly dressed any better for work – '

'But you've never been into work,' he pointed out softly. 'If you had, Cleo, I'd have remembered.'

'Oh! You were out,' she told him airily. 'I popped in once or twice on the off chance. I'm surprised Miss Super-Efficient Taylor didn't mention it.'

'But I'm more surprised that *you* didn't,' he countered, the edge to his voice unmistakable.

'Well, I guess it didn't seem important at the time. And since you weren't there, I took myself off to lunch.'

'And conveniently forgot to mention it later?'

Cleo's face hardened. 'What is this, Travis? The third degree? I didn't mention calling in because I forgot. It simply slipped my memory. Satisfied?'

'And if I'm not?'

'More wine, Travis?' John Rossington's emollient voice sliced across the tension.

More wine. What a tempting thought. But no, better not. Not on top of the brandy. Loosen his tongue and heaven only knew what might come pouring out. And besides, something else had just struck him. In half an hour's time, when this cosy family group broke up, he would be led upstairs to a huge fourposter bed in a hearts-and-roses suite that wouldn't look out of place on a honeymoon. And Cleo would expect him perform. Like a prize stud, he appreciated grimly, he'd be expected to do his duty.

Oh, God! What a mess.

He switched his gaze from Cleo's half-defiant, half-mulish expression to her father's anxious face, his soft grey eyes full of silent suffering. With a shock, Travis realized the man looked ill. He shook his head. 'Thanks, John. But, no,' he demurred. 'It's getting late. I'll stick with coffee.'

'But, sweetheart, I've ordered champagne.'

'Fine. You drink it. I'm sticking to coffee.' He turned away, loosening his tie, dropping his jacket into a heap on the nearest chair.

'But I don't understand. We're not driving home. That was the whole point of staying over, Travis. We're alone. Just you and me. And I've missed you.' She lowered her voice, her expression coy as she sidled across the room, positioning herself squarely in front of him. And when Travis didn't move, didn't react, she reached out, sliding her hands slowly from the clenched muscles of his stomach to the powerful barrel of his chest, her thumbs caressing the hard nub of his nipples as exploring fingers moved upwards to his shoulders.

'Darling, I've missed you,' she repeated huskily, raising her face and parting her lips in silent invitation of a kiss.

Travis stifled a groan. He needed that drink . . . needed to stay sober just as badly . . . was caught firm between a rock and a hard place.

He licked his lips, took a deep breath. 'Honey, I've missed you, too. But it's been one hell of week at work and I'm bushed. Let's go to bed – to sleep,' he amended hastily. 'And in the morning – '

'Sleep? Oh, I get it.' Cleo's face tightened. She pushed him roughly away. 'You're still sore. Why, Travis, why don't you believe me?'

'Let's just say that I find your selective memory hard to swallow.'

'Selective? Don't be so ridiculous. I've told you, I simply forgot. It isn't important.'

'But it is to me.'

'But I don't see why.'

'No.'

Impasse. Two sets of stormy eyes, the atmosphere thickening. And Travis was tired, too tired to argue and besides, it could go on all night, this pointless niggle about something and nothing. And at the end of the day, what did it matter? Face it, Travis, you're just looking for an excuse, provoking a row, clutching at straws in an effort to stall her. Man or mouse? he wondered fleetingly, a wry smile touching his lips.

Watching him, Cleo's face softened. 'Sweetheart.' She moved back into the circle of his arms. 'What are we doing?' she asked, her hands cupping his face and drawing his head nearer to her own.

Her lips brushed his and Travis groaned, part need, part loathing, because he could take her easily enough; could pick her up and lay her down upon the wide expanse of bed and bury himself in her body, because Cleo, a tiger in bed, would do the rest. And the most jaded of men couldn't help but respond. How many men? he wondered fleetingly, hating himself for the thought, for the double standards that existed in his mind. For a virtuous woman is priced above rubies. Billie. Billie had turned him down. Almost at the point of no return, Billie had turned him down. How many men? he wondered. Why did the thought of Billie in another man's arms, another man's bed, fill him with hate and anger?

Soft, insidious fingers were moving over his body, tugging his shirt free from the waistband of his trousers, brushing fleetingly against the bulge below. He felt himself harden, fought for control, heard Cleo's low growl of approval and knew he was fighting a losing battle. He had to be fair. Cleo – or Billie. He couldn't make love to one with the image of the other engraved upon his mind. It would be sweet release for his body, he knew, but torment for his soul.

And still the battle raged, the imperative physical need beginning to gain the upper hand. Her hands had moved upwards, snapping open the buttons of the shirt, pushing the fabric free of his shoulders. As her fingers raked the dark mass of hair that covered his chest and brushed the nub of his nipples, Travis held himself rigid, didn't touch, didn't speak, simply accepted the woman's knowing touch. How easy to give in. Cleo would never know, he argued within himself. She was a full-blooded woman and she wouldn't be short-changed, he'd make sure of it. She'd never know and hell, how he needed her, yet needed Billie more. Billie.

He made a grab for Cleo's wrists, pulling her up sharp. 'Whoa, there, lady,' he insisted with what he hoped was playful admonishment. 'Too much, too soon,' he explained shakily, unable to meet her gaze. 'You're all woman Cleo, but after five long weeks, if we move too fast now, I'll leave us both frustrated. Five minutes,' he promised, slipping free of her grasp and heading for the bathroom. 'I need a shower. A cold one,' he explained with another tight smile. And then . . .

Oh, God. And then.

Cleo smiled smokily. 'I'll be waiting,' she murmured huskily. She padded across to the bed, turned down the corner of the duvet and, supremely confident that Travis would be watching, she swung round and with slow deliberation snapped the poppers on her blouse, exposing the firm, tiny breasts beneath. Holding his gaze, she brushed her thumbs against her nipples, a calculated gesture that in the past would have been sure to make his blood boil. 'I'm right here, sweetheart,' she murmured thickly.

He took his time. Stalling again. He stood under the icy jets of the shower and punished his body. He couldn't do it. Somehow he had to go out there and explain to the woman he was supposed to love and marry that he'd changed his mind. That he was chasing a dream but preferred that to the reality. He loved Billie. Hated Billie. Wanted to punish Billie, destroy her as she'd destroyed him. So, why not punish Billie? Console himself with Cleo. You'll hurt Cleo, he told himself, and Billie would never know – or care.

The battle raged on and on. What the head doesn't know the heart doesn't grieve for. Cleo will never know, not unless you tell her. If you walk away now, she'll never understand. Stay, and she'll never know the difference. Fool. Fool. Fool. The spirit indeed is willing, but the body is weak. And yes, right now he needed to say his prayers, because he had to decide, and he had to decide now. No turning back, Travis. Climb into Cleo's bed now and you're committing yourself – for ever.

The phone rang as he opened the bathroom door, the mobile phone in his jacket pocket.

'Leave it,' Cleo hissed from the depths of the bed.

Travis shook his head. 'If it's the mobile at this time of night, it's trouble,' he told her, fastening the towel more securely round his waist as he padded across the room.

He kept his back turned, was aware that she'd slipped out out of bed to come to stand behind, naked and inviting but he wouldn't look, wouldn't touch, held himself rigid as she brushed herself against him.

'Kent,' he bit into the mouthpiece. He listened in silence, his face growing darker by the moment. 'I'm on my way.'

'Travis!' Cleo wailed but he simply pushed past, retrieving shirt and trousers on the way.

'Sorry, honey. That was Johnson, the security guard at the office,' he explained tersely, perching on the edge of the bed and not stopping to towel dry his still-damp body, a stupid mistake since it took him twice as long to wriggle back into his clothes. He swore eloquently under his breath. 'There's been a fire in the workroom,' he added, tucking his shirt into the waistband and standing to zip up his fly. 'Sorry, Cleo, I'll have to go. I'll take your car?' Half-statement, half-query, his racing mind vaguely aware that Cleo had started to pull her clothes on. 'No – you stay here,' he insisted with a tight, reassuring smile. 'No point in ruining the night for both of us. And there's nothing you can do, probably precious little that I can do, but I'll have to go over.' He dropped a light kiss on the top of her head. 'I'll pick you up tomorrow. And I'll phone. As soon as I can, I promise that I'll phone.'

Thank goodness he was sober. Given that he'd started the night with a large brandy, somewhere along the way the decision to stay off the wine had been the right one. And that other decision? he asked himself as he eased the car out onto the main road and headed for the outskirts of the city. Was that the right one, too?

But, since he hadn't been put to the test, he'd never know.

Until next time.

CHAPTER 13

Arson. Travis couldn't believe it, didn't want to believe it. And yet, standing in the ruins of the workroom, ankle-deep in water and with the pungent smell of burning in his nostrils, he was beginning to face the unpalatable truth. Someone had a grudge. Against Giddings? he wondered. Or Travis Kent?

Billie. No. He balled his fist, hammered at the smoke blackened wall. No! No! No! It wasn't Billie. It couldn't be Billie. Not this time. And yet he couldn't escape the fact that someone hated him enough to risk their life torching a highly flammable building.

'It's a professional job,' the fire officer had explained once the flames had been brought under control. 'Kids larking about would smash a few windows, drop a burning rag through. This little lot was deliberate, well spaced-out and planned. Another five minutes and the place would have been an inferno. As it is, sir, you were lucky.'

Lucky? Travis had groaned aloud, but the officer had been emphatic.

'Thanks to your security guard, we caught it in time. You might not believe it now, but you'll have a clearer picture in the morning. Smoke and water damage mostly. A couple of weeks and you'll be back in business.'

A couple of weeks? Months more like, Travis had railed silently, remembering the door that had slammed as he was leaving last night and wondering how close he'd been to coming face to face with the culprit. And business meant money, contracts postponed or lost. Yet the fire chief was right in a way. It could have been worse. The offices were safe and that was something to be thankful for.

He drove home. There was nothing he could do that he couldn't do from the comfort of his own four walls. He made a mental list as he drove along, sifting it back and forth as he juggled the priorities.

Phone Cleo. Local radio broadcast to staff – no – better do that first. Doubtless the news would have spread as swiftly as the fire, but the workforce was entitled to more than idle gossip. And they'd be worried about their livelihoods. That is, most of them would, Travis amended, his lips tightening at the thought that someone could deliberately set out to ruin him. Still, no time for idle speculation. That was a job for the police. Back to the important things. Phone Donna. More than likely she'd be happy to drive across, be on hand to take letters, make and answer phone calls, hold the fort while he drove back to York to pick up Cleo.

Industrial cleaners, Portacabins, machine hire. His mind ran on. They could be up and running again by the end of the week, he decided, determined to make it a reality. And, in a warped sort of way, it might have done the company a favour. A refurbished building with a purpose-built workroom and a batch of new equipment. It was a pity about Billie's computers, but thank heavens he'd taken the time to back up the system. Everything was salvageable. It was just a matter of time.

Thinking of time, he ran his hand along his aching jawline, felt the early morning rasp of stubble, and the realization that he'd been up all night finally hit him. Hell, but he was tired.

The shrill ring of the phone woke him. He jerked upright in the chair, his fuddled mind slow to clear. Nine twenty-five. What the hell-?

'Travis? Oh, Travis,' Cleo sobbed as Travis stiffened, the thought of resurrecting last night's niggle almost the final straw. And he should have phoned her, he thought belatedly. He'd promised. And he would have done, too, but for the events of the night catching up on him. 'Something's happened,' Cleo wailed. 'It's Daddy. He didn't get up for breakfast and when Mummy went to wake him

237

he had these terrible pains in his chest and – '

'Easy, Cleo,' Travis cut in, urgently yet softly. 'I'm here. Take your time. Just tell me what the problem is.'

Which is why, ten minutes later, he found himself heading back to York.

'It never rains but it pours,' he'd murmured to Donna who'd arrived as he was leaving. But at least he was leaving things in capable hands. If anyone could bring order out of chaos, Donna could.

He went straight to the hospital, Cleo having pulled herself together and taken a taxi there. He found Cleo and her mother in a small private waiting-room; one look at their faces was enough to put his mind at rest.

'Thank heavens,' he murmured when Suzanne had finished explaining. No one actually said so but the dreaded words 'heart attack' had been uppermost in everyone's thoughts.

'They're keeping him in for tests and observation,' Cleo added, her exquisite face pale and pinched beneath the ubiquitous mask of make-up. 'A couple of days and they'll probably discharge him. Until then, Mummy will move into The Swift with me. It's handy for the hospital and, well, we just want to be near him.'

'Of course you do.' Travis hugged her reassuringly, aware of an overwhelming sense of relief. It was good to know that John was in no danger but, if

238

the truth were known, Travis was even more relieved that, for a few days at least, her father's illness would keep Cleo out of his hair.

'Sorry, Mr Kent, but we're stopping work.'

Sorry? Travis leaned back in his chair and studied the woman through hooded eyes. There'd been rumblings of discontent for weeks now, so he wasn't really surprised. Furthermore, he might just have nailed his culprit. No, not the arsonist. Without hard proof he could hardly pin that on her, though he wouldn't mind betting that the two were linked. But sorry? Oh, no. He'd spotted the gleam of triumph in her eyes. Sorry was the last thing this hard-nosed woman was feeling.

He smiled, leastways his mouth did. The warmth didn't reach his eyes. He waved an airy hand. 'Sit down, Mona. We might as well be civilized. I'll order some coffee and then you can tell me what the problem is.'

'I'll stand, if you don't mind.'

Travis shrugged. 'Whatever you prefer,' he murmured, not the least put out. He buzzed for coffee, sat and waited in silence until Donna brought it through, allowed the cafetière to brew for a couple of minutes and then poured the first cup, his movements slow and deliberate. Not stalling, just wondering how far he could push the woman. Because if he could provoke her into losing her temper, Travis might just learn a thing or two.

'Help yourself to cream and sugar,' he invited pleasantly, sliding the cup and saucer across the desk.

Mona shook her head. 'Not for me. And if you don't mind, I haven't come to socialize.'

'No. Of course not.'

The woman's face hardened and Travis made a mental note. She was quick, brighter than he'd expected. She'd caught his thinly veiled touch of sarcasm. In that case, it wouldn't do to underestimate her. But at least the gloves were off. Once the problem was out in the open, he could handle it. And he was sure that he could handle it. Once he'd finished, Mona Watts would be given her marching orders.

'So – ?' He poured himself a coffee, pointedly left the first cup to cool on the edge of the desk, pointedly waited for Mona to show her hand. His mouth tightened. She was the one with the grievance, and he wasn't about to make things easy for her. He took a long, satisfying drink from his cup and then sat back, arms folded across his chest, eyebrows raised in casual enquiry.

'We're walking out,' she blurted out at last. 'The girls aren't happy. They've been working in those huts for weeks now – '

'Hardly huts,' Travis interrupted, 'and it is just a temporary measure. The workroom – '

'Won't be ready till after Christmas, and it's no joke, all cooped up in those chicken sheds with the wind howling through the gaps in the windows.'

'But why did no one tell me? I'll get onto it straight away. A few draughts are easily put right.'

'Maybe so,' she ackowledged. 'But it's more than that. The lighting, for a start.'

'Oh?

'It's those strip lights. They're straining the girls' eyes. All that close work – '

'Extra lighting,' Travis murmured, jotting it down on the pad in front of him. He smiled across. 'Anything else, Mona?' he enquired pleasantly.

'As a matter of fact, yes,' she snapped. 'I've been discussing it with Health and Safety. It's cramped, there's no room to move. If there was a fire – '

'Precisely,' Travis bit. 'That's exactly why you're working in the mobiles. The fire, remember? And before you quote the Health and Safety directive, chapter, verse and book, let me remind you, Mona, the fire department was consulted and the arrangements in place meet all of their stringent requirements. Next?'

'The rest room.'

'Not enough beds?' he quipped, the sarcasm undisguised this time. He'd summed the woman up and was rapidly tiring of the game. She'd been stirring. Nothing more, nothing less. And though she'd brought the workforce to the point of anarchy, he was equally sure that they could be persuaded to see sense. It was the run-up to Christmas for a start; most of the women had families, children to buy for. And in the high-tech nineties computers and computer games were sure to feature large, the kind of toys that didn't come cheap. Whilst they might deny themselves, the women wouldn't dream of denying their children.

'It's all right for you,' Mona hit out. 'All nice and cosy with your wall-to-wall carpets and coffee and biscuits at the drop of a hat. We're roughing it over there and it's not fair. It's gone far enough – '

'I couldn't agree more,' Travis cut in, baring his teeth in a semblance of a smile. He stood up, moving quickly round the desk, saw the flicker of fear in the woman's eyes as he swept past her and suppressed the surge of satisfaction. It wasn't over yet, but it soon would be, and then Mona Watts would rue the day she'd crossed him. As he recalled once threatening Billie, Mona would be out of a job, and without references – she'd be unemployed and unemployable.

Billie. The fire went out of his belly. Is that what he'd really done to Billie, forced her out of his life, out of the job she seemed to love, into the cold, harsh world of unemployment? It was no more than she deserved, he argued, sweeping out of the office and across the yard to the largest of the three mobiles that would have to serve until the work-room was back in commission. Judging from the noise, the women had already stopped work and were congregating there.

But it was Billie, not the women, who filled his mind. Because Billie had gone. She'd disappeared. And if she'd found another job in the trade, Travis would have heard by now on the grapevine. So – he faced the unsavoury fact. He'd ruined her. For the sake of a lost contract he'd ruined her. And the contract didn't matter. It never had. It had always been the trust.

Silence fell as he appeared in the doorway, Mona Watts breathless and ignored in his wake. Travis strode to the head of the room, to the makeshift canteen with its jumble of plates, cups, sandwich boxes, newspapers, magazines and the music system that for once was switched off. He glanced around, spotted a large cardboard box under a nearby table and, picking it up, emptied the polystyrene padding it contained into a bin. If he was aware of the tension in the room, he gave no indication, could have been alone for all the notice he took of anyone as he produced a marker pen from an inside pocket and wrote a single word on the side in large black letters. SUGGESTIONS.

Smiling, he held the box up for everyone to see. 'I've spoken to Mrs Watts and we've agreed on a range of improvements that I'm sure you'll all be happy with. But just in case there's anything we've forgotten, suggestions can go in here. And that goes for the grievances as well. If you're not happy, simply jot it down on a piece of paper and pop it in the box. Anonymously or otherwise. And I can promise you, every single one will be acted upon.' There was a ripple of noise – approval, Travis judged – and so he let it run its course, his eyes sweeping over the sea of heads, searching each and every face for signs of trouble and, as he'd expected, finding none. Satisfied, he nodded, raised his hand and the silence fell again. 'And in recognition of some excellent work being done in difficult circumstances, there'll be a flat-rate increase for everyone. Call it an early Christmas bonus,' he added, naming a more-than-generous sum, and he swept out again before the room could explode into a riot of sound. 'My office. Now!' he growled over his shoulder at Mona Watts who stood scowling in the doorway, then followed him to his office.

'You can't fire me. I've done nothing wrong,' she insisted with a defiant toss of her head.

Travis looked her up and down, his lips curling in distaste. 'No. I don't suppose you have. Technically, at least. But you and I know different, don't we, Mona? So you'll resign forthwith, you'll take a very generous pay-off, and you'll never darken this door again. Oh, and Mona – ' He paused, wrote a company cheque, swung it round on the desk so she

could read the amount and let the moment hang
before he slid it towards her, not quite relinquishing
a thumbhold on one corner. And then he moved his
hand, keeping his eyes fastened on her face. 'If
you'll tell me who's behind all this,' he invited
softly, 'I'll double it.'

'Go to hell,' she spat, snatching up the cheque
and heading for the door.

Travis smiled grimly. She'd be back. When the
money ran out, she'd be back. He'd stake his life on
it. And then he'd have his arsonist.

'I'm sorry, darling. I know it's been weeks since
we've spent any time together but Daddy's not fit
enough to drive and Mummy thinks it would be
best if I do the chauffeuring. I know it spoils our
plans for Christmas but – '

'Mummy and Daddy come first,' he interrupted
drily. 'It's all right, Cleo,' Travis relented. 'I
understand.'

'You do? Honestly and honestly, Travis?'

'Honestly and honestly, Cleo.' He grinned, was
glad that Cleo couldn't see his face. Trust Suzanne
to let nothing, not even her husband's illness, stand
in the way of her plans. The Snellings were expecting them and she simply couldn't let Lady Mary
down. The fact that the Rossingtons could well
afford a chauffeur had clearly slipped her mind.
Or had it, Travis mused? After all, Suzanne was a

calculating bitch, would be aware of the impact of arriving in style in a chauffeur-driven car. So why lean on Cleo? Unless . . . Ah yes! Travis smiled, switched the phone to his other ear to free his right hand, and began to sign the pile of letters Donna had placed silently in front of him. But, of course . . . the Snellings had a son, one of Scotland's most eligible bachelors, and it didn't take a genius to follow the workings of Suzanne Rossington's mind. Clever, clever Suzanne. She hadn't given up hopes of that title for her beautiful, only daughter, and was using John's illness as a lever. It explained a lot, not the least Cleo's continued absence in London.

'Daddy's still a bit fragile,' Cleo was explaining, 'so we'll do the journey in stages. We'll stop off at the Churchland-Gores – you remember, Mummy's friends near York? – so what I was thinking – '

'Dinner at The Swift?' Travis cut in.

'Exactly. And if you book a room for the night,' she suggested coyly, 'we could probably manage an extra course or two . . .'

And this time, Travis realized, frowning as he replaced the handset, there'd be no wriggling out of things. It said a lot for his sense of humour that he added the silent rider, no wriggling out of things – and especially his clothes.

He wore a black suit. Funereal. Symbolic. As he swung the car into the car park, he was aware that he'd reached a decision. If he was being honest, the decision had been made for weeks, but since he hadn't seen Cleo alone since the night of the fire, he'd never been put to the test. Trial by fire. Hardly. But it wasn't going to be easy.

'Darling! Oh Lord, how I've missed you,' she murmured throatily, a dozen heads turning as she rose and glided towards him. Travis felt his stomach clench. He'd almost forgotten how good she looked, how good she was to be with. And when she raised her face for a kiss, touched his lips with hers, he had to brace himself not to pull away. She looked good, felt good, tasted good. His sense of humour surfaced again. Just a like a chocolate bar – or some age-old TV ad for a product he could no longer identify.

The condemned man ate a hearty dinner. He was ravenous, and Cleo, in blissful ignorance, enjoyed her meal, enjoyed the attentions of a bevy of penguin-suited waiters who seemed to outnumber the diners by three to one and who moved around the tables like a formation dance team: perfect coordination, silver-domed plates carried high, swung down simultaneously, lids removed with a flourish. The food was superb but, as the meal progressed, Travis began to feel the twinges of unease. How to break it to her gently? There was never going to be a right time to break an engagement. But he'd already left it too long, should have driven down to London weeks ago and been honest with Cleo.

He glanced up to find Cleo's green, cat-like eyes fastened on him. 'Let's skip dessert and go upstairs,' she suggested, dabbing the corner of her mouth with the napkin. 'You *did* book the room?' she added as an afterthought.

Travis had the grace to look ashamed. 'Well, no,' he admitted. And then he took the coward's way out. 'I didn't think there'd be time.'

'Coming from the man who made love to me standing up in a lift between floors in that hotel in Rome,' Cleo said in clipped tones, 'that takes some believing.'

'Ah, yes, Cleo. But I was younger then and we were – '

'In love? That *is* what you were going to say, Travis?'

'Still at the novelty stage,' he contradicted mildly. 'Hot-headed, hot-blooded. More quantity than quality,' he explained, aware from Cleo's stormy expression that whatever he said now would be taken badly.

'And now that the novelty's worn off it's once a week, once a month if I'm lucky?'

'Hardly,' he murmured, praying Cleo would her voice down.

'Precisely. Hardly. Hardly ever, in fact. Not even a wham, bam, thank you, ma'am, these days, hey, Travis?'

'When we're two hundred miles apart? Have

some sense, Cleo. I'm in Felbrough, you've been in London – '

'And never a weekend free to pop down and see me?' she needled him.

'Hell, Cleo. You know I've hand my hands full at work – '

'Ah, yes. Work. I might have known you'd put your precious company before me.'

'Not at all. But between the fire and your father's illness – '

'Excuses, excuses. You're just trotting out excuses. Face it, Travis, you're stalling. You don't love me at all. Well?'

And how to answer that without hurting her? But isn't that what he'd decided, to let her down gently? He ran his fingers through his hair. How the hell to let a girl down gently? Yet given her mother's manipulations, if Cleo arrived in Scotland fresh from a broken engagement, it might work out best for everyone. He didn't love Cleo. And in that case, she had a right to know.

'We can't talk here,' Cleo whispered furiously, aware, like Travis, that heads had begun to turn, that curious glances were coming their way.

'No. I'll book a room. To talk, Cleo. Understand? That's what we're here for.'

They rode the lift in stormy silence, side by side in the small, bronze-mirrored space. No chance of making love here, Travis acknowledged grimly, when not even so much as their glances touched.

Cleo's anger dissipated the moment they crossed the threshold. As Travis closed the door and leaned back against it, she spun round, her smile bright as she ran the palms of her hand across his chest, urgent fingers plucking at the buttons of his shirt. Travis froze.

'Kiss me,' she murmured urgently, linking her hands behind his neck and urging his face down to hers.

Travis jerked away and Cleo laughed, reached out to pull at the folds of his shirt, one hand slipping down to cradle the bulge at his groin. He grabbed at her wrists. 'This isn't a good idea, Cleo. We need to talk.'

'I'd rather let my body do the talking,' she told him coyly, thrusting her pert little breasts out. Since she was braless, as always, the dark points of her nipples stood out beneath the flimsy, pale fabric of her blouse.

Travis closed his eyes. Resist. Resist everything except temptation. Oscar Wilde, he identified, inconsequentially. Because Cleo had begun to rub against him and he was feeling himself rise. Sex. Sex on a plate. Not love, he reminded himself. He'd be using her. And he'd hate himself – later, in the dark hours of the night when the demons were active in his mind. So – he pulled away, saw the shock of disbelief in Cleo's emerald eyes and inwardly flinched. He was over the worst. He'd resisted.

The phone by the bed rang. Cleo shot him a glance of pure venom before snatching up the receiver.

Travis fastened the buttons that Cleo had all but ripped loose. Over the worst? Hardly. Cleo might have guessed, but he still had to tell her. And though he'd give the world not to hurt her, she had the right to know. He'd tell her now.

Cleo put the phone down. She spun round, her face beginning to crumple.

'What is it? For heaven's sake, Cleo, what is it?' Travis demanded as the tears began to trickle down her cheeks.

'It was Mummy. Daddy's feeling ill again.'

'I'll drive you back. We'll talk on the way.'

Only they didn't, of course. Only a prize cad would choose a moment like this to let a girl down. And whatever else he was, Travis hoped he hadn't sunk that low.

Suzanne Rossington greeted them at the door.

'False alarm, darling,' she reassured brightly as Cleo darted up the steps. 'I hope I haven't spoiled your evening? Just a touch of angina, thank goodness. He's taken one of those tablets the specialist prescribed and has gone for a lie down. Run up and say hello, there's a darling, but don't stay too long. Ah, Travis.' Suzanne's hard gaze bounced across the hall way. 'How sweet of you to drive Cleo back. But we mustn't stand here all night. Come in, Travis. Come and meet the Churchland-Gores . . .'

'Bitch,' Travis murmured on the lonely drive home. Because he'd seen through her. It had been a calculating and deliberate act, Travis would stake his life on it. Suzanne had cleverly guessed her daughter's intentions and had dragged Cleo back on the pretence of her father's failing health. And the irony was that by choosing to interfere, Suzanne had scuppered the very thing she was angling for. Until they were given the space to have that talk, officially at least, Cleo and Travis were still engaged. Thanks to Suzanne.

More tears. Donna's, this time. Now what? Travis wondered, dropping his brief case onto a low-backed chair and crossing the outer office.

Donna gazed up at him, a wealth of misery in her soft brown eyes. 'I'm sorry, Mr Kent, but something awful has happened. It's the computers. I switched my machine on as normal and there was nothing there. There's simply nothing there. It's all been wiped clean.'

'Everything?' Travis stifled a spurt of irritation. It was unlike Donna to panic yet she'd clearly got it wrong. Wrong time of the month? he wondered, aware that female hormones did go to pot, and with disastrous effects on occasion. But it was out of character for Donna. She was always so cool, calm and collected, and besides, he'd backed the system up himself last night. 'It's all right, Donna,' he quickly reassured her. 'There's probably a fault on your machine. Dry your eyes, there's a good girl, and then put the kettle on. I'll check next door.'

Only next door was exactly the same. The screen was uncompromisingly blank and nothing Travis did made the slightest bit of difference.

'It doesn't make sense, Donna,' he acknowledged wearily. 'I backed the system up myself last night. I know I did.'

What next? he wondered, sitting at his desk and running his fingers through his hair. Fire, flood, pestilence, the proverbial plague of locusts? And all since Billie had walked out and disappeared. Billie. He looked up. He had to find Billie. He wasn't a superstitious man by nature, but everything had begun to go wrong the moment Billie walked out. And he'd been harsh. He couldn't turn the clock back, but he could at least try to make amends. And, come hell or high water, he'd find out who was doing their best to close him down . . . which gave him an idea . . .

'Come back and work for you? It's a nice thought, but I'm more than happy pottering about the garden and looking after my cats. Thanks, Mr Kent, but no thanks.'

253

'Travis, Anna. The name's Travis. We're old friends, for goodness' sake. And it would only be for a couple of months, just to get things sorted.' He smiled winningly. 'I'll make it worth your while.'

Anna smiled too. 'I'm sure you would,' she murmured. She had to admit that, with the worst of the winter to come and a never ending stream of vet's bills, a little bit extra even for a month or two would more than welcome. 'Tell you what, how about a coffee while I think it over?'

'Thanks, Anna. Coffee would be lovely.'

He sat back and listened to the comforting sounds that came from the kitchen, the rattle of crockery, the tinkle of spoons on saucers, the whistle of the kettle as it came to the boil. He felt at home, as he had done in Billie's cottage, and was beginning to feel like a miniature ball-bearing rattling round the dome of St Paul's in his own mausoleum of a house.

And Anna looked well, the retirement, not to mention the confinement with cats, clearly a tonic. Cats. They seemed to be everywhere, and a matching pair of tabby and whites had been turfed off the chairs in the sitting-room so that he and Anna could sit down. Affronted, they'd given a haughty swish of their tails and promptly curled up in front of the glowing fire.

'So – ' Anna regained her seat, stirred her coffee thoughtfully. 'What's the problem?'

'What isn't the problem?' he quipped, filling her in on the recent disasters.

Anna nodded. 'I'd heard about the fire, of course. Who wouldn't, in a place like Felbrough? But I hadn't realized things were quite so bad.'

'No. And it would have been a lot worse if the fire had spread to offices. But the workroom's back in commission at the end of the month and, despite all the delays, the order books are overflowing.' And with the files on the hard-disc unit recovered, thanks to some computer whiz kid, it should be all systems go. 'Things are almost back to normal,' Travis explained, resisting the urge to cross his fingers. 'But I need someone I can trust in the workroom.'

'So you thought of me?'

'Why not? You know the job inside out and the girls know and like you.' He grinned disarmingly. 'You're the obvious choice. And they'll talk freely in front of you. They trust you. Someone's out to get me, Anna. And I need to flush them out before something else happens. If not . . .' He paused, spread his hands, his expression suddenly solemn. 'Next time there's a fire, someone could be killed.'

Anna looked shaken. 'You don't seriously think they'd go that far?'

Travis shrugged. 'They've tried it once. It's my bet they won't be happy till they've closed the place down.'

He caught a movement out of the corner of his eye and turned his head. A young cat had appeared in the doorway, his black and white face and smudge of a nose all too familiar. Travis almost dropped his cup, the jolt to his stomach a physical blow. Was she here? Could Billie have been here all this time?

The cup rattled loudly in the saucer as Travis placed it on the table beside him. He leaned forwards, extending his hand. 'Hello, boy. Remember me?' Clearly he did, or he recognized a friend, at least. The cat advanced into the room, brushed against his legs, allowed Travis to tickle the soft spot behind his ear, topaz eyes inscrutably appraising. Satisfied, he jumped up, trod several circles of Travis's lap and then curled up in purring contentment. Travis looked up. Anna was watching him carefully. 'He's Billie's cat.' It was a statement, not a question and he held Anna's gaze, his eyes silently pleading. The silence was oppressive but Anna wasn't about to make it easy for him. He swallowed hard. 'How is Billie?' he asked softly.

'Billie's fine,' Anna conceded, 'in the circumstances.'

'Oh?'

'Her aunt died. Her mother's sister. The day she lost her job,' Anna expanded, rubbing salt into his wounds. And why not? She was Billie's godmother and was bound to feel protective.

'Billie – '

256

'Isn't behind this trouble at Giddings,' Anna cut in fiercely.

His head shot up, the pain slicing through. 'Don't you think I don't know that? Oh, Anna, Anna, what the hell do you take me for?'

'A suspicious man, and why not?' she conceded brusquely. 'When things start going wrong, it's easy to point the finger. And Billie's not here to defend herself.'

No. The hope died. He could see that now. She wasn't living with Anna. The cottage was barely big enough for one. The hand stroking the cat paused for a moment. 'Will you tell me something, Anna?'

'If I can.'

'I know Billie's not responsible, but because of you she does have this irrational hatred of Giddings.'

'Me?' Anna looked bemused.

'You worked at House of Marianne. When Giddings took over, you lost your job,' he explained patiently.

'Ah, yes,' Anna chuckled. 'I'm beginning to see what you're driving at. But you're wrong, Travis. It has nothing to do with me. For House of Marianne read Marianne Housman.'

'A first-class designer,' he agreed. 'A contemporary of my mother. And, if I remember rightly, she was the driving force behind the company. Until she married and her husband took over the reins.'

'Exactly. And Marianne Housman is my oldest friend.' There was the briefest of pauses, the merest hint of hesitation, and watching her, an icy trickle ran down Travis's spine. 'She's also Billie's mother.'

'Is? But – Billie's mother is dead – isn't she?' he stammered. But Anna didn't reply, didn't need to. The truth was written loud and clear in her solemn grey eyes. Oh, hell! Travis slumped down into the cushions. It was beginning to make sense. It was still a bit hazy around the edges, but where Billie was concerned, he was beginning to understand.

CHAPTER 14

'More coffee, sir?'

Travis glanced up from the report he was reading. 'Thank you, no,' he told the smiling stewardess. 'But I wouldn't say no to a brandy.'

'Coming right up.'

Travis swallowed a smile. Coffee. Blanket. Pillow. Slippers. Magazine. Brandy. Refreshments. Headphones. You name it, the girl had fallen over herself to provide it over the past few hours. With several more to pass before they landed at Logan International, he might as well make the most of it. And, whilst service with a smile was all part of the job, Travis had forgotten the pleasure to be had from a harmless flirtation. He and Cleo had never really known a starry-eyed stage; as for Billie – He brought his thoughts up sharp. Did all roads have to lead to Billie? he chided himself, and yet that was an unfortunate choice of phrase given the way he was feeling.

Billie. Heaven knew where she was. For all his

probings and cajolings, he'd got precious little out of Anna.

'Billie's fine,' she'd insisted when Travis had pressed her. 'And, no, she isn't working, but she's hoping to sort something out in the next couple of weeks.'

'In the trade? Without references?' Travis had asked, but Anna had been evasive.

'It's – all up in the air at the moment. I'm not sure of Billie's plans myself yet.'

'And if you were, you wouldn't tell me – hey, Anna?' he'd challenged.

Anna had flushed and Travis had chuckled.

'You're hardly flavour of the day,' Anna had pointed out tartly. 'Condemning Billie out of hand.'

'Ah. So she told you?'

'Not exactly. But enough for me to plug the gaps.'

Just like Travis, in fact, since that was all he had to go on. Flimsy – yet damning evidence.

'From Billie's point of view, it wasn't looking good,' Travis had countered almost pleadingly. It still wasn't. Someone *had* leaked those plans and only two people had had access to them.

'Maybe not,' Anna had allowed. 'I only know that Billie was hurt, hurt and upset and then arrived home to even more bad news.'

'Yes.' Travis had swallowed hard. 'Awful timing.' Bloody awful timing.

'Yet, in a way,' Anna had mused, cutting across his thoughts, 'it gave her something to focus on, took her mind away from work. Hardly a blessing in disguise, but . . .'

Always a but, Travis had supplied silently.

He'd stood up to leave, certain from Anna's tight expression that he'd be wasting his time repeating the offer of a job. Like Billie, Anna wouldn't work for Giddings again if it was the last company on earth.

Reaching the door he'd paused, so many things running through his mind, the need for someone – Anna, if not Billie – to understand that he'd had no choice. On the face of it – then and now – Billie was guilty as charged. And yet, what could he say that wouldn't make things worse?

He'd risked another glance at Anna's solemn face and, swallowing hard, had taken the plunge. 'Tell Billie – when you see her – if she needs that reference, she only needs to ask. She's good at her job, one of the best. And no one can ever take that away from her.'

Anna's expression had lightened. 'Thank you, Travis. I doubt she'll take you up on it, but it's nice to know the offer's there.' She'd stood at the top of the steps, flanked by a colony of cats that had appeared out of nowhere and condescended to see him safely off the premises.

'Goodbye, Anna,' Travis had called through the

open window of his car. 'See you around some time.'

'See *you* on Monday,' she'd called back cheerfully, and the dark cloud that had been following him around all day had magically disappeared. 'Nine o'clock sharp,' she'd added. 'And I must confess, I'm really looking forward to being back at work.'

And for a fortnight, at least, it had all been plain sailing. Too soon to relax, of course, but Travis was keeping his fingers crossed.

'Magazine, sir?'

Travis came back to the present, realized he'd loosened his grip on the report he'd been reading, that it had slipped from his grasp and closed to under its own momentum. For the past half-hour at least, he'd been sitting, gazing into space.

'Yes. Why not? All work and no play . . .' he chided himself, flashing her a winning smile, and the girl flushed, dropped the glossy selection she'd been holding, and knelt to scramble wildly at his feet.

'Here, let me.' Travis joined her, the stewardess's fluster growing by the second.

'I'm terribly sorry – '

'Hey, no problem,' Travis reassured, gathering the pile together. He stood them on end, tapped them on the floor, edges perfectly aligned as with a flourish, he handed them back to her.

'Thank you.'

Under the cake of make-up she coloured again, and Travis wondered if skilled use of a trowel was a condition of the job. From a distance there was an aura of glamour that didn't withstand closer inspection, not in daylight, at least.

He didn't particularly like make-up, had always been thankful that Cleo used it so skilfully. Not that anything Cleo did was any of his business any more. And as for Billie – He stifled a sigh. Why drag Billie in? Fresh-faced Billie who managed to look stunning with little more than a hint of lipstick. But her appearance wouldn't come as a shock to a guy when he woke to find her head next to his on the pillow. The knife blade twisted.

'You haven't chosen a magazine,' the stewardess pointed out, her expression quizzical.

Travis decided he'd been daydreaming again and, since they were little more than halfway there, could hardly blame it on jet lag. He flashed her another bright smile. 'You're right. Just leave me a handful, any will do.'

He regained his seat and placed the magazines on the fold-down table in front of him. He could have moved down the plane to the informal seating area, but he wasn't in the mood for conversation. Half an hour's reading followed by a cat nap would be just what he needed to help break the tedium of the journey. And then back to business. If nothing else, he needed to finish that feasibility study before they landed.

Flicking half-heartedly through the pages, he realised he wasn't in the mood and might as well do some work, after all. He was shuffling them back together when the bottom one slid from his grasp. Travis made a grab at it. *Better Homes and Gardens.* It looked more interesting than the others, but he was more tired than he realized and it wasn't long before his eyelids began to drop. He stifled a yawn. Time for that nap. The magazine flicked shut, images skipping past like the frames of a magic lantern. And then a single word leapt subliminally off the page.

Travis jerked upright, clumsy fingers riffling the pages. Too fast, he missed it, cursed eloquently and forced himself to take a deep breath. More haste, less speed, he silently rebuked himself, and started at the front again, each page carefully thumbed and just as carefully scrutinized. Then he found it, tucked in with the other advertisements. A ten-centimetre box. Housman. The Housman Design Centre. Right there, on the outskirts of Boston. And though it might be a long shot, he sure as hell was going to follow it up.

Easier said than done, he discovered on landing. 'Mr Kent? Bill Morris. Welcome to Boston.' The young financier offered his hand. 'I have a driver and car waiting, so it's straight down to business. It's a hectic schedule and there's no time to waste.'

And so it proved, every second of his three-day visit carefully accounted for. Working breakfast. Working lunch. Working dinner. And Travis was bored. Give him the British way of doing business any day.

By the last afternoon he was desperate. And if the North American branch of Giddings depended on the next few hours alone, then tough. As far as Travis was concerned, he'd done more than enough already.

'Cancel the four o'clock meeting.'

Bill Morris, who'd stuck like glue to Travis's side from the moment he'd landed, turned a whiter shade of pale. Even the stripes in Bill's suit seemed to blanch under the shock of such a sacrilege. 'But, Mr Kent – '

'No buts. I'm taking a break. If it's that important, Bill, *you* attend the meeting.'

He slipped out before giving him time to react, took the lift – elevator, he amended – to the ground floor and paused on the threshold. Mentally weighing the time it would take to summon the driver and car, he stepped out into the street and hailed a passing cab.

The driver whistled as Travis gave the address. 'Other side of town, mister. It'll cost.'

'It'll be worth it.' And it would, too, just to put

his mind at rest. It was a long shot, but something in his bones told Travis he was on the right track. It was a clue. And it might just give him a lead to Billie. If he was wrong, well, he'd just have to accept it, but if he was right – Travis swallowed hard.

When the car braked, skidded to a halt, Travis looked up.

'Is this the place?'

Small, discreet for the States where everything came larger than life and was unashamedly ostentatious. Travis pushed open the door.

The receptionist smiled, rose to her feet. 'Can I help you, sir?'

But his glance had already moved on, through the half-open door to her right that was clearly marked Private, and on to the office beyond.

The woman there had back to him, was replacing files on a shelf. Tall for a woman, five feet nine, Travis hazarded. Slim, long, honey-brown hair caught at the nape of her neck in a midnight velvet bow. And impeccably dressed in a knee-length, powder-blue suit. Not a hint of the tomboy.

Travis felt the breath leave his body.

'Sorry, sir. You can't go in there.'

The receptionist had moved to his side, but Travis barely noticed her, his whole attention riveted on the woman ahead.

'Can't I?'

He stode forward, pushed the door wide. And as the woman turned, a smile of greeting dying on her lips, fireworks exploded in his head.

'Hello, Billie.'

CHAPTER 15

'Hello, Billie.'

Just like that. No hint of a warning, no premonition. Just 'hello, Billie' out of the blue.

And for a moment, a wonderful, heart-stopping moment, it was the most beautiful sound in the world. And then – Anna, oh, Anna. How could you? I trusted you. Oh, Anna!

Billie swallowed hard. She barely moved, barely breathed, her legs turning to jelly as the heat ran through her. But outwardly, at least, she didn't react. She had her pride – heaven knows it was probably all she had, but at least she managed to hang on to her dignity.

'Travis? W-what a surprise,' she stammered absurdly, licking her dry lips. Surprise? He was the last man on earth she would have expected to walk through that door; she wasn't sure that the vision was real, that with the stresses and strains of the past few weeks, she hadn't simply conjured him up from a vivid imagination.

Her gaze flicked past him to the flustered girl hovering in the doorway. Because Travis had bypassed reception, Billie wondered idly, or because Travis seemed to have that effect on the female of the species?

'It's all right, Celeena,' Billie reassured. 'Mr Kent's – ' She paused, searching for inspiration. Ex-boss, colleague, neighbour, friend, lover – almost – once, she mused as the pain scythed through. 'Mr Kent and I know each other back home.'

Home. Where everything had gone wrong, because Travis hadn't trusted her. And she'd loved him too much to live with that knowledge. Past tense? she asked herself. Or present? And she crossed to the desk, taking refuge behind it, glad of the solid block of wood between her and the man who'd come within a hair's breadth of destroying her. Gazing up into those velvet black eyes, seeing a gamut of expressions chase across his face, Billie stared truth hard in the eye. She loved him. Always had, always would.

She waved an airy hand, her control stretched almost to breaking point. 'Take a seat, Travis, and I'll order some coffee. I take it you do have time?'

He nodded, seemed about to speak, changed his mind and took the chair that Billie had offered, simply sitting, simply waiting, watching Billie as a hawk does its prey.

And Billie, too, lapsed into silence, a million and

one things running through her mind. But since Travis had taken the trouble to seek her out, he could be the one to break that silence. A resolution quickly made and just as quickly broken because Billie couldn't bear the silence, couldn't look at Travis, couldn't *not* look at Travis, couldn't fathom the welter of emotion in the depths of his eyes.

'So – what brings you here?' she asked at last.

'To Boston? Or the Housman Design Centre?' he stalled. He spread his hands. 'Would you believe . . . coincidence, Billie?' he asked with a touch of humour.

'No, Travis,' she returned primly. 'Where you're concerned, nothing's left to chance. When you walked through that door, you knew exactly what – or who – to expect. Anna – '

'Not guilty, Billie,' he cut in quickly. 'Anna told me nothing, absolutely nothing.'

'So how did you know where to find me?' she asked in all innocence.

'What makes you think that I was looking for you?'

Billie's chin shot up. Too cruel. But then the truth often does hurt. Of course Travis hadn't been looking for her. Why should he? He hated her. She'd come between Travis and his precious company and for that he could never forgive her. Only he was wrong.

Tears stung the backs of her eyes but Billie blinked them away. Cry? When she'd done nothing wrong? Oh, no! She was past crying for Travis, for any man.

Glancing across, she angled her head, her expression carefully neutral. 'Fine. Well, I guess that takes care of the preliminaries, Mr Kent. And since this clearly isn't a pleasure trip, it has to be business. Giddings' business. So – ' She picked up her pen, flicked the notepad to an empty page and raised a quizzical eyebrow. 'What can I do for you?'

'Have dinner with me tonight.'

'Why?'

'Does there have to be a reason?'

'Like I said, where you're concerned, there's always a reason.'

'In that case, take your pick.' He raised a hand, a finger snapping neatly into place for each. 'Because I'm a stranger in town. Because we're old friends. Because I'm flying home tomorrow.'

Tomorrow? Billie's heart sank. Yet why should she worry? There'd be four or five direct flights to London; if by some fluke they'd booked the same one, she was travelling economy, Travis was sure to be first class. The chances of coming face to face with Travis had to be remote. But then, fate had a habit of playing tricks. Why else should Travis turn up here of all places?

'Friends?' she queried. 'Don't make me laugh. If

271

we were the last people on earth, we'd still not be friends,' she stated coldly.

'We were more than friends at one time, Billie,' he pointed out softly.

'Past tense, Mr Kent. And believe me, where friendship's concerned, we never ever came close.'

'Not even that night at Fleet?'

'Especially not that night at Fleet. I – '

'Didn't react, didn't respond, didn't come alive?' he challenged, his eyes pinning her.

Billie flushed. 'I didn't even want to be there, remember?' she pointed out, and when the images flashed through her mind, a man and a woman almost naked on a bed, she hastily smothered the memory, the need, the pain. 'It was business, pure and simple,' she informed him. 'Just like everything Travis Kent does, in fact.'

'Oh, Billie, not everything, I assure you,' he almost purred. 'That night at Fleet, believe me, the pleasure was all mine.'

'Until I turned you down.'

'Ah, yes.' His face hardened. 'The rugged Viking. How is he? Taking care of his precious jewel, I hope?'

'Mind your own business,' she spat the words out.

The coffee arrived. While Celeena fussed, poured, simpered and blushed to the roots of her bleached blonde hair as she handed Travis his cup,

Billie had to dig her nails into the palms of her hands, because she wanted to scream, and scream from the rooftops.

'Thank you, Celeena,' she said instead.

'Yes, thank you, Celeena,' Travis echoed with his best damsel-slaying smile. And then, quick as as a flash, he switched his gaze to Billie. Surely he hadn't missed her naked stab of anguish?

She dropped her eyes, the coffee cup blurring. Why? Why had he come? Why now? And yet, she was going home tomorrow and had already begun to face the fact that, sooner or later, she and Travis would meet. Because he'd have heard. Because he'd have realised. And because he'd do his best to close her down. As far as Travis was concerned, she was finished in the trade. It was all a matter of time. Only – did she have news for Travis.

'So – why are you here?' she asked, tiring of the game of cat and mouse.

'As you rightly said, business,' he murmured pleasantly.

'Here? With Housman Design? Or Boston?' she asked.

Travis spread his hands again. 'Why not both?' he murmured enigmatically.

Why not, indeed? Billie echoed, but silently. Absurd though it sounded, it could be the truth. If she was thinking of crossing the Atlantic to open an independent branch of Housman Design in

Leeds, why shouldn't Travis do the reverse and launch Giddings on the North American market?

'Stalling, Travis? That's not like you,' she mocked. And then she remembered. 'But you're hardly likely to tell *me* your plans, hey, Travis?'

'If the cap fits, Billie . . .?'

'And if it doesn't?' she challenged.

'It seemed pretty conclusive three months ago.'

'But appearances can be deceptive, Travis.'

'Not with the evidence stacked waist-high, Billie.'

'Ah, yes. Evidence. A set of plans. And just two people who could have leaked them.'

'Exactly.'

So – 'Never heard of pillow talk?' she asked saccharine sweetly.

'Oh, I see. Well, that explains a lot of things. You couldn't wait to tell the rugged Viking. I should have guessed, shouldn't I?'

'Wrong, Travis. I wasn't thinking of me.'

'You surely don't think *I* leaked those plans?' he asked incredulously.

'Why not? One of us did – apparently.'

'And since it wasn't me – '

'Take a bow, Billie!' she supplied. She smiled grimly. Well, at least she knew where she stood. Travis believed it. Even now, he believed it. And the knowledge hurt every bit as much as it had then.

'Did you want something in particular?' she enquired briskly when he made no effort to return to the subject of business. And since he hadn't come looking for her, the visit had to be business.

'Not precisely,' he admitted.

'Just idle curiosity, then?'

'Let's just say, I'm sizing up the opposition.'

'It must be quite a bonus, discovering we're old friends.' The sarcasm was veiled, but Billie knew Travis wouldn't have missed it.

'Old friends, rivals, lovers . . .' He let the sentence hang, black eyes fastened on her face, daring her to contradict.

Only Billie was learning. She'd had six long weeks of coping with the pain, with the knowledge that the man she loved hated and despised her.

'Rivals?' So *that*'s why you're here? Giddings of Boston. Hmm . . .' She angled her head, as if testing the name on her tongue for effect. 'Yes, it has quite a ring to it, Travis.'

'Almost as good as Housman of York,' he mocked.

Billie smiled, one of those cat-that-got-the-cream smiles. Because Travis didn't know. He was matching pit for pat but he didn't know. It was guesswork, pure and simple. And he was wrong. So – if he hadn't done his homework, he really hadn't been expecting Billie. That cutting remark had been the truth. And she was glad, since it cancelled out the advantage of Travis walking in and taking her by surprise.

Watching her, his whole expression hardened and Billie could almost see inside his mind. He was in the dark and, for a man like Travis, always so supremely in control, it had to be galling.

'Housman of York,' he repeated, oh so softly, folding his arms and watching her through half-hooded eyes. 'Or House of Marianne?'

'Meaning?'

'Come now, Billie, don't be coy. You know exactly what I'm driving at. Marianne Housman of House of Marianne. You're not denying there's a connection?'

Billie went cold. She was wrong. Travis *had* done his homework. She might have known not to under-estimate him. 'Since you've clearly discovered a link, I'd be foolish to deny it,' she admitted calmly, a lot more calmly than she was feeling.

'Precisely.' It was Travis's turn to smile a know-ing smile; Billie had a mental picture of herself as an insect squirming on a pin in some particularly cruel schoolboy experiment. 'Which brings us neatly to the point, Billie.'

'Oh?'

'The missing link. That all-important piece of the jigsaw: Billie Taylor's irrational hatred of Giddings. I've always known it was there, Billie, but I just couldn't fathom out why. Even allowing for Anna, it didn't make sense but . . .' He paused, spread his hands, deliberately spun the moment out as Billie felt the hairs on the back of her neck begin to prickle out a warning. 'But now I've found it. And it was under my nose all the time. Marianne Housman. Marianne Taylor *née* Housman,' he added with the merest hint of triumph.

'Ten out of ten, Travis, for detection work at least. So what exactly does it prove?'

'Billie's revenge. An eye for an eye, a tooth for a tooth. And a company for a company. Giddings for Housman, in fact.' He angled his head, an eyebrow raised in almost casual enquiry. 'And I'm right, aren't I, Billie? Leaking those plans was the first step in a clever campaign to force Giddings out of business. Your campaign.'

'You're mad!'

'Believe me, Billie, I've never been more sane.' He smiled, an ugly snarl of the lip and, reading the truth as Travis believed it, something in Billie's heart died. He believed it. Nothing else mattered. 'So – spare me the excuses, Billie. I haven't come four thousand miles to listen to your lies.'

'No? So why have you come?' she enquired politely. Deep inside she was crying, but she refused to let the pain float to the surface. That would come later, in the dark hours of night when Billie was alone, never so alone. It was a trick she'd learned when her father had died and her mother had gone to pieces and the sympathy of friends had proved overpowering. Someone had to be strong.

And at the end of the day, no one else could cope for her. Life had to go on, and there would be life without Travis Kent – or Travis Kent's approval – she reminded herself.

'I've told you. Business. And the slight matter of our unfinished business, Billie.'

'Sheer speculation, Travis. And if I could just remind you, we're not in England now.'

'Meaning?'

'This is Boston and the name over the door is Housman, not Giddings.'

'You're threatening me?'

'On the contrary, you're threatening me,' she countered coolly, folding her arms and leaning back in her chair. 'I'm merely pointing out a fact.'

'And matching thrust for thrust like an expert, hey, Billie?' he needled her.

The atmosphere thickened – not a sound, not a whisper, just two pairs of eyes, smouldering with hate. And right now, yes, she hated him, every bit as much he hated her. Because he believed. Because he hadn't asked. Here, as he had done in Felbrough, Travis had condemned her out of hand. Judge, jury and Lord High Executioner. Billie had her pride. She was innocent, but she'd be damned if she'd explain, damned if she'd beg. If Travis wanted to believe, then why should she be the one to shatter his illusions?

Travis leaned forward. 'Billie – '

The knock at door followed by Celeena's appearance cut him off. Billie spun round, relief and irritation battling for position in her mind. The receptionist smiled, her eyes sliding past Billie and across to Travis.

'Yes, Celeena?' Billie queried as the girl fluttered her obscenely long lashes.

'Sorry, Miss Taylor. There's a query at the front desk. If I could just find the file . . .?' she murmured almost breathlessly.

Billie nodded. Why not? At least with the girl in the room she and Travis wouldn't be sparring. And since it was getting them nowhere, the time had come to call it a day. Travis could leave.

Ignoring Celeena and Travis both, Billie reached for her notepad, jotting down the things she had to do before she flew home: papers to sign, packing to finish, laundry bill, phone bill, keys to be returned to the agent. Order a cab for the trip to the airport? she mused. Probably not necessary. Time enough once she was ready to leave, but she made a note in any case. Phone Anna. Anna. Just what *had* Travis wormed out of Anna? she asked herself, glancing up.

Travis hadn't moved, was watching her intently. Billie almost smiled. Poor Celeena. All that attention-seeking clatter going on in the background and yet Travis's eyes were fastened on Billie.

And yet, if Cleo was anything to go by, surely

Travis had a penchant for petite, green-eyed blondes. Billie's mind skittered away from the thought. Why plunge the knife in? Travis could manage that without any help from her.

Travis. He'd done her a favour, she decided. He'd turned up out of the blue and caught her off guard, yet she'd held her own. Facing him again in England would be child's play. Her lips tightened. Hardly. But she'd coped today, and she'd coped well. Yes, he'd definitely done her a favour.

Celeena sidled out and Billie let her pen fall from her fingers. Ignoring Travis, she slipped out of her chair and crossed to the window, pushing aside the blind. It was a bitter cold day and though traffic was heavy, there were few pedestrians braving the flurries of snow.

'Isn't it time you were going?' she murmured without turning.

'Why?'

'Something to do with time, business and money,' she explained. 'And you are flying home tomorrow.'

'Exactly. Which brings us neatly back to my original suggestion. Dinner,' he reminded. 'To-night.'

'I'd rather starve,' she explained, swinging round, leaning back against the wall and eyeing him coolly.

'With a figure like yours, I find that hard to

believe,' he pointed out slyly, warm eyes sliding over her body, top to bottom and back again and lingering for a heart-stopping moment on the rapid rise and fall of Billie's breasts, clearly visible beneath the severe cut of the jacket.

'And is this the girl who needed fattening up on the way to Pellaton?' she needled as the currents of heat began to swirl in her veins.

'Very true, Billie. But I was wrong, as I discovered for myself at Fleet.'

Fleet. Billie blushed afresh at the memory – man and woman, mouth against mouth, tongues exploring moist and heated depths, her near-naked body stretched out against his on the bed; the touch of his lips, his lips circling her aching breasts, nuzzling and tugging at the proudly jutting nipples; his hands touching, caressing, loving. And then long, slender fingers gliding across the soft white skin of her thighs, his expression smoky as Billie trembled at the touch, wanted the touch, hardly dared breathe as Travis slid a single finger under the lace of her panties and – Oh, God! she almost groaned aloud, remembering – the need, the shame, the want, the superhuman effort it had taken to deny him. Because she *had* wanted him – wanted him, ached for him, needed him. Needed him now, if she was honest. Despite the contempt, the hate, the anger, the shame, she wanted him.

'So – it's settled then?'

The sound of his voice snapped Billie out of her trance.

'No, Travis. It is not settled. You have the cheek to walk in here, repeat some ridiculous accusation for which you haven't a scrap of proof and then have the gall to ask me out to dinner. And why, Travis? So you carry on where you've just left off, insulting me? Thanks, but no thanks. The very idea's enough to choke me.'

'I'm – '

'Just leaving,' she told him abruptly. 'Remember?'

'Trying to – '

'Goodbye, Travis. And don't forget to close the door behind you.'

'Fine. I'll pick you up at eight. I'm sure the simpering Celeena will have your address.'

'As it happens, she doesn't,' she informed him coolly. 'But since you've taken the trouble to notice the poor girl, why not do yourself a favour, and take Celeena out to dinner?'

'And be bored rigid in less than five minutes? Thanks, Billie, but no thanks. I like a little more spirit in my women, not to mention the odd spot of grey matter when it comes to brain cells.'

'And if I'd made that remark,' Billie snapped, 'I'd be labelled catty.'

'Catty – but truthful,' he admitted as the atmosphere shifted, as Billie recognised a subtle change in tack.

'Eight o'clock, Billie? For old time's sake?' he asked almost pleadingly.

'Give me one good reason,' she stalled, aware that, like water on a stone, Travis had worn her down, that if they spent the evening wrangling then at least she'd be alive, that Travis would have bounced her out of limbo and into hell. Heaven would be nicer but, Billie mentally shrugged, beggars can't be choosers.

'One reason? I can think of dozens,' he told her softly, rising leisurely to his feet, crossing the room and coming a halt in front of her.

'Oh?' she murmured, resisting the urge to fold her arms across her chest. It was the closest they'd been since Travis had arrived and she was shockingly aware of the man beneath the sophistication of the Savile Row suit. And he was all man, she reluctantly acknowledged. She tilted her head, the gesture unwittingly aggressive.

'Prickly as a hedgehog,' Travis murmured, a smile playing about the corners of his mouth.

'I beg your pardon,' Billie snapped, stiffening.

'Like I said, prickly as a hedgehog. Relax, Billie, I'm not about to eat you.'

But since he was closing in, Billie wasn't about to chance it. She moved to her left, was brought up short by his hand reaching out to touch the wall beside her, side-stepped right, only to discover that he'd rapidly out-thought her there as well. She froze, eyeing him warily. Two inches either way, and his hands would be touching her shoulders.

'Travis!' she warned.

He laughed. 'Now that I've found you, Billie, I've no intentions of letting you go. Not unless to agree to see me later,' he almost growled.

'Found me? But you weren't looking for me — remember?' she needled.

'Ah, yes.' He had the grace to look ashamed. 'It was a cheap little gibe. But hell, woman, you've only yourself to blame.'

'Me? And how do you work that out?' she asked incredulously.

'Simple.' He closed in, dipping his head, his lips brushing hers, just the lightest of touches really but enough to make her blood boil.

Billie gasped, her lips parting with the shock, and Travis growled, gathering her close, his tongue sliding through into the hot, moist depths as his mouth claimed hers, branded hers. And having fought the battle and lost, Billie gave up the struggle, allowing herself to slump against him. She felt the hardness of his body as he ground his hips against hers; lips, tongue, hands and mouth, the taste, the touch, the unique body smell of Travis blocking out the world and creating exquisite torment in her mind.

Hours later, it seemed, Travis raised his head. 'Woman, you drive me crazy,' he murmured thickly. 'Is it any wonder I don't know what I'm saying?'

CHAPTER 16

'You look – wonderful,' Travis murmured, his heated glance travelling over her.

'Thank you.'

He looked pretty good himself, she could have replied, but didn't, suddenly very shy and very, very nervous. It was ridiculous, really, since they'd known each other for months, had worked together, laughed together, fought tooth and nail on more than one occasion, and shared that weekend away at Fleet, almost reaching the point of making love. So – it was hardly a first date, hardly a date at all since Travis was happily engaged. And yet she licked her dry lips, allowed Travis to take her arm as he guided her into the diners' bar.

She'd arrived by cab, turning down Travis's offer of his driver and car. Her lips had twisted in wry amusement. Trust Travis to do things in style. Everyone else in Boston took a cab or the trolley or the T-train, but not Travis Kent. Drop Travis in the middle of the Sahara and he'd manage to conjure up a motorized camel train. In fact, she wouldn't be surprised to learn that he was flying home tomorrow by private jet.

'So what's it to be?' Travis asked once Billie was seated. 'Martini? Manhattan? Bourbon on the rocks?'

'Gin and tonic, please,' she requested demurely. When in Rome might be a good maxim, but she'd stick to what she knew, and once she judged she'd had enough, she could easily switch to tonic water and lime.

'So – ' Travis raised his glass; brandy, Billie guessed, from the pale amber colour of the liquid. 'Here's to old friends.'

'Hardly,' Billie reminded tartly, and when Travis frowned she spread her hands. 'Okay. I give in. Truce,' she conceded with a smile. 'For tonight, at least.'

'And if we manage that, Billie, it will be a miracle,' Travis agreed.

The drink helped, took the edge off her nervousness, but having polished off the first with comparative ease, Billie was determined to make the next last.

The waiter carried her glass through to the restaurant and Billie was conscious of the heads that turned, curious female heads that switched rapidly from Billie to Travis with a perceptible nod of approval. Lady killer. She swallowed a smile. No wonder he was arrogance personified. And why not? With his height and physique, Travis would be every woman's dream. Combine it with his dark, brooding looks and the understated power of money and the result was sure to be explosive. And yet, Billie mused, Travis didn't seem to play the field. He was engaged, of course, but that wouldn't stop some men from playing around.

The menu, like the drinks' list, was full of exotica as well as the traditional New England favourites of broiled veal chops, Boston beans and scrod, and a gourmet's choice in seafood. Billie kept to things she knew. 'Avocado mousseline and then the fillet steak, medium rare,' she ordered, half-daring Travis to mock her choice.

He didn't, opting for steak himself, T-bone, of course, and rare to medium.

'How are things in Felbrough?' Billie asked, cutting into her steak and discovering it was cooked to rosy pink perfection. She was acutely aware of the man, of Travis's smoky gaze fastened on her face, and found the pockets of silence disturbing.

'Hasn't Anna filled you in?' Travis queried.

'I haven't spoken to Anna for a week or so,' Billie admitted, frowning. She *had* phoned, several times, but Anna never seemed to be in.

Travis ran through the list of disasters.

'It never rains but it pours,' Billie observed, unwittingly echoing Travis's thoughts in the aftermath of the fire.

'No. But touch wood, with Anna back at the helm, the worst is behind me, Billie.'

'Anna?' Billie almost dropped her fork. No wonder she hadn't been in when Billie had phoned. She was much too busy – working for Travis. Oh, Anna! How could you?

'Ah. I see.' Travis looked solemn. 'Anna hasn't told you?'

'I'm not Anna's keeper, Travis, any more than she is mine. She'll tell me in her own good time.'

'Yes.' He paused, considered, spoke. 'I called round. To Anna's, I mean, when I had the idea of offering her the job. Smudge is fine. I thought you'd like to know.'

'Why, thank you, Travis. And to think I didn't know you cared. In fact, since most people can't tell one cat from another, I'm amazed you recognized the wretch among Anna's considerable brood.'

'Like his owner, Billie, he's instantly recognizable,' Travis explained, surprising her all over again.

It was beginning to make sense, his inside information about her mother. And yet Travis had been quick to insist that Anna had told him nothing. So, either he was lying, Billie mused, being economical with the truth, or he'd followed up the

289

clues that Billie herself had dropped.

It served to underline how little she knew about him, how little they knew about each other. Working so closely together, they'd built up a mutual bond of trust and yet that had fallen at the first big hurdle. Could she trust Travis? she asked herself. She'd like to think so, but the sobering fact was, Billie couldn't be sure. It was academic in any case. She no longer worked for Giddings and she and Travis had nothing else in common. In fact, now that she'd had time to think about it, the whole idea of having dinner with Travis was absurd.

'Is the steak overdone?' Travis asked, cutting into her thoughts.

Billie gave a start of surprise. 'Yes, no! No, the steak is fine,' she insisted with a tight smile.

'So why the scowl, the glance that would curdle milk straight from the cow?'

'Just – thoughts,' she stalled, aware that she had coloured guiltily, though what she had to feel guilty about, she wasn't quite sure.

'And what happened to that truce we'd called?' he enquired mildly.

'Did I speak? Have I complained?' Billie asked with an edge to her tone.

'You didn't need to. Your face spoke volumes. What have I done now, for heaven's sake?'

Her smile was brittle. 'Nothing. Absolutely nothing. Eat your meal, Travis, before it gets cold.'

He seemed about to speak, frowned, changed his mind, finished his steak in silence.

'Dessert, Billie? Fresh fruit salad and cream, *sour* cream,' he emphasized tartly once the main course had been cleared. 'Lemon cheesecake – that should be sharp enough even for you. Or how about the – '

'Chocolate gateau, thank you, Travis. And point made.' She smiled sweetly. 'It's a lovely meal, let's not spoil it, hey?'

'Agreed.' He reached across the table, hand outstretched, palm uppermost. 'Friends?' he asked, and Billie paused, knowing she couldn't refuse without seeming churlish, and placed her hand in his.

Friends, rivals, lovers, she remembered as the touch of skin on skin created havoc in her mind. Rivals, undoubtedly, once she returned to England, but as for the others . . . Billie shook her head. It was wishful thinking, on her part, at least.

They lingered over coffee, the atmosphere in the restaurant warmer than the bar.

It was strange being with Travis again. She hadn't known a soul when she landed; though she had made friends and met the cousin and family she'd barely heard of, for the most part she'd kept herself to herself. What with the funeral and meetings with lawyers and the invaluable few weeks she'd spent at Housman's, Billie had been too busy to socialize, too busy or too tired. The little free

time she had allowed herself had been spent famil-
iarizing herself with the city's history, riding the
trams or simply soaking up the atmosphere on the
streets.

It crossed her mind to wonder how close she'd
been to bumping into Travis on one of her forays.

'It's a lightning visit,' he explained when she
asked. 'A pity, really. It would have been nice to
see something other than the four walls of assorted
boardrooms.'

Yes. Billie could only agree. In just a few short
weeks she'd grown to love the place. Boston was
surprisingly compact and better seen on foot, a
curious mix of trendiness and tradition, from the
upmarket Beacon Hill with its narrow cobbled
streets and gas lights and grand Victorian town
houses, to the high rise blocks and brownstones
that co-existed happily elsewhere.

'But there's nothing to stop you coming back,'
Billie pointed out. 'I assume you are thinking of
launching Giddings over here?'

'Unless I blew it this afternoon,' Travis agreed.

'Blew it?'

'Coming to find you. I ducked an important
meeting.'

'But you weren't looking for me, remember?' she
reminded him.

Travis grinned. 'No. And cross my heart, that
was the truth, Billie. I was following a hunch. I

hoped it might point the way to you. But I never for a moment expected you to be here.'

'Why?'

'Why what?'

'Why come looking for me? We hardly parted the best of friends.'

'No.'

'So . . .'

There was a pause, and Billie held her breath, watching the shadows chase across his brow. Would he cross his heart and give her the truth this time? And would she recognize it if she heard it? she mused.

'You wouldn't believe me if I told you, Billie,' he conceded at length. 'But that day when you – we,' he corrected, 'lost the Haige contract, I was angry, sure enough, and I blew up, but I didn't intend driving you out of the country, Billie.'

'Don't flatter yourself, Travis, you didn't. My mother's sister died and I flew out for the funeral. And since I was jobless, I decided to stay on for the experience.' There were one or two other little details, but she'd no intentions of revealing them to Travis . . . not yet, at least.

'Yes. Anna told me. I'm sorry, Billie.'

'My, my, Anna has been busy,' Billie drawled, irrationally hurt by what she saw as Anna's defection. 'So what else did she tell you? That Aunt Janey was a Housman, too? That she and Mum were twins, that the American company has gone from strength to strength? What a disappointment, Travis, discovering your influence doesn't reach across the Atlantic. Finished in the trade? Oh, no. Believe me, Billie Taylor's only just beginning.'

'I didn't – '

'Don't lie!' she hissed. 'You knew what you were saying and you knew exactly what you were doing. You wanted to ruin me. Still do, since you still believe that I leaked those plans. And not just the plans, hey, Travis? Why not spit it all out and get it over and done with? The computers, the strike threat, the fire. Were they Billie Taylor's fault, too? Is that what you believe? What the hell do you take me for?' she demanded icily. 'A potential murderer?'

'I don't – '

'What? You don't *know*, is that it?' she asked, near to tears but determined to hide it. 'Such touching confidence in your staff, Travis, in your assistant. Such overwhelming trust,' she added bitterly.

'Will you please lower your voice – no, better still,' he bit out, leaning towards her, his eyes as black as thunder as they pinned her fast, 'will you please shut up for the odd thirty seconds or so and allow me to get a word in edgeways?'

'Why? So that you – '

'Can explain, Billie,' he interrupted, surprisingly mildly. 'I simply want to explain. But, of course, if you don't want to listen – '

'You didn't listen to me,' she hissed, 'that day in Felbrough. You – '

'Just assumed? Yes, you're right,' he agreed solemnly. 'I jumped to conclusions. But you didn't help yourself, Billie.'

'I might have known it would be my fault,' she cried out bitterly. 'Just like those plans – '

'No!' He banged his fist down hard on the table, causing the cutlery to rattle and Billie jumped.

'No, what?'

'No, I don't believe you leaked those plans.'

'So – but – I don't understand. Who did?' she asked as the fight went out of her.

Travis's expression was bleak. 'That's just it, Billie. I don't know. I honestly don't know. But if it's any consolation, I'm sure it wasn't you.'

The tears welled then and Billie blinked them away, escaping to the powder room and taking her time. So Travis didn't blame her, didn't hate her any more. It didn't help, she decided absurdly. It ought to but it didn't and she could see why. As long as Travis had believed it, it had given Billie a focus. Take the focus away and she was left with the emptiness of loving him and having nothing in return. And once she was back in England, working in an industry where the Giddings' name held sway, she'd be conscious of Travis whichever way she turned. But she could sell the cottage, move to Leeds, escape from him that way. No. Tempting

295

though it seemed, she couldn't sell the cottage. It was her mother's home, too, and as long as there was hope that Marianne could improve enough to come home, the cottage would always be there for her.

Billie dabbbed at her eyes, pulled a face at her reflection in the huge bank of mirrors. Thank heavens for small mercies. Since she hadn't been wearing mascara, nothing had run!

Travis was waiting outside and Billie forced a smile.

'Brandy?' he asked, leading the way to the lounge.

They paused on the threshold. It wasn't exactly crowded, but it was noisy, with a pianist idly picking out a tune on the instrument in the corner. Billie spotted the vacant loveseats. Somehow she couldn't see herself and Travis cosily installed on one of those.

Travis grinned. 'I think not,' he murmured and then he paused.

Billie eyed him warily. She didn't know what was going through his mind, but she wouldn't mind betting it was sure to unnerve her.

'There's always my room,' he suggested, holding her gaze. 'My suite,' he elaborated quickly. 'The sitting-room's large enough to throw a party and there's not a bed in sight, Billie, I promise you.'

'What makes you so sure the thought of a bed unnerves me?' she asked defiantly.

Travis smiled. 'Fine. My suite it is. And then I'll call a cab, take you home.'

'Don't be ridiculous.' Billie tossed her head. 'I don't need a chaperone, Travis. I've been riding around Boston in cabs for weeks, and with never a moment's harm, I assure you.'

'At this time of night?' he queried pointedly. And Billie hid a smile. He clearly didn't like *that* idea but she wasn't about to enlighten him.

They had the lift to themselves, a four-by-four-foot box of mirrors. Billie didn't know where to look, was suddenly very, very nervous. This wasn't a good idea, she decided, too late to wriggle out of it. It was difficult enough being alone with Travis in a crowd but alone in a hotel bedroom – sitting-room, she quickly reassured herself . . .

She ran her hands down the folds of her dress, wiping slightly moist palms dry. It was new and the first time she'd worn it and Travis's praise had been balm to a battered ego. Not just his words at the start of the evening, but the eloquent flash of approval that had gone with them. It was a fit and flare dress in soft, sapphire blue wool, the neckline a daringly deep V that reached to the valley between her breasts. It skimmed her body like a well-fitting glove, the skirt dipping to just above her calves. Demure, yet suggestive, Billie had loved it on sight. Right now, she wondered just how suggestive and whether Travis would take it as an invitation she hadn't intended. She licked her dry lips. She was being ridiculous, she decided, but it didn't help.

The sitting-room did. 'Wow! You were right. It *is* big enough to throw a party,' she declared as Travis threw open the door.

Not one, but three large, striped, Chesterfield sofas were grouped around a central coal-effect fire. Travis tossed his jacket over the arm of one as Billie sank down into the middle one. It was bliss, unashamed luxury, even viewed through the eyes of an interior designer, and for once, Billie wasn't disapproving.

He poured the drinks, holding up a heavy leaded goblet for Billie's inspection and at the same tilting the bottle.

'Whoa!' Billie implored as he angled his head in enquiry. 'That's more than enough. It's late already so I shan't stay long. Can't deprive a guy of his beauty sleep, hey, Travis,' she murmured with an attempt at lightness. 'And I'd hate you to miss that early flight.'

'Oh? And how do you know what time my flight is?' he queried, carrying the drinks across and coming to sit beside her.

He was close, unnervingly close, but Billie refused to wriggle away, refused to let the nerves show. 'Just woman's intuition,' she explained with a smile. 'Naturally I've checked on the flight times.

I'll be flying home myself soon,' she reminded him. Very soon, she underlined silently. She was right, he *was* booked on an early flight. She could relax.

'You're not planning on settling in the States, then?' he queried, turning his body sideways and leaning back against the bolstered arm of the sofa. It gave Billie a few extra precious inches of space and she began to breathe more evenly.

'No, Travis, I'm not settling in the States, tempting though it sounds to get away from you.'

'Ouch!' He winced playfully. 'It's been a rough few weeks, hasn't it, Billie?'

'And that's an understatement if ever I heard one,' she agreed. She sipped her drink, slowly, determined to make it last.

'And I haven't helped, hey, Billie?'

'Conscience pricking, Travis?' she queried, but not unkindly.

'If the cap fits, Billie . . .'

'You said it,' she pointed out, but she was smiling, as was Travis. The banter was simply that, light-hearted banter. And yet it was more than that, she decided, suddenly uneasy. She'd dropped her guard, was flirting almost, and where Travis was concerned, that was courting danger.

'I ought to go,' she murmured, draining her glass. 'If you'd care to call that cab?'

'I don't, as it happens, but I guess I haven't much choice. I'll come with you, see you home.'

'There's no need,' she insisted, rising, placing her glass carefully down on the table in front of her. 'I'll be perfectly safe, I assure you.'

'And I assure you, no gentleman would dream of allowing a lady out alone at this hour of the night in a strange city. And ten minutes either way will hardly affect my beauty sleep.'

'No.' Billie swallowed another smile. Dark shadows under his eyes and an early morning stubble would probably add to the attraction.

She'd worn a jacket but had left it in reception, had nothing to collect but her clutch bag. She'd dropped it on a chair, now stooped to retrieve it, all the time shockingly aware of Travis.

He'd crossed to the phone, palmed the receiver. Nearly done, she told herself. A five-minute wait for the cab, a ten-minute journey home. And then goodbye. Until tomorrow, maybe. Yet the chances of coming face to face with Travis at the airport had to be remote. She was economy, he'd be first class, she was flying out to Gatwick, he could be Heathrow. But perhaps it would be easier just to tell him?

Travis put the phone down, his expression tight as Billie raised an enquiring eyebrow.

'Don't go,' he said simply. 'Please, Billie. I'd like you to stay.'

'I – ' She halted, suddenly confused. Stay. What was he offering? A night of pleasure before he flew

300

home to Cleo? A night of love? Love? Fine chance, she told herself, her lips twisting, and yet the decision had already been made, had never been hers to make in the first place. 'I – Oh, God!' she said at last.

CHAPTER 17

His face lit up. He was across the room in an instant and then Billie was in his arms, such strong, comforting, protective arms, and it was the most natural thing in the world to raise her face for a kiss, taste the warmth of his lips against hers, and she opened her mouth, craving the touch, craving the harshness, the raw, frenetic need igniting like blue touch paper.

'Oh, Billie,' he breathed almost reverently, pausing, cradling her face in his hands. 'Oh, Billie, Billie, I want you,' he murmured in anguish.

Billie smiled, brought her hand up to his mouth. 'Hush, sweetheart,' she murmured, and Travis laughed aloud, a wonderful sound that made her heart sing. He caught at her hand, turned it palm upwards, nuzzled it with his mouth, his lips, his tongue, kissing, licking, caressing, every tiny touch sending currents of heat swirling through her.

Billie went weak at the knees, would have slumped but for Travis holding and caressing, his arms enfolding as his lips sought hers again, punishing, demanding. She opened her mouth, lips parting in delicious invitation, tasting, responding, her tongue pushing though and meeting his, performing an age-old love dance with his. And still the kiss went on, mouth to mouth, skin to skin, nerve endings jangling as the need, the unashamed need pulsed through her veins.

While his mouth played havoc with hers, his hands were pleasuring her body, skimming across her curves, the barrier of clothes heightening the tension. Travis wanted her – every touch, every kiss, every nuance of expression told her that he wanted her. And best of all, most frightening of all, she felt his hardness pressing in her groin and knew that she wanted Travis every bit as much as he wanted her.

He paused, raised his head, a million and one questions in the swirling depths of his eyes. And Billie gazed back, every single question answered, every single answer 'yes'. Yes! Yes! Yes! And Travis smiled, dipped his head to brush her lips with his, fleetingly, lovingly, urgently as he slid a hand down to hers, threaded his fingers with hers, drew her slowly, inevitably, towards the bedroom.

A nervous tongue moistened dry lips, an unwittingly erotic gesture and Travis groaned, pulled her to him, almost crushed the breath from her body as he held her, simply held her, and Billie felt the pounding of his heart beneath her cheek and smiled inside.

I want you, Billie,' he said simply, a quizzical expression in his eyes, a thousand and one doubts in his eyes, and again Billie smiled, answered yes with every breath: She was brimming over with love, and the answer yes was written loud and clear in her bright sapphire eyes.

He drew her to the bed, paused, looked, sought a response, received one in Billie's trembling lower lip, bent to still the tremble with his own, the touch igniting her all over again.

With hands not quite steady, Travis reached out, tugged at the zipper and peeled the dress away from her shoulders. As it fell to her feet, Billie stepped out of it, just her stockings, bra and panties standing between her and complete loss of her modesty. And she was proud, because Travis was feasting his eyes, his glance reverential, adoring.

He smiled, shrugging himself out of his shirt, tossing it uncaringly into a corner of the room. It was Billie's turn to reach out, to touch, to run her fingers through the mass of hair that covered his chest, her thumb brushing against a nipple that hardened to the touch, sending fresh shivers of heat running through her.

'Hell, woman,' Travis murmured, pulling her back into the safety of his arms.

And this time it was skin against skin, Billie's

breasts tightening, aching to spill free of the lacy black bra she hadn't deliberately worn with Travis in mind. Oh, no? She smiled, leaning back in his arms as Travis's mouth began to feather the stem of her neck with a million tiny kisses. Who was she kidding? The stockings, and the matching bra and panties may have been bought to please herself but their choice at the start of the evening had been calculated. She'd needed to look good, from the top of her head to the tips of her toes. She'd needed to feel good and yes, she'd thought of Travis. Standing naked before the mirror in her bedroom, she'd thought of Travis and her nipples had hardened, darkened, and she'd remembered another time, another place, when she'd lain almost naked before him. She'd wanted him then; she wanted him now.

His mouth moved down, his lips nuzzling the hollow at the base of her throat, and then moved on, lower again, Billie swaying back in his arms as deft fingers snapped the catch of her bra, just as deftly tugged it free, and Travis gasped aloud at the sight of the firm, full breasts that screamed out for his touch.

'You are the most wonderful, wonderful woman in the world,' he told her, almost reverently, and the currents swirled afresh in Billie's mind, the want, the need, the raw, aching need for Travis to look, to touch, to taste suddenly unbearable.

She arched her back, bringing her proudly jutting

nipples almost to the point of contact with Travis's powerful chest – almost – and then she paused, felt the current jump the gap between them, heard Travis's growl of pleasure as he crushed her against him.

'Witch. My wonderful bewitching Billie,' he murmured and his hands slid round, thumbs stroking the undercurve of her breasts, a fleeting touch that ignited Billie all over again, and she gasped as his hands took the full weight of her breasts, lifting and cradling while his thumbs rubbed against the rosy nipples which hardened and strained for more and more and more. With a growl of delight, Travis dipped his head, taking the first aching nipple into his mouth, tasting with his tongue, almost rolling it on his tongue, and then he was kissing, sucking and kissing, the resultant tug in the pit of her stomach turning her legs to water. Tidal waves of want threatened to swamp her and Billie began to moan, a primitive, animal sound that began deep in her throat and reverberated inside her head, inside her mind.

And, while his mouth suckled hungrily on one breast, his hand kneaded the other, pulsing, squeezing, his palm alternately cupping and denying the straining nipple and almost bringing Billie to screaming pitch.

She pushed hard against the hand and the fingers closed round, tweaking the nub between finger and thumb.

'Oh, God! Oh, my God!' Billie murmured but Travis had moved on, the cradling hands pushing her breasts together, allowing his tongue to nuzzle the valley between, allowing his lips to switch from one straining tip to another and back again.

And then her breasts were free again, and as his hands slid into the curve of her waist, his mouth explored the planes of her belly in ever-decreasing circles towards the dimple of her navel. He was kneeling at her feet and Billie gazed down in wonder, her fingers threading the silk of his hair. And she loved him – oh, how she loved him. As she smiled, he raised his head and their glances locked and the messages flowed between them: love, given and received, the bittersweet taste of passion roused and not yet sated.

'I want you,' he told her solemnly, his black eyes seeing to the centre of her soul. He came to his feet, cradled her face between his hands, dipped his head to taste her mouth, a soft, gentle, reverent touch that fanned the flames of Billie's desire. Then it was Billie's turn to kiss, to touch, her mouth moving against his, the raw, aching need spiralling out of control as instinct took over.

She pushed her body into his, urged her mouth to meld with his, allowed her hands to range the rippling muscles of his back, a soft, sensuous massage of dancing fingers.

Travis laughed, grinding his hips against hers,

and Billie felt the straining hardness of his manhood and trembled in part fear, part desire.

'I want you,' he whispered fiercely against her ear. 'This is how much I want you!' And he captured her hand and guided it down to the bulge at his groin. As Travis came alive beneath her fingers, the strength of his arousal created fresh needs, stoked the fears.

'Oh, my love,' she almost choked. And Travis smiled.

'Now?' he asked.

Billie nodded, her eyes brimming, tears of love, tears of wonder. He loved her. Surely he loved her? And since he loved her, it couldn't be wrong, it was all too wonderful to be wrong.

With infinite patience, Travis drew the stockings down from Billie's thighs, over her knees, waited for Billie to raise each foot in turn before he peeled them free of her long, long legs. And then his mouth retraced the path, ankle to knee, a million tiny kisses, and higher again, the soft, inner skin of her thighs trembling beneath the touch.

Reaching the apex of her legs, he halted, glanced up at her. Billie held her breath. Smouldering black eyes held her gaze. He didn't move, hardly seemed to breathe, and then a single finger slid inside her panties. Travis paused, his eyes dark swirling pools, unblinking and compelling, and Billie waited, simply waited. The finger moved, parted the curls, slid into the secret, sensitive part of her and Billie gasped, and gasped again as he found the nub and moved his finger so gently backwards and forwards. And Billie was moaning aloud, swaying backwards, filled with the exquisite pain of pleasure. And still he held her gaze, refused to allow her to look away.

'I want you, woman,' he told her fiercely. 'And I want you now.'

He was on his feet, his eyes fastened on her face, deep black pools swirling with passion. Billie watched as trousers followed shirt into the corner of the room and then, naked and proud, his magnificent, lightly tanned body gleamed in the soft glow of the wall lamps. It was Billie's turn to feast her eyes. And she was afraid, afraid and happy because she'd roused this tiger of a man and unleashed his power. After tonight, her world would never be the same again. Travis, wonderful, wonderful Travis, would turn it upside down.

He opened his arms and Billie's smile brimmed as she stepped across. With arms folded round her, Travis gave another growl of pleasure, hugging her, his hands slipping down to caress the curve of her buttocks, slipping beneath the lace, easing the lace over her hips and allowing the damp scrap of fabric to flutter to the floor.

'You're mine,' he growled, his fingers kneading the taut flesh. 'You're all mine and I want you *now*.'

And, before he'd finished speaking, he'd swept her into his arms, cradling her close as he carried her across to the enormous bed. Billie trembled as he placed her carefully on the duvet before stretching out beside her. But he didn't touch, simply looked, propping himself up by an elbow, his eyes travelling her body, his mouth curving into a smile of satisfaction, and Billie's heart soared. He loved her, he wanted her, he needed her, and best of all, he found her body pleasing. Tall, gawky, anything-but-petite Billie Taylor had the ability to please a man, and not just any man. This man. She loved this man. She smiled, and Travis's smile of pleasure broadened.

He dipped his head to kiss her and the touch was electric. A tiny pause, a gasp, pleasure, shock, need, and then he was kissing her with a frenzy more than matched by her own. They were together on the bed, arms and legs entwined, skin against skin, the currents swirling, the passion mounting, the need spiralling out of control as Travis eased his body down onto hers. Billie parted her legs and guided him inside.

Travis thrust hard, met with a resistance and faltered but, as the shock registered in his eyes and he made to pull away, Billie arched her back, her hands on his buttocks, urging him down, and then he was filling her, the moment's pain an exquisite stab of delight before the waves began to roll, minds and bodies perfectly matched as the explosions began.

'Billie! Billie!' he called out and they were pulsing together, the rhythmic thrusts of his body quickening the need till the release came – man, woman, mind to mind, body to body in a single mind-blowing, electrifying climax.

Hours later, it seemed, she opened her eyes. He was gazing down with love and her heart soared, and then his eyes darkened, shadowed with revulsion, and Billie went cold.

'Travis?' she murmured as he turned away, swung himself upright, sitting on the edge of the bed, his back rigid, his head bowed. 'Wasn't it – wasn't I – any good?' she stammered, scrambling to a sitting position and hugging a pillow to her chest in an effort to hide her nakedness.

'Good? *Good?*' His head jerked round, eyes nuggets of jet and Billie winced at the fury. 'Woman, you were magnificent,' he told her.

'But – '

'Yes, but. Always the but,' he derided almost wearily as something vital in Billie's mind died.

Cleo. She should have known, should have remembered. Travis loved Cleo. And making love with another woman made Travis unfaithful. He'd made love to Billie, had enjoyed making love to Billie, but she wasn't Cleo. Now he despised himself for the weakness, probably despised Billie more.

Billie felt the tears sting, struggled to hold them at

bay. Cry? Embarrass them both? Oh, no. She owed him that, at least.

'I'm sorry,' she said instead.

'*You*'re sorry?' he snapped. And then the anger died. 'No, Billie,' he contradicted her flatly, running his fingers through his hair in a strange, despairing gesture that made Billie want to cry all over again. 'I'm sorry. You've done nothing wrong, nothing to be ashamed of. But it shouldn't have happened. I shouldn't have let it happen.'

'Fine,' she conceded, struggling to understand. 'So we made love. So it was a mistake.' A mistake on his part, at least. 'We're mature adults, Travis. These things happen. And Cleo – '

'Cleo? What the hell does she have to do with this?'

'But you – she – '

'Were all washed up weeks ago,' he explained as the ice began to thaw, though imperceptibly.

'But – then – I don't understand,' she said simply. 'What have I done wrong?'

'Nothing, woman. Nothing at all. But don't you see, that's just the point? I have. I've taken you, taken something precious and I didn't know, never realized. Don't you see, Billie, I've taken something irreplaceable.'

'But it happens to most women sooner or later,' she countered almost pleadingly. He was ashamed. He'd been part of the most wonderful moment of

312

her life and yet Travis was ashamed of it.

'Maybe,' he conceded bitterly. 'But not with me.'

Ah. So she had been gauche. When he'd told her she was magnificent, he was simply being kind. Still, it was her first time, and *she* hadn't been shortchanged. And if she never, ever, made love again, she'd have something wonderful to hold on to. Wonderful – yet in Travis's mind, sordid, she realized as the pain scythed through her.

She moved, reached for her clothes, sat on the edge of the bed as she slipped on the still-damp panties, fastened the bra with fingers that shook. Back to back and a chasm apart when, less than half an hour ago, they'd been in heaven. She reached for her stockings, decided not to bother and crumpled them into a ball before dropping them on the floor. She would push them into her clutch bag later.

'Why, Billie?' he said as she stepped into her dress. He'd turned and, was watching her. Having to dress in front of a man who so openly despised her seemed obscene. 'Why didn't you explain?'

'Explain?' She tugged at the zipper, tilted her chin in defiance. 'Oh, sure. Let's have an action replay,' she mocked. 'Sorry, Travis, can't go to bed with you tonight. I'm a virgin, you see. Twenty-two years old and still a virgin. But if you'd care to hang around for a day or two,' she sneered, 'I'll find someone else to do the breaking in for you.'

'Don't – '

'Don't what? Don't tell the truth? Don't rub salt in the wound? Most men would have been proud,' she railed, was aware that by hitting back at him she was probably hurting herself more. 'Quite a notch in their belts, a real live virgin. But I might have known you'd take it another way. Well, *you* might be ashamed,' she informed him defiantly, 'but I'm not,'

'Ashamed? Yes, I'm ashamed,' he rasped, moving round the bed and coming to stand in front of her. So near, yet so far away, she thought, the sight of his naked body sending fresh needs surging through her wayward mind. 'But of me, you little fool. Not you. Don't you see? I didn't have the right.'

'Well, if that's all that's bothering you, worry not, Travis. I granted you the right,' she reassured him with a flippancy that was sheer bravado. 'You might be an expert but, believe me, if I'd wanted you to stop, I'd have stopped you. That night at Fleet – '

'Yes, Billie. That night at Fleet. I despised you, hated you, pictured you making love with another man and hated you. Because *I* wanted you, I'd never wanted anything so badly in my life. And then you turned me down.'

'The prerogative of a real live virgin,' she jeered, and she was crying inside, hating him, hating herself more. 'Only, not any more, hey, Travis?'

He snatched at her arms, fingers biting cruelly into the soft flesh as he tugged her closer to his blazing face. 'Why didn't you tell me?' he demanded in anguish. 'The most precious thing in the world and that night at Fleet you let me sneer, belittle, mock, insult you. Why, Billie? Why the hell didn't you tell me?'

'And if I had, would you have believed me?' she asked softly as the anger drained away.

He swallowed. 'No,' he said at last, releasing her. 'No.' And then, softly, so softly she had to strain to hear the words, 'I'm sorry, Billie.'

'Yes.' Billie's turn to swallow hard. 'But if it helps, Travis,' she murmured, swinging away and heading for the door, 'I'm not.' She paused in the open doorway, watching him, but Travis refused to turn, refused to look her in the face. She choked back the tears. 'Travis?'

'Go away, Billie. Go and sit down. I'll get dressed and then I'll take you home.'

'But I don't want to go home,' she said simply. And it was true. She couldn't be sure, but she thought – hoped – that she was beginning to understand some of his reactions.

'No?' He shrugged, indifference oozing from the pores of his skin. 'Fine. Make yourself at home. Choose yourself a sofa, Billie.'

'And what's wrong with the bed?' she queried softly, aware that she could be making a terrible mistake but she had to try. For her own peace of mind, she had to try.

315

He shrugged again. 'You take the bed, I'll take the sofa. It makes no odds to me.'

'But it's such a big bed,' she pointed out coyly, moving back across the room. 'And I'd feel all alone. Come to bed, Travis,' she murmured huskily, coming to a halt behind him. 'Come back to bed with me.' And she reached out, slid her hand into the slight curve of his waist and round to the planes of his belly, aware of his manhood springing into life. Her fingers travelled downwards.

Travis snatched at her hand, swung round, his expression bleak. Billie's hopes died. So – she was wrong. She'd misread the cues and now she was making a fool of herself.

'After the way I've treated you?' Travis queried coldly. 'I might be good in bed, Billie, but I'm not that good.'

'I don't agree,' she told him. 'I wanted you. I still do.'

A ghost of a smile crossed his features. 'Thank you.'

'For what?'

'For not crying. For not ranting and raving. For letting me make love to you. For giving me something uniquely precious. For trying to understand. For being so forgiving.'

'There was nothing to forgive,' she told him simply.

'No? A virtuous woman is priced above rubies.

316

And, yes, Billie,' he emphasized urgently, 'I did say it. And if many a true word is spoken in jest – or anger – then that insult really has come home to haunt me.'

'It doesn't matter,' she told him, blue eyes silently pleading. 'Not to me. Don't punish yourself, Travis. Don't go on punishing me.' He didn't react, didn't speak; though his eyes were fastened on her face, Billie couldn't decipher the expression in their swirling depths. But at least she'd tried. He didn't want her. Fine. Her lips twisted. No regrets. She'd tried. He'd turned her down. It had been a calculated risk and it had backfired, but if she hadn't made the effort, the doubt would have festered in her mind. Nothing ventured, nothing gained. Nothing gained anyway. No – that wasn't true, either, she realised as the room blurred, as she swung away for good this time.

She reached the door as Travis's voice sliced across to stop her. 'Billie!'

She halted, her heart thumping so loudly that it seemed to echo round the room and round and round inside her head. She didn't speak, didn't turn, couldn't bear to look, to see the expression in his eyes when he spoke. She was afraid. Goodbye was such a cold and final word.

'Don't go, Billie,' he said a lifetime later. 'Please, Billie, I really do need you to stay.'

CHAPTER 18

Billie closed her eyes. She wasn't asleep, simply remembering, replaying the tape in her mind, recalling each and every moment. And feigning sleep gave her the privacy she craved to be alone with her thoughts, took away the need for conversation with a perfect stranger.

They'd made love, talked, made love again. 'Why, sweetheart?' he'd asked in one of the still, quiet moments. 'Why didn't you tell me? If I'd known, I'd have taken things more slowly.'

'And spoiled all the fun?' she'd quipped, banishing the shadows in his eyes. And yes, she had finally understood. He'd been ashamed, had despised himself for the insults at Fleet, had been horrified to think he'd taken something he wasn't entitled to. And so he'd lashed out – at himself, at Billie, hurting both in an effort to wipe away the stain. In making love again, Billie had been able to banish the pain, purge the guilt. She wanted him and needed him, too, she'd pointed out, and then she'd proved it.

And so the night had passed. And when she opened her eyes to daylight, Travis had been there beside her, a smile of indulgence playing about the corners of his mouth as he gazed steadily down at her.

'Good morning, sleepyhead,' he'd greeted her softly. 'Sweet dreams?'

'Have you been watching me all night?' she'd asked, her heart singing. Such wonderful dreams, she could have confided, but didn't, since the dreams could never come close to matching the reality.

'Hardly,' he'd murmured, laughing. 'Since we spent half the night exploring one another's bodies.'

'Only half?' she'd teased, and Travis had dipped his head, his mouth a much too fleeting touch, and she'd snaked her hand behind his neck, pulling him back into her arms, the kiss deepening, the need rising and Travis had laughed again, pulling free and stripping away the duvet, exposing Billie's milky white body, the rosy nipples that hardened beneath his knowing gaze.

'Too soon,' he'd murmured smokily. 'You, my beautiful wanton, need cooling off, and I've just the thing in mind.'

He'd led her to the bathroom which, like the sitting-room and bedroom, was big enough to house a family of ten and still leave space to swing a cat. They'd climbed into the enormous sunken tub

319

and, like naughty children, poured an entire bottle of bath foam under the running water. Bubbles and foam had filled the room, and Billie had giggled as they'd crept up her nose, giggled and sneezed alternately. And when they'd finished cavorting like a pair of dolphins, they'd turned their attentions to the serious business in hand.

'You first?' he'd asked, holding out the bar of soap.

'Certainly. If sir would care to stand?'

Sir did, and when she'd finished with him and all his delicious bits and pieces, it had been Travis's turn.

'If madam would care to stand . . .?'

'How could a girl refuse?' she'd teased, and started to tremble the moment Travis slid the soap across the first of her curves, an erotic glide of soap, hands and fingers that roused her yet denied her, a desperate Billie reaching out to draw him close.

'Don't move,' he'd commanded thickly. 'Woman, I defy you to move.'

Faced with such a challenge, what could she do but try, holding herself rigid as every inch of skin was explored, caressed, lathered, from the tips of her fingers, along the length of her arms and into the hollow beneath that she'd never dreamt could feel so erotic, across her taut shoulders and back, down into the left curve of her waist, just skimming the top of her buttocks, across to the right curve of her waist, every touch, every movement, kindling tiny explosions in her mind. Though the effort nearly killed her, she'd stood perfectly still, her body still, her insides in turmoil.

And then he'd spun her round, the smouldering message in his eyes filling her with fire. 'So far, so good,' he'd murmured huskily, but if Billie's appearance was calm, Travis's body had betrayed him. The laughter gurgled in her throat as she'd reached out to touch him, to palm the delicate sacs, laughing again as Travis jerked himself away from her.

'No, woman,' he'd commanded huskily. 'Not yet. Too soon. Much, much too soon.' And then the soapy fingers had circled her breasts, spiralling so very slowly towards the centre, Billie's nipples refusing to conform as they hardened, ached for his touch, jutting fiercely. Travis had smiled, bending, his tongue flicking the tip of each, briefly, much too briefly, the heat running through her like molten lava.

She'd closed her eyes as he'd moved down her body, bypassing the junction of her legs, down one leg – lift, foot caressed, toes teased – across to the next – lift, foot caressed, toes tugged – and then the long, long journey upwards. He paused to tickle the tender spot behind a knee and on again, the soft inner skin of her thighs tingling beneath his touch. And then . . . Billie groaned inwardly as Travis paused, teasing, tantalizing, testing; of course, she had to pass the test and continued to hold herself rigid, the self-denial exquisite torture.

He'd soaped his hands, allowed the bar to fall unheeded and reached out to grip her slippery body with his fingers while his thumbs massaged the tops of her thighs, nearer and nearer to that dark and damp inviting triangle, nearer and ever nearer, just skimming the edges, a rhythmic circling, a mind-blowing swirl. Billie began to moan, the sound echoing round the room, a haunting, primeval love song.

Then the trembling began, at the epicentre deep inside, uncontrollable, her legs turning to jelly, the need spiralling out of control as the probing fingers paused, plunged, plundered, turning Billie into a quivering mass of nerve endings.

'Travis! Oh, lord, Travis!' she'd implored and he'd laughed, stepped out of the bath, swung Billie into his arms and carried her, steaming and dripping, back to the bed.

'Now, Billie,' he'd growled, gazing down but holding himself aloof. 'If you want me, you'll have to beg.'

'And if I don't?' she'd enquired, the expression on her face carefully non-committal.

'If you don't – what?' he'd asked.

'If I don't beg, of course,' she'd told him smokily, and he'd growled again, stretching out beside her and gathering her to him, rolling over onto his back and pulling her on top of him, the hands that cupped her buttocks the most delicate restraint.

'Then I'll just have to teach you how, won't I, my pretty maid?' he'd told her solemnly. And then the kissing had started, the hands on her body rousing her to even dizzier heights. Then he'd flipped her back onto the pillows, trailed his mouth from the hollow in her throat, down to the valley between her breasts. He'd cupped her breasts, pushing them together, deepening the valley, and then his tongue had pushed between them, greedily lapping and sucking and then, sated, yet insatiable, the nuzzling mouth moved on, nipple to nipple, tasting, teasing, biting as his hands and fingers probed and stroked, downwards now, almost there, threading the curls yet skirting the screaming centre of Billie's existence. Then he paused, drew back, knelt astride her legs and leaned forwards to pinion her arms with a vice-like grip of velvet fingers.

'If you want me, Billie,' he'd reminded her thickly, 'then beg.'

And, since she couldn't move because he'd pinned her beneath him, couldn't reach out for his manhood so was powerless to use her hands to drive him to the fever pitch he'd roused in her, she simply smiled.

'Now!' she said. 'I want you now! I want you to kiss me. I want your mouth and hands to caress me. I want you to touch every inch, every hollow, with your mouth, your lips, your fingers, your mouth again. And, when your body aches as mine does, when I've denied you the final taste, when you're ready to beg as I am, then, Travis, and only then,' she emphasized huskily, 'will I offer myself to you.' And she smiled again, a muted smile of triumph because she'd turned the tables, put the onus firmly back on Travis, had given him her answer. She wanted him, but he wanted her every bit as badly and she'd prove it.

He'd smothered a groan. 'Witch,' he'd murmured knowingly. 'But since your wish is my every command . . .'

The first touch ignited her. Billie writhed beneath him, biting hard on her tongue, determined not to ask, to force Travis to capitulate, but clever, clever Travis knew her well, played her like a virtuoso, enough, no more, enough to bring her to the edge and then –

'Travis! Travis! Please, Travis!' she'd called out in anguish.

'Please, Travis, what?' he'd growled, black eyes smouldering.

And, since he'd asked so nicely, Billie told him, two small yet eloquent words of command. Shock registering on his face – shock, and then delight as Travis moved to obey, parting her legs and thrusting hard between them, driving, punishing, the punishing rhythm easing as Billie matched him pulse for pulse, as the ocean waves rolled, surfed, reached a massive, towering peak that seemed to hang in the air before crashing and exploding into a myriad scattered droplets.

'Shouldn't you be packing?' she'd asked when the breakfast had arrived.

'Is that a hint, Billie, that you wish to be rid of me?'

'Hardly,' she'd murmured, curled up on the sofa, enveloped in one of the soft towelling robes the hotel provided for guests, her damp hair tied up in a turban. Watching her wriggle in to the robe, Travis had frowned, clearly preferring to see her naked. 'But I'd scandalize the staff,' she'd pointed out and he'd given in.

'I've plenty of time,' Travis explained, easing the cork from the bottle of chilled champagne.

'Champagne! At this hour?' Billie had laughed.

'And why not? It's a special day – for me, at least,' he'd told her fiercely, handing her a glass.

It was dry, and the bubbles escaped up her nose, but Billy had to admit it was delicious, decadent but delicious. And it was a special day for her, oh yes, it was a day she'd remember all her life.

'So what time's your flight?' she'd asked, swallowing the disappointment when he told her. In less than an hour, he'd be on his way to the airport and Billie would have a day to kill, another twelve hours before she'd follow him across the Atlantic. It was on the tip of her tongue to tell him then, but no, she'd surprise him, arrive home out of the blue.

'Come and eat,' he'd urged, kneeling on the rug beside the coffee table and patting the floor beside him.

Billie obliged, diluting her champagne with the freshly squeezed orange juice.

'Croissant? Muffin? Cereal? Strawberries and cream? Or I can order something hot, if you'd rather?'

'Croissants will be lovely,' she'd assured him, and Travis had nodded, pulling one apart, dipping the corner in the pot of strawberry jam and feeding Billie from his fingers. As his fingers brushed against her mouth, her lips, already swollen from an ecstasy of kissing, began to tremble all over again.

They shared the rest of the sweet French bread, Travis refusing to allow Billie to help, tugging the rolls apart, dipping, offering, tasting his own, his black eyes alternately smouldering and solemn as they rested on her face. And then he bent to kiss her mouth, to lick away the residue of jam, and the currents ran through Billie like a flame.

Travis smiled. They had no need for words. They were together and they were alone and nothing else in whole world mattered. He reached for the dish of strawberries, took one, dipped it in the cream and offered it to Billie. This time he allowed her to reciprocate and so the erotic meal went on, touch for touch, bite for bite, the tension mounting all over again, because she ached for him, knew from his face that he ached for her. It was only a matter of time – the waiting, the denial, were part of the foreplay – but they would wait.

Travis drained his glass. His gaze was molten. Billie trembled. Without a word she freed her hair from the towelling turban, allowed the damp locks to tumble dishevelled down her back. And then she tugged at the belt of her robe, allowing the robe to fall open, her breasts to spill free. She raised her chin, swollen lips parted in silent invitation.

Travis groaned. He caught her to him, kissing her, fiercely, briefly, urging her down on the rug as his mouth sought her aching breasts, his hungry lips devouring, his hands ranging her body. As Billie writhed beneath him, he pushed himself inside, higher and higher, harder and harder, the tension mounting, the rhythm perfect, the tempo gathering pace until the release came.

Sated and exhausted, Travis smiled down at her. 'And this, my love, is something else we must discuss, and soon. Babies,' he'd added, sensing Billie's confusion. 'Carry on like this, and we'll have a house full before next Christmas.'

'And would you mind?' she'd asked, her voice carefully neutral.

'If it means I have to share you with them, too

right I would,' he'd told her. And then he'd grinned. 'Now one or two I could probably cope with, along with the cats.'

And quite what he meant by that, Billie didn't have the courage to ask.

They'd showered and dressed, separately, aware that with passions running high, they'd never reach the stage of leaving if they touched each other again.

'I'll order my car, take you home,' he'd said at last. He'd packed and was ready to leave, would leave the hotel at the same time as Billie.

Billie shook her head. 'There's no need,' she'd insisted. 'I'll take a cab. I hate long, drawn-out goodbyes. And besides,' she'd added with gleam in her eye, 'we'd probably never make it, would scandalize your driver, not to mention have us both arrested before we'd gone halfway up the street.'

Travis had grinned. 'When are you coming home, Billie? You *are* coming home?' he'd asked, suddenly uncertain.

'Soon,' she'd promised him. And again, it was on the tip of her tongue to tell him, and again she made the decision to keep the surprise.

On leaving the room he'd kissed her, slowly and tenderly. They'd taken the lift to the ground floor, hand in hand and silent in the small glass compartment, and when Billie glanced at their reflections, a wealth of emotion came back at her.

Travis collected Billie's jacket, ordered her cab.

'I'll phone you, the minute I'm home. If madam would care to leave her number?' he'd said at last, attempting to lighten the moment.

Billie joined in. 'Madam would. But let me phone you. I take it you're driving straight to Felbrough?'

'Uh-uh.' He'd grimaced, shaken his head. 'I couldn't take the long drive on top of all this. Domestic flight to Leeds-Bradford. I should arrive home by mid-afternoon – British time tomorrow, I mean. Which means you getting up at the crack of dawn to call me.'

'Oh, I think I can manage that easily enough,' she allowed with a smile. She'd still be in London, she'd calculated quickly, sleeping off the effects of the flight, had pre-booked a hotel room. But she'd phone him, leave the surprise till later.

And then it was goodbye. Such a cold word. Such a final word. But in twenty-four hours or so they'd be together. Billie was luckier than Travis, she'd realized the moment he'd waved her out of sight. She knew that she'd be seeing him soon, very soon.

She slept, was amazed the flight could be over so quickly. And since she'd managed to sleep through the second meal break, she was ravenous.

By the time she cleared customs, Billie was feeling lightheaded. She wandered out into the concourse, cocooned in her own rosy world. She was tired, of course, and her body clock was haywire, but it was more than that. She was walking on air and the radiance showed in her face.

She'd stop for something to eat, an old-fashioned English breakfast of bacon and eggs with all the trimmings, would savour the memory of the breakfast she'd shared with Travis and, despite the expense, she'd take a taxi direct to the hotel.

She'd travelled down by train all those weeks ago, judging the car unreliable and now she was glad, would be able to sit and dream all over again on the train home. In fact, she decided, with a secret little smile, in her present state she'd be a positive danger on the roads.

It was Cleo she saw first, the hackles rising on Billie's neck as the cold green eyes met hers across a sea of heads, appeared to be looking straight through her.

What on earth was Cleo doing here? Billie wondered. Stupid question, really, since it was obvious she was meeting someone off a plane. Travis? No. Not Travis. His flight would have landed eight hours or more ago. Then Cleo waved to someone out of sight away to Billie's left, her smile broadening as she dashed across a gangway. Curious, Billie turned her head, saw Cleo launch herself into the man's arms. Travis. It couldn't be Travis. The man had his back to her. Same height, same build, same suit, she realised as the nausea swamped her. Of course it was Travis. She loved him, for heaven's sake. She could pick him out of a capacity crowd at Wembley Stadium with her eyes closed. Cleo spun round in his arms, appeared to be sifting the crowd for someone – for Billie?

Billie stood rigid, the breath punched from her body. It was strange the things you think of in a crisis. She'd forgotten to phone Anna, she thought suddenly. She ought to do it now, let Anna know she was safely back in England, send her love to Smudge. And someone near by dropped an open can of cola, as the mole-coloured splashes on her trousers would later confirm. She didn't heed the boy's stammered apologies, didn't notice the fuss, but the smell must have registered, that distinctive aroma of caramel – for years to come, the slightest whiff in a café or a bar would be enough to trigger the nausea. And, last but not least, Billie would never forget the expression in Cleo's eyes – that ugly flash of triumph that Travis caught and swung round to investigate, his own smile dying on his lips.

For a moment, nothing. And then Billie moved, darting away as fast as she could manage given the hindrance of the luggage trolley.

'Billie – '

'No. Don't. Don't say a word. I really don't want to know.'

'But at least let me explain.'

'No.' No explanations, no regrets. 'Just leave me alone.'

'Please, Billie – '

'Go away,' she hissed. 'Leave me alone. Go!' Get out of my sight, get out of my life, she tagged on silently, bitterly, wondering where she'd heard those words before. And then it hit her. His words. The words that had haunted her for weeks. Until last night when all the love had driven it away. Love. Fool, she berated herself. He'd never promised love, never even hinted at it.

He grabbed hold of her, pulling her up short.

Billie angled her head. 'Remove your hand,' she requested icily, 'or I'll scream.'

'Don't be ridiculous – ' He broke off as she opened her mouth, dropped his hand, fell into step beside her.

Billie ignored him. There were too many things running through her mind to pay heed to man who'd gone pale beneath the the early-morning shadow of stubble.

It explained such a lot, she realized, the things that had been vaguely there at the back of her mind and which, like a lovesick fool, she'd chosen to ignore. No false promises, no declarations of undying love. She'd been too shy to tell him how she felt herself, hadn't noticed Travis's omission – until now, when it was so glaringly obvious she'd clearly been in a dream. Dream. Nightmare. A nightmare of her own making, since she'd been stupid enough to drop her guard and trust him. Trust. Always a question of trust.

'Billie – '

They'd reached the taxi rank, the cold, damp English air beginning to permeate. Home. Only she wasn't going home – ever. Forget the dream, she'd sell the cottage, move to Leeds. There'd be nursing homes in Leeds and her mother would soon settle in. Though she couldn't avoid hearing about Travis on the business grape vine, she'd do her best to block him from her mind.

'Billie! For goodness' sake, woman, will you stop and listen?'

He pulled her up short, the grip on her arm sending waves of heat surging through her, heat and desire. She spun round, her eyes spitting flames. 'Why?' she demanded, loving him, hating him, even now aching for him. 'To more lies, Travis? Sorry, I've neither the time nor the inclination. Now run along, there's a good chap, the lovely Cleo's waiting.'

'Cleo and I – '

'Are all washed up? Were all washed up weeks ago?' she said scornfully. 'Yes, Travis. I remember. There's nothing wrong with my memory. And there's precious little wrong with my eyesight. Now go away and leave me alone. We're through.' Not that we ever got started, she added silently. It was sex, on his part at least. Good sex, too, but just a straightforward biological function like eating, sleeping, crying, creating babies. Babies.

She went icy cold. Babies enough to fill the house by Christmas, she remembered. What on earth would she do if she was pregnant?

For the second time she shook herself free, pushing the luggage trolley towards the back of the queue.

'Why, Billie?' he asked. 'Why won't you let me explain?'

'You lied,' she said simply. 'About Cleo. About the flight you were booked on. If you were to swear on the Bible that this is London, England, I wouldn't believe you now. Trust. I trusted you. But never again,' she informed him icily, choking back the tears. 'I wouldn't trust you – or any man – as far as I could throw him. Not again. Not ever.'

'Billie!'

She stopped dead on the kerb, didn't turn, didn't acknowledge him at all, tried hard not to listen.

'I was wrong. About you, remember? So now it's your turn. If you want the truth, you know where to find me.'

'Under the nearest stone,' she murmured, and then she swung round, her eyes pools of hate. 'The truth, Travis, is something you wouldn't recognize if it hit you in the face.'

CHAPTER 19

'Why, Anna? Why didn't you tell me?'

Anna shrugged apologetically, her face creased with worry. 'It didn't seem important,' she explained. 'Travis is often away for days at a time. And when he said the States, it never crossed my mind that he meant Boston. Is it so important?'

'Only to me. He took me by surprise, caught me off guard.' Swept me off my feet, made love to me, lied to me, broke my heart, she tagged on bitterly. But at least the cramping pains in the pit of her stomach meant one thing less to worry about. She wasn't pregnant. But if her body was functioning to order, her mind refused to conform. Travis. She breathed him, lived him, ate, drank and slept him. He filled her mind. Despite the resolution, he filled her mind. And she loved him. Fool, fool, fool, after everything he'd done, she loved him still.

And there wouldn't even be work to fill the long empty days, not for a while at any rate. Empty days, empty nights, her glaringly empty life.

'So what are your plans?' Anna enquired over sandwiches and soup in her small but cosy kitchen. 'You'll need a job, for a while, I suppose.'

'Hmm.' Billie glanced up, her hand pausing in mid-stroke. Smudge was curled up on her lap, unhygienic, she knew, but she needed something warm, something tactile to help soothe her frayed nerves. The cat pushed his damp nose into the palm of her hand, nudging Billie to continue. 'Go back to work for Giddings?' she quipped with a flash of her old humour. 'Could you picture Travis's face if I turned up on Monday morning to ask for my job back?'

'I don't see why not,' Anna mused. 'You did nothing wrong. And Travis said – ' She stopped, broke off in confusion.

'Travis said, what?' Billie queried carefully.

'He said to tell you that if you needed references, you only had to ask.'

'Well, I don't. Not from Travis. Not from Giddings,' she told Anna grimly. 'Until Aunt Janey's money is released, I'll get by.' Somehow. 'How's Mummy?' she asked, changing the subject abruptly. She would have gone straight to the nursing home but, by the time she'd reached Felbrough, it had grown late and her mother would have been in bed.

'Marianne's fine. She seems more aware of things lately and the doctors are quietly optimistic. I didn't say anything sooner, Billie, because I didn't want to raise your hopes, but if the improvement continues, there's no real reason why Marianne shouldn't come home.'

Home. Just when Billie was planning on selling it. Just when she was planning on moving to Leeds. Man proposes, God disposes. Ah, well. Billie smothered a weary sigh. She'd just have to rethink her plans.

She left Smudge at Anna's, booked herself into Felbrough's only decent hotel. She couldn't face the cottage. Time enough tomorrow when Travis would be at work and she could wander the house and garden she loved without fear of prying eyes. Not that Travis could pry given the catproof fence he'd erected all those months ago.

And with time on her hands, she'd decorate, do all the things in her own home she normally did for others. Raggle-taggle cottage, Mr Kent? Not for much longer, she scorned. She'd have someone round to take care of the gardens and deal with the outside paintwork, but the rest of the transformation would be down to Billie. And Aunt Janey's legacy, of course.

Aunt Janey's legacy. Too much to leave sitting idle. Barely enough to set her up in business. There'd been no strings attached, Billie had discovered. The money was Billie's to do as she pleased – as long as Marianne was provided for. So Aunt Janey must have known. She'd kept herself informed of the situation in Felbrough and had cared enough to make her sister's life finally secure. But what to do with the money? Too much – and yet not nearly enough to set herself up in opposition to a company like Giddings.

It was Anna who gave her the idea.

'Where's the point in starting my own business?' Billie railed when the subject came up a few weeks later. 'The mighty Travis Kent would simply trample me into the ground.'

'Now you're being neurotic.'

'Not neurotic, realistic. Daddy – '

'Oh, Billie.' Anna shook her head, grey eyes full of compassion. 'It didn't happen,' she murmured softly. 'Not the way you think – '

'But Giddings – '

'Yes, I know. I was involved, too, remember? But it wasn't as straightforward as you think.' She'd been drying cups on the draining board and absentmindedly dropped the cloth she'd been using into the sink full of water, before wiping damp hands down the sides of her skirt. 'Oh, Billie,' she said again, taking a chair and pulling it up close. 'It's been playing on my mind for weeks but I couldn't break your mother's confidence. But Marianne's getting better. Facing the past is part of her therapy and she agrees with me that it's time you were told.'

'Told? Told what?'

'The truth. The truth about Giddings. You can't blame Giddings, Billie.'

'But – '

'No, Billie, listen,' Anna entreated softly, taking Billie's hand. 'You were young and you idolized your father. Your mother didn't have the heart to shatter the illusion. But you're old enough to take it now. Your father lost the company, Billie. Drinking, gambling, wild ideas that went drastically wrong. The Giddings' offer was a godsend, far more than Housmans deserved. And when Richard gambled his way through that as well . . .'

He couldn't live with the shame, Billie supplied silently, vaguely aware at the back of her mind that she'd always known that there had to be something more than the loss of the family business behind her father's suicide. She swallowed hard. Poor Mummy. Poor Daddy. And poor Anna, putting up with Billie's rantings and ravings without a word of complaint.

She forced a smile for Anna, wonderful Anna who'd cared enough to shelter Billie from the harsh facts of life. 'I can see now why you didn't mind working for Travis, why you happily betrayed me by going back when I lost my job.'

'Betrayed you?'

'That's how it seemed when I heard,' she admitted. 'And to add insult to injury, I didn't even hear the news from you.' And if she was wrong about that, blaming Travis and his family for her own family's failings, what else could she be wrong about? But, no. Billie stiffened. Where Cleo was concerned, Billie had seen the evidence for herself. 'So – how are things at Giddings?' she steeled herself to ask.

'Fine. Touch wood, things have settled down. I'll give it a few more weeks and then think about retiring, for good this time. Travis can do without me. He misses you, of course,' she threw out as an afterthought.

'Oh, of course!' Billie almost choked on her drink.

'Well, it stands to reason,' Anna explained completely unrepentant. 'He lost a good designer, not to mention his second-in-command. Travis relied on you, Billie. He could trust you.'

Trust her? But he hadn't, had he? Not when it mattered, at least. Any more than Billie now trusted him. 'You mean he hasn't found a replacement yet?'

Anna shook her head. 'He doesn't say much but I wouldn't mind betting he'd have you back tomorrow.' She paused, looking thoughtful, and Billie wondered what was running through her mind. 'Why not give it a try, Billie?'

'I'd rather starve,' Billie snapped. And then, aware that she'd sounded harsh, 'Thanks, Anna, but no thanks. When you retire, Travis will just have to manage without either of us.'

'Hmm. I suppose he will. But he's working too hard, all hours of the day and night. Almost as if he's driven by demons.'

Good! Let's hope they're the same demons that torment me night after night, Billie railed evilly, though silently. She was almost flattered. 'Hasn't he advertised? For an assistant, I mean? After all, it's a job with prospects. There'll be no shortage of bright, young hopefuls.'

'Young and hopeful, maybe,' Anna agreed. 'The postbag's bulging. But bright? Heaven only knows what they teach them at those colleges these days. How to twiddle their thumbs, by the looks of things.'

'Now there's an idea,' Billie mused as something struck her. She let the thought sink in and then she smiled broadly. 'Anna, you're a marvel!'

She drove herself hard, driven by demons, she acknowledged, but she had to do something to fill the hours – the long, empty hours of the day, the interminable hours of the night – and at least by wearing herself out, she stood a chance of snatching a few precious hours of sleep.

And, having poured her heart into the cottage, she turned it back into a home she could be proud of, a home fit for her mother who would be strong enough for weekend visits soon, the doctors had assured her. Billie then switched her attentions to Aunt Janey's legacy and her future.

Her future. Billie Taylor's special plan. Eat your heart out, Travis Kent, she jeered, having set the ball in motion. And look out, Giddings. Because Billie Taylor was about to make a success of things.

CHAPTER 20

A birthday card? Hardly, since her birthday wasn't till June. And since the news hadn't broken yet, too early for congratulations. But definitely a card, she decided, picking the envelope up off the mat and turning it over to study the neatly printed name and address, the smudged postmark that might or might not have been York. Billie shrugged. She ripped it open, drawing out the contents, a single, unfolded sheet of card, and then she gasped.

'The management and staff of Giddings request the pleasure of the company of Miss Wilma Jane Taylor at The Starling Room, The Swift Hotel, York for a double celebration: the occasion of the sixtieth birthday and the retirement of Miss Anna Miller.' The time and date followed and underneath the RSVP, someone – Travis, Billie realized as the printing blurred – had added a handwritten post-script: 'Please come, Billie. We can't let Anna down, not on her special day. Travis.' Not: best wishes, Travis. Or: love, Travis. Just: Travis. And why not?

He was nothing to Billie, she was nothing to him. But clever, clever Travis had out-thought her – did he really know her so well? she wondered, the idea disturbing. Because Travis had known how Billie would react. He'd known, and now he'd made certain that Billie would attend. Let Anna down? Not Billie.

She entered the room alone, her eyes sweeping across a sea of heads. She was late, but better late than never, she decided. And it really had been a battle. Spend an evening in the same room as Travis, watching Travis and Cleo talking, dancing, heads together as they whispered words, shared lovers' secrets? Or let Anna down?

Anna was in the centre of a crowd, spotted Billie and came across at once, her face beaming.

'Billie! I was beginning to think you weren't coming.'

'Happy birthday,' Billie murmured, hugging Anna fiercely. Not coming? No. It might have been a battle but Travis had known Billie better than she knew herself. 'And happy retirement,' she added with a smile. 'I take it's for good this time?'

'Unless a certain young lady has need of my services?' Anna queried with eloquent lift of her eyebrow. 'The rumours are flying thick and fast, Billie. Isn't it time you let your godmother into the secret?'

'No secret,' Billie reassured her. 'And I'll tell you all about it soon.'

Anna linked arms, drawing Billie back across the room. 'There's a hot and cold buffet later,' Anna explained. 'So there's plenty of time to take to the dance floor and work up an appetite. But come and have a drink first.'

'Champagne! My, someone's honoured,' Billie murmured drily as Anna summoned a passing waiter.

'Yes. I've been lucky. I've had a lovely day and, thanks to Travis, I'll have a night to remember all my life.'

'Ah, yes. But it's no more than you deserve,' Billie pointed out, raising her glass. And though Giddings' money it might be, it was nice to know that Travis had taken the time and the effort to arrange a special tribute to Anna. And thinking of Travis . . . Billie's lips twisted. Who was she trying to kid? She was always thinking of Travis.

'Where is the great man?' she enquired tartly.

'Travis? Oh, he'll be here later,' Anna explained. 'Being the boss, he didn't want to put a damper on the festivities by arriving too soon. He said he'd pop in for an hour and then slip away again when no one's looking. Worried, Billie?' she added unexpectedly.

Billie took a long, slow sip of her ice cold wine. 'About Travis? Should I be?' she stalled, aware of the giveaway spots of colour in her cheeks.

'Oh, Billie.' Anna shook her head, her grey eyes fleetingly troubled. 'I'm not blind, love. I see things. And I do understand. And if you ever need to talk . . .'

Billie smiled. 'Thanks, Anna. But no thanks. Where Travis is concerned, there's nothing to say.' Nothing. It was over, finished, finished before it began. Only that wasn't true either, Billie acknowledged as the pain scythed through her. It would never be over. Their single night of love was etched into her mind. Love. Her lips twisted. But it was true. On her part, at least.

There was a commotion at the door and Billie turned, the colour draining from her cheeks. Travis. Complete with an attractive dark-haired girl almost hanging on his arm, and an official photographer. But no Cleo, Billie noted, faintly puzzled. And then she realised. A works' outing? A knees-up with the hoi polloi? Hardly Cleo's scene at all. And yet Billie was surprised that Cleo could bear to let Travis off the leash, if only for an hour.

As if sensing her scrutiny, Travis looked up suddenly. Billie froze as her eyes locked with his across the room. Oh, hell, how she wanted him! Even now she wanted him and the rest of the room retreated, the noise, the laughter, the movement and colour little more than a blur. Just Billie and Travis alone in a crowd.

A pair of hands slid around her waist, male hands. 'A hug for old time's sake, Billie?'

'Tony! Oh, Tony, it's good to see you.' And she twisted round, flung her arms around his neck and hugged him close as Tony dipped his head, kissed her, little more than a peck, really, but it was balm to Billie's aching heart. Tony's hand slid down, his fingers threading with hers. 'Come on. I've someone I'd like you to meet.'

No prizes for guessing who, Billie smilingly acknowledged, as Tony led her to the table where Heather was sitting with her pretty young sister-in-law.

Tony's new bride was just what Billie would have expected, very shy and clearly very in love with her husband.

'Billie Taylor?' she murmured, her voice a soft Scottish burr. Her nose creased in the effort of remembering. 'But, of course, I've heard such a lot about you from Heather. And I had the most wonderful wedding dress, thanks to you. Won't you sit down?'

'Sandy's a nurse,' Tony explained as Billie took the chair she was offered.

'Given your line of work, lots of things in common, then,' Billie murmured with a return to humour.

'Oh, sure, Billie,' Tony drawled goodnaturedly. 'We can discuss the merits of bedpans over romantic candle-lit dinners for two.'

347

'I don't know about the bedpans, but the dinners would be nice,' Sandy added, clearly tongue in cheek.

Billie smiled. They were happy and it showed, and she was glad. Tony deserved it.

'You're very lucky,' she told him, when Tony remembered his manners and asked Billie to dance.

'And don't I know it.' He grinned broadly and then he sobered. 'But what about you, Billie? Is there no one special in your life?' he probed, and Billie swallowed hard.

'Footloose and fancy free,' she insisted, forcing a smile.

'Either that, or the men around here go about with their eyes closed,' Tony riposted, his warm glance sweeping over her.

Compliments from Tony? My, my, Sandy had worked wonders, Billie decided. But it was nice to know that someone had noticed.

And she *had* dressed with care – for Travis? she'd wondered fleetingly – having splashed out on one of Heather's creations, a full-length, off-the-shoulder cream silk sheath that defied all Billie's efforts to conceal her underwear. She'd settled in the end for a pair of the briefest of briefs and self-support stockings but still felt next to naked. But it was worth it. She could hold her own in any crowd, could take the opulent surroundings in her stride. She might be crying inside, but to anyone watching she was confident and happy, the life and soul of the party. Only Anna, caring, loving, wise old Anna saw more than Billie intended, her gaze unexpectedly solemn whenever Billie happened to catch her eye. Seeing Anna's concern, Billie made an effort, sparkling like the bubbles in the champagne she was drinking, courtesy of Travis. Travis. And his very generous gesture to Anna. It was more food for thought, Billie realized, beginning to think that in many ways she'd misjudged him. And having discovered the truth about House of Marianne and the Giddings takeover, she was sharply aware that an apology to Travis was long overdue.

'Thank you, Billie. It takes courage to admit that you're wrong, but you've never been short on that, have you?' he observed when Billie spotted him alone at the bar and seized her opportunity.

It was strange, really. When she'd mentioned an apology, there'd been a flicker of hope in his eyes followed by an equally unexpected stab of pain. And then the shutters had come down and Travis was back in control, draining his glass, reaching for another, offering one to Billie who politely declined. There would be hours yet, she knew, and she had no intentions of dropping her guard, allowing the mellowing influence of alcohol to cloud her judgement or render her maudlin.

Travis shrugged, his glance sweeping over Billie, very much as Tony's had done not ten minutes earlier. Though he missed not a single detail, Billie was sure – the rise and fall of agitated breasts beneath the flimsy material, the hard thrust of nipples that had a life of their own where Travis was concerned – there was nothing insolent in his warm perusal of Billie's body. And Travis knew, knew every line, every curve, could probably describe Billie's underwear – or lack of it – with indecent precision.

'You're still seeing the rugged Viking, then?' he tossed out unexpectedly.

'Oh, but Tony's – '

'A fool if he lets you slip through his fingers,' Travis cut in harshly. 'And how long's it been now, Billie? A year, eighteen months? And still no hint of wedding bells?'

'Perhaps Tony prefers his woman a little less shop-soiled,' Billie snarled. Unfair of her, she knew, but there was nothing rational about her anger, or the feelings she had for Travis. Besides, he'd no room to talk, engaged to Cleo, making love to Billie, turning up tonight with yet another woman in tow.

'Don't – '

'Don't what? Don't say it like it is, Travis?'

'Don't put yourself down. You've done nothing to be ashamed of.'

'Well, I am. Ashamed. Disgusted. Sickened. Shall I go on?'

350

'Plucky. Prickly. Proud. And magnificent in bed. Shall *I* go on?'

'And give the whole room something to talk about? Will you please lower your voice?' she muttered.

'Why?'

'Because whatever we had between us that night was –'

'Special?'

'A mistake. But a private mistake. And that's the way I'd like to keep it.'

'Perhaps that's part of the problem, Billie. Too many secrets from the man you're supposed to love.'

'Whilst you, of course, told Cleo all?'

'As a matter of fact, no,' he informed her, his face tightening. 'I told Cleo nothing. You surely didn't expect me to?'

'Where you're concerned? I wouldn't know what to expect.'

'No. I don't suppose you would. And that's another of your problems,' he tossed out bitterly.

'And what's that supposed to mean?'

'Trust. Or in your case, lack of it.'

'I simply took my lead from you,' she pointed out sweetly. 'And before you say it, yes, that was a problem. Past tense, Travis, since I make a point of learning from my mistakes.'

'How very gratifying. I'm almost flattered, Billie.'

'Well, you shouldn't be. It wasn't meant as a compliment.'

'No?'

'No!'

He shrugged. 'You've grown hard, Billie.'

'And do you care, Travis?'

'If part of it is down to me, then yes.'

'Well, don't flatter yourself. I am what life has made me – life, Travis, not a single, sordid night.'

'And is that how you view it? The loving, the kissing, the touching, the sharing? *Sordid?* Oh, Billie.' He shook his head. 'You really don't understand, do you?'

'Where you're concerned, only too well, believe me,' she hissed.

'Smile, folks. Closer together now, and say che-eese.'

At the sight of the photographer, Billie froze. Travis swore eloquently under his breath and then tugged her close, his hand snaking around her waist as the cameraman repeated his instruction.

'Smile,' Travis whispered against her ear. 'For Anna's sake, if no one else's.'

The moment the flashbulb went off, Billie jerked free.

'Afraid, Billie? Of me? Afraid that if I touch you, you'll melt into my arms? Not so hard after all,' he crooned with a shrewd, assessing glance.

'Wishful thinking, Travis. You might be good in

bed, but you're not that good,' she castigated cruelly.

'I wish I could say the same for you, but I'd be lying, hey, Billie?' he challenged, a backhanded compliment if ever she heard one. Because Travis knew. Billy was lying and he knew. Clever, clever Travis had seen beyond the insult and he'd simply turned the other cheek, made Billie's gibe seem cheap and nasty, which it was, she realized. And he didn't need Billie's seal of approval. Travis was good in bed, and, of course, Travis knew it.

A waiter approached with a trayful of drinks.

'Allow me,' Travis murmured, handing Billie a glass.

She took it without speaking, remembering the last time she'd shared champagne with Travis. A celebration meal. Just like tonight in fact. And thinking of tonight, Anna's special night . . . She took a deep breath.

'I haven't had time to thank you,' she murmured.

Expressive eyebrows rose. 'Believe me, Billie, the pleasure was all mine,' he retorted solemnly.

Billie flushed. 'Do you have to bring everything back to the level of sex?' she demanded coldly.

'Why not? It's a healthy human pastime like eating and sleeping, breathing, making love. Making love, Billie. So much nicer than the cold and clinical mechanics of sex, even good sex.'

'I wouldn't know,' she said.

'No? Well, well. You do surprise me. The rugged Viking's clearly in for a surprise, whenever the happy occasion occurs.'

'Don't be so revolting,' she rasped. 'And will you please stop calling him that,' she added viciously. 'His name's Tony, for heaven's sake.'

'Someone taking my name in vain, Billie?'

'Tony!' Billie went cold, wondering how much Tony had overheard. Travis, she noticed, was completely unperturbed.

'Hardly,' she stalled, flashing him a weak smile. And since the two men stood eyeing one another warily, she took another deep breath. She'd introduce them. At least with Tony in earshot, the conversation would return to normal, if normal could be used to describe anything Travis ever did, and as soon as she could without making it obvious, she'd make her escape.

'Tony Massie,' she murmured. 'Travis Kent. I don't think you two have met.'

'Correction, Billie,' Travis growled. 'We met on your doorstep several months ago.'

'Ah, yes,' Tony murmured. 'I remember now. The car had broken down, Billie, and I slept on your settee. And you – '

'Were returning the cat who'd spent the night howling in my garden,' Travis interrupted. He flashed Billie a strange, half-apologetic glance. 'I was rude, I seem to remember. And jumped to the sort of conclusions a gentleman just doesn't voice. My apologies. With hindsight, Massie, I'm surprised you didn't sock me one.'

Hindsight? Or a better knowledge of Billie? she mused. Since the two men shook hands and appeared to have buried the hatchet, she allowed her mind to wander.

Travis was jealous, she decided. Jealous of Tony. How strange. And how typical of Travis. He'd taken her virginity and stamped his mark upon her body and whilst he didn't want her, he couldn't stomach the idea of anyone else having her. Or rather he *did* want her, just didn't want the commitment of a relationship based on anything more than sex. And why should he? He had his commitment already – Cleo. And if Billie had been stupid enough to settle for that, how on earth had he hoped to get away with it? The lover next door? she fumed silently. It was too close to home, didn't make sense. Billie would have known, for heaven's sake. He could hardly maintain the fiction that he and Cleo were all washed up with Cleo's car coming and going up the lane. And yet, Billie mused, now that she came to think of it, she hadn't noticed Cleo's car, not recently. Not that Billie had been looking. But if she could spot the white Mercedes now and again, surely she'd have noticed the equally distinctive Lotus Elise?

'Tony?'

The two men swung round as Sandy approached.

Tony smiled, holding out his hand. 'Sorry, sweetheart. I know I was supposed to be fetching the drinks, but I got waylaid by Billie and her friend.'

'So I noticed. But Heather says to leave the drinks for now, we're going in to eat.' She flashed a warm smile at Billie and then smiled shyly up at Travis, blushing to the roots of her hair at the intent stare that came back at her.

'I don't believe we've met,' Travis murmured with one of his damsel-slaying smiles. 'If we had, I'd definitely have remembered.'

'Allow me,' Billie drawled. And it was her turn to smile. 'Travis Kent, meet Sandy Massie. Sandy and Tony are staying with Heather,' she explained when Travis didn't react. 'On route from Scotland and their honeymoon.' She caught the flash of surprise that he didn't quite mask and smiled again. 'Quite a night for revelations, hey, Travis?' she couldn't resist needling him as she swung away.

She found Anna. 'Shall I fetch you something to eat, or would you rather come and choose?'

'Bless you, Billie. My legs are aching with all this dancing. I keep forgetting that I'm not as young as I used to be.'

'You're as young as you feel,' Billie reminded.

'Well, I feel perfectly ancient,' she retorted and Billie laughed. At least someone was enjoying herself.

Someone else was enjoying himself too, she noticed, pulling up short in the doorway and scanning the buffet. Travis. Travis and the girl, dark heads close together deep in conversation. Billie felt the breath leave her body. Ridiculous, really. Now had it been Cleo she'd steeled herself to face her. But another girl, a younger girl . . . If Travis *was* playing the field . . . That made Billie just another one-night stand, she thought as the waves of disgust swept through her. And yet, surely not? Even Travis wouldn't have the nerve to flaunt another girl in public, would he?

'Ah, yes. I was wondering when you'd notice,' Anna murmured in answer to Billie's carefully casual enquiry. She nibbled thoughtfully on an olive.

'So?' Billie felt a prickle of alarm.

'She's Helen Breitling, Travis's new assisant,' Anna explained.

'Oh! But she's so young,' Billie murmured absurdly, an equally absurd stab of resentment catching her off guard. Only natural, she supposed. Travis would have replaced Billie sooner or later but, since the weeks had gone by and Travis hadn't bothered to re-advertise, she'd half convinced herself that he couldn't replace her, not because she was indispensable but because of everything they'd shared. Shared? Ha! Her lips twisted bitterly. It might have been something precious to Billie, but for Travis it was little more than a one night stand.

And Travis Kent's new assistant she might be, but Billie wasn't blind. She saw the way the girl's eyes followed him around, lit up whenever Travis happened to glance across, the way she hung on his every word when Travis was speaking. Jealous? Yes! Yes! Yes! Fool that she was – had she no shame? – wanting him, even now, knowing the sort of man he was. Billie ached to feel his arms around her, have his lips caressing hers, have his hands ranging her body. She squeezed back the tears, the mouthful of food sticking in her throat.

'Excuse me,' she murmured to Anna. 'I'm just popping to the Ladies'.'

She wove her way through the couples who were beginning to drift back on to the dance floor. How much longer? she wondered. Travis would pop in, stay for an hour and then leave, Anna had reassured her, hours ago now it seemed. Back to Cleo, Billie had assumed, since Cleo had chosen not to attend. But now . . .

'Ah, Billie.' Travis stepped across her path and Billie stumbled, gasping as his hand shot out to steady her. 'Falling for my charms again, I see,' he murmured drily and Billie flushed.

'Hardly,' she bit out, 'since you're otherwise engaged.' Her eyes were bright, brittle pools and Travis followed the line of her gaze before whistling lightly under his breath.

'Oh, Billie,' he chided softly. 'I do believe you're suffering from a touch of the green-eyed monsters.'

'Don't be ridiculous,' she said, her chin snapping up. 'I was simply stating the obvious.'

'And jumping to conclusions. Still, why should I have a monopoly on that?' he added enigmatically. 'Come across and let me introduce you.'

'I don't – '

'Yes, you do,' he contradicted, and he took her hand before she had time to react, the touch of skin on skin sending waves of heat surging through her traitorous body. And yes, smouldering black eyes proclaimed, he'd logged her reaction.

But hadn't been indifferent himself, Billie decided with a glance of pure defiance. And why not? Travis was a very physical man. And Cleo alone, Billie was beginning to appreciate, would never be able to satisfy someone as insatiable as Travis. Would any woman? she wondered, the knife blade twisting.

'Helen, sweetheart, this is the girl wonder you've had the misfortune to replace,' he explained, black eyes dancing with amusement. 'Billie Taylor, Helen Breitling.'

'How do you do?' Billie murmured as the pain scythed through. *Sweetheart*. Oh Travis, did you have to flaunt her here, rub salt into the wound? 'And how are you finding things at Giddings?' she added politely, wanting to hate the girl who'd stepped into her shoes but aware of nothing but warmth in her soft black eyes. No wonder Travis was besotted.

'Very well,' Helen admitted, 'considering the mammoth task you've left me. And take no notice of Travis. He was a fool for letting you go in the first place, and he knows it. I hear you're planning on going it alone?'

'Not exactly,' Billie murmured warily. Since she hadn't yet told Anna, she was loath to let Travis in on her plans. The news would break soon she knew, but until then Travis, like the rest of the world, would simply have to wait. 'I – '

'Don't have to say a word, Billie,' Travis cut in coldly. 'We understand perfectly.'

'I doubt it,' Billie snapped. 'But you needn't worry, I won't be treading on your toes. When Housman Design moves into Leeds, your precious Giddings' empire will be safe.'

'Leeds? A double celebration, then, since Giddings are moving in the opposite direction. Ironic, really. Perhaps we ought to raise a glass, wish each other well?'

'Boston?' Billie half-stated, half-queried as the anger died.

Travis smiled. 'Boston. You know it well, I believe?'

'Very well,' she murmured. 'Since I spent several weeks there. It's a lovely city.'

'I wouldn't know. I saw very little. Too busy tied up with business to make time for pleasure.'

'Cruel, Travis. Too cruel,' Billie snapped as the pain tore through her.

'But then life often is, don't you find?' he countered harshly.

'Am I missing something here?' Helen put in, her quizzical glance switching from Billie's strained face to Travis's tight-lipped mouth and back again.

Billie swallowed hard. Poor Helen. Getting caught in their crossfire. Little did she know. 'No,' she murmured flatly. 'Just Travis and I reminiscing.' And, like old times, each one going for the jugular.

'Hmm. Well it sounded like fireworks to me. You'd have been good for Giddings, Billie. And kept Travis on his toes. But since you're opening up in Leeds soon, you might just give him a run for his money.' She smiled an impish grin and gave Travis a playful thump on the arm. 'Looks like you've met your match, brother.'

'Brother?' Billie's chin snapped up.

'Half-brother,' Travis acknowledged; though he smiled, the light didn't reach his eyes. 'What was it you were saying earlier, Billie? Quite a night for revelations. Quite a night, indeed.'

Impossible man. He'd known. Of course he'd known. And like an expert angler he'd cast the line, baited her, hooked her, and then he'd reeled her in. And she'd no one to blame but herself for jumping to conclusions.

She danced, wearing herself out with the music, refusing to look for Travis among the mass of swaying, jiving bodies, and yet aware that if Travis had been on the dance floor, Billie would have spotted him at once. He'd probably gone, she decided, relief and disappointment jostling for position. He'd have done his regulation hour or so, and duty over, he'd slip back to the loving arms of Cleo.

'My dance, I believe,' said a familiar voice from behind and that was another misconception buried, because Travis was very much still here, and the fight – flight surge of adrenalin was another revelation. She was glad. Exquisite torture. Because she loved him, loved every line of his wonderful, taut body, loved every nuance of expression. And he'd betrayed her. He'd taken her, loved her, lied to her. And, heaven help her, she still loved him. But Travis was promised to Cleo, she acknowledged, rubbing salt into the wound, and Billie, driven by demons, simply had to goad.

'Where is the dear lady? Not ill, I hope?'

'Cattiness isn't becoming, Billie.'

'Can't a girl ask a civil question? I'm just surprised she's let you off the leash, that's all.'

'Cleo's – otherwise engaged,' he explained enigmatically.

The music changed to something slow and smoochy.

'Not so fast,' Travis growled, his hand snaring Billie's wrist as she made to swing away. And he pulled her into the hard lines of his body, his hands slipping down her back to the swell of her buttocks, his cheek resting against her hair as they shuffled round the dance floor, and Billie dreamed. For a whole five minutes she allowed herself to dream, breathing him, touching him, inhaling his unique body smell. They were together and they were alone, alone in a crowd, and his hands on her body pulled her close, held her close, fingers and thumbs describing tiny erotic circles that seared Billie's skin, and the heat spread out, the heat, the want, the need, the raw aching need she had for Travis. And thigh to thigh, hip to hip, she felt the straining hardness of his manhood and knew that he wanted her every bit as badly.

And when the music came to end, Travis paused and gazed down at her. Billie's heart turned over as she read the message, misread the message, wanted to believe the message in the deep, dark pools. And then he smiled. As Billie's lips parted in silent invitation, Travis dipped his head.

CHAPTER 21

She woke late, a legacy of a disturbed night's sleep. Travis. She hadn't been able to get him out of her mind. Travis mingling with the crowds, Travis looking stunning in dress shirt and dinner jacket. Travis laughing, smiling, dancing. Travis with Billie. Travis with Billie in his arms. Travis with Anna, thanking Anna, kissing Anna, kissing Billie. No – that's where the dream became a nightmare. He hadn't kissed Billie, but he'd held her, cradled her close as they'd shuffled round the dance floor. And he'd wanted her. Hip against hip Billie had felt his hardness and, despite the lies, she'd wanted him. And for a whole five minutes she'd allowed herself to dream, because she'd wanted him. And then Travis had dipped his head and Billie had known he was going to kiss her, she had ached for him to kiss her. Only he mustn't. Never. Ever. Because the need would be more than she could live with. Need. Want. Lust. No, it was more than lust. Lust she could cope with. But the

gaping chasm where her heart should be was
something else again. And so Billie had pulled
away, had seen the flash of pain in his eyes but
had closed her mind to his hurt, saying a swift
goodbye to Anna and making her escape. Escape.
Only there was no escape. Not from Travis.

Luckily it was Sunday. She fed Smudge and then
padded back to bed with a cup of tea and the
morning papers, desultory news mostly but, as
she'd expected, Billie's new venture had made the
home and garden supplement.

'Billie Taylor, the promising young Giddings'
designer whose resignation last October sent shock
waves rippling though the trade, is planning to do
for interior design what Prue Leith did for cookery.'
Billie smiled at the rhetoric. But it was all there, the
college course that she would teach part-time, the
freelance she hoped to expand into a fully fledged
business, and last, but not least, Billie's tribute to
her mother and Aunt Janey, the Housman scholar-
ship to Harvard. One student a year, maybe, but a
once-in-a-lifetime opportunity for a bright young
hopeful.

Billie felt her first glow of pleasure. It *was* going
to happen, she told herself, allowing herself to
believe it. She really was going to make it happen.

Smudge padded in and devised a new game,
burrowing under the papers. In an effort to divert
him, Billie made a tunnel of the sports page, and

when he managed to demolish that, she tugged the rest out of reach. Only Smudge, being Smudge, liked this game better, a paw shooting out quick as a flash to hook an inside corner. The rest of the section came away cleanly and Billie folded it in half before placing it out of his reach.

'Now, wretch!' She froze. Smudge was sitting in the middle of the society page, the game forgotten as he groomed himself, and unbelievably, incredibly, Cleo's face stared up from between his front paws. Cleo, in technicolour glory, complete with wedding dress and veil. Married? Oh, Travis! Billie screamed silently. Not a word, not a hint, not even a whisper. Too, too cruel, Travis. How could you? How could you hold me, dance with me, react so physically – and then leave me to find out like this? And instead of shooing the cat away, she knelt, attempted to read the caption, but made no sense of the snatch of words and finally lifted an unprotesting Smudge into her arms.

'The bride, whose surprise engagement to the Honourable Jamie Snelling was announced on New Year's Eve, was given away by her father . . .'

She didn't see the rest, the page blurring as waves of relief swept through her. And yet it didn't help. How could it? New Year's Eve. While Billie was in Boston. And Travis – Billie went cold. Dear God, what had she done?

'Oh, Smudgie,' she moaned, holding the cat close

366

and rocking back and forth as the tears scalded her cheeks. 'What on earth have I done?'

'Billie?' He masked the surprise. 'This is indeed an honour.' He waved an airy hand. 'Come in. Let me make you a coffee.'

'It isn't a social call,' she told him primly.

'No? Well, a coffee won't hurt, surely?' he chided, and Billie moved forwards, across the threshold, allowing Travis to lead her through to the kitchen. 'We could drink it in the lounge,' Travis explained. 'But it's cosier in here.'

'Yes.' Wonderfully cosy. It was the first time she'd seen inside the house, and probably the last, she tagged on bitterly. And though the hallway hadn't registered, she now had time to gaze around, aware that she wanted to look anywhere but at Travis, but didn't want to appear nosy either and so settled for the sort of swift, appraising glance a designer would give a new commission. First impressions. Very impressed. All warm, poppy reds, and shelves and shelves of cookery books interspersed with plants.

'Thank you.' She accepted the coffee, cradled the cup between her hands and ignored the plate of biscuits. Food would choke her. Brandy would have helped, she decided, wondering why she hadn't thought to take a quick slug of Dutch courage before coming round to face him. And yet she knew the answer to that as well. Because Travis deserved an apology, and he deserved one straight from the heart. Stone cold sober. So – no easy way to say it:

She lifted her chin. 'I'm sorry, Travis. For jumping to conclusions at the airport. I couldn't have been more wrong, could I?'

He shrugged, his features impassive. 'It doesn't matter, Billie. Not really. It simply makes us quits, that's all. I didn't trust you. You didn't trust me. Cleo didn't trust either of us. She was jealous, you see,' he explained flatly, when Billie raised an eyebrow. 'Even though we'd called it a day, she was jealous of you, resented your place in my life. And the irony is, if I'd caught the plane I was supposed to, none of this would have happened. If you'd told me you were coming home that day, we'd have travelled together and it wouldn't have happened. And if Cleo hadn't been there to meet her fiancé, it wouldn't have happened. We were in the wrong place at the wrong time with Cleo. Quite a heady cocktail. And Cleo took advantage.'

And now it was too late, Billie realised. She'd blown it. She'd jumped to conclusions and she'd blown it.

Leaden footsteps carried her to the door.

'Billie?'

She stopped, turned, stood and waited.

'Thanks. For coming to explain, I mean. I'm not

sure I'd have had the guts. Like I said last night, you're a plucky lady. Always were, always will be.'

'Yes.' She was strong. Outwardly at least. But Travis wasn't there to hear the sobs that racked her body night after night. He didn't wake to a pillow sodden with tears. He didn't love her. He'd never professed to love her. And she was wrong to hate him. He hadn't taken something precious, he'd given her something precious. He'd taught her body how to love, and one day, maybe, if she could bring herself to trust another man, then she'd be glad, glad of her single night of love with Travis. Heaven help another man, she thought, a fleeting smile lighting up her face at the thought of another man having to live up to the promise of Travis.

'Billie?'

'Travis?' she murmured warily, aware of the scrutiny, wondering if her thoughts were plastered across her brow.

'That night in Boston. We were good together. Try not to hate me.'

'Hate you?' Her lips twisted bitterly. 'No, Travis. I don't hate you. Believe me, I've never hated you.'

'Never, ever, Billie?' he asked incredulously.

'Never, ever, Travis,' she agreed solemnly. And it was true. How could she hate the man she loved?

She reached the door to the hall way as Travis moved across to intercept, his arm snapping into place and barring the way.

Billy halted, suddenly confused. 'What are you doing?' she asked.

'Just a hunch,' he murmured enigmatically. 'But don't let me detain you. Feel free to leave.'

And have to push past, *touch* him? Billie shivered. Outwardly calm she might be, but that was more than a girl should have to endure.

Almost as if reading her mind, Travis reached out, a single finger tracing the angle of her jaw and Billie jerked back as if stung.

'Hmm. Just as I thought,' Travis murmured.

Billie licked her dry lips. 'Can I go now?' she asked politely.

'Certainly. Feel free to leave any time you want to.' He smiled, didn't move, and Billie felt just the tiniest prickle of apprehension.

'Would you move your hand, please?' she asked as calmly as possible.

'Why?'

'Why?'

'Yes, why?'

'So that I can get past, of course,' she explained absurdly.

He nodded, moved his hand and Billie breathed a huge sigh of relief, the relief lasting less than a second. Like a partner on a dance floor, Travis stepped smartly into the breach, not filling the doorway completely, but the resultant gap too narrow for Billie to squeeze through unscathed.

Her chin snapped up, her startled eyes colliding with his.

'Don't let me keep you,' he insisted as Billie licked her dry lips.

She took a deep breath. 'Travis – '

'Billie?'

'I'd like to leave.'

He shrugged. 'Fine. Be my guest.' He gave a bow, his outstretched arm waving her past.

Only Billie didn't move, hardly dared breathe. He was playing with her. Like a cat with a mouse he was playing with her, and that block of ice she called her heart began to glow. He hadn't lied, she reminded herself. He had finished with Cleo. And though he'd promised Billie nothing, had never said the words, for one night at least she'd been sure they had a future together.

But he doesn't love you, the voice of reason niggled. What price a lifetime spent with a man who doesn't love you? Lifetime? Her lips twisted bitterly. Hardly. As with Cleo, Billie would be just a passing phase. Good in bed, fun to be with, till the novelty faded or a new, improved version came along. Good while it lasted. Could she cope with that? Could she live with the pain that would follow, the pain she'd been living with for the past few weeks, only worse, much, much worse, since there'd be weeks, months, years of loving to come to terms with? Always assuming she lasted that long. Not a single night, Billie. And if a single night can break your heart, think, think of the damage a hundred nights, a thousand would do. If she lasted. If. If that's what Travis was offering.

She angled her head, met his gaze unflinching. 'I'd like to get past, please.'

'No problem,' he agreed. But still he didn't move, didn't smile, didn't bother to wave her on, simply returned her gaze, black eyes heavy with challenge.

Billie felt the anger surge. Playing games. Playing games with her heart, her life. Fine, so Travis can love them and leave them, off with old and on with the new like a shabby piece of clothing. But not with Billie. And yes, she'd just been given an answer. She loved him. And it was all or nothing. A casual affair wouldn't do. All – or nothing. And since Travis had promised her nothing, that's what she'd settle for. Nothing. No Travis, no love, no sex, nothing. And she'd cope. She'd have to. And she'd start right now.

She pushed past, felt the heat of his body, heard the sharp hiss of indrawn breath – his breath, she registered as her knees turned to jelly – but she didn't stop to wonder why, simply dashed across the hallway, choking back the tears. She had to escape, get out of the house and into the safety of the cottage. And she half-ran, half-stumbled down the driveway.

Reaching the gates and out of breath, she paused,

blinking back the tears. He hadn't followed, she realized, absurdly disappointed. He'd simply let her go. And why not? She meant nothing to Travis, nothing. The tears began to trickle and she brushed them away with the back of her hand.

Home. Nearly home. Only not for much longer. Anna could have the cottage. It was the perfect solution. Anna and her cats. And when Mum was fit enough to visit, at least she'd feel at home.

She reached the front step as a man stepped out from around the corner of the house. Billie stopped short. 'Travis!'

'The very same,' he agreed solemnly.

'But – ' How the hell had he managed to arrive at her front door before she had?

'Simple. I followed your example. The short cut,' he added, having clearly read her mind. 'The Billie Taylor special. Through the fence. Or in my case, over it.'

'You jumped the fence?'

'An Olympic gold in pole vaulting, Billie? No.' He smiled, the light reaching his eyes for once, and deep inside Billie smiled. She did love him. Just couldn't live with him unless he loved her too. 'The ladder,' he reminded. 'Another Billie Taylor special.'

So that explained how, but said nothing about why. And though she was itching to ask, Billie refused to put the thought into words.

She swung away, heading round the back. Since she couldn't push past Travis to get to the front door, she'd go in though the kitchen, assuming she could shake him off. But since he'd taken the trouble to come, there had to be a reason. She'd get rid of him faster if she asked, she reasoned, sharply aware that he'd followed, that he was near enough to reach out and touch.

She halted. 'Did you want something?' she enquired politely, folding her arms across her chest, a giveaway gesture she knew, but she had to do something with her arms, with the hands that were itching to reach out and touch.

He smiled. 'Past tense, Billie. And present,' he murmured enigmatically.

'Cut the riddles, Travis. I'm not in the mood for games,' she snapped.

'Oh? And what are you in the mood for?' he asked, and though he didn't seem to move, the gap between them narrowed imperceptibly.

Billie fought the urge to take a step back. 'Nothing. I'm busy. And time is money, remember?

'Ah, yes. The Billie Taylor Design School. Congratulations, Billie. The papers are full of it. I hear it's a roaring success.'

'Hardly,' she snapped. 'Since the course doesn't start until September. But it will be.'

'So sure, Billie? Always so sure,' he drawled. 'Yet another Billie Taylor special,' he mocked, and as the light died in his eyes, the hope died in Billie's. Because whatever Travis wanted, it wasn't what Billie had been foolishly hoping.

'Not always,' she bit. 'I was wrong about you for a start – '

'Yes, woman. Very wrong. But like I said, that makes us quits.'

'Well, I'm sorry.' She swallowed the lump in her throat. He'd never know just how sorry. 'I've said I was sorry, Travis. What more do you want?'

'Oh, Billie. If only you knew. If only you knew,' he repeated wearily.

So – why had he come? Why was he standing there, that bleak expression in his eyes? If he hated her, why should he care? If he hated her, why should the hurt show? Billie was hurting, but Billie loved him. She hurt because she loved him. So, why did Travis hurt? Put like that, the answer was glaringly obvious. And Travis, like Billie, was afraid.

She took a deep breath. 'At the airport, you said if I wanted the truth, then I'd know where to find you.'

He nodded, no reaction, no curiosity, nothing. Just a curt dip of the head.

She licked her lips. 'So, here I am. I made the effort to find you. Now I want the truth.'

'About Cleo? But you've worked that out for yourself, Billie.'

375

'No. Not Cleo. About me. You and me.'

'You and me?' He laughed, a harsh sound that grated on the air. 'You and me don't exist, Billie.'

'But we might have, Travis. We were good together. *You said* we were good together.'

'Past tense, Billie,' he reminded cruelly. 'Since you didn't want to believe in us.'

'Present tense, Travis,' she countered softly. And then, softer still, 'Please, Travis.'

'Please, Travis, what?' he asked, his face uncompromisingly grim. But there had been a flicker of recognition in his eyes, a flicker of something else that might just be sheer imagination, but Billie had come too far to back out now.

She almost smiled, remembering that night, that question, her pithy reply that had shocked him. She couldn't use those words now, not yet at least. But there were other words, equally small, equally potent. And she'd nothing to lose but her pride.

'Love me,' she said simply.

He flinched, nostrils flaring white as black eyes continued to fix her with their steely stare. 'No!' he snarled viciously, almost cutting the air with an imperative slice of his hand. 'Don't. Don't cheapen yourself, Billie. I might be good in bed, but I'm not that good. Oh you'd enjoy it, never fear,' he allowed. 'But you'd wake up tomorrow and you'd despise yourself all over again. If you need a man, Billie, do yourself a favour and find one you can love.'

'I think I have,' she told him softly. 'I think I found him weeks ago and stupidly, idiotically, hadn't the sense to see it. Leastways,' she corrected, 'I knew how I felt. My own feelings were never in doubt. I gave you my body, Travis. But that night in Boston I gave you something much more precious than my virginity.'

'A virtuous woman,' he agreed, but there was no sting in the words. Just indifference.

So. She was wrong. But at least she'd tried. The story of her life, she was beginning to think. With grim echoes of her school reports. Billie works hard. Billie tries hard. Billie cries hard – deep down inside. She raised her chin, watching Travis through a blur of tears.

Why didn't he go? she wondered. Why didn't he leave her in peace? He still hadn't explained what he'd come for but it didn't seem important now. Nothing did. She sniffed, swung away, reaching for the handle.

'Billie.'

'Travis?' she queried, without bothering to turn her head.

'Say it again.'

'Say what again?'

'Something about your feelings. I think, *hope* I understand. But I'm not sure. And I need to be sure.'

'*You* need to be sure? You've got a nerve, Travis

377

Kent,' she fumed, her back straight, her shoulders rigid. 'You keep me in limbo but *you*'ve got to be sure. Talk about arrogance personified.'

'But it doesn't stop you loving me, hey, Billie?' Question, not statement, she noticed, catching the shadow of doubt in his tone.

'No, Travis,' she agreed solemnly as something began to glow deep inside. 'It doesn't – won't – won't ever stop me loving you.' She turned to face him. 'I love you,' she said simply, her eyes fastened on his face. 'I've probably always loved you. And if you want me, Travis,' she added equally simply, 'you know where to find me.' She allowed herself a fleeting smile as the devil inside her surfaced. 'Top of the stairs,' she murmured smokily. 'And first door on the left. Oh, and Travis – don't leave it too long. I should hate to fall asleep while I'm waiting.'

'Sleep? Who said anything about sleep?' he growled, then he was up the steps in an instant and had scooped Billie into his arms. 'Billie, Billie, Billie! Oh, woman, I love you!' he said fiercely, then his mouth came down, smothering her gurgle of delight, his lips moving urgently against her. Billie melted against him, her lips opening, allowing his tongue to find hers, entwine with hers before sweeping down into the secret, moist corners. And while his mouth created chaos, his hands were roaming her body, holding, caressing, stroking, teasing, stoking, the need already spiralling out of control.

378

Billie raised her head, her lips swollen with desire. 'Let's go inside,' she murmured throatily. 'If we stay out here, Travis, we'll scandalize the cat.'

He glanced down, spotted the familiar black and white face with his snub of a nose watching them with feline inscrutability from the bottom of the steps. 'And that will never do,' Travis agreed solemnly.

Hand in hand they reached the lounge. Travis paused on the threshold, kissing her again, softly, tenderly, and suddenly it was all too much for Billie. Top of the stairs? They stood no chance of reaching the bedroom. She'd wanted him for so long, she simply couldn't wait any longer, and her trembling fingers plucked at the buttons of his shirt, pulling the material free of the waist band of his trousers and brushing against the bulge beneath, and as the thrill ran through her, she laughed, felt Travis respond and snaked her fingers down to cradle and caress, to feel the heat, the strength of him.

Travis growled, his hands urgently tugging at her blouse, pulling it free from the waistband of her jeans, his fingers snapping the buttons, his mouth following the trail, gliding from her throat to the valley between her breasts and creating havoc with each and every touch. And it was Billie's turn to moan, the ache in the pit of her stomach exquisite, the ache in her straining breasts unbearable. Travis nuzzled her nipples through the material of her bra, nuzzled, nibbled, sucked the hard nubs that thrust themselves forwards, aching for his touch, his lips, his mouth, his teeth, his fingers. As Travis drew away his eyes fastened on the damp circles that his mouth had made, the deep pink halos with their rigid inner buds and he groaned at the sight, rubbed the hard nubs with his thumbs before pulling her breasts free of the cups of her bra, kneeling to nuzzle, to kiss, to suck, to tease with his fingers, mouth and tongue. Then his hands were moving down to her waist, his lips exploring the plains of her belly as his fingers popped the button on her jeans, lowered the zipper, peeled the faded denim material over her hips and down her never-ending legs, his tongue following, his tongue and the feathered touch of fingers, fingers that glided back along the soft, sensitive inner skin of milky white thighs. Then paused for an exquisite, tantalizing moment at the hem of her panties.

He glanced up, eyes smouldering pools, the need, the want, the ache, the love in his eyes all the reassurance that Billie ever needed and she smiled down at him.'

'Love me,' she murmured thoatily, her fingers threading his hair.

And Travis smiled. 'Oh, yes, Billie. I love you,' he told her solemnly. 'But when I lay you down on the rug that's not what I intend doing, my love.'

'Oh?' she growled as the thrill ran through her. 'And just what do you intend doing?' she queried smokily, dropping to her knees and facing him.

And he smiled, leaned forwards, whispered in her ear, two wonderfully eloquent words that sent the blood rushing though her veins.

'Oh, good,' she murmured, slipping free of his arms and down onto the rug to lie in front of the glowing fire. And as she waited for Travis to shake himself free of his clothes, she brought her hands up to her breasts, cradled her breasts, offered her breasts, her eyes bright with promise, her lips bruised and swollen and aching with desire.

He was beside her in an instant, reaching for the panties she'd deliberately not removed, his growl of pleasure music to her ears, and he feasted his eyes for a moment, his sultry glance travelling the length of her, and then he reached out to touch, his finger brushing gently through the soft hair at the junction of her legs. Though the touch was featherlight, Bille arched towards him, Travis growling as she thrust herself against his hand, her need all consuming. As his fingers threaded through and homed in on the secret, sensitive part of her, Billie felt the heat, trembling, wanting, needing, her legs parting, her body moving against his hand, his fingers. His fingers, oh God, what magic he could weave with those fingers, backwards and forwards along the the tiny nub of her existence, backwards and forwards as the tremors began, an earthquake building up, Billie's body convulsing and then Travis was inside her, thrusting, plunging, faster and faster and faster until the explosions began and the rest of the world ceased to exist.

'Sorry, sweetheart,' he murmured a lifetime later. 'I needed you so badly there wasn't a cat in hell's chance that we'd make it to the bedroom.'

'So you couldn't make it to the bedroom – *this* time,' she emphasized smokily, curling up in his arms in the warm glow of the fire and letting the silence of love envelope her.

She might have slept, probably only dreamed, such wonderful dreams.

'You touched me. When I called round this afternoon. You wouldn't let me pass,' she reminded, a query in her voice.

'Ah, yes. I was testing.'

'Oh?'

'Something Anna said, hinted at last night at the party. So I was testing.'

'And?'

'You reacted. It raised my hopes, so when you bolted – '

'You followed!'

'Exactly. And then I chickened out.' He raised himself on one elbow, eyes dark pools in the soft glow of firelight. He touched her lips, a single finger that caressed, loved, reassured, himself as much as

Billie. 'You seemed so hostile, racing down that drive like bat out of hell.'

Billie laughed at the description. 'Yes. And then you frightened the living daylights out of me. Is it any wonder I was hostile?'

'What a pair of fools we've been.'

'No, my love,' she contradicted huskily. 'Not foolish, simply afraid, afraid to trust our emotions

'Trust. Always the trust. We can rebuild the trust, can't we, Billie?' he asked softly.

'No,' she told him solemnly, aware of the pain in his eyes, sharing the pain because she knew the words had hurt him. And she cradled his face in her hands, her thumbs gently stroking the angle of his jaw, her expression unwavering. 'We can't rebuild something that didn't exist in the first place, Travis. But we can start again – if you want to.'

'If? Billie! Oh, Billie – '

'I'll take that as a yes, then?' she teased.

'Woman, you'd better believe it,' he insisted, kissing her all over again.

Billie nestled her head securely on his shoulder. 'Next problem, Mr Kent . . .'

'Mmmm, my love?'

My love. How wonderful it sounded: 'My house or yours?'

'After we're married? Hmmm . . . Mine, I think. Think of all those rooms, Billie, lots of rooms for babies and cats.'

'Not to mention making love . . .'

'Talking of which . . .'

'You're insatiable.

'Where you're concerned, too right I am. Complaining?'

'Only when I think of all the time we've wasted.'

'So let's make up for lost time,' he suggested, his lips exploring her mouth as his hands began to roam the curves of her body.

Billie rolled free, coming to her feet and standing like Venus before him. 'You, my love,' she murmured throatily, 'need cooling down, and I've just the thing in mind. Follow me, Travis.'

She led the way upstairs to the minuscule bathroom she'd so recently revamped, glad now that she'd created extra space by ripping out the ancient bath and installing a shower in its place. And since she was wearing nothing more than a smile, she simply stepped into the cubicle, pulled Travis in behind and wrapped her arms around him.

'Like I said,' she almost gurgled, feeling him rise against her. 'You need cooling off.' And she turned the dial, allowed the ice-cold jet of water to play across his back, laughing again as Travis cursed eloquently before scooping her even closer, and he pushed her back against the wall and it was Billie's turn to gasp at the ice-cold contact of the tiles against her buttocks. Unrepentant, Travis laughed, and he thrust against her, the sting of

the water forgotten as, unerringly, he slipped inside her, the strange contrast of searing heat and
cold heightening the tension, and Billie was pinned,
trapped, powerless to move, just her hands, her
hands and mouth touching him, tasting him, loving
him, the tension mounting as Travis continued to
thrust, now hard and demanding, now languid and
slow, stoking the fires with unhurried deliberation
until Billie was ready to scream out with frustration.
And then he pulled back, the flash of knowledge in
his smoky black eyes followed by a searing flash of
desire as Travis plunged, his hands slipping round
to grip her buttocks and her feet were no longer on
the ground as Travis held her, pinned, suspended,
and thrust hard and fast into her. Billie arched her
back, her breath short, sharp and laboured as the
pleasure grew, as the waves of heat began deep
inside, an avalanche of want and need and love
that Travis had created, and then the lights exploded in her mind and Billie cried out with the
pain, the bittersweet pain of reaching a climax,
again, and again, and again, as Travis continued
to drive himself deep into Billie's quivering body.

'Oh, Billie,' he told her solemnly later, much later
when their racing hearts had calmed. 'That was out
of this world. Oh, Billie, you really are amazing.'
And he cradled her face in his hands, gazing down
with all the love she never thought to see. And
Travis dipped his head, kissed her, spun the dial

on the wall round to warm and allowed the jets to wash over them as the trembling in her body slowly ebbed away.

'And to think, next door, there's a wonderful sunken bath that hasn't been christened yet, not properly at least,' he murmured when Billie reached up to kiss him, draw him out of the shower and into her bed.

'I should think not,' she replied, pretending to be scandalized, remembering the sunken bath in Boston and the erotic experience of sharing it with Travis. And yes, there had been a momentary stab of pain when the image of Cleo sprang into her mind, but just as quickly slipped out again. So Travis had a past, had shared part of his life with someone else. It wasn't important. It was the present that mattered now, the present and the future.

More love, wrapped in fluffy bath towels this time, words of love as they sprawled on Billie's bed, glass of wine in hand, courtesy of Billie who'd treated herself in private celebration of her plan.

'We won't let business come between us, will we?' she asked doubtfully when Travis raised his glass in joint tribute to Giddings of Boston and Housman UK.

'Nothing will ever come between us,' he told her fiercely, and then he explained. 'I've no proof but, the leaked plans, the sabotage, the arson, the strike attempt, everything points to Cleo.'

'But, why?' Billie asked incredulous. 'I thought she loved you.'

'I doubt Cleo ever really loved anyone but Cleo,' he demurred drily. 'But you're right in a way. She wanted me but hated the thought of settling in Felbrough.'

'And that was her way of driving you back to London? But someone could have been killed,' Billie recalled, horrified.

'It doesn't matter now,' he reassured her, hugging her. 'She's gone and she can't hurt either of us ever again.'

And Billie smiled, settled down, curled up again, content. There was nothing to come between them, only the shadows of the past and they'd buried those today.

Another lifetime passed.

'I didn't thank you. For Anna's party, I mean.'

'You didn't have to. It was no more than Anna deserved. She kept me sane,' he explained when Billie raised an enquiring eyebrow. 'When you walked out and things were going wrong, I remembered Anna. There were times, Billie, when I'd have closed the place down but for Anna.'

'Because of me? Oh, Travis.'

He hugged her. 'Because of you. Because I loved you. Because I'd loved you from the day you dropped into my life, hissing and spitting like a she-cat.'

'A hoyden in the grass,' she reminded. 'You were annoyed, worried about your precious garden.'

'Worried about you, more like. You could have been killed, for heaven's sake.'

'And to think you cared. All those months and I never knew you cared.'

'Never, Billie? Never, ever? Not even when I kissed you?' he asked incredulously.

'Especially not when you kissed me. The kisses were wonderful, but the moment they were over you made it clear you were simply playing games.'

'Trying to prove a point? Yes. You're right,' he agreed as Billie nodded solemnly. 'I was trying to prove that you needed me, wanted me, couldn't live with without me. And then you'd glance across with your ice-cool composure and I'd needle, goad, say everything but what I really wanted to say.'

'But you must have known. You kept on telling me how much I wanted you,' she pointed out.

'Ah yes. But who was I really trying to convince, my love? And since you were practically engaged – '

'To Tony? Hardly,' she laughed. 'Believe it or not, we were just good friends.'

'And fool that I am, I jumped to the wrong conclusions, nearly blew it.'

'No more than I did with Helen. I liked her,' Billie confided. 'Even though I tried hard not to. You were right, I was jealous. Jealous because she'd taken my place at work and because she seemed to mean so much to you. I thought you'd found another woman and you were flaunting her in front of me. But once we'd met, I couldn't help but like her. I'm glad she's your sister.'

'Good. Because she's pencilled herself in as chief bridesmaid.'

Billie laughed. 'But how could she possible know when we didn't know ourselves?' she queried, glowing inside.

'Woman's intuition. She's known for weeks that something was wrong and that it had nothing to do with Cleo. One look at the two of us together last night was enough for Helen to have us wedded, bedded and all the children named.'

'Hmm. Looks to me like she's mixed the order up,' Billie murmured drily, her heated gaze travelling the length of Travis's naked body.

'Precisely. But not by much, hey, my love?' he told her fiercely, and then, suddenly unsure, 'You don't want a fuss, do you, Billie?'

'York Minster, hundreds of guests, a frothy white dress and a ten-layer wedding cake?' she queried, features impassive. 'Not to mention a white Rolls Royce and a round the world honeymoon. What do you think?' she challenged.

'I think – hope – that you're joking. But if that's what you really want – '

'I want you,' she told him simply. 'Just you, and always you. Anna, Helen, a couple of friends, Mum if she's up to it. But most of all, just you and me. Our day, our wedding, our life.'

'And our love,' he murmured. 'And talking of which . . .'

'More love?'

'More love,' he agreed, spreading her hair across the pillow and gazing down, black eyes smouldering with desire.

And Billie began to tremble. He didn't touch, didn't speak, simply continued to watch her, Billie's need growing, his need growing, the physical sign of his need filling her with pride because Travis loved her, wanted her, needed her and now they belonged, they would always belong.

'For ever and a day,' Travis told her solemnly, dipping his head to kiss her swollen lips. 'For ever and a day. Trust me, Billie.'

'I do,' Billie murmured huskily. 'And I will. For ever and a day.'

**THE EXCITING NEW NAME
IN WOMEN'S FICTION!**

PLEASE HELP ME TO HELP YOU!

Dear *Scarlet* Reader,

As Editor of *Scarlet* Books I want to make sure that the books I offer you every month are up to the high standards *Scarlet* readers expect. And to do that I need to know a little more about you and your reading likes and dislikes. So please spare a few minutes to fill in the short questionnaire on the following pages and send it to me. I'll send *you* a surprise gift as a thank you!

Looking forward to hearing from you,

Sally Cooper

Editor-in-Chief, *Scarlet*

QUESTIONNAIRE

Please tick the appropriate boxes to indicate your answers

1 Where did you get this Scarlet title?
Bought in Supermarket ☐
Bought at W H Smith or other High St bookshop ☐
Bought at book exchange or second-hand shop ☐
Borrowed from a friend ☐
Other _____

2 Did you enjoy reading it?
A lot ☐   A little ☐   Not at all ☐

3 What did you particularly like about this book?
Believable characters ☐   Easy to read ☐
Good value for money ☐   Enjoyable locations ☐
Interesting story ☐   Modern setting ☐
Other _____

4 What did you particularly dislike about this book?
_____

5 Would you buy another Scarlet book?
Yes ☐   No ☐

6 What other kinds of book do you enjoy reading?
Horror ☐   Puzzle books ☐   Historical fiction ☐
General fiction ☐   Crime/Detective ☐   Cookery ☐
Other _____

7 Which magazines do you enjoy most?
Bella ☐   Best ☐   Woman's Weekly ☐
Woman and Home ☐   Hello ☐   Cosmopolitan ☐
Good Housekeeping ☐
Other _____

cont.

And now a little about you –

8 How old are you?
   Under 25 ☐   25–34 ☐   35–44 ☐
   45–54 ☐   55–64 ☐   over 65 ☐

9 What is your marital status?
   Single ☐   Married/living with partner ☐
   Widowed ☐   Separated/divorced ☐

10 What is your current occupation?
   Employed full-time ☐   Employed part-time ☐
   Student ☐   Housewife full-time ☐
   Unemployed ☐   Retired ☐

11 Do you have children? If so, how many and how old are they?
   _____
   _____

12 What is your annual household income?
   under £10,000 ☐   £10–20,000 ☐   £20–30,000 ☐
   £30–40,000 ☐   over £40,000 ☐

Miss/Mrs/Ms _____
Address _____
   _____
   _____
   _____

Thank you for completing this questionnaire. Now tear it out – put it in an envelope and send it before 31 January 1997, to:

Sally Cooper, Editor-in-Chief

SCARLET
FREEPOST LON 3335
LONDON W8 4BR
Please use block capitals for address.
No stamp is required!   QUTRU/7/96

Scarlet titles coming next month:

RENTON'S ROYAL Nina Tinsley

Sarah Renton is troubled. **Renton's Royal**, her one abiding passion, is under threat. Her rivals for power and success are other Renton women – who each have their own reasons for wanting to take over from Sarah. What these women all discover, in their search for success, is that passion and power make dangerous bedfellows . . .

DARK LEGACY Clare Benedict

Greg Randall haunted Bethany Lyall's dreams . . . and her every waking moment too. Before Bethany could follow her heart, though, she had to conquer the demons from the past and face the dangers in the present. Of the *three* men in her life, only Bethany could decide who was her friend, who was her enemy and who would be her lover!

WILD JUSTICE Liz Fielding

Book One of **The Beaumont Brides trilogy**:

Fizz Beaumont hates Luke Devlin before she even meets him! So Luke Devlin in the flesh is a total shock to her, particularly when he decides to take over her life. Fizz is so sure she can resist him, but then he kisses her – and her resistance melts away . . .

NO DARKER HEAVEN Stella Whitelaw

Jeth *wants* Lyssa. Lyssa wants marriage without romance. Jeth offers excitement and passion, but his son, Matt, offers uncomplicated commitment. Against her will, Lyssa is caught up in an eternal triangle of passion.